SAVING FISH
from
DROWNING

AMY TAN

G. P. PUTNAM'S SONS

New York

SAVING FISH

from

DROWNING

G. P. PUTNAM'S SONS
Publishers Since 1838
Published by the Penguin Group

Penguin Group (USA) Inc., 375 Hudson Street, New York, New York 10014, USA ·
Penguin Group (Canada), 90 Eglinton Avenue East, Suite 700, Toronto, Ontario M4P 2Y3,
Canada (a division of Pearson Penguin Canada Inc.) · Penguin Books Ltd, 80 Strand,
London WC2R 0RL, England · Penguin Ireland, 25 St Stephen's Green, Dublin 2, Ireland
(a division of Penguin Books Ltd) · Penguin Group (Australia), 250 Camberwell Road,
Camberwell, Victoria 3124, Australia (a division of Pearson Australia Group Pty Ltd) ·
Penguin Books India Pvt Ltd, 11 Community Centre, Panchsheel Park, New Delhi–110 017,
India · Penguin Group (NZ), Cnr Airborne and Rosedale Roads, Albany,
Auckland 1310, New Zealand (a division of Pearson New Zealand Ltd) ·
Penguin Books (South Africa) (Pty) Ltd, 24 Sturdee Avenue,
Rosebank, Johannesburg 2196, South Africa

Penguin Books Ltd, Registered Offices: 80 Strand, London WC2R 0RL, England

A joint publication of G. P. Putnam's Sons, a division of Penguin Group (USA) Inc., and
The Random House Publishing Group, a division of Random House, Inc.

ISBN 0-399-15301-2

Printed in the United States of America

BOOK DESIGN BY AMANDA DEWEY

This is a work of fiction. Names, characters, places, and incidents either are the product of the
author's imagination or are used fictitiously, and any resemblance to actual persons, living or
dead, businesses, companies, events, or locales is entirely coincidental.

While the author has made every effort to provide accurate telephone numbers and Internet
addresses at the time of publication, neither the publisher nor the author assumes any responsibility for errors, or for changes that occur after publication. Further, the publisher does not have
any control over and does not assume any responsibility for author or third-party websites or
their content.

The evil that is in the world almost always comes of ignorance, and good intentions may do as much harm as malevolence if they lack understanding.

—ALBERT CAMUS

A pious man explained to his followers: "It is evil to take lives and noble to save them. Each day I pledge to save a hundred lives. I drop my net in the lake and scoop out a hundred fishes. I place the fishes on the bank, where they flop and twirl. "Don't be scared," I tell those fishes. "I am saving you from drowning." Soon enough, the fishes grow calm and lie still. Yet, sad to say, I am always too late. The fishes expire. And because it is evil to waste anything, I take those dead fishes to market and I sell them for a good price. With the money I receive, I buy more nets so I can save more fishes.

—ANONYMOUS

SAVING FISH
from
DROWNING

· a note to the reader ·

THE IDEA FOR THIS BOOK began with a bolt of lightning and a clap of thunder. I was walking on the Upper West Side in Manhattan when I was caught without an umbrella in a fierce summer downpour. I spotted a possible shelter: a handsome brownstone building with gleaming black double doors. A brass plaque read: "American Society for Psychical Research." Lured by the possibilities within, I rang the bell, and spent the rest of the day perusing the Society's archives.

Like the first public library that I visited as a child, the room was jammed floor to ceiling with the leather and cloth spines of old books—little tombstones of ideas and history clothed in midnight blue, purple, brown, and black, the titles imprinted in fading gilt letters. In the center of the room were tall stools, a narrow wooden table, and cabinets housing Dewey Decimal cards. Within "A–Ca,"

I found entries for "Automatic Writing," descriptions of archived "messages from the unseen world." They were written in various languages and orthographies, including Chinese, Japanese, and Arabic, reportedly transmitted to people who had no knowledge of the received language. The messages from royalty and famous personages were noteworthy for having signatures "verified by the experts."

I was especially impressed with the transmissions received from 1913 to 1937 by an "ordinary homemaker" in St. Louis, Pearl Curran, who had no formal education past the age of fourteen, and was the recipient of stories from a garrulous ghost named Patience Worth. Patience purportedly lived in the 1600s and wrote of medieval times. The results were volumes of antiquated prose, with intimate knowledge of colloquialisms and social manners of olden days, a language that was not quite Middle English and yet contained no anachronisms past the seventeenth century. One of her page-turners began in this breezy way: "Dew-drop soggeth grasses laid low aneath the blade at yester's harvest..." Aside from the stolid prose style, there was good reason to either admire or loathe Patience Worth and Pearl Curran. One of the novels was dictated in a span of thirty-five hours.

There was another case in the archives that fascinated me even more. The writings were recorded by a medium named Karen Lundegaard, who lived in Berkeley, California. She had received in fifty-four sessions a rambling story that was part rant, part memoir, delivered by a spirit named Bibi Chen.

The name startled me. There was a well-known woman by that name in my hometown, San Francisco. She had been a socialite and the owner of a landmark shop on Union Square, The Immortals, which sold decorative Asian antiques. She died under bizarre circumstances that were never fully explained. Karen Lundegaard described Bibi Chen accurately: "A petite, feisty Chinese woman, opinionated, and hilarious when she didn't intend to be."

I had a passing acquaintance with Bibi Chen, but I could not say I knew her personally. We exchanged brief hellos at the usual fundraisers for the arts or the Asian-American community. Her name was often boldfaced in the social columns, and she was much photographed wearing dramatic garb, along with a multicolored braid and false eyelashes as thick as hummingbird wings.

Karen had transcribed Bibi's voice in pencil on yellow legal pads. This began as spastic marks and jerky false starts, then gave way to pages of frantic squiggles and drunken scrawls, and gradually loped into the smooth shape of handwriting. It was as if I were seeing the electroencephalogram of the brain-dead being resuscitated, a marionette whose strings had been yanked into animation. Page after seamless page flowed with generous application of exclamation points and heavily underlined phrases, the style most beginning writers are cautioned against using.

When I returned to San Francisco, I met with Karen Lundegaard several times at her bungalow stuffed with arcana and, by her description, "tag-sale items." She was quite frail, debilitated by metastatic breast cancer, which she had long known she had but for which she had been unable to get adequate treatment because she lacked medical insurance. ("If you mention anything about me," she said, "tell people that.") Although she was ill, she welcomed my peppering her with questions. Her sessions with Bibi Chen, she said, were professionally gratifying, because the spirit came through with great clarity. The connection to other spirits, she explained, was often indistinct, similar to mobile phone calls that go in and out of range. "Bibi has a *very* pushy personality," she told me. I wondered if I might witness an automatic writing session. Karen promised to try, but said it would have to be later, when she felt better. "Receiving" drained her energy.

However these writings came to be, I decided the material was irresistible. In a city known for its characters, Bibi Chen was the genuine article, a true San Franciscan. Without giving away her story, I will mention only that she talked about eleven tourists missing in Burma, who were the subject of news headlines for weeks, a story readers may well recognize. While Karen Lundegaard may have constructed from what she had already read in the news, her writings contained details that were not reported, according to people I later interviewed.

Whether one believes in communication with the dead or not, readers are willing to suspend disbelief when immersed in fiction. We want to believe that the world we have entered through the portals of another's imagination indeed exists, that the narrator is or has been among us. And so I have written this story as that, fiction inspired by Karen Lundegaard's automatic writings. I retained Bibi's religious and racial comments that may be offensive or humorous, depending on the reader's politics. A few people who were part of the real events asked that I not use their names. And while I was not able to confirm some details that Bibi gave, I left in those I found interesting. Hence, there may be errors of fact. Then again, the nature of many people's recollections entails some degree of embellishment, exaggeration, and the bias of opinion.

Although you may think this book was as effortless to write as those dictated by Patience Worth, I relied on the assistance of many to assemble the pieces. For interviews, I thank people too numerous to name, but you know who you are. I am grateful to the Asian Art Museum in San Francisco and the American Society for Psychical Research in New York for opening their doors to me. I hope readers will visit their collections and give generously to their coffers.

At the time of this writing, foreign writers and journalists were still not allowed in Burma, so I was not able to see the mentioned locations firsthand. Thus I appreciated the videos of the country lent to me by Vivian Zaloom. Bill Wu provided expert commentary on

Buddhist art that is found in China and along the Burma Road and corrected some of Bibi's interpretations of cultural influences. In some cases, I deliberately let stand her errors of interpretation, and I hope that Dr. Wu will forgive me for that. Mike Hearn of the Metropolitan Museum of Art in New York offered additional insight on the Chinese aesthetic. Robert and Deborah Tornello of Tornello Nurseries untangled what is found in a bamboo rainforest, and Mark Moffett's *The High Frontier: Exploring the Tropical Rainforest Canopy* gave me a bird's-eye view of the ecosystem with vivid and visceral pleasure; Mark Moffett has no relation to the character in this book with the same name. Ellen Moore organized the reams of information collected and kept distractions at bay. Animal behaviorist Ian Dunbar furnished insight on dog behavior and training principles, but the methods and philosophy depicted in this fiction do not accurately represent his.

While it is impossible to corroborate the thoughts and motives of the Myanmar junta, I have included "Bibi's report" as fictional imaginings of fictional characters. This may have clouded the line between what is dramatically fictional and what is horrifyingly true. Let me briefly say, the truth of Bibi's story can be found in numerous sources citing the myth of the Younger White Brother, the systematic killing of the Karen tribe, and even the military regime's ban on reporting losses by its national soccer team. I apologize for any glaring inaccuracies, most of which are no doubt mine, but some may be "Bibi's." Editors Molly Giles and Aimee Taub deleted chaos on the page and clarified where I was going and why I was lost. Anna Jardine exterminated an infestation of embarrassments.

One final and important acknowledgment: I posthumously thank Karen Lundegaard, who gave me her blessing to use the "Bibi writings" in whatever way I wished, who tirelessly answered questions, and who welcomed me as a friend. Karen succumbed to her illness in October of 2003.

Tourists Flee Burma,
Fears Over 11 Missing Americans

By May L. Brown
Special Field Report for the *San Francisco Chronicle*

MANDALAY, December 31—In the glossy, air-conditioned bar of the Golden Pagoda Hotel, pampered tourists escape the humidity with cocktails charged at upscale American prices. But none are celebrating the coming New Year in the wake of reports that 11 Americans on an art expedition in Burma have been missing for almost a week under "suspicious" circumstances. The jittery hotel guests exchange rumors ranging from drug-running and hostage-taking to revenge by disturbed Nats, mischievous spirits in Burmese superstition.

The tourists, four men, five women, and two children from the San Francisco Bay Area, were last seen on December 25 at Inle Lake as guests of the Floating Island Resort. Before dawn on Christmas morning the Americans and their Burmese guide climbed into two piloted longboats to watch the sunrise. The jaunt normally takes 90 minutes. The passengers never returned, nor did the longboats and their crews.

The 61-square-mile lake, surrounded by pine-studded peaks, is a tangle of inlets to isolated villages and flotillas of tomato-growing paddies. The resort is in the mountainous region of southern Shan State, whose eastern border is the gateway to the Golden Triangle, notorious for its heroin trade. In past years, the region was closed to tourism because of warfare by ethnic tribes against the military government. Local tour operators emphasize the area today is trouble-free, citing that many resorts are even operated by the former warlords of other tribes.

The 11 tourists were first reported missing by another member of their group, Harry Bailley, 42, a British-born celebrity dog trainer featured on the television series "The Fido Files." Bailley declined to join the sunrise adventure because he was ill with food poisoning. When his friends failed to return for lunch and dinner, he notified resort management, who, Bailley complained, did not immediately contact local authorities.

On December 26, the group's 26-year-old Burmese guide, Maung Wa Sao, called "Walter," of Rangoon (Yangon), was discovered unconscious by two 10-year-old acolytes from a monastery in In-u, near the opposite end of the lake. Maung was suffering from scalp lacerations, dehydration, and a possible concussion. From his hospital bed, he talked to Shan State military police and claimed no recollection of what had happened from the time he climbed in the boat until he was found in the crumbling ruins of a pagoda.

Shan military police did not contact the U.S. Embassy in Rangoon (Yangon) until December 29. "Our office is working intensively with the Burmese military regime," said U.S. consular staff Ralph Anzenberger. "The disappearance of 11 Americans on holiday is of great concern to all. For now, the identities of the missing are being withheld, given the uncertainty of what the situation might be."

He declined to confirm reports that one of the missing women is a prominent journalist and activist for a human rights organization, Free to Speak International. The military regime does not knowingly grant entry to foreign journalists, Anzenberger said. But Philip Gutman, spokesperson for Free to Speak in Berkeley, told the *Chronicle*, "[She's] written stories about oppression, all of which are credible and well-documented." Gutman feared that the Burmese military regime may have detained the journalist and her companions, and that they may have joined a reported 1500 political prisoners. "They've been known to lock up anyone who criticizes them," Gutman pointed out. "Their notions of human rights are pretty perverse."

Gutman also acknowledged that the journalist has participated in rallies in support of Burma's opposition leader, Aung San Suu Kyi, "the Lady," whose party's landslide victory in the 1990 elections was illegally overturned by the junta. Aung San Suu Kyi, who has been under house arrest since 1989, was awarded the Nobel Peace Prize for 1991. She has repeatedly called upon other governments to apply pressure on the junta by ceasing commerce with Burma. The U.S. imposed sanctions on new business development in 1997.

But that has not prevented tourists from flocking to an exotic destination at a bargain price. Tourism has steadily increased, that is, until now.

"We sincerely respect the Lady," confided one Burmese tour operator, under condition of anonymity. "But to be honest, the government treats the people better when the tourists are coming. When the tourists are not coming, the gentle people are punished, not the government."

Today, military police in gasoline-belching motorboats began another day searching along the shores of Inle Lake. Meanwhile, white-gloved staff at the Golden Pagoda Hotel in Mandalay are busy carrying out luggage. "Sure, it makes us nervous," says departing guest Jackie Clifford, 41, a biotech investment consultant from Palo Alto, California. "We were going to fly to Bagan tomorrow to see all those incredible temple ruins. Now we're seeing if we can book a flight to a Thai resort instead."

She will have to stand on line. Many other guests have left for the airport to make similar arrangements.

A Brief History of My Shortened Life

It was not my fault. If only the group had followed my original itinerary without changing it hither, thither, and yon, this debacle would never have happened. But such was not the case, and there you have it, I regret to say.

"Following the Buddha's Footsteps" is what I named the expedition. It was to have begun in the southwestern corner of China, in Yunnan Province, with vistas of the Himalayas and perpetual spring flowers, and then to have continued south on the famed Burma Road. This would allow us to trace the marvelous influence of various religious cultures on Buddhist art over a thousand years and a thousand miles—a fabulous journey into the past. As if that were not enough appeal, I would be both tour leader and personal docent, making the expedition a truly value-added opportunity. But in the wee hours of December 2nd, and just fourteen days before we were to leave on our expedition, a hideous thing happened . . . I died. There. I've finally said it, as unbelievable as it sounds. I can still see the tragic headline: "Socialite Butchered in Cult Slaying."

The article was quite long: two columns on the left-hand side of the front page, with a color photo of me covered with an antique textile, an exquisite one utterly ruined for future sale.

The report was a terrible thing to read: "The body of Bibi Chen, 63, retail maven, socialite, and board member of the Asian Art Museum, was found yesterday in the display window of her Union Square store, The Immortals, famed for its chinoiserie. . . ." That odious word—"chinoiserie"—so belittling in a precious way. The article continued with a rather nebulous description of the weapon: a small, rakelike object that had severed my throat, and a rope tightened around my neck, suggesting that someone had tried to strangle me after stabbing had failed. The door had been forced open, and bloody footprints of size-twelve men's shoes led from the platform where I had died, then out the door, and down the street. Next to my body lay jewelry and broken figurines. According to one source, there was a paper with writing from a Satanic cult bragging that it had struck again.

Two days later, there was another story, only shorter and with no photo: "New Clues in Arts Patron's Death." A police spokesman explained that they had never called it a cult slaying. The detective had noted "a paper," meaning a newspaper tabloid, and when asked by reporters what the paper said, he gave the tabloid's headline: "Satanic Cult Vows to Kill Again." The spokesman went on to say that more evidence had been found and an arrest had been made. A police dog tracked the trail left by my blood. What is invisible to the human eye, the spokesman said, still contains "scent molecules that highly trained dogs can detect for as long as a week or so after the event." (My death was an event?) The trail took them to an alleyway, where they found bloodstained slacks stuffed in a shopping cart filled with trash. A short distance from there, they found a tent fashioned out of blue tarp and cardboard. They arrested the occupant, a homeless man, who was wearing the shoes that had left the telltale imprints. The suspect had no criminal record but a history of psychiatric problems. Case solved.

Or maybe not. Right after my friends were lost in Burma, the newspaper changed its mind again: "Shopkeeper's Death Ruled Freak Accident."

No reason, no purpose, no one to blame, just "freak," this ugly word next to my name forever. And why was I demoted to "shopkeeper"? The story further noted that DNA analysis of the man's skin particles and those on both the blood-spattered trousers and the shoes confirmed that the man was no longer a suspect. So who had entered my gallery and left the prints? Wasn't it an obvious case of crime? Who, exactly, caused this freak accident? Yet there was no mention of a further investigation, shame on them. In the same article, the reporter noted "an odd coincidence," namely that "Bibi Chen had organized the Burma Road trip, in which eleven people went on a journey to view Buddhist art and disappeared." You see how they pointed the shaking finger of blame? They certainly implied it, through slippery association with what could not be adequately explained, as if I had created a trip that was doomed from the start. Pure nonsense.

The worst part about all of this is that I don't remember how I died. In those last moments, what was I doing? Whom did I see wielding the instrument of death? Was it painful? Perhaps it was so awful that I blocked it from my memory. It's human nature to do that. And am I not still human, even if I'm dead?

The autopsy concluded that I was not strangled but had drowned in my own blood. It was ghastly to hear. So far none of this information has been of any use whatsoever. A little rake in my throat, a rope around my neck—this was an accident? You'd have to be brainless to think so, as more than a few evidently were.

At the postmortem, photos were taken, especially of the awful part of my neck. My body was tucked into a metal drawer for future study. There I lay for several days, and then samples of me were removed—a swab of this, a sliver of that, hair follicles, blood, and gastric juices. Then two more days went by, because the chief medical examiner went on vacation in Maui, and since I was an illustrious person, of particular renown in the art world—and no, *not* just the retail community, as the *San Francisco Chronicle* suggested—he wanted to see me personally, as did esteemed people in the professions of crime and forensic medicine. They dropped by on their lunch hour to make ghoulish guesses as to what had happened to cause my premature demise. For days, they slid me in, they slid me out, and said brutish things about the contents of my stomach, the integrity of the vessels in my brain, my personal habits, and past records of my health, some being rather indelicate matters one would rather not hear discussed so openly among strangers eating their sack lunches.

In that refrigerated land, I thought I had fallen into the underworld, truly I did. The most dejected people were there—an angry woman who had dashed across Van Ness Avenue to scare her boyfriend, a young man who jumped off the Golden Gate Bridge and changed his mind halfway down, an alcoholic war vet who had passed out on a nude beach. Tragedies, mortal embarrassments, unhappy endings, all of them. But why was I there?

I was stuck in these thoughts, unable to leave my breathless body, until I realized that my breath was not gone but surrounding me, buoying me upward. It was quite amazing, really—every single breath, the sustenance I took and expelled out of both habit and effort over sixty-three years had accumulated like a savings account.

And everyone else's as well, it seemed, inhalations of hopes, exhalations of disappointment. Anger, love, pleasure, hate—they were all there, the bursts, puffs, sighs, and screams. The air I had breathed, I now knew, was composed not of gases but of the density and perfume of emotions. The body had been merely a filter, a censor. I knew this at once, without question, and I found myself released, free to feel and do whatever I pleased. That was the advantage of being dead: no fear of future consequences. Or so I thought.

WHEN THE FUNERAL finally happened on December 11th, it was nearly ten days after I died, and without preservation I would have been compost. Nonetheless, many came to see and mourn me. A modest guess would be, oh, eight hundred, though I am not strictly counting. To begin, there was my Yorkshire terrier, Poochini, in the front row, prostrate, head over paws, sighing through the numerous eulogies. Beside him was my good friend Harry Bailley, giving him the occasional piece of desiccated liver. Harry had offered to adopt Poochini, and my executor readily agreed, since Harry is, as everyone knows, that famous British dog trainer on television. Perhaps you've seen his show—*The Fido Files*? Number-one ratings, and many, many Emmy Awards. Lucky little Poochini.

And the mayor came—did I mention?—and stayed at least ten minutes, which may not sound long, but he goes to many places in a day and spends far less time at most. The board members and staff of the Asian Art Museum also came to pay respects, nearly all of them, as did the docents I trained, years' and years' worth, plus the people who had signed up for the Burma Road trip. There were also my three tenants—the troublesome one, as well—and my darling repeat customers and the daily browsers, plus Roger, my FedEx man; Thieu, my Vietnamese manicurist; Luc, my gay haircolorist; Bobo, my gay Brazilian housekeeper; and most surprising to say, Najib, the

Lebanese grocer from my corner market on Russian Hill, who called me "dearie" for twenty-seven years but never gave me a discount, not even when the fruit had gone overripe. By the way, I am not mentioning people in any order of importance. This is simply how it is coming to me.

Now that I think of it, I would estimate that *more* than eight hundred people were there. The auditorium at the de Young Museum was crowded *beyond belief*, and hundreds spilled into the halls, where closed-circuit television monitors beamed the unhappy proceedings. It was a Monday morning, when the museum was usually closed, but a number of out-of-towners on Tea Garden Drive saw the funeral as a fine opportunity to sneak into the current exhibit, *Silk Road Treasures from the Aurel Stein Expeditions*, a testimony, in my opinion, to British Imperial plundering at the height of cupidity. When guards turned the interlopers away from the exhibits, they wandered over to my funeral fête, morbidly lured by copies of various obituaries that lay next to the guest book. Most of the papers gave the same hodgepodge of facts: "Born in Shanghai . . . Fled China with her family as a young girl in 1949 . . . An alumna of Mills College and guest lecturer there, in art history . . . Proprietor of The Immortals . . . Board member of many organizations . . ." Then came a long list of worthy causes for which I was described as a devoted and generous donor: this league and that society, for Asian seniors and Chinese orphans, for the poor, the ill, and the disabled, for the abused, the illiterate, the hungry, and the mentally ill. There was an account of my delight in the arts and the substantial amounts I had given to fund artist colonies, the Youth Orchestra with the San Francisco Symphony, and the Asian Art Museum—the major recipient of my lagniappes and largesse, before *and* after death—which enthusiastically offered the unusual venue for my funeral, the de Young, in which the Asian was housed.

Reading the roster of my achievements, I should have been bursting with pride. Instead, it struck me as nonsensical. I heard a roar of voices coming from every bit of chatter from every dinner, luncheon, and gala I had ever attended. I saw a blur of names in thick, glossy programs, my own displayed in "Archangels," below those in the fewer-numbered and more favored "Inner Sanctum," to which that Yang boy, the Stanford dropout, always seemed to belong. Nothing filled me with the satisfaction I believed I would have at the end of my life. I could not say to myself: "That is where I was most special, where I was most important, and that is enough for a lifetime." I felt like a rich vagabond who had passed through the world, paving my way with gold fairy dust, then realizing too late that the path disintegrated as soon as I passed over it.

As to whom I had left behind, the obituary said, "There are no survivors," which is what is said of airplane crashes. And it was sadly true, all my family was gone—my father, of a heart attack; one brother, of alcoholic cirrhosis, although I was not supposed to mention that; the other brother a victim of a road-rage accident; and my mother, who passed from life before I could know her. I don't count my stepmother, Sweet Ma, who is still alive, but the less said about her the better.

The choice of an open-casket ceremony was my fault, the result of an unfortunate aside I had made to a group of friends at a tea-tasting party I had hosted at my gallery. You see, I had recently received a ship's container of fantastic items that I had found in the countryside of Hubei Province. Among them was a two-hundred-year-old lacquered coffin of paulownia wood made by a eunuch singer who had performed in palace theatricals. In death, most eunuchs, except those in the upper echelons of service, were given only the most perfunctory of burials, without ceremony, since their mutilated bodies were not fit to appear before spirit tablets in the temples. In yesteryears, people rich and poor prepared for the netherworld by making their coffins long before they ceased to hear the cock crow-ing the new day, and the fact that this eunuch was allowed to make such a grand coffin suggested that he was someone's pet—the prettier boys often were. Alas, this adored eunuch drowned while fishing along the Yangtze, and his body went sailing without a boat, swept away to oblivion. The eunuch's parents, in Longgang Township, to whom his possessions had been sent, faithfully kept the coffin in a shed, in hopes that their son's wayward corpse would one day return. The subsequent generations of this family grew impoverished by a combination of drought, extortion, and too many gifts to opera singers, all of which led to their losing face and their property. Years went by, and the new landowners would not go near the shed with the coffin, which was reputed to be haunted by a vampire eunuch. Derelict with neglect, the shed was covered with the dirt of winds, the mud of floods, and the dust of time.

Then, when a newly rich farmer started construction of a miniature golf course to adjoin his family's two-story Swiss-style villa, the shed was unearthed. Amazingly, the coffin had only superficial rot and not much cracking from shrinkage; such is the quality of paulownia, which, though lightweight, is more durable than many harder woods. The exterior had more than fifty coats of black lacquer, as did its short four-legged stand. Beneath the grime, one could see that the lacquer bore whimsically painted carvings of sprites and gods and mythical beasts, as well as other magical motifs, and these were continued on the interior lid of the coffin as well. My favorite detail was a playful Tibetan spaniel on the portion of the lid that would have been opposite the corpse's face. Having been protected from sunlight, the interior art on the lid was still exquisitely colored against the black lacquer. Neat bundles of paper lined the bottom, and I determined them to be a short history of the intended tenant of the coffin and the same man's unpublished poems, tributes to nature, beauty, and—most intriguing—romantic love for a lady from her youth through premature death. Well, I *presume* it was a lady, though one never knows with some Chinese names, does one? The coffin contained two other objects: a smaller lacquer urn with the name of the eunuch's dog, the Tibetan spaniel, and a small ivory-rimmed box in which three calcified peas rattled about, said to be the eunuch's manhood and its two accompaniments.

I could immediately see the coffin was both a millstone and a treasure. I had a few clients—people in the film industry—who might have liked this sort of odd decorative piece, particularly if it still held the petrified peas. But the proportions were awkward. The top extended beyond the length of the coffin like the duck-billed prow of a ship. And it was monstrously heavy.

I asked the farmer to name his price, and he spit out a number that was a tenth of what I was mentally willing to pay. "Ridiculous," I said, and started to leave. "Hey, hey, hey!" he shouted, and I turned back and uttered a sum that was one-third his initial offer. He doubled that, and I retorted that if he was so enamored of a dead man's house, he should keep it. I then split the difference and said I wanted the infernal box only to store some surplus items I had bought, after which I would chop up the coffin for firewood. "It has lots of room for storage," the farmer boasted, and upped the ante a wee bit. I heaved the biggest sigh I could muster, then countered that he should make arrangements for his men to deliver it to Wuhan harbor for shipment with the rest of my brilliant bargains. Done! *Voilà tout!*

Back in San Francisco, once the coffin arrived, I put it in the back room of my shop and did indeed use it to store antique textiles woven by Hmong, Karen, and Lawa hill tribes. Soon after, I had guests over for the tea-tasting. We were sampling different *pu-erh tuo cha*—which is, by the way, the *only* tea that improves over time; anything else, after six months, you may as well use for kitty-cat litter. With the fifth tasting round, we had come to the gold standard of aged teas, a twenty-year-old vintage of the aptly named "camel breath" variety, which is especially pungent but excellent for lowering cholesterol and extending the life span. "But should I die sooner than later," I jokingly said, "then *this*"—and I patted the enormous funerary box—"this magnificent vessel to the afterworld, the Cadillac of coffins, is what I wish to be buried in, and with the top raised at my funeral so that all can admire the interior artistry as well. . . ."

After I died, more than a few from that tea-tasting soiree recalled my quirky remark. What I said as a witticism was described as "prescient," tantamount to a "last wish that *must* be honored," et cetera, ad nauseam. And so I was made to lie in that shipwrecked coffin, *not*, fortunately, with the shriveled parts of the eunuch. The ivory-rimmed box with the ghoulish relics disappeared, as did the container with the bones of the eunuch's beloved Tibetan spaniel—although why anyone would want to steal those sad contents as souvenirs is beyond *my* imagination.

The museum staff in charge of conservation and restoration did a minor bit of spit and polish, though no repair of chips or cracks. Such is their attitude about maintaining authenticity. A Chinese preservationist would have made it look as good as new, and painted it a nice, bright lacquer red and shiny gold. Because the coffin was rather deep, the bottom was filled with styrofoam in the shape of edamame pods, and over that went a layer of velvet—*beige polyester*, it was most dreadful. That was how I came to be exhibited in the museum auditorium, lying in a large black-lacquered coffin carved with celestial animals and the name of its intended tenant, who no doubt would seek me out with an eviction notice shaking in his hand.

Had I seriously been making arrangements for a premature death, I would have asked to be cremated like the Buddhist high monks, poof, gone, without attachment to the body. As for a suitable receptacle for my remains, no single urn would have sufficed. I would have chosen nine boxes of different and delicate proportions, all from The Immortals, say, a meander-patterned box from the Southern Song

dynasty, a round *tao yuanming* for collecting chrysanthemum flowers, and—my absolute favorite, which I had overpriced on purpose—
a simple Ming brush box made of black-lacquered leather. I used to
open it, inhale, and feel the poetry streaming over my face.

The nine well-chosen boxes would have been arranged on a table
during the reading of my will, three rows across, three down, like the
three tosses of I Ching coins—both random and meaningful. Nine
friends, equally chosen with thought from the best of society, would
each have been asked to select a box with a portion of my ashes. Per
my request, they were to take me along on a trip to a lovely place—no
sedentary fireplace mantels or Steinway piano tops for me—where
they might scatter my ashes but keep the box as a memento. The
boxes, being museum quality, would have increased in worth over the
years, and made people remember me "with growing appreciation."
Ah-*ha*, they would laugh upon reading that part. Thus, my ashes
would have taken a more lighthearted and peripatetic course, and I
could have avoided that abhorrent spectacle of an open coffin.
But there we all were, me included, waiting our turn to view the
macabre.

One by one, these friends, acquaintances, and strangers from the
different times of my shortened life stood by the casket to say
farewell, adieu, zai jen. Many people, I could tell, were curious to see
what the morticians had done to cover up the mortal wound. "Oh
my God!" I heard them whisper noisily to one another. To be honest,
I, too, was shocked to see how outlandishly they had prepared me for
my debut with death. A shiny silver scarf was wrapped into a puffy
bow around my lacerated neck. I looked like a turkey with aluminum
foil, about to be put in the oven. Even worse, Bennie Trueba y Cela,
the docent who grieved for me the most—that is to say, with the
greatest display of wracking sobs—had given the mortuary a photo
taken during an expedition that a group of us had made to Bhutan
three years before. In that picture I looked strong and happy, but my

hair was awful—no hot water to wash it for three days. It hung in long greasy strands, the crown was plastered down, and there was a big groove around my forehead where a sun hat had been glued to my scalp with heat and sweat. Himalayas, ha— Who knew it would be so hot there when trekking? Who knew that Bennie would later give this same photo to a mortuary girl to show her what I looked like "in the best of times"? And that that silly girl would give me this same mashed-down Himalayan hairdo and color my skin as dark as a Brokpa maiden's, so that now people would remember my face all wrong, like an old mango that had shrunk and shriveled?

Not that I expected everyone to say, "Oh, I remember Bibi, she was beautiful." I was not. I had a keen eye for beautiful things since girlhood, and I knew my faults. My body was as small and short-legged as a wild Mongolian pony's, my hands and feet as thick as unread books. My nose was too long, my cheeks too sharp. Everything was *just a little too much*. That was the legacy of my mother's side of the family, insufficient excess, too much that was never enough.

Yet I was not dissatisfied with my looks—well, when I was younger, yes, multiply so. But by the time I became a young woman, I knew it was better to be unforgettable than bland. I learned to transform my faults into effect. I darkened my already thick eyebrows, put big-stoned rings on my knobby fingers. I dyed my muddy hair in long streaks of bright gold, red, and lacquer black and wove them into a massive plait that striped the entire length of my back. I adorned myself with layers of unlikely colors, clashing tones married by texture or design or flow. I wore large pendants and medallions, clown-green gaspeite where people expected cool imperial jade. My shoes were my own design, made by a leather worker in Santa Fe. "You see how the toes are curled in the Persian slipper tradition?" I remarked to those who stared too long. "Why do you suppose the Persians started doing that?"

"To show they were upper-class," one person said.

"To point their feet to heaven?" another ventured.

"To hide curved daggers," a man guessed.

"I'm afraid the answer is less fascinating than that," I would say before revealing the fascinating fact: "The curled toes *lifted* the hems of long skirts to prevent the wearers from tripping as they walked the long carpeted halls to pay obeisance to their shah. And thus you see, they are merely practical." Every time I said this, people were highly impressed, and later, when they saw me again, they would say, "I remember you! You're the one with the fascinating shoes."

At the funeral, Zez, the curator at the Asian who oversaw restoration of ancestor commemorative paintings, said I had a style that was "absolutely memorable, as emblematic as the best portraiture of the Sackler collection." That was a slight exaggeration, of course, but it was heartfelt. I certainly felt pings and pangs in my own late heart. There was even a moment when I could sense the ache of others. I was suffused with shared grief—at last, to feel so deeply—and I was glad, truly this time, that I did not have children, no dear daughters or sweet sons to feel the kind of pain that would have come from losing me as their mother. But all at once, this sadness-gladness evaporated, and I settled into more reflective thought.

To think, in all my life no one had loved me wholly and desperately. Oh, I once believed that Stefan Cheval cared for me in that way—yes, *the* Stefan Cheval, the famous one with the controversial footnote. This was eons ago, right before that pink-skinned congressman declared his paintings "obscene and un-American." My opinion? To be perfectly honest, I thought Stefan's series *Freedom of Choice* was overwrought and clichéd. You know the one: gouache overlays of U.S. flags draped over images of dead USDA-stamped livestock, euthanized dogs, and computer monitors—or were they television sets back then? In any case, heaps and heaps of excess to show immoral waste. The reds of the flag were bloody, the blues were garish, and the whites were the color of "discharged sperm," by Stefan's own description. He was certainly no Jasper Johns. Yet after

Stefan's work was condemned, it was vociferously defended by First Amendment rights groups, the ACLU, scads of art departments at top-notch universities, and all those civil libertarian types. Let me tell you, it was *they* who conferred upon the work grandiose messages that Stefan never intended. They saw the complexities of meaningful layers, how some values and lifestyles were judged more important than others, and how we, as Americans, needed the shock of ugliness to recognize our values and responsibilities. The rivulets of sperm were especially frequently cited as representing our greed for pleasure without regard to mess and proliferation. In later years, the mess referred to global warming and the proliferation to nuclear weapons. That's how it happened, his fame. Prices rose. The mere mortal became an icon. A few years later, even churches and schools had posters and postcards of his most popular themes, and franchise galleries in metropolitan tourist centers did a brisk business in selling his limited-edition signed serigraphs, along with prints of Dalí, Neiman, and Kinkade.

I should have been proud to have such a famous man in my life. Socially, we were an ideal duo. As to pleasures of the boudoir, I would discreetly admit that there were innumerable wild nights that met the standards of Dionysus. But I could not give up my work to be an addendum to his. And he was always gone to give a paid lecture, to attend the trustees' annual dinner at the Met in New York, or to drop by ritzy benefits, several a night, for which he would jump out of a dark-windowed Town Car, lend his conversation-stopping presence for twenty minutes, then move along to the next party. When we were together, we enjoyed playful verbal banter. But we were not tender. We expressed no gushing sentiments one might later regret. And so, the seasons passed, the blooms faded, and nature took its course of inevitable decay. Without argument or discussion, we started to neglect each other. Somehow we remained friends, which meant we could still attend the same parties and greet each other with a pretend kiss on the cheeks. Thus, we circumvented becoming fast talk-talk. We were, at best, gossip on a slow day. Speaking of which, a friend told me Stefan now suffered from major and paralyzing depression, which I was sad to hear. What's more, she said his signed giclée reproductions, the ones finished off with brushstrokes of clear acrylic swish-swashed here and there by his own hand, were selling on eBay starting at $24.99, no reserve, and that included the frame. As I said, it was quite sad.

I had other men as steady companions, and with each of them I experienced a certain degree of fondness but no heartsickness worth mentioning. Well, plenty of disappointment, of course, and one silly episode of cutting up a negligee bought for a night of passion, an impetuous disregard for money, since the gown was worth far more than the man. But I ask myself now: Was there ever a true great love? Anyone who became the object of my obsession and not simply my affections? I honestly don't think so. In part, this was my fault. It was my nature, I suppose. I could not let myself become that *unmindful*. Isn't that what love is—losing your mind? You don't care what people think. You don't see your beloved's faults, the slight stinginess, the bit of carelessness, the occasional streak of meanness. You don't mind that he is beneath you socially, educationally, financially, and *morally*—that's the worst, I think, deficient morals.

I always minded. I was always cautious of what could go wrong, what was already "not ideal." I paid attention to the divorce rates. I ask you this: What's the chance of finding a lasting marriage? Twenty percent? Ten? Did I know any woman who escaped having her heart crushed like a recyclable can? Not a one. From what I have observed, when the anesthesia of love wears off, there is always the pain of consequences. You don't have to be stupid to marry the wrong man.

Look at my dearest friend and the trustee of my estate, Vera Hendricks. She is one very smart lady, has a doctorate in sociology from Stanford, is the director of one of the largest nonprofit foundations for African-American causes, and she is often included in the Hundred Most Influential Black Women of America. In any case, as smart as Vera is, in her younger years she made the mistake of marrying a jazz drummer, Maxwell, whose job, it seemed to him, was to stay out and smoke and drink and tell jokes, then come home in the early hours of the morning. And he was not black, mind you, but Jewish. Black and Jewish, that was no small aberration among couples in those days. His mother reverted to Orthodoxy, declared him dead, and sat shiva for weeks. When they moved from Boston to Tuscaloosa, Vera and Maxwell had to fight the world to stay together. Vera confided that people's hatred toward them was their raison d'être as a couple. Later, when they lived in the liberal environs of Berkeley, where mixed marriages were the norm, the fights were just between the two of them and were mostly about money and drinking, among the most common causes of marital discord. Vera was a reminder to me that even intelligent women make stupid mistakes in their choice of men.

As I approached forty, I almost persuaded myself to marry and have a child. The man loved me deeply and spoke in the romantic verbiage of destiny and diminutive nicknames that are too embarrassing to repeat. Naturally, I was flattered and also touched. He was not handsome in a conventional sense, but I found his genius to be powerful, and thus an odd aphrodisiac. He was socially inept and had a number of strange habits, but on the basis of DNA alone, he was an ideal partner for procreation. He spoke of our future child as part angel, part wunderkind. I was intrigued with the idea of a child, but inevitably it would arrive in a package called motherhood, which raised memories of my stepmother. After I refused the man's numerous entreaties to marry, he was shattered to the depths of his being. I felt quite guilty until he married another woman, six months after. It was sudden, yes, but I was pleased for him, really, I was, and I continued to be pleased when they had a child, then another and another and another. Four! There was so much to be pleased about, wasn't there? One was the most I would have had, and for years I thought about that child that never was. Would she have loved me?

Look at Vera's two daughters, I often mused—they have always adored her, even in their teens. They were the progeny that people can only dream of. Might my child have had similar feelings for me? I would have seated her on my lap and brushed her hair, smelling the clean scent. I imagined myself tucking a peony behind her ear, or clipping in her hair a pretty barrette speckled with emeralds. And we would look in the mirror together and know we loved each other so much that tears would spring to our eyes. I realized much later that the child I imagined was my young self, who had longed for just such a mother.

I admit that whenever I heard that certain offspring of friends had turned into misfits and ingrates, I received the news with schadenfreude, and also was relieved to have missed the entire spectrum of parental frustration and despair. What could possibly be more socially devastating than having your own child declare that she hated you, and in front of your less-than-best friends?

This question came to me as I watched Lucinda Pari, the director of communications for the Asian Art Museum, rise and approach the lectern to provide her own contribution to my eulogy. She had once told me that I was like a mother to her. Now here she was at my memorial, praising my virtues: "The money from Bibi Chen's estate"—she paused to toss her sleek curtain of hair like a racehorse—"money derived from the sale of her *deluxe* three-unit apartment building and *gorgeous*, bridge-view penthouse on Leavenworth, in addition to her store, the *legendary* Immortals, and its *enormously* successful online catalogue business, on top of a personal collection of Buddhist art—a very fine and well-regarded collection, I might add—has been willed in trust to the museum." Loud clapping ensued. Lucinda's talent has always been to mix drama and exaggeration with dull facts so that words balance out as believable. Before the applause could turn thunderous, she held up her palm and continued: "She leaves us with an estate estimated to be—wait a minute, here it is—*twenty million* dollars."

Nobody gasped. The crowd did not jump up and cheer. They clapped loudly, but I wouldn't say wildly. It was as if my bequest had been expected, and an ordinary amount. When the room quieted all too soon, she held up a plaque. "We will be affixing this in commemoration of her generosity in one of the wings in the new Asian, to be opened in 2003."

One wing! I knew I should have specified the degree of recognition I should receive for my twenty million. What's more, the plaque was a modest square, brushed stainless steel, and my name was engraved in letters so small that even the people in the front row had to lean forward and squint. This was the style Lucinda liked, modern and plain, sans serif type as unreadable as directions on a medicine bottle. She and I used to argue in a friendly way about the brochures she had expensive graphic artists design. "Your eyes are still young," I told her not too long ago. "You must realize, people who give vast amounts of money, their eyes are old. If you want this style, you should give people reading glasses to go with it." That's when she laughed in a not-so-joking way and said, "You're just like my mother. There's always *something* not right."

"I'm giving useful information," I told her.

"Like my mother," she said.

At my funeral, she said those words again at the very end, only this time she was smiling with tearful eyes: "Bibi was like a mother to me. She was terribly generous with her advice."

MY OWN MOTHER did not give me advice, terrible or otherwise. She died when I was a baby. So it was my father's first wife who raised my two brothers and me. She was named Bao Tian—"Sweet Bud"—which was not quite suitable. We, her stepchildren, were obliged to call that old sour-mouth by the affectionate name of Sweet Ma. Whatever emotional deficits I had, they were due to her. My excesses, as I have already said, were from my mother.

According to Sweet Ma, she would have been my father's only wife had she not insisted that my father take a concubine so he could seed some descendants. "It was my own idea," Sweet Ma boasted. "I wasn't forced to accept the arrangement, not at all."

As the fates would have it, Sweet Ma was unable to bear children. Soon after she married she caught a spotted-skin disease—it might have been measles, or chickenpox, but was definitely nothing as serious as smallpox. The aftermath of this illness, she lamented, blocked off the path to the warm springs of her body, and thus, she did not have sufficient heat to incubate the seeds of babies. Instead, this useless warmth rose in her body and continued to break out as blisters on her face and hands, and perhaps the rest of her, which we couldn't see, nor did we want to. Time and time again, she would wonder aloud over what she had done in a past life to deserve such a barren fate. "What small transgression for such bitter punishment?" she cried as the red dots rose. "No children of my own, just the leftovers of others" (meaning my brothers and me). Whenever she ate anything that disagreed with her, from unripe kumquats to veiled insults, her face was soon decorated with crusty splotches that resembled maps of foreign countries. "Do you know where India is?" we would ask her, and swallow our giggles. To soothe herself, she scratched and complained incessantly, and when she ran out of things to say, she would look at me and criticize my mother for endowing me with such ugly features. In time, she scratched her eyebrows bald, and when she did not draw them in with mean black slashes, she resembled a Buddhist nun with knots on her forehead, bulging with anger.

That is how I remember Sweet Ma, always running a sharp finger along her hairless eyebrows, chattering nonsense. My older brothers managed to escape her grasp. They were immune to her influence and treated her with blank-faced disdain. Thus, all her arrows fell on me as her solitary target.

"I tell you this," Sweet Ma would say to me, "only so you won't be stricken sick to hear it from someone else." And she would tell me once again that my mother had been a tiny girl like me, but not as squat, barely seventy pounds at age sixteen when my father took her in as his breeding concubine.

"Itty-bitty though she was," Sweet Ma said, "she was excessive in everything she did. She ate too many pears. She showed too much emotion. Why, when she laughed she could not control herself, and would fall to the floor in a fit of giggles until I slapped her back to her senses. What's more, she slept all night long, yet yawned all day. She slept so much her bones turned soft. That was why she was always collapsing like a jellyfish out of water."

During wartime, when the price of fatty pork had tripled, Sweet Ma could be heard to declare: "Though we have money enough, I'm content to eat meat sparingly, just for the taste and certainly not more than once a week. But your mother, when she was alive, her eyes were like those of a carrion bird, ready to pounce on any dead flesh." Sweet Ma said a decent woman should never show eagerness for food or any other kind of pleasure. Most of all, she should "never be a burden," this being what Sweet Ma strived not to be, and she desired in particular for my father to acknowledge this as often as she did.

In those days, we lived in a three-story Tudoresque manor on Rue Massenet in the French Concession of Shanghai. This was not in the best of the best neighborhoods, not like Rue Lafayette, where the Soongs and the Kungs lived, with their villas and vast, multiacred gardens, croquet lawns, and pony carts. Then again, we were not the kind of family to rub our bountiful luck into the faces of our inferiors. All in all, our house was still quite good, better than most people could say they live in, even in comparison with today's multimillion-dollar San Francisco homes. My father's family had a longtime cotton mill business and the department store Honesty, which my grandfather had started in 1923. It was maybe one degree less prestigious than the department store Sincerity, and while our store was not as large, our merchandise was just as good, and in the case of cotton goods, the quality was even better for the same price. All my father's foreign customers said so.

He was a typical high-class Shanghainese: absolutely traditional in matters of family and home, and completely modern in business and the outside world. When he left our gates, he entered another realm and adapted himself to it like a chameleon. When necessary, he could speak in other languages, and the accent was absolutely particular to the tutor he had chosen for reasons of class distinction: the English was Oxford, the French was Right Bank, the German was Berlin. He also knew Latin and a formal kind of Manchu into which all the literary classics had been translated. He wore pomade in his sleeked-back hair, smoked filter-tip cigarettes, and conversed on subjects as wide-ranging as riddles, the physiology of different races, and the curiosities of other cuisines. He could argue persuasively on the mistreatment of China in the Treaty of Versailles and compare the political satire in Dante's *Inferno* with Tsao's earlier version of *A Dream of Red Mansions*. When he stepped back through the gates of our family home, he reverted to his private self. He read much, but seldom spoke, and truly, there was no need in a household whose women worshipped him and anticipated his needs before they ever occurred to him.

His foreign friends called him Philip. My brothers' English names were Preston and Nobel, which were auspicious, sounding like the word "president" and the name of the prestigious prize that comes with a lot of money. Sweet Ma chose the name Bertha, because my father said it was close-sounding to "Bao Tian," and my mother had been known as "Little Bit," which was how she pronounced the Western name Elizabeth, which my father had given her. My father called me Bibi, which was both a Western name and short for Bifang, the name my mother bestowed on me. As you can imagine, we were a worldly family. My brothers and I had English- and French-speaking tutors, so we could receive a modern education. This also gave us secret languages that we could use in front of Sweet Ma, who knew only Shanghainese.

One time, Nobel reported that our Bedlington terrier, whom Sweet Ma detested, had left a small offering in her room—*"Il a fait la merde sur le tapis"*—and because the pattern in the rug masked the appearance of fresh fecal deposits, our stepmother could not figure out why every room in the house stank until it was too late. The boys had a fondness for adding surprise elements to Sweet Ma's vials of medicines and snuff bottles. *Caca d'oie*, collected from the scummy shoals of our goose pen, was a favorite because it encompassed the trifecta of disgusting things: foul, slimy, and bilious green. To hear them tell me what they had done left me laughing helplessly on the floor. I so miss my brothers!

More often, however, my brothers were not at home to buffet Sweet Ma's assaults upon me. Whenever I sat before the keys of the piano, Sweet Ma recounted my mother's poor musicianship as a possible cause of mine. I defended my mother once, telling Sweet Ma that my father had recently told some guests that she "could make Chopin's *Fantaisie Impromptu* sound like fast-running water in a spring brook."

"Ssss!" Sweet Ma countered with irritation. "That was said to guests who are *foreigners*. They expect inflated talk. They have no shame, no propriety, no standards of excellence. Besides, *any* schoolgirl can play that easy song, even *you*, if you practiced a little harder." And then she poked the side of my head for good effect.

Sweet Ma said that my father did not need to inflate *her* worth, because they had a complete understanding. "Superfluous words are not necessary when the marriage is balanced, in perfect harmony," she told me. "And that is because our union was fated to be."

At the time, it did not occur to me to question what she said, and my brothers had no opinions on love, or if they did, they would not share them with me. I was thus left to assume that a good marriage was one in which the husband respected the wife's privacy. He did not intrude in her life, visit her rooms, or bother her with questions. There was no need to speak to each other, since they were of the same mind.

But one day my uncle and his family came for a visit several months long. My cousin Yuhang and I kept each other company morning to night. We were like sisters, although we saw each other only once a year. On that particular visit, she told me that she had overheard her parents and their friends gossiping—which, at the time, was the only way anyone learned the truth. The gossip had to do with the union between Sweet Ma and my father. It had been agreed to before their births. In 1909, two comrades from different life circumstances vowed that if the revolution to end the Ching dynasty succeeded and they were still alive to see it, their families should be united by marriage. Well, the Ching was overthrown in 1911, and the comrade with a son had a reputation so high it was said to have reached the heavens. That would be my father's family. The other had a daughter, and his household clung to earth like the rotted roots of a tree about to tilt over with the next small gust. That would be Sweet Ma's household. When the poor comrade with the daughter ran into the rich one with the son, he mentioned their earlier vow, incompatible in status though their lives were. It was widely known, the servants said, that my grandfather was a man of high morals for forcing his eldest son to marry a girl so plain, so lacking in any charms that would compensate for her embarrassingly meager dowry. No wonder the son took on a concubine as soon as he could.

Of course, Sweet Ma reported things differently: "Your mother," she said, "was the daughter of a concubine to a family of only middle status. The concubine had given birth to ten healthy babies, all boys except one. That one girl, while weedy in looks at age sixteen, held promise for being as baby-prolific as her mother. I suggested her to your father, and he said I was wife enough. But I insisted that a stallion must have mares, and mares produce broods, so he mustn't be a mule."

According to Sweet Ma, the relationship my father had with my mother was "very polite, as one should be toward strangers." In fact, my father was much too kind, and my mother learned to take advantage of this. The way Sweet Ma described it: "She was a schemer. She'd put on her rose-colored dress, twirl her favorite flower hairpin, and with eyes dishonestly lowered, she would raise that simpering smile of hers toward your father. Oh, I knew what she was up to. She was always begging money to pay off the gambling debts of her nine brothers. I learned too late that her entire family was a nest of snake spawn. Don't you grow up to be like them, or I'll let the rats in to chew you up at night."

According to Sweet Ma, my mother proved true to her breeding and excelled at becoming pregnant every year. "She gave birth to your eldest brother," Sweet Ma said, counting on her fingers. "Then there was your second brother. After that, three blue babies, drowned in the womb, which was a shame but not so tragic, since they were girls."

I came along in 1937, and Sweet Ma was there to witness my dramatic arrival. "You should have seen your mother when she was nine months pregnant with you. She looked like a melon balanced on chopsticks, teetering this way and that. . . . Early in the morning, that's when her water broke, after making us wait all night. The winter sky was the color of spent coal, and so was your mother's face. . . . You were too big to come out between her legs, so the mid-wives had to slice her nearly in two and pull you out like a fatty tape-worm. You weighed over ten pounds, and you had bloody hair down to your shoulders."

I shivered when she said that.

"Bifang your mother named you, though heaven knows I tried to persuade her to choose something else. 'Good-reputation jade' sounds like an advertisement poster, in my opinion, what pleases the ear of those who don't know better. '*Bifang, bifang*, buy your *bifang* here!' Ha, *fang pi* would be a better name to call you, a fart, yes indeed, that's what you were, all right, a stinky little fart that shot out of her bottom."

Sweet Ma held up a hairpin for me to see but not touch. "She named you Bifang because your father gave her this ugly thing to commemorate your successful birth." It was a hairpin with a hun-dred tiny leaves carved out of bright imperial-green jade. Within the branches were peony blossoms made of tiny diamonds. The shining hairpin, when placed in the hair, suggested a glorious spring. Upon seeing that hairpin for the first time, I knew why she named me Bi-fang: I was her precious jade, her budding treasure, her glorious spring. *Bifang.*

Sweet Ma tried to change my school name as well. "I like the name Bibi," I said. "Father calls me that."

"Well, there's nothing good about that name, either. It's especially common. Your father had a Dutch customer whose wife was named Bibi. He asked the Dutch lady if that was an unusual name in her country. And she said, 'Heavens, no. "Bibi" can be French, it can be German, Italian even, so really, it is found everywhere.' And your fa-ther clapped his hands and said there was an expression that meant exactly that: *bibi jie shi*—can be found everywhere. If it was found everywhere, he said, to be polite, it must be popular, very much in fa-vor. To my way of thinking, if it's found everywhere then it must be a common nuisance, like flies and dust." The day Sweet Ma said this, she was wearing my mother's hairpin, the one she said was so ugly. I wanted to pull it out. And because I could not, I said in my strongest voice that I had already chosen Bibi as my school name and I would not change it. Sweet Ma then said if I was old enough to choose my name, I was old enough to know the true circumstances of my tiny mother's death.

"She died of excess and dissatisfaction," Sweet Ma divulged. "Too much but never enough. She knew I was your father's first wife, the most respected, the most favored. No matter how many sons she had, he would probably one day turn her out the door and replace her with another."

"Father said that?"

Sweet Ma did not confirm or deny. Instead she said, "You see, respect is lasting. Fondness is passing, a whim for a season or two, only to be replaced by a new fancy. All men do this. Your mother knew this, I knew this. Someday you will, too. But rather than accept her situation in life, your mother lost all control of her senses. She began to crave sweets. She couldn't stop eating them. And she was thirsty all the time, drinking like the genie who swallowed the ocean and spit it back up. One day, a ghost saw how weak she was in spirit and entered her body through the hole in her stomach. Your mother fell to the ground, twitching and babbling, and then she was still."

In my made-up memory, I saw my tiny mother rise from her bed and go over to a pot of sugared black sesame seed soup. She dipped her fingers to taste if it was sweet enough. It was not. She added more lumps of sugar, more, more, more. Then she stirred the hot, dark paste, tipped bowlful after bowlful into her mouth, filling her stomach to the level of her throat, the hollow of her mouth, until she fell to the floor, wet and drowned.

When I developed diabetes, just five years ago, I thought my mother might have died of the same thing, that her blood was either too sweet or not sweet enough. Diabetes, I found, is a constant battle of balance. Anyway, that was how I knew my mother, through the faults I inherited: the crooked lower teeth, the upward scrunch of the left eyebrow, the desire for more than could ever be satisfied in a normal person.

The night we left Shanghai forever, Sweet Ma made one more show of her endless sacrifice. She refused to go. "I would be useless over in America, unable to speak English," she said coyly to my father. "And I don't want to be a burden. Besides, Bifang is almost thirteen, too old now for a nursemaid." She glanced in my direction, waiting for me to contradict her with vigorous protests.

My father said: "Don't argue about this. Of course you're coming." He was in a hurry, because waiting for him was the gatekeeper, a mean man named Luo, whom we all disliked. He had made arrangements for our hasty departure before Shanghai fell completely under Communist control.

In front of my brothers, our grandfather, and the servants, Sweet Ma continued to argue, again looking for me to say the correct words. I was supposed to fling myself at her feet, knock my head on the floor, and beg her not to leave me. And because I did not do so, she became more determined to extract this plea from me. "Bifang doesn't need me," she said. "She already told me so."

It was true. Only that morning, I had said similar words to her. She had been berating me for sleeping too long. She called me Rotten Soft Bones. She said I was just like my mother, and if I didn't cure myself of these bad habits, I, too, would meet a terrible demise. I was not quite awake, and in my longing to cling to sleep, I placed my hands over my ears and thought I was shouting in my dreams: "Stop, you moaning milk-cow." And the next thing I knew, Sweet Ma was slapping me back to my senses.

Now there I was with my family, about to flee in the middle of the night, with gold and diamonds stuffed into the soft bodies of my dolls, and there was this: my mother's hairpin. I had stolen it from Sweet Ma's dresser and had sewn it into my coat lining.

Gatekeeper Luo urged us to hurry, and Sweet Ma was still staging threats not to go. We were all supposed to plead for her to change her mind. My mind went in a new direction. What would happen if Sweet Ma *did* stay behind? How would my life change?

Pondering such thoughts made my chest ticklish and weak. I felt my knees and spine growing soft. This always happened when I anticipated anything good or bad, whenever I came close to allowing myself to feel the extremes of emotion. Since my mother had been the same way, I feared that I, too, would one day lose control and fall into a heap and die of excess. I had thus learned to push down my feelings, to force myself to not care, to do nothing and let things happen, come what may.

Silence would now decide my fate. "Speak," Father coaxed. "Apologize."

I waited in silence. "Hurry now!" he scolded. A minute must have passed. My legs were growing weak again. Push it down, I told myself, push down your wish.

Father finally broke in and repeated to Sweet Ma: "Of course you're coming," but Sweet Ma beat her chest, shouting, "It's finished! I would rather have the Communists run a bayonet through me than be forced to go with that wicked child!" And she lurched out of the room.

When we boarded the boat to Haiphong, I reflected in terror over what I had done. I stood on the deck as the boat pulled away, the black sky clotted with stars and galaxies, and I imagined what bright life awaited us in a new land just over the horizon. We were going to America, where joy was so abundant you did not have to consider it luck.

I pictured Sweet Ma alone in our family house on Rue Massenet, the rooms still richly furnished, but ghostly, empty of life. Soon the soldiers with bayonets would come into the house and smash its cap-italist symbols, and all the while, Sweet Ma would sit in her usual chair, telling the revolutionaries she didn't want to be a burden. Per-haps they would punish her anyway for her bourgeois life. They might slap her browless face—I could picture it so clearly—the cruel men shouting for her to use her hair and tears to mop the floor. They would kick her thighs to hurry her up, aim a boot at her bottom. As I relished this scenario, playing it over and over in my mind, I became weak-limbed with fear and exhilaration, a strange combination that made me feel truly malevolent. I sensed I would be punished in my next life. I would become a cow and she the crow who would peck my flanks. And with that image in my mind, I suddenly felt bony fin-gers pluck my cheek, pinching until I tasted blood.

It was Sweet Ma. Father had gone back and insisted three more times that she come. Though her dignity was shaken, she had al-lowed herself to be pulled from her chair and carried screaming to the waiting car that whisked them both to the wharf. Thus, Sweet Ma returned, more determined than ever to put some sense into my brain by beating the evil out of my body. How lucky was I that she continued as my dim guiding light.

Sweet Ma tried to shape my mind, pounding it like dumpling dough. And the more she tried, the more I became like my mother, so she said. I was greedy, she warned, and could not fill my heart with enough pleasure, my stomach with enough contentment, my body with enough sleep. I was like a rice basket with a rat hole at the bot-tom, and thus could not be satisfied and overflow, nor could I be filled. I would never know the full depth and breadth of love, beauty, or happiness. She said it like a curse.

Because of her criticism, I acted as if I were even more deficient in feeling, particularly toward her. I found that a blank face and a bland heart were the very things that made Sweet Ma's eyebrows bulge to bursting. My reasoning was this: How could I be wounded when I didn't care? In time, I felt I was growing stronger and stronger. My legs no longer buckled, and I learned to hide from pain. I hid my deepest feelings so well I forgot where I had placed them.

I remember the terrible night I realized that Sweet Ma's curse had come true. It was a year after I started university life, and I had returned home at Sweet Ma's command to join the family celebration of the Autumn Festival, what is traditionally a time of thanksgiving. Now here we were, my father and brothers and I, at the usual gathering of distant relatives and Chinese friends, both longtime citizens and the recently immigrated. We were in the backyard of a second cousin's house in Menlo Park, about to view the full moon rise. We carried paper lanterns with sputtering candles, and walked toward the swimming pool. And in that pool, I saw the moon appear and shimmer, a golden melon and not just a flat disc, as it had always appeared to me before. I heard people moan with happiness. I saw their mouths pop open, the rims of their eyes drip with tears.

My mouth was closed, my eyes were dry. I could see the moon as clearly as they, and I could even appreciate its special glories. But why didn't I flood in the same way? Why was their happiness tenfold what I felt? Did I lack the proper connection between the senses and the heart?

And then I realized that this was my habit. To hold back my feelings. To keep my knees from buckling. And with that knowledge, I was ready to feel whatever I wanted, as fully as I wanted. I gazed at the moon and willed myself to feel all the emotions. I waited for joy and awe to wash over me. I was determined, I was ready, I was anticipating, expecting, hoping . . . but nothing happened. My legs stood strong and straight.

That night of the moon viewing I realized I would always be deficient in great feeling. It was because I never had a proper mother while I was growing up. A mother is the one who fills your heart in the first place. She teaches you the nature of happiness: what is the right amount, what is too much, and the kind that makes you want more of what is bad for you. A mother helps her baby flex her first feelings of pleasure. She teaches her when to later exercise restraint, or to take squealing joy in recognizing the fluttering leaves of the gingko tree, to sense a quieter but more profound satisfaction in chancing upon an everlasting pine. A mother enables you to realize that there are different levels of beauty, and therein lie the sources of pleasure, some of which are popular and ordinary, and thus of brief value, and others of which are difficult and rare, and hence worth pursuing.

But through my formative years, I had only Sweet Ma. That woman with her parched innards tried to push upon me her notion of good things—telling me to be glad I was not as bare-dressed as a tree in winter, to be grateful that the little skeleton of a girl lying in a gutter was not me, to recognize that the shade of a willow tree in unbearable heat was a happy sacrifice I could make to those who were either older or younger than I was, which was everybody, as it always turned out. I followed Sweet Ma's instructions so that eventually I could feel not naturally, but only carefully.

When my father died, I felt loss and sadness, to be sure, but not the turmoil or devastation that my brothers and stepmother showed. With romance, I felt pangs of love, yet never the passion that overcame my friends.

But then I discovered art. I saw for the first time nature and pure feelings expressed in a form I could understand. A painting was a *translation* of the language of my heart. My emotions were all there—but in a painting, a sculpture. I went to museum after museum, into the labyrinths of rooms and that of my own soul. And there they were—my feelings, and all of them natural, spontaneous, truthful, and free. My heart cavorted within shapes and shadows and splashes, in patterns, repetitions, and abruptly ending lines. My soul shivered in tiny feathered strokes, one eyelash at a time.

And so I began to collect art. In this way, I was able to surround myself with the inexpressible, to exult in the souls of others. What a lifelong debt I owe to art!

As for Sweet Ma, she remained her bitter, complaining self. When my father died, I put her in an apartment in my building and hired a housekeeper who could keep things tidy and cook Chinese food for her. Sweet Ma never lifted a finger, except to scold me or anyone else who was unlucky enough to cross her path. When she became infirm, I put her in the best of senior residences, at great expense to myself. She was not grateful. She called it Death's Waiting Room. For years, I told myself to be patient, knowing she would soon die. Surely her explosive anger might cause a similar effect on the blood vessels or her brain or heart. She was nearly ninety-one and I only sixty-three when I passed her by and flew out of this world.

Oh, how she wept. She recalled our past together as such a rosy relationship that I wondered if she was more senile than I thought. Or could it be that she had actually had a change of heart? When I discerned the answer, I changed my mind about her as well. Whereas I once looked forward to her end, I now wish her a long, long life. Let her not leave Death's Waiting Room and join me as her companion in the afterlife.

WHEN THE FIRST PART of my funeral ended, the crowd drifted down the steps of the de Young Museum and onto Tea Garden Drive. My casket was sealed with wax, placed on dollies, and quickly wheeled to a delivery bay, where a hearse was waiting. The hearse drove out of the parking lot, just as giggly children from the Chinese American International School—of which I had always been a generous benefactor—left the bandshell in the Music Concourse with their sweet-sounding instruments and filed behind the hearse. From the green wooden benches rose another two dozen students wearing white sackcloth—loose jackets, pants, and caps, costumes left over from the previous year's spring pageant. They fell in behind the band. Two sturdy boys on stilts held up a poster-mounted photo of me in my Himalayan hairdo. A wreath of flowers framed my blown-up face and its too-broad smile. Dear me, it looked as if I were campaigning to become Mayor of the Underworld!

In a short while, the mourners, as well as a dozen or so tourists on rented Rollerblades and a few dozen more who had been expelled from the gates of the Japanese Tea Garden, gathered behind the band, following the busy hand signals of the museum staff. The flutes trilled, the cymbals tinkled, the drums rumbled, and a flock of fat pigeons flew up with a windy flapping of wings, and that was how we began our walk to pay tribute to "a great lady lost."

Though it was December, the weather was sunny and without wind, which made everyone feel enlivened, unable to grieve with true despair. Those who had signed up for the ill-fated Burma Road trip were ambling in a cluster toward the rear. They were the ones I decided to join, listening at the back of their minds. As we were circling the concourse, Harry Bailley brought up the subject of canceling. "What fun would it be without our Bibi?" he said in that rich baritone that I have always loved listening to on his television show. "Who would tell us what to savor, what to see?" All very touching questions.

Marlena Chu was quick to agree. "It just wouldn't be the same," she said in an elegant voice, tinged with an accent shaped by her Shanghainese birth, her childhood in São Paulo, her British teachers, and her studies at the Sorbonne. She came from a family of former vast wealth and power, who were reduced on their exodus to South America to becoming merely comfortably well-off. Marlena bought fine art as a professional curator for private collections and commissioned sculptural installations for corporations setting up their international headquarters in far-flung places. I also happened to know that she had a potential new client in Milan. She would have been relieved to have a legitimate reason to cancel the Burma trip. However, her twelve-year-old daughter, Esmé, who dreamed of helping Burmese orphans and had bragged to her teacher and classmates of this noble cause, would have protested unceasingly had she been told they were now going to fashionable Italy instead.

How I knew all this, I had no notion at first, didn't even wonder how I knew. But I sensed others as clearly as I sensed myself; their feelings became mine. I was privy to their secret thoughts: their motives and desires, guilt feelings and regrets, joys and fears, as well as the shades of truth within what they said, and what they refrained from saying. The thoughts swam about me like schools of colorful fish, and as people spoke, their true feelings dove through me in a flash. It was that shocking and effortless. The Mind of Others— that's what the Buddha would have called it.

Whatever the case, with this enlarged consciousness, I eavesdropped on my friends as they discussed the upcoming Burma trip. "To tell the truth," I heard Roxanne Scarangello say, "I've been asking myself why I even agreed to go to Burma." This was a small jab at her husband, Dwight Massey, who had booked them on the trip without gaining her full enthusiasm. It could be argued that she had never said no, not absolutely. While she was busy with a critical part of her research, she told him to make the arrangements but said she wouldn't mind another trip to the Galápagos, so she could further document ecological changes and their effects on the endemic species of the islands. That was the topic of her forthcoming book. She was an evolutionary biologist, a Darwin scholar, and a MacArthur fellow.

Her husband was a behavioral psychologist who had once been her student; he was thirty-one, twelve years her junior. His specialization was the neurological differences between males and females, "often erroneously referred to as differences in mean IQ," Dwight would say, "rather than different fluencies in regional areas of the brain." He was now assisting with the research project of another scientist, investigating the means by which squirrels were able to bury nuts in a hundred-some places, without any discernible pattern except a roughly circular one, and then months later find the nuts again. What strategies did females use to bury and find the nuts? What strategies did the males use? Were they different? Which were more efficient? It was an interesting project, but it was not Dwight's. He was an underling. His career thus far had been determined more by the universities where Roxanne was sought.

Dwight had worshipped Roxanne unquestioningly when they first paired up—this was ten years back, shortly after she appeared in *Esquire*'s "Women We Love" issue. He was twenty-one, her brightest student. In recent times he more frequently competed with her intellectually, as well as physically. Both Roxanne and Dwight were appallingly athletic and loved very much to perspire. So they had much in common. But if you were to meet them for the first time, you might think, as I did, that they were an unlikely couple. She was muscular and stocky, round-faced and ruddy-complexioned, with a demeanor that was at once smart and friendly. He was lanky, had sharp-angled facial features that made him look roguish, and his manner seemed combative and arrogant. She evinced confidence, and he acted like the nippy underdog.

"It's the ethics that bother me," Roxanne now said. "If you go to Burma, it's in some ways a financial collusion with a corrupt regime."

Marlena stepped in: "Roxanne makes a very good point. When we signed up, it seemed that the regime was improving matters. They were on the verge of some kind of rapprochement with that woman, the Nobel Peace Prize winner—"

"Aung San Suu Kyi," said Dwight.

"—and to go," Marlena continued, "when many are honoring the boycott, well, it's similar to crossing a picket line, I think—"

Dwight cut her off again. "You know what kind of people blindly follow boycotts? Same ones who say that eating hamburgers means you approve of torturing cows. It's a form of liberal fascism. Boycotts don't help anyone, not real people. It just makes the do-gooders feel good. . . ." Wherever he really stood on the matter of boycotts, Dwight keenly wanted to make this trip because he had learned only a year before that his great-great-grandfather on his mother's side had gone to Burma in 1883, leaving his wife and seven children in Huddersfield, a city of industry in Yorkshire. He took a job with a British timber company, and, as the story was reported in the family, he was ambushed by natives on the banks of the Irrawaddy in 1885, the year before the British officially took over old Burmah. Dwight felt an uncanny affinity toward his ancestor, as though some genetic memory were driving him to that part of the world. As a behavioral psychologist, he knew that wasn't scientifically possible, yet he was intrigued by it, and lately, obsessed.

"What is the point of *not* doing something?" he went on arguing. "Don't eat beef, feel good about saving cows. Boycott Burma, feel good about not going. But what good have you really done? Whom have you saved? You've chosen to vacation in fucking Bali instead. . . ."

"Can we discuss this more rationally?" Vera said. My dear friend despised hearing people use sexual expletives for emphasis. Invoke religion instead, she'd say to those in her organization—use the "damn" and "God Almighty" that show strength of conviction. Use the f-word for what it was intended, the deep-down guttural pleasure of sex. And don't bring it into arguments where hearts and brains should prevail. She was known to have kicked people off projects at work for lesser linguistic offenses. She observed that Dwight was smart and abrasive, and this combination was worse than being simply stupid and annoying. It made people want to pummel him to bits, though they might have agreed with some of what he had to say.

"Sanctions worked in South Africa—" Marlena began.

"Because the oppressors were white, and rich enough to feel the pinch," Dwight finished. "The U.S. sanctions in Burma are pretty ineffectual. Burma does most of its trade with other Asian countries. Why should they care if we disapprove of them? Come on, what's the incentive?"

"We could reroute to Nepal," another from our little group said. That would be Moff, an old friend of Harry's from boarding school days at École Monte Rosa in Switzerland, which they had attended while their diplomat fathers were assigned to countries without English-speaking schools. Moff was interested in Nepal because he owned a bamboo farm near Salinas, and, as it happened, he had been doing research on harvestable wood products in the Nepal lowlands and the possibility of living there six months out of the year. His name was actually Mark Moffett, but he'd been known as Moff since Harry started calling him that in boyhood. The two friends were now in their forties and divorced. For the last four years they had made a ritual of traveling together during winter holidays.

Moff figured that his fifteen-year-old son, Rupert, would love Katmandu as much as he had at that age. But his ex-wife would no doubt throw his Nepalese singing bowls at his balls if he took their son to that "hippie place." In the custody battle for Rupert, she had accused Moff of being a drug addict, as if he had been smoking crack 'round the clock rather than just taking a few friendly tokes of weed every now and then. It had been a battle to get her to let Rupert go with him to China and Burma for the holidays.

Vera cleared her throat to get everyone's attention. "My dear fellow travelers, I hate to tell you this, but to change or cancel anything now means forfeiting the entire deposit, which, by the way, is one hundred percent of the cost since we are now just days from our departure date."

"Good Lord, that's outrageous!" Harry exclaimed.

"What about our trip insurance?" Marlena said. "That would cover it. Unexpected death."

"I'm sorry to report Bibi didn't buy any." Why was Vera *apologizing* for my sake? As everyone murmured varying degrees of shock, dismay, and disgust, I shouted and pounded my fist into my palm to make my point. But no one could hear me, of course, except Poochini, who perked his ears, raised his nose, and yelped as he tried to sniff me out.

"Shush," Harry said, and when Poochini was quiet for five seconds, Harry stuffed another piece of desiccated liver into my darling's mouth.

For the record, let me clarify the facts. While I ultimately did not buy the insurance, I most certainly brought the subject up, at least twice. I remember specifically that I went over how much extra per person it was for the insurance, to which Harry had responded with his usual "Good Lord, that's outrageous." What did he mean by "outrageous"? Did he want me to buy the damn insurance or not? I'm not some dog he can train by saying, "Good, Bibi. Shush, Bibi," until I know what he wants me to do. I then went on to detail the cost for various plans, from simple trip cancellation, through emergency medical evacuation in a helicopter and transfer to a Western hospital. I explained the variations in policies on preexisting conditions, and whether, for example, a broken bone or a bite from a possibly rabid dog would qualify for evacuation. And who was listening? Nobody except Roxanne's half sister, Heidi Stark, who worries about *everything*. "Bibi, is there malaria at that time of year?" "Bibi, should we bring anti-venom for snakes?" "Bibi, I read about a woman who got epilepsy from being bitten by a monkey in Madagascar." On and on she went, until Harry put his hand on her shoulder and said, "Heidi, love, you needn't be so grim. Why not anticipate an excellent time?"

The trouble was, they *all* anticipated an excellent time. What was grim was forgotten; the encephalitic monkeys were shooed away, as was the need for insurance—that is, until my funeral. Then it be-came *my* fault that they could not anticipate an excellent time, *my* fault that they could not cancel the trip. How quickly they turned into petulant creatures, as whiny as children following their mother on a hot day of errands.

The hearse rolled, the band marched, and my friends trudged along the eucalyptus-lined lane, past throngs of gaping people spilling out of the California Academy of Sciences building, the tod-dlers clinging to their rubber replicas of dinosaurs and shouting with glee to see this unexpected parade.

"Woof-woof! Love your show!" some voices called out.

Harry nodded to his fans. "Quite embarrassing," he said in a low but pleased voice. With his television smile still affixed, he turned back to our group and, now infused with bravado by public worship, said heroically: "Well, what to do? The deed is done, the die is cast, best to make a go of it, I say. To Burma."

Vera nodded. "No one could be as wonderful as our Bibi, but there's the practical matter of finding another tour leader. That's the simple imperative."

"Someone knowledgeable about Burma," Marlena added. "Some-one who's been many times. That Asian art expert, Dr. Wu, perhaps. I hear he's fantastic."

"Top-notch," Harry agreed.

"Whoever we get for a tour leader," Dwight added, "we should have them cut out half of the cultural-museum shit and add in more bicycling or trekking activities instead."

Heidi chimed in: "I also think we should each research something about Burma, like its history, politics, or culture. Bibi knew so much."

One by one they acquiesced, but not before offering amendments and disagreements, then even more complicated refinements and caveats—an omen of things to come.

By the time we reached John F. Kennedy Drive, the band was playing a squeaky version of "Amazing Grace" on the two-stringed *erhu*, and I had been forgiven by the group for not having bought trip cancellation insurance. As two motorcycle police held traffic at bay, the hearse sped off, and I bid my body a silent adieu. Then Harry asked the rest of the travelers to join him in a circle for a team high five, intoning, "May Bibi join us in spirit."

So that was how it came about. They hoped that I would go. How could I not?

· 2 ·

MY PLANS UNDONE

Almost everything I had planned came undone. My original itinerary began thusly: My friends, those lovers of art, most of them rich, intelligent, and spoiled, would spend a week in China and arrive in Burma on Christmas Day.

It started as planned: On December 18th, after nearly two days of travel and two stopovers, we arrived in Lijiang, China, the "Land Beyond the Clouds." My group was met by the best tour guide of the region, one I had used on a previous trip. Mr. Qin Zheng was an athletic young man, who wore designer-label jeans, Nike sneakers, and a "Harvard"-emblazoned pullover. My friends were surprised that he looked so Western, and except for the Chinese accent, he could have been one of them. He narrated the sights they could still appreciate as twilight approached.

From the window of the deluxe air-conditioned tour bus, my

friends and I could see the startling snowcapped peaks of Tibet glinting in the distance. Each time I have seen them, it is as amazing as the first.

Vera was jingling and jangling on the bumpy bus ride. She wore a profusion of ethnic-style jewelry around her neck, and encircling both wrists and ankles, and this was complemented by a colorful caftan, sized extra-large, though she was hardly fat, merely tall and big-boned. Since turning fifty, ten years ago, she had decided that her usual garb should be no less comfortable than what she wore to bed. Thrown over her shoulders was another of her trademarks: a raw-silk scarf printed with African motifs of her own design. Her hair, dyed taupe brown, had been shorn into a springy cap of baby's tears.

Seated next to her on the bus was the newly designated tour leader, Bennie Trueba y Cela, who began to read aloud the commentary I had meticulously appended to the itinerary months before: "Many believe Lijiang is the fabled city of Shangri-La that James Hilton described in his novel *Lost Horizon*. . . ." In remembering me, Vera chuckled, but her eyes stung with tears and she used her scarf to wipe away the wetness on her smooth cheeks.

I confess I was overwhelmed with self-pity. Since my death, it had taken me some time to accustom myself to the constant effusion of emotions. Whereas I had lacked dimension of feeling my entire life, now, through others, there was width, volume, and density ever growing. Could it be that I was sprouting more of the six supernatural talents that Sakyamuni received before he became the Buddha? Did I have the Celestial Eye, the Celestial Ear, along with the Mind of Others? But what good did it do me to have them? I was terribly frustrated that whenever I spoke, no one could hear me. They did not know I was with them. They did not hear me vehemently disapprove of suggested changes to the careful tour plans I had made. And now look, they had no idea that the "commentary" I had planted in the itinerary was often meant to be humorous asides that I would have elucidated upon during the actual tour.

The remark about Shangri-La, for example: I had intended to follow that with a discussion about the various permutations of "Shangri-La" notions. Certainly it is a cliché used to lure tourists to any site—from Tibet to Titicaca—that resembles a high mountainous outpost. Shangri-La: ethereally beautiful, hard to reach, and expensive once you get there. It conjures words most delightful to tourists' ears: "rare, remote, primitive, and strange." If the service is poor, blame it on the altitude. So compelling is the name that right this minute, workmen, bulldozers, and cement trucks are busily remodeling a hamlet near the China–Tibet border that claims to be the true Shangri-La.

I would have brought up the link to geography as well, the descriptions of the botanist Joseph Rock, whose various expeditions for *National Geographic* in the 1920s and early 1930s led to his discovery of a lush green valley tucked in the heart of a Himalayan mountain topped by a "cone" of snow, as described in his article published in 1931. Some of the inhabitants there were purported to be more than a hundred fifty years old. (I have met demented residents at old-age homes who have made similar claims.) James Hilton must have read the same article by Rock, for soon after, he used similar descriptions in penning the mythical Shangri-La. Voilà, the myth was hatched, delusions and all.

But the most interesting aspect to me is the *other* Shangri-La alluded to in *Lost Horizon*, and that is a state of mind, one of moderation and acceptance. Those who practice restraint might in turn be rewarded with a prolonged life, even immortality, whereas those who don't will surely die as a direct result of their uncontrolled impulses. In that world, *blasé* is bliss, and passion is *sans raison*. Passionate people create too many problems: They are reckless. They endanger others in their pursuit of fetishes and infatuations. And they self-agitate when it is better to simply relax and let matters be. That is the reason some believe Shangri-La is so important as the antidote. It is a mindset for the masses—one might bottle it as Sublime Indifference, a potion that induces people to follow the safest route, which is, of course, the status quo, anesthesia for the soul. Throughout the world you can find many Shangri-Las. I have lived in my share of them. Plenty of dictators have used them as a means to quell the populace—be quiet or be killed. It is so in Burma. But in art, lovely subversive art, you see what breaks through in spite of restraint, or even because of it. Art despises placidity and smooth surfaces. Without art, I would have drowned under still waters.

THERE WAS NOTHING PLACID about Wendy Brookhyser. She had come to Burma with an itch in her brain and a fever in her heart. She wanted to fight for Burmese rights, for democracy and freedom of speech. She could not tell anyone that, however. That would be dangerous. To her fellow travelers, Wendy said she was the director of a family foundation. And that was indeed the case, a foundation set up by her mother, Mary Ellen Brookhyser Feingold Fong, the "marrying widow," as she was unkindly called in some circles. In her position as director, Wendy had never done much more than attend an occasional meeting. For that, she received a salary sufficient for a carefree lifestyle with regular infusions from her mother for her birthday, Christmas, Chanukah, and Chinese New Year. Money was her birthright, but since her teens, she was adamant she would not become a party-throwing socialite like her mother.

Here I must interject my own opinion that the aforementioned mother was not the senseless schemer her daughter made her out to be. Mary Ellen gave the best parties to draw attention to worthy causes. She didn't simply write checks to charities like other nine-digit doyennes who had generous pocketbooks but not the time to amplify their compassion. She was utterly involved, financially and morally. I knew this because Mary Ellen was a friend of mine—yes, I believe I can call her that, for we chaired a fair number of events together. And she was quite the compulsive organizer, one who attended every boring planning meeting. I'm afraid I had a rather embarrassing habit of dozing at some of those. Mary Ellen was all about details; she knew if the proposed dates for events conflicted with the social calendars of the big money-givers. And because of her social web, she could line up celebrities to generate "publicity heat," identifying the singers, movie stars, or athletes who could be inveigled on the basis of their family background of genetic disease, mental illness, addiction, cancer, murder, sexual abuse, senseless tragedy, and other sorts of unhappinesses that fuel causes and then galas for causes. She also kept a meticulous record of those black-tie events for which she had bought tables at the highest level, and whose event chair might then be vulnerable to the unspoken but well-understood system of payback. It was all based on connections and intimate gossip, don't you see. In any case, I knew I could always count on Mary Ellen to contribute yearly to Self-Help for the Elderly by pointing out that it served those with Alzheimer's, the illness to which her first husband had succumbed; he was, by the way, the one who practically invented PVC pipes and made a huge fortune distributing them. Ernie Brookhyser. Perhaps you've heard of him. One of the many benefits Mary Ellen had attended was for the Asian Art Museum. During the live auction, she was high bidder for the Burma Road trip—paid thrice the value, I was pleased to see. She then gave the trip for two to Wendy as a birthday present.

Wendy had first thought to refuse the trip and also rebuke her politically unconscious mother for thinking her daughter might holiday in a country run by a repressive regime. She had fumed about this over lunch with a former Berkeley housemate, Phil Gutman, the director of Free to Speak International. Phil thought the all-expenses-paid trip might be useful for "discreet information-gathering." It could be a humanitarian project, and a necessary one. Wendy might masquerade as a pleasure-seeker, go along with the happy-go-lucky tourists, and when the opportunity presented itself, she could talk to Burmese students, have casual conversations with natives to learn who among their neighbors, friends, and family members were missing. Free to Speak might later float her report as a spec piece for *The Nation*. But Phil also underscored that she had to be extremely careful. Journalists were prohibited from visiting Burma. If caught rummaging around for antigovernment views, they and their informants would be arrested, possibly tortured, and made to disappear into the same void into which thousands had gone before them. Worse, the government there would deny that it detained any political prisoners. And there you would be, invisibly imprisoned, forgotten by a world that had secretly concluded you must have had some degree of guilt for getting yourself in such a jam. You see what happened to that American woman in Peru, Phil said.

"Keep the rest of the group ignorant of your activities," he cautioned Wendy, "and no matter how strongly you feel, don't engage in activities that would jeopardize the safety of others. If you're worried, I might be able to rearrange my schedule and come with you. You said there were two tickets, didn't you?"

Their conversation drifted from lunch into dinner. Phil made suggestive remarks, picking up on the flirtation they had had while housemates, which Wendy never acted on. She thought he looked spongy, like a Gumby toy with bendable limbs and no muscle. She liked hard bodies, tight butts, chiseled jawlines. Bad Boy Scout was her version of sexy. But the more they talked and drank, the more impassioned Wendy became about the plight of other people, and that impassioned sense transformed into sexual passion. She saw Phil as an unsung hero, a freedom fighter, who would one day be as admired as Raoul Wallenberg. With these heroics in mind, she let

Phil think that he had seduced her. He was an awkward lover, and when he nibbled her ear and said nasty words, she had to suppress her laughter. Back in her apartment and alone in her own bed, she wrote about the experience in her journal. She was pleased that she had had sex with him. It was her gift to him. He deserved it. But would she do it again? Not a good idea. He might start thinking that the sex was more meaningful than it was. Besides, he had so much hair on his back it was kind of like having sex with a werewolf.

When Wendy departed on the Burma Road trip, it wasn't Phil who was with her but a lover of one month's duration, Wyatt Fletcher. He was the adored only child of Dot Fletcher and her late husband, Billy, the Barley King of Mayville, North Dakota, a town whose motto flaunted: "The Way America Is Supposed to Be!" This was a town that fully came together when its native sons fell into trouble, particularly when the trouble was no fault of their own.

Wendy adored Wyatt's style, for instance, the fact that he could not be coerced or co-opted. If something or someone disagreed with him, he simply "moved on," as he put it. He was tall, slim-hipped, hairlessly muscled in the chest and back, towheaded and perpetually bronzed as those of Norwegian extraction can be. Wendy believed they were complements of each other. I, however, do not think opposites necessarily are. She was short and curvy, with a mass of curly strawberry-blond hair, skin that easily sunburned, and a sculpted nose, courtesy of a plastic surgeon when she was sixteen. Her mother had homes in San Francisco, Beaver Creek, and Oahu. Wendy assumed Wyatt was from a blue-collar family, since he did not talk much about his parents.

In one sense, Wyatt could be called homeless; his bed was whatever guest room of well-heeled friends he was bumming in for the month. What he did for a living depended entirely on where he was staying. In the winter, he found odd jobs in ski shops and snowboarded in his spare time, and for housing, he shared floor space with his ski patrol friends and a few indoor squirrels. He had spent the previous summer bicycling on the fire roads of Mount Tamalpais, accompanied by two Scottish deerhounds that belonged to his ex-girlfriend's parents, the absentee owners of a countrified wood-shingled mansion in Ross, which was where he house-sat and resided with the hounds, in the quaint pool house with its hammock, billiards table, and oversized rock fireplace. The spring before that, he crewed on a private luxury yacht that took ecotourists around the fjords of Alaska. Several of those well-heeled clients offered him future house-sitting employment, "gigs," he called them. All in all, he was an easygoing charmer whose predictable rejoinder, "Like, whatever," to any remark or question was synonymous with his lack of direction and encumbrances in life.

As vacuous as my descriptions may make him sound, I rather liked Wyatt. He had a good heart toward all, whether they were former teachers, girlfriends, or employers. He was not cynical about those of us who were wealthy, nor did he envy or take excessive advantage of us. He remained pleasant and respectful to everyone, even the meter maid who ticketed the car he had borrowed. He always paid the ticket, by the way. I would say he had one of the finest attributes a human being can have, in my opinion, and that is kindness without motives. Of course, his lack of motivation was another matter.

During the bus ride into Lijiang, Wyatt dozed, and Wendy gave everyone who was awake the benefit of her stream-of-consciousness observations. "Omigod, look at those people on the side of the road. They're smashing rocks, turning them into gravel to pave the road. . . . Those faces! They look so beaten down. Does the government think people are machines? . . ." Though Wendy had only arrived in China, she was already sharpening her sensibilities about despotic rule.

LIKE ANY EXUBERANT PUP, Wendy needed to learn "shush." That's what Harry Bailley thought. He was sitting across the aisle from her and Wyatt. He had forgotten that he had once possessed the dedication of an activist. In his youth, now some twenty-plus years past, he, too, had wanted desperately to sink his teeth into important causes. He had vowed to resist complacency, abhor apathy, "to make positive, incremental change and leave an imprint after this tenure on earth."

Years before, a much younger Harry had led the movement to abolish aversive dog-training methods, those that relied on leash-jerking, shock collars, and rubbing the dog's face in its feces. When he finished veterinary training, he did doctoral studies in the behavioral sciences department at UC Berkeley, investigating pack behavior, how dogs instinctively learned from higher-ups and taught protocols to lower-downs. Dog temperament was not ingrained from birth, he noted. It could be shaped by interaction with other dogs and people and by tasty bribes. Anyone who understood basic Skinnerian principles could tell you that when given positive reinforcement, dogs respond more quickly and consistently to what humans want, and they learn new behaviors more quickly through luring, shaping, and capturing.

"If your doggie has your very expensive alligator purse in his mouth," Harry would say in his seminars, "offer to trade him a piece of hot dog. Oh goodie, pant-pant, and he'll drop the purse at your feet. What's the lesson here? Put your overpriced purses and pumps where Pluto can't get to them! Then go and get him a smelly old tennis ball. The game is simple: Ball in your hand, treat in his mouth. Even if he's a basset hound, he'll turn into an impressive retriever if you do enough trades."

And through such commonsense advice, Dr. Harry Bailley became the Dog Trainer of Dog Trainers, the founder of the well-regarded International Society of Canine Behaviorists, the inventor of humane training devices (patents pending), the star of *The Fido Files*, and now the well-qualified owner of my dear, dear Poochini. I'm afraid I never did much training with him, and naughty Poochini had already chewed off the spines of some of Harry's collection of first-edition books.

"You must inform your clients, gently but firmly," he often told his disciples at lectures. "Dogs are not people in fur coats. No, indeed. They don't speak in the future tense. They live in the moment. And unlike you and me, they'll drink from a toilet. Lucky for us, they are perfect specimens of how operant conditioning and positive re-inforcement work, and beautifully so if only we learn how to apply the principles properly. Their human handlers have got to be absolutely objective about what motivates their poochies—so quash their tendency to ascribe Muggum-wuggum's barking, growling, and counter-surfing to anthropomorphic motives such as pride, revenge, sneakiness, or betrayal. That's how we speak of our ex-wives, former lovers, and politicians. Remember that *Canis lupus familiaris* is driven by his own jollies, which are usually harmless to others but can be detrimental to white carpets and Italian shoes. The fact is, dogs mark territory and they masticate. And if dogs resemble *Homo erectus* in any respect, it is in those traits of the poorly socialized male. Both do what pleases them: they scratch their balls, sleep on the sofa, and sniff any crotch that comes their way. And you, the brilliant dog trainer, must *train the owners*—that's right, those barely evolved humans holding those rolled-up newspapers in hand like cavemen's cudgels—you must train the humans to show the dogs what lucky canines *prefer* to do other than nip and yowl, or use the leather sofa as a chew toy. Ah! 'Prefer' is the operative word, isn't it? . . ."

Harry Bailley believed in training people early, before they could inflict any lasting damage upon the wee and impressionable pooches. "Puppy classes!" he would exhort on his television show. "A great equalizer, the perfect socializer, far better than those bore-and-snore book clubs that are all the rage on the other channel. Doggie classes, what a *fantastic* way for singles to meet. Strong, sensitive men. Woof! Loyal, long-limbed ladies. Woof-woof! And all those sweet, slurpy puppies. Picture their tails wagging—the *doggies*, you scalawags." And as his TV clients and their dogs tangoed to "Sit," "Down," "Stay," and "Come," Harry would ham it up to make everyone feel successful, proud, and continually motivated. "Lure your dog. That's right, dangle that cheese bit above his nose, now back until he sits. Steady, steady . . . *Yessss!* Bingo! Give him the jackpot right away. He's got it. *You've* got it. Only five point two seconds that time. Good Lord, you two are *fast!* What a fantastic team!" The dogs panted. The humans, too.

Harry revolutionized dog training. Everyone said so. In the early days, he went so far as to believe his notions of dog behavior could be applied to anything, from toilet training to international politics. He said so in seminars: "Which works faster: beating and humiliating a dictatorship, or luring it to follow a better and more rewarding model? If we call upon the country only to pummel it for being bad, how likely is it to come seeking our humanitarian advice? Isn't it utterly obvious?" And then Harry would dangle a hundred-dollar bill and bob it up and down so that people in the front row would nod dutifully in agreement. He was rather cocky in those days.

In more recent years, Harry had become less focused on the bad behavior of dog owners and governments and more on his own virility, which he feared might share the fate of endangered species— going, going, gone. He still had his hairline, though it had grayed on the sides—excellent credentials for authority. His physique was still trim; expensive tailored suits helped give him that effect. The damn trouble was, he had an enlarged prostate, the typical benign prostatic hyperplasia that afflicts many men, more annoying than harmful. But by God, Harry would moan, it shouldn't strangle a man's best friend before he's even turned fifty! He was troubled that he had to urinate frequently, and the more he strained, the more he issued

forth only driblets, much to his shame at public urinals. He was educated enough to know that the force of urinary flow—or lack
thereof—was not a correlation of sexual prowess. Yet he feared that
his personal plumbing, which had once spurted those two essential
fluids as forcefully as the nozzle on his garden hose, might soon become choked off like a water-saving shower head, and unsatisfying
not just to him but to the woman of the moment as well.

He searched the Internet for information that might indicate the
prognosis of his sex life should his condition worsen. Ejaculatory
backfiring was one worry. Could women really tell? He found a web-
site on prostate problems, with messages from men who shared the
same annoying condition. Several posters suggested that daily ejacu-
lations might slow down the hyperplastic activity and keep the pelvic
muscles better toned. The message board was also littered with invi-
tations to join porn sites where sufferers could find instant relief for
one flat rate. Great, Harry thought, the answer is to masturbate like
a kid with a magazine as your one-night stand. No, thank you. He
grew more determined to find a lovemate—one would do nicely in
this day and age of protected sex and privacy angst—one incredibly
wonderful woman he could have and hold, who would understand
when parts of him sputtered and gave out, for now or forever. Harry
was desperate for love and sex, and for the first time, in that order.

Lovely, sleek Marlena Chu had boarded the bus to Lijiang ahead
of him and had taken a window seat, while her daughter, Esmé,
raced to the aft of the bus and flopped lengthwise on the long bench.
Ye gods, an opportunity. Harry pretended to pass Marlena before
reversing to inquire quietly whether she might have any aspirin.
Women adore helping creatures in pain; Harry knew that, as well as
the fact that ladies always carry remedies for menstrual cramps and
headaches. As Marlena began to dig through her purse, he sat down
next to her and waited puppylike for his treat.

Although Harry had seen Marlena at many social gatherings in

San Francisco, here in this mountain valley in China, she looked positively exotic. Why was that? Why had he not sought her out before? Could it really be that he had overlooked her because she was past a certain dewy-skinned age? But look at her now. Everything about her was smooth and elegant: her hair, her face, her clothes, and especially her movements and gestures. When applying insect repellent, she looked like a goddess. Such grace, such style. She wore a simple black sleeveless sheath and a large colorful pleated scarf, wound and wrapped, so that it resembled a sarong, an origami shawl, a sari, the multiple effects waiting to be undone by a breeze, a whisper of consent in the night.

Naturally, he worried that his friend Moff might have similar thoughts. The two men often did when it came to women. He glanced over at Moff, who was staring right this moment at Heidi as she reached into the overhead rack to pull out a neck pillow from her rucksack. Moff's son, Rupert, who had been playing with a deck of cards, also stared openly at the young woman's breasts. Harry had noticed that Moff had given Marlena a number of second glances, his eyes drifting down the length of her figure, lingering on her buttocks. By sitting next to her, Harry hoped this territorial hint would find its way into his friend's brain, stir some cognition where impulsive behavior and primitive reflexes now resided. Moff could be thickheaded exactly when you didn't want him to be.

There was that time, Harry recalled, when they were both at a café in Stinson Beach, and Harry had clearly indicated his interest in the café's owner by saying to Moff: "What gorgeous peepers. Huge hazel irises, fourteen millimeters in diameter, I reckon." Harry had a fixation about eyes. And Moff had answered, "Really? Hadn't noticed." The next day Harry was back at the café and ordered eggs sunny-side up. The woman was friendly, but it was hard to move in more closely; she was like those hand-shy dogs in shelters that had been beaten by previous owners. But he loved the challenge of transforming untrusting creatures into licking maniacs. Take it slowly, he cautioned himself. No sudden moves.

The next day, she wasn't there. He learned later that Moff had wooed the pants off her by asking if he could drop her somewhere on his refurbished Harley. She rode with him down the coast to Monterey, shedding almost every stitch of clothing and flinging it into the Pacific. After two rapturous months, Moff had to break things off because of "serious differences in expectations." She responded by spray-painting his motorcycle pink. Harry was more upset than Moff about this report. Blast it! Moff had turned her into a Cerberus hellhound who wanted only to lunge and kill anyone with a penis. He had utterly ruined her as far as future dating was concerned. Adding insult to injury, Moff had also said to him, "Those hazel irises you admired so much? Colored contact lenses, my friend."

What the devil did women see in Moff? Harry tried to imagine him from a female's perspective. . . . He was taller than average (meaning, taller than Harry, who was five-feet-ten), had a passable build, lanky and no flab. But he was a complete washout when it came to proper clothes. His boyhood pal wore the same jungle-safari shirts and baggy short pants no matter what the season or event. And the shoes, well, they were more working-class boots, greased with dirt and flecked with paint. His hands were callused, like an ordinary laborer's. He wasn't the sort to buy a woman flowers or speak to her in endearments, not like Harry. And Moff's hair was a mess, long bushy locks gathered into a ponytail, and a receding hairline accentuating a massive forehead. The latter made him appear superbrainy, which he was, Harry acknowledged, though he also knew that Moff had been kicked out of school for truancy and smoking pot by the time he was sixteen, and thus was forced to become an autodidact.

What knowledge Moff possessed had come from reading, roaming the streets, and taking odd jobs in his youth, many of them in dockyards where he did inventory for import-export companies, the rest in backyards in Miami and Los Angeles, where he pruned hedges and cleaned pools. His interest in bamboo began in the 1970s, when he grew walls of it to camouflage his marijuana plants. Keen to make his cannabis as powerful per puff as possible, he devoured books on horticulture, particularly those related to genetic enhancement. Later, bamboo cultivation itself superseded his nefarious grass-growing interests—and why wouldn't it, when bamboo regenerated so quickly, just like marijuana, but without the legal hassles? And thus he made the 1980s transition to capitalist farmer, shipping containers of "live product," as he called it, to the lobbies of new office buildings, remodeled airports, and luxury hotels around the world. (Harry didn't know at the time that Moff and Marlena had quite a few clients in common. Then again, neither did Moff.)

All right, so Moff had an unconventional business, Harry granted him that. And by calling himself a "plantation owner," Moff made himself highly attractive to women with romantic illusions. They probably thought the plantation was idyllic, like the set for a dinosaur movie, and indeed, it had been used for that purpose on several occasions. But Moff himself had not a whit of romance in his brain. His plantation was intentionally situated near the Laguna Seca Raceway in Salinas, and that was where he took his dates—a factor in a man's favor if a woman's idea of a good time was smelling crankcase oil and getting her eardrums blown out by the rpms of Le Mans prototypes. Inexplicably, there was no shortage of women in that category.

Perhaps, Harry thought, he should just be direct with Moff, inform him straightaway that he was interested in Marlena, strongly so. "Old chum, I hope you don't mind, but you know . . ." and Harry would indicate with a nod that the lady in favor was Marlena. He imagined Moff would reply with a "Ho-ho," then clap his hand firmly on Harry's back, thus sealing their understanding. Marlena, while unaware of the pact, would subconsciously sense the respect these two men shared and never violate it by bedding both of them.

"Have you noticed the trees along the roadside?" Marlena now said to him. Harry peered out the window and in doing so leaned his chest against her arm, his cheek hovering close to hers. The tree trunks were painted white halfway up.

"It's been that way mile after mile," she continued, "like a white picket fence."

My God, Harry thought, her voice was liquid amber, light and mysterious. "An insecticide," he concluded.

She frowned. "Really? I thought it was so the drivers could see the road at night."

He backpedaled: "Brilliant deduction. Dual-purpose white. Kills bugs, saves lives."

"Watching the trees can be hypnotic, though," she added. "Not great for drivers."

"Is that why I'm feeling dazed?" He stared into her eyes.

Out of protective instinct, she did a quick deflect. "Probably jet lag."

He wished he could see her eyes more clearly, but the light was too dim. He could tell how responsive a woman was from the way her pupils reacted. If they pulsed into superdilation, that meant she was open to flirtation, and sex within hours if not minutes was a strong possibility.

Marlena smiled, then yawned. "I can't wait to fall into my bed."

"Funny," Harry quipped, "I'm looking forward to the *exact* same thing." He gave his best version of a puppy panting.

She raised one eyebrow, acknowledging the naughty ambiguity of his response. He grinned, and she returned a small smile that was neither rebuke nor acceptance. "The trees," she ventured again, her voice a little higher, "are they poplars? It's hard to see the shape of the leaves. Most of them have already fallen off."

Cheek to cheek, they stared into the darkness, at the blur of whitened trees.

To help my friends find the right sensibilities for viewing Lijiang, I included in their itinerary the translated sentiments of a local amateur archivist: "Throughout the last eight centuries, the frequent earthquakes of this region, some measuring to a greatness of 7.0, have rattled the teeth of its citizens, and shaken a few foodstuffs from the cupboards, but not our determination to stay. Because of its beauty, Lijiang is a place no one can ever leave willingly. But if you must go, by peaceful old age or by tourist jet, look down from the sky, and you will notice that Lijiang resembles an ancient ink stone used for centuries to write poetry celebrating its antiquities and self-replenishing virtues."

This tribute to his hometown was quaint, and perfectly expressed. But of course, most of my friends did not bother to read it.

As I had planned, the group checked into the best hotel Lijiang had to offer. The Glorious View Villa was in the newer, rebuilt section of town, directly across the street from the historic old town with its ramble of lanes, small canals, and aging courtyard homes with their snaky gray tiles and sun-dried mud bricks. The newer hotels of Lijiang were bland but provided one essential tourist attraction: private toilets and baths. The Glorious View had other markings of luxury: a marble-floored lobby lined with uniformed staff, who had received extensive training in greeting customers with happy faces and cheerful phrases: "Welcome!" "You're welcome!" "You're most welcome!"

The rooms themselves were small, dull, and dimly lit by energy-saving fluorescent bulbs. The twin beds, sheets, and towels were newer and cleaner than those of any other hotel in the city. The carpets had only a few watermelon stains. A small amount of toilet paper was doled out each day, adequate if one had intestinal fortitude. More was available on request or by theft from the supplies cart in the hall that was monitored by a surveillance camera. The Glorious View Villa was, in fact, the best hotel in the whole of the Naxi Autonomous Region, but for a group used to staying at a chain no worse than the Four Seasons, "best" should have been thought of as a restricted comparative term, not a fixed standard of excellence.

This distinction was lost on Roxanne and Dwight, who tried the knobs on the bedside consoles, the ubiquitous fixture of Chinese hotels. They duly clicked to appropriate notches marked "Lights," "TV," "Stereo." The lights remained lit, the television stayed black, the radio silent. "How can this be a first-class hotel?" Roxanne groused. "This place is the pits."

Because Lijiang had been described as "historic," "remote," and "near the Tibetan foothills," Roxanne had imagined they would be staying in a nomadic tent–style villa. The floors should have been beaten earth covered with yak hides, the walls adorned with colorful tapestries. She wanted saddled and snorting camels waiting outside, in lieu of battle-scarred taxis and tens of thousands of tourists, most of whom were Chinese. But it was only Dwight who was snorting. He nuzzled his wife's breasts, his usual sign that he wished to mate. I use the word "mate" deliberately. They were both desperate to have a baby before it was too late. For this trip, she told him, she had brought along the thermometer, and the last reading indicated it was prime time. She wasn't in the mood, but this was not about lust.

"I can't believe they make beds even smaller than twins," Roxanne said. She pointed disparagingly at the twin bed with its headboard permanently nailed to the wall, a good six feet apart from its match. "Honey, see if you can get us a room with a king-sized bed. If we have to pay more, so be it." And Dwight dashed down four flights of stairs—no slow elevators for him—in pursuit of this mission. A baby was at stake, his scion, a cross between two future Nobel laureates. By the time he returned to inform his wife that king- and queen-sized beds were deemed imperialist, Roxanne was sonorously asleep.

Across the hall, Harry Bailley, alone in his hotel room, replayed the conversation he had had with Marlena. She was flirting with him, he was damn sure of it. So what should he do to step things up a bit? And what about that midge of a daughter of hers? What a surprise to learn Esmé was already twelve. She looked like an eight-year-old, an elfin sylph with her pixie haircut, pink T-shirt, and jeans. She still had a child's body, not a hint of adolescence on the horizon. But at twelve, the girl could take care of herself and would be less of an obstacle to his gaining Marlena's solitary affections. In any case, three weeks lay ahead of them, plenty of time to figure out logistics and ways that a prepubescent could amuse herself without the company of her delightful mother. Esmé, love, here's ten dollars. Why don't you run off into the jungle and give a dollar to each monkey you find?

Harry peered into his wallet. There they were: two condoms. He briefly considered the other attractive single woman in the group, Heidi, younger half sister to Roxanne. She had a certain beguiling quality: big wondering eyes, limber legs, tumbling bunches of blond hair. And those breasts on such a tiny rib cage—they could not possibly be real. (In fact, they were.) Harry, an expert in animal structure, had convinced himself he knew better. They pointed and didn't sway; he had noticed that many times. What's more, the nipples sat too high, as if they were doilies floating on balloons. No doubt about it, they were not the bona fide mouthable chew toys. He had slept with a half-dozen women with artificial bosoms, so he should know. His friend Moff had also slept with many of the same type of inflated woman—a few, in fact, *were* the same, not surprising since the two vacationed at the same Club Meds—and Bamboo Boy swore he could not tell the difference. Tut, tut. That was more telling of Moff, Harry secretly opined. A superior lover, such as he, knew instantly. Naturally endowed women reacted with intense shivers when their nipples were caressed with a feather, an edge of silk, a silky tongue. The reactions of women with implants were a second or two off, or sometimes, to Harry's horror, entirely absent, especially if their eyes were closed so they could not gauge when to pretend. This left Harry feeling as if he had fondled a corpse.

Two demerits to Heidi for the implants, Harry decided. Marlena's breasts were smaller, but they would react lusciously to his touch, and these days, that was far sexier than size. Also in Marlena's favor, she was relaxed, older than Heidi to be sure, but with a confident maturity he was ready for. Heidi was young, cute, and a little neurotic, a combination that would become in a short time less young, less cute, and more neurotic. She was always so worried about things going wrong—was it clean, was it safe? If she's on the lookout for problems, Harry thought, she's going to find them. The best thing for her to do is be on the lookout for good things. It's how they train people to train dogs. If you're keen to spot bad behavior that you must punish, you will see only bad behavior. Catch the dog doing something good and reward him, and you'll start seeing good behavior all the time. God, if only more people knew the principles of dog behavior. Wouldn't the whole world be great?

Marlena's child, Esmé, was thinking of dogs as well, one in particular: a tiny Shih Tzu puppy with runny eyes and a cough, which she had seen in the hotel's beauty parlor late at night. The beauty parlor with its pink lights had odd hours and even odder services. It provided not haircutting or styling but the companionship services of three beauties, who looked not much older than Esmé. One of the girls owned the puppy and said there were others—seven fingers' worth. This puppy was maybe three months old, she guessed, and a "very good dog." As she said this, the puppy squatted and let out a stream. It was also for sale cheap, the girl went on without hesitation, only two hundred kwai, about twenty-five American dollars.

"Where's the mother dog?" Esmé asked.

"Muzzer no here," the girl replied.

"It's an orphan?"

And the beauties were quick to assure her, "Fun, fun. Guarantee you money-back."

Unlike Esmé, who still preferred T-shirts and jeans, the beauties were swathed in tight dresses and perched on chunky-heeled shoes. They carried key chains slung on low-hipped belts, attesting that they owned cars, or at least had privileges to them. In their well-manicured hands, they gripped petite cell phones, always at the ready to offer their services. Harry had received just such an offer a half-hour after checking in. A voice cooed in a Texas twang and Chinese tones: "Hello, honey, you lonesome tonight?" And though Harry was tempted, he was also a veterinarian who was well aware of the precise opportunistic methods by which parasites and deadly viruses travel. Down, boy. Good boy.

Bennie Trueba y Cela had received a similar call and had laughed uproariously. "Sweetie, you've got the *wrong* number," he said. He had the girth and robustness of his Texan mother, and the sensual lips and extravagant gestures of his Spanish father, who died a month after Bennie had announced to him by letter that he was gay. This sent Bennie to a psychiatrist to examine his problems with other people's anger, disappointment, and criticism. "My father's death was like a complete rejection." He said some variation of this at almost every session, making it sound each time as if it were a sudden epiphany.

Bennie's room at the Glorious View Villa was the one that would have been mine, across from Vera's at the end of the hall. The hotel liked to please tour leaders and gave them rooms with a mountain view, that of Jade Dragon Snow Mountain. Its numerous jagged peaks did indeed recall a sleeping dragon with a ridged back. When I was last here and was told I had a mountain-view room, I was suspicious of what this meant, for I have been in hotels that claimed to have panoramas but had only the poetic hint of one. And on one unpleasant occasion, I snapped back the curtain to see that the view was indeed that of a mountain, only it was placed right against the window, the dark rock obscuring all light and emitting the dank smell of a cave.

Bennie took a deep breath and inhaled inspiration from the mountain. The group had originally hoped to secure Dr. Bill Wu as tour leader, and a wise choice that would have been. He was a dear friend from the days when he and I were teaching at Mills College. But he was busy leading another group on an intensive study of the thousand Buddha carvings of the Dunhuang caves. Bennie had a few years of docent experience, but unlike me, he had never been to Burma or China and knew little about either country or its art. He had cried with gratitude when told after my funeral that he had been chosen the new leader. (That was after several other possibilities had been ruled out.) Thus appointed, he vowed to help in any way he could—by organizing luggage collection for transport, confirming airline reservations and passport needs, doing the hotel check-ins, arranging matters with the local guides provided by China's and Burma's offices of tourism, anything that would ensure that everyone had a marvelous, first-class adventure.

Pleasing people was his greatest joy, he liked to say. Unfortunately, he often promised what was humanly impossible, and thus made himself the target of people's ire when reality replaced intention. It was that way with his business. He was a graphic artist, and his lover, Timothy, was an art director. Bennie pledged impossibly fast turn-arounds, special design elements and paper stock upgrades thrown in for free, a budget twenty percent lower than what any other firm had submitted, which later grew to be twenty-five percent higher than anyone else's. (He had inherited this technique of estimates and overruns from his father, who was a building contractor.) There were always unavoidable, perfectly legitimate reasons for the overruns, of course, and in the end he endeared himself to the clients, for they were always ecstatic with the final product. He was, in fact, a very talented designer. But by going away to China and Burma for three weeks, he risked missing his deadlines—again.

On the other hand, the current project was for the Asian Art Museum, and Bennie believed that they, of all people, would understand. He even convinced himself that I, dearly departed Bibi, was sending him signs to lead the tour in my permanent absence. For instance, he found a message in a fortune cookie: "Go where your heart leads you." A book on Burma popped into his hands when he was in a bookstore. That same day, while purging his files, he happened upon an old invitation to a fund-raiser for the Asian, for which I was listed as a patron and he as having provided a donation in kind. I assure you, I was incapable of sending any such billets-doux. And had I been, I would have been far less subtle. I would have advised Bennie to stay home.

To his credit, Bennie did conscientiously study the itinerary I had prepared. Before the departure date, he had called the various tourism offices in China and Burma to confirm that all arrangements were still locked in. He was so obsessed with making sure everything was right that he ate cashews constantly to assuage his gnawing anxiety. He later switched to pistachios and sunflower seeds, since shelling them required slowing down his consumption. Nevertheless, he gained several pounds, which meant his goal to shed twenty before the trip had to be increased to "a little more." Going to Burma would aid in that direction, he believed. With the heat and all the running around he would have to do, the fat would melt away like glaciers transported to the Gobi.

As he eased into bed that first night in Lijiang, he was confident that all plans would run as smoothly as the second hand on his Rolex. The bed seemed awfully hard, but he would sleep well, no doubt about that. On the plane, he had been forced to stay awake because there were no electrical outlets for powering up the continuous positive air pressure machine he used for his obstructive sleep apnea. He had feared he would fall asleep and snore loudly or, worse, stop breathing while flying at thirty-nine thousand feet over the Pacific. With transfers in Seoul, Bangkok, and Kunming, he had gone ages without sleep, and when the plane touched down in Lijiang, he was hallucinating that he was back at the San Francisco airport and late for his departure.

Now that he was safe and sound in the hotel, he slipped the sleep mask over his face, adjusted the CPAP machine to the high-altitude setting, cranked the pressure up to fifteen, then lay back with his head in a horseshoe-shaped neck brace. He silently thanked me for my wisdom in suggesting that the group sleep in late the first morning, then leisurely rise to enjoy "A Taste of Winter Delicacies" at a picturesque local restaurant. I had chosen the menu myself: sautéed ferns, pine needles in a spicy sauce, north-wind mushrooms with their tiny caps, cow-liver mushrooms, large and smooth black, oh, and best of all, a lovely braised white reed whose texture is somewhere between asparagus and endive. Bennie was happy to transition from sleep to food.

Dwight had other ideas. At seven a.m., he managed to roust Roxanne and Heidi, as well as the young and the restless, Rupert, Esmé, Wyatt, and Wendy. They went jogging through the old town, where they risked ankle wrenches while dodging Tibetan spaniels and Pekingese lying on the uneven stone-paved lanes. Rupert and Esmé zoomed past Dwight. Rupert had the same coloring and features of the local kids, Dwight noticed. I would say, however, that Rupert's height and his earrings, two on the upper part of one ear, were glaring signs that he was not from these parts. But Esmé could easily have passed for a child from Lijiang. The majority of the inhabitants were the result of centuries of bedtime mergers among Han Chinese, a dozen Yunnan tribes, and over the ages, British opportunists, European explorers, passing nomads, and fleeing Jews. The populace was an unplanned and lovely mix, no two ever the same, just like art.

It was a thrilling, vertiginous run—the smell of morning fires, steaming cauldrons, and fire-snapping grills, the awesome snowy peaks. "Coming up behind you," they would shout, and then pass successive clusters of Naxi women with their crisscross halters to which were secured ninety-pound loads of pine needles pressing on their backs.

Our early-morning risers spent forty-five minutes aerobically seizing their lungs at an altitude of seven thousand eight hundred seventy-four feet and a temperature of forty-eight degrees, then chanced upon the perfect place to breakfast. What luck: there they were, sitting among the locals on long benches, gulping down with proletarian gusto bowls of thick spicy noodles and chives, a breakfast that well suited them, since their confused stomachs had been crying that it was time for a flavorful dinner and not a bland breakfast.

At nine, the nip in the air was gone, and when the hale and hearty returned to the hotel, they were ready for more adventures. They rang up the others, gurgling over what delights were to be seen while running about in the fresh alpine air as opposed to dozing in a dreary room. Soon everyone was in the lobby, so that they could meet up with the local guide and be on their way.

Bennie announced that there had been a slight change in plans. He quickly assured them that it was all for the better. He had had a phone call earlier that morning from a man who told him that their guide from yesterday, Mr. Qin, had experienced an unavoidable problem. (The problem was that another tour leader, who knew of Qin's merits, had, with a few dollars pushed into helpful hands, pirated him away.) Bennie assumed the original guide or a member of his family had taken ill. The voice at the other end of the line said Bennie could choose from one of two available guides. One was an older man born and raised in this province and an expert on every square inch of the area, from the tops of the highest mountains to the rocks down below. Besides knowing English and Mandarin, he could speak several minority dialects, including Bai, his native tongue. He was excellent, energetic and happy, and everyone was pleased with his services, in spite of "his recent loss."

"What loss?" Bennie had asked.

"His arm," the voice on the phone said. "He misses his arm."

"Oh. I'm sorry. What about the other one?" Bennie asked.

"That arm no problem."

"I mean the other guide."

The voice described a woman, younger than the man, but not too young. She had no losses. Formerly, she was from the big city, Chengdu, and was reassigned to here. Formerly, she was a teacher. Because she was new to the area, she was not as experienced as the older man, but she had studied intensively, so she was also very good.

"What kind of teacher?" Bennie asked.

"English," came the answer.

"So that's who I picked," Bennie explained to the group. "I could tell they were trying to stick me with this old guy that nobody wanted. But I managed to get the English teacher, who sounded more hip and up-to-date on things."

A minute later, the former English teacher walked in. She wore oversized glasses with lenses so shiny that it was hard to see her eyes. Her hair had undergone a tragic experiment; her sister-in-law, who hoped to work in a beauty salon one day, had subjected her to a permanent, and no matter how much she tried to tame the tightened curls, her hair was a battle of tufts that all jutted out in opposing directions. She wore a drab blue top with wide lapels and white buttons, complemented by matching unattractive slacks. It was never my nature to judge people solely on appearances, but I had a bad feeling.

She stepped forward timidly and in a barely audible voice said, "So pleasing meet you in Lijiang." This was how the group met the stiff and reticent Miss Rong, a name that everyone pronounced "wrong" from start to end.

If I could have stopped this fiasco by jumping back into the living, I would have done so. Miss Rong was not local to the area, not even to Yunnan Province. She spoke no minority dialects, had no training in art and culture. The one-armed man, by the way, was an excellent guide, the most knowledgeable of all the guides. But Miss Rong was at the bottom of a very deep barrel. She was not able to talk about the ravishing mountain meadow scenery or give insight into the history of Lijiang, its two ancient families, the customs of the Naxi or any of the other tribes in the area. She had memorized information and stated the number of square kilometers, the population, the percentage of economic growth in key areas of industry and agriculture. I had to hear it only once. "The old city," she said in a heavy accent and with the stiffness of recitation, "is protect by UNESCO. You know UNESCO. For that reason, Lijiang will stay ancient with economic developing, and because therefore, you can inspect the authentic historical site with special law for snacks selling, tailor, barber, and tourist traps."

"So what's up for today?" Bennie asked in a nervously cheerful tone. He hoped she would improve once she loosened up. Miss Rong began to outline the day's activities. The more she talked, the worse her English seemed to be. Everyone had a hard time understanding her. Bennie pretended he did not. A discussion ensued among my friends, led by Dwight, about changing the plans a bit, including perhaps a bike trip the next day instead of the temple visit, and a hike rather than the tour of the UNESCO site. Miss Rong looked blank-faced as English words ran past her ears. "And we should cancel this 'Taste of Winter Delicacies,'" Dwight said. "I don't want to sit in a tourist restaurant and eat what all the tourists eat." He went on to brag about the native cuisine they had eaten that morning, how they sat among the locals, and it was completely spontaneous, not a tourist activity, but a real experience. The noodle soup was also delicious. My friends made affirmative responses. "Sounds great."

Dwight turned to the speechless Miss Rong and let spew a rapid assortment of words she could not follow: ". . . authentic . . . no buffet . . . no touristy restaurant . . . no strict schedule." He was very stern, she sensed, had so many prohibitions to not do this, not do that. But what? What he did not want was not entirely clear. The tongue-tied Miss Rong could answer only, "This no problem."

Bennie also had no objections to the suggested changes. He had wanted to please and was mortified that he had instead chosen a guide who was nearly unintelligible. "Terrific. Let's do it!" he said of the new plan. He secretly mourned not eating winter delicacies. Sautéed ferns—lost to spontaneity, alas.

A further powwow led to the consensus that they should set forth immediately on a bus ride to Stone Bell Mountain, where they might do some hiking. They gathered what they needed for the day, which for everyone except Heidi was hardly more than what they wore, some camera gear, journal books, and sketch pads. Soon they boarded the bus and were on their way, hooting and cheering, "To Stone Bell Mountain," as Roxanne took a group shot with her camcorder. This would be their habit from now on: to change plans and announce their new fate as if it were a better course.

Two hours into the bus ride, several people yelled that they had seen a roadside restaurant with an authentic local look about it. The bus pulled into a dusty lot in front of a one-room hovel. Being famished, Bennie declared this an oasis befitting a possible write-up in *Travel & Leisure*. The quaint stools and low table with its antique plastic tablecloth had transformed into an al fresco mirage. . . . The group stepped off the bus, shed their jackets, and stretched. The air was warm. Moff and Rupert headed for the nearest clump of trees. The others sat at the tables. Bennie took out a sketch pad, Wendy had her soft leather journal with its nearly pristine lined pages, and Roxanne looked through the viewfinder of her omnipresent digital camcorder. What luck that they had come upon this rustic eatery (which even the locals eschewed with authentic disdain). What luck for the cook (promoted to "chef" by Wendy) and his waitress wife. They had not seen a hapless customer in three days.

"What shall we order?" Bennie asked the group.

"No dog!" cried Esmé.

"How about snake?" joked Rupert.

"You don't suppose they eat cats?" Heidi added, and shuddered at the thought.

Miss Rong conveyed this message in Mandarin to the chef: "They don't wish to eat dog, but want to know if you serve the famous Yunnan dish Dragon Meets Lion." The cook sadly informed her they had had no deliveries of fresh snake or cat recently. But, his wife interjected, they would gladly serve their finest. That turned out to be a bit of something that resembled pork, and might have been chicken, rice twice reheated, and all of it invisibly sprinkled with cockroach legs coated with little microbes that feed off human intestinal lining. This *plat du jour* was washed down with plentiful bottles of warm beer and cola.

Harry Bailley drank three local ales and ate nothing. Dear friend that he is, I know he is quite the fussy eater, who prefers Languedoc with this peasant dish, Sancerre with that, and it should be this vintage, served at that temperature. Beer was already a concession for him, let alone a lukewarm bottle that was not Guinness stout. Having drunk three, he was in urgent need of a loo. He was slightly inebriated, and because the restroom was unlit, he nearly fell into the abyss. Catching himself, he then observed both visually and viscerally the level of hygiene practiced in this restaurant. Good God, that hole in the floor that passed as a toilet was only a *suggested* target. It was also evident that quite a number of deathly ill people with bloody bowel disorders had found refuge there. Furthermore, toilet paper was not to be found, nor water with which to wash one's hands. Abominable! Thank God he had not partaken of the fare.

Heidi also did not indulge in the roadside picnic. She had eaten the protein-rich soy bar she carried in her daypack, where she also stored a bottle of water, along with the heating coil she had used that morning to disinfect the water. In the same pouch she had two mini-bottles of antibacterial disinfectant, a half-dozen alcohol wipes, a doctor-prescribed needle and syringe in case she was in a head-on collision and needed an operation, her own nonporous eating utensils, a pack of moistened towelettes, chewable antacid tablets for coating the stomach before and after eating (this, she had read, could ward off as much as ninety-eight percent of the common nasties that cause travelers' diarrhea), a plastic funnel with a six-inch retractable tube for urinating while standing, nonlatex gloves for handling the funnel, an epinephrine injection pen in case she went into anaphylactic shock from an exotic insect bite, extra nine-volt batteries for the portable air sanitizer she wore around her neck, lithium batteries for the anti-nausea device worn on her wrist, as well as Malarone tablets for preventing malaria, anti-inflammatories, and a prescription bottle of antibiotic for bacterial gastrointestinal diseases. More preventatives and remedies, including a bag of intravenous fluid, were in her suitcase back at the hotel.

Heidi and Harry were thus spared from dysentery this time, she by anxiety, and he by snobbery. From years of experience, the bus driver, Xiao Fei, who was called "Mr. Fred" for American convenience, had an intestinal tract and immune system conditioned to resist infection. Some in our group, by virtue of their inherited robustness in warding off disease, would overcome the invaders before any symptoms manifested. As for the others, the dysentery consequences of this *Shigella bacillus* culinary adventure would not be felt for another few days. But the bacteria had already begun their descent into foreign guts, and would wend their ways into intestinal tracts and into bowels. The bus would take a similarly tortuous, winding route along the Burma Road, where soon the forces of fate and *Shigella* would meet up with them.

SUCH WAS THEIR KARMA

Lateness, I would have reminded my friends, is one of the deadly sins on a group tour, not to be tolerated, and punishable by the fates in any number of unforgiving ways. But this rule and warning were not established early on, and after that mistake of a lunch, my friends spent an additional twenty minutes locating everyone so they could board the bus.

Rupert had taken off down the road to check out the rock-climbing possibilities, and because he was fifteen and utterly unable to discern the difference between five minutes and fifty, not to mention between private and public property, he had managed to climb a stone wall and trespass into a courtyard housing six hens and a disheveled rooster. Roxanne was capturing arty footage with her camcorder of Dwight walking down a deserted road. Wendy had located some photogenic children who belonged to the sister of the chef's wife, and she busied herself taking pictures with a very expensive Nikon while Wyatt made faces to make the kids laugh. Bennie was adding shading to the sketch he had made of this local Chinese bistro, a dilapidated building at a crossroads that appeared to lead to nowhere. Mr. Fred, the bus driver, had wandered across the road to smoke a cigarette. He would have stayed closer to the bus, but Vera, who wanted to board, had asked with exaggerated waves of her hands that he not contaminate the air around her. Miss Rong was in the front seat, studying a book of English phrases. Moff also got on the bus, and lay down at the back for a five-minute nap. Heidi boarded and applied a disinfectant to her hands, then put some on a tissue and wiped down the armrest and grab bar in front of her. Marlena and Esmé were doing their best to use the latrine with its perilous pit. Bad as it was, they preferred privacy to open-air cleanliness. Harry had gone searching for a better loo and in doing so saw a pair of interesting red-breasted birds with twitchy eyes.

This tendency for people to wander off was already becoming a habit, with Rupert and Harry vying for first place in being the most dilatory. When everyone had finally been rounded up, Miss Rong counted heads: the black lady, the plump man, the tall man with horsetail hair, the kissing girl, the man who drank too many beers, those three with baseball caps, another two with sun hats, and so on, until she reached eleven and had to start over again. At last, she found the requisite twelve. She gave the signal to the bus driver with a triumphant *"Zou ba!"* and off they went.

The bus's transmission and shock absorbers were put to the test as Mr. Fred lurched into oncoming traffic and in Russian-roulette fashion passed slightly slower vehicles on the uneven road. The combination of bad suspension and frightful suspense was ideal for inducing motion sickness in almost everyone. Heidi felt no queasiness whatsoever, thanks to her anti-nausea wrist device. And Rupert was also unaffected and was even able to read from a black-covered paperback, Stephen King's *Misery*, which held as its ignominious bookmark a page of the notes I had worked on so laboriously.

Stone Bell Temple lay ahead. I had hoped my friends might learn about the importance of its holy grottoes and their carvings, many created in the Song and Tang dynasties, with the more recent ones completed in the Ming, several hundred years in the past. By seeing a medley of ancient Nanzhao, Bai, Dai, and Tibetan images, they might have sensed how streams of minority tribes' religions had joined the dominant—and often domineering—Chinese river of thought. The Han Chinese have always been good at absorbing motley beliefs yet maintaining their own as paramount. Even the Mongols and Manchus, who had conquered and ruled them since the thirteenth century, had assimilated Chinese ways and had virtually become Chinese themselves. Think about this, I would have said to my charges: as we go into this temple, think about the influences of tribes, invaders, and rulers upon one another. You see remnants of their effects in both religion and art, in essence those areas that are expressions of the spirit.

The bus rumbled on. The tribe they were about to meet was the Bai, and my twelve friends would have a profound effect on them, and vice versa.

"Hey, Dad," Rupert called out, holding up the page from my notes, "get this." He began to read what I had written: "'One of the shrines is most aptly named the Grotto of Female Genitalia.'" Rupert snickered through his nose in an unattractive way and neglected to read further, where I had written the following: "Many tribes in this region believe that creation begins from the womb of darkness. Thus, there is a profound reverence for grottoes. This particular grotto is unspectacular but delightful, and contains a rather plain and small shrine, about twenty inches in width and twenty-four in height, and carved simply in the shape of a vulva surrounded by labia onto which have been inscribed tributes over the centuries to fertility. The grotto symbolizes fertility, and fertility is fervently worshipped in China, for to lack fertility is to lose one's family line, and a family without heirs is consigned to oblivion, darkness, and the permanence of death."

No, sad to say, my queasy friends did not read this, although their imaginations had become quite fertile. The Grotto of Female Genitalia: What could such a curiously named place look like? Collectively, the women envisioned a primordial cave emanating warmth, mystery, comfort, safety, and innate beauty. The men pictured a cleft in the mountain with overgrown bushes behind which was a tiny entrance that led into a moist cave, and Bennie's imagination further embellished it as dark, slimy, and filled with screeching bats.

Before they reached their destination, however, the travelers saw large domed ovens on the left side of the road, smoke spewing from their vents. What were they baking? Miss Rong made rectangular shapes with her hands, and pointed to homes and walls. Loaves of bread? Oh, bricks and tiles! Marlena suggested a photo stop, Wendy agreed, and Vera, ignoring the groans of the men, who believed a shopping spree was about to take place, raised her palm to order the bus driver to pull over.

Esmé was the first to see the water buffalo on the right side of the road. It appeared to be stuck, with mud up to its belly. Why was it blindfolded? And why were those men whipping it? Wendy began scribbling madly in her journal. Bennie sketched a quick impression.

Miss Rong happily explained that this was how the mud was "smashed" so it would be soft enough to place in the molds. And the buffalo's eyes were covered so the beast did not know it was going in circles. All twelve travelers were now transfixed as the buffalo plowed its wretched Sisyphean route. 'Round and 'round he stumbled and lurched, haphazardly and endlessly, his great body heaving to take another breath, his nostrils flaring with fright as the whip came down across his hindquarters.

"Man, that is one miserable existence," Roxanne said. The others echoed similar sentiments.

Esmé was close to tears. "Make them stop."

Miss Rong tried to ease their discomfort. "This is karma," she tried to explain in her rudimentary English. "Past life this buffalo must be doing bad things. Now suffer, so next life get better. . . ." What she was trying to say was this: Your situation and form in life are already determined before you are born. If you are a buffalo suffering in mud, you must have committed wrongs upon others in a previous existence, and thus, you deserve this particular reincarnation. Perhaps this buffalo was once a man who killed an innocent person. Maybe he was a thief. By suffering now, he would earn a much cushier reincarnation in the next go-round. It's an accepted way of thinking in China, a pragmatic way of viewing all the misfortunes of the world. You cannot change a buffalo into a man. And if a buffalo does not mash the mud, who else would do this job?

Miss Rong blithely continued her philosophical talk: "So family must having a house, house must having bricks, buffalo must having smash mud. Do not be sad, this the way of life. . . ." She enjoyed the opportunity to inform her charges of Buddhist ideas. She had heard that many Americans, especially those who travel to China, love Buddhism. She did not realize that the Buddhism the Americans before her loved was Zen-like, a form of not-thinking, not-moving, and not-eating anything living, like buffaloes. This blank-minded Buddhism was practiced by well-to-do people in San Francisco and Marin County, who bought organic-buckwheat pillows for sitting on the floor, who paid experts to teach them to empty their minds of the noise of life. This was quite different from the buffalo-torture and bad-karma Buddhism found in China. Miss Rong also did not realize that most Americans, especially those with pets, have great sympathy for animals in misery, often more so than for miserable humans. Animals, with their inability to speak for themselves, the pet lovers believe, possess innocence and moral purity. They do not deserve cruelty.

If only Miss Rong could have posed the situation in better English and with more comprehensible cases of comparison: For a man who rapes and murders little girls, what is a satisfactory punishment? Should he not be turned into a beast of burden who lives in mud and is whipped every waking hour so that he might learn what suffering is and thus become a better being in his next incarnation? Or should the villain be paraded about town to the jeers of a crowd, as they do in some countries, placed in a burlap bag, tossed over a cliff, and then dismembered so that he will have to walk sans penis in hell? On the other hand, as has been described in both Christian and Chinese hells, would it be more just if he were consigned to a vat of oil, one that boils eternally and in which each moment is as unbearable as the first dip of the toe, so that his horror is endless, without any hope whatsoever of redeeming himself? Given my present state, I weighed which of these various hells was least horrific and thus most appealing, and I hoped that my current state of limbo would not lead to my learning which was true. I hoped I would not come back as a mud-smashing water buffalo.

Thus saddened by this tour of Buffalo Torture, the travelers continued their bus journey to the grottoes. As the road climbed into the mountains, Marlena and Harry were interested in taking note of the scenery. It was an excuse to lean their faces together and make small talk. "Those are poplars, I believe. . . ." "Look, eucalyptus." "What are those?"

Moff, who was sitting behind them, answered in a bored voice: "Willows."

"Are you sure?" Harry said. "They don't look it."

"Not all willows are the grand weeping variety."

He was right. These willows were a scrubby, fast-growing kind that can be cut back often for kindling. Higher up, the willows gave way to long-needled pines, and trudging along the road was a pha-lanx of Naxi women collecting the fallen needles.

"What do they use those for?" Marlena called out to Miss Rong.

Miss Rong struggled to say it was for the animals. Everyone assumed she meant that the animals ate the needles, which is not so. In the winter, the animals nest in the needles to stay warm, and in the spring, the Naxi women use the manure-soiled needles as fertilizer when they plant the new crops. With a limited diversity of life, there is greater diversity of purpose.

"Where are the men?" Wendy demanded to know. "Why aren't they out there breaking their backs?"

"Yes, very lazy," Miss Rong joked. Then she added, "They play outside, do poetry." She was partly right. The rest she knew but didn't know how to verbalize clearly, so I will translate: In China, there is a saying made popular after the revolution: Women hold up half the sky. In the Naxi Autonomous Region, women have always held up the whole sky. It is a matriarchal society, where the females do the work, handle the money, own the houses, and raise the children. The men, meanwhile, ride on the backs of shooting stars, so to speak. They are bachelors, boyfriends, and uncles, roaming from bed to bed at night, not knowing which children they have fathered. They take the animals out to graze early in the morning, they bring them back at dusk. In the mountain pastures, they roll their cigarettes and smoke, and when they call the animals, they lure them with love songs. They sing at the top of their lungs, which extract oxygen much more efficiently than those of most Americans. So Miss Rong was correct in what little she said. The men do poetry. To hear a song sung in the mountains is always poetry.

At the entrance to the temple park, the bus stopped and my friends jumped out for camcorder documentation of their arrival. They gathered behind a sign, "Sincerely Welcoming You to Farmous Grottoe of Female Genitalia." Harry had his arm around Marlena's waist. The others arranged themselves in various positions according to height. Roxanne held the camcorder. Meanwhile, Miss Rong had gone to pay the park entry fee. She stepped up to an old man sitting in a tollbooth the size of an upright coffin. He spoke to Miss Rong in the Bai dialect that was common in that region, telling her, "Hey, be careful today. We may get a thundershower any minute, so stay off the high ridge. Oh, and one other important matter—please note, the foreigners should avoid going to the main grottoes between the hours of two-thirty and three-thirty, because a television crew from CCTV will be filming a documentary there. Sorry for the inconvenience."

Miss Rong, who was ashamed to let both the man and her charges know she did not understand Bai, nodded briskly in return. She believed he was just reminding her that as an official tour guide she was required to take her tourists to the state-approved souvenir store. Each time she had been asked to be a substitute tour guide, the main office had reminded her of this as her foremost duty.

Before embarking on the trail, several of our group made a visit to the restrooms, two gender-assigned concrete pavilions with an open trough through which a paltry stream of water constantly ran, failing, however, to wash away the deposits. Heidi donned a face mask before entering, turned on her air purifier, and retrieved from her pack various germ-fighting supplies. The other women crouched and buried their faces in their sleeves, trying not to retch. In the men's latrine, Moff let out a gusher strong enough to jet-spray gum off a sidewalk, while Harry, standing at the other end of the trough, focused his mind and squeezed his muscles—lats, abs, quads, and glutes—and out came a meager trickle. Though he had not attained relief, he zipped up quickly, not wanting to prolong his humiliation.

Let me add here that I am most emphatically *not* in the habit of watching or talking about people's private business. I also abhor scatological humor and salacious gossip. But these are things I knew with these Buddha-like talents I now possessed, the Celestial Eye, the Celestial Ear, the Mind of Others. Furthermore, I report these intimate details that are salient only so that you might better judge later what occurred and why. Just remember: Throughout history, many a world leader was injudiciously influenced by his malfunctioning bladder, bowels, and other private parts. Didn't Napoleon lose at Waterloo because he couldn't sit in a saddle, on account of hemorrhoids?

At one o'clock, the eager travelers began their downward trek into the canyon that was the heart of Stone Bell Mountain. They were slightly disoriented from jet lag, the bouncy bus ride, and retreating motion sickness. Miss Rong's version of English did not help matters. She was trying to recall which English words meant "east," "west," "north," and "south," and eventually she translated her directions thus: "Descend shady side, see temple grotto, ascend sunny side up, return the bus." Of course, such terms are relative to the time of day. In fact, they rely entirely on the assumption that sunny and shady remain constant even after the sun has been completely obliterated by storm clouds as black as the tumbling seas.

To those who might visit the Lijiang region one day, let me assure you that winter is an excellent time for travel. It is the dry season. Even in late December, the days are usually warm and pleasant, while the nights are brisk but easily managed with a sweater or light pullover, unless, of course, you are someone like Heidi, who prefers layers—a down vest with Gore-Tex waterproofing, microfleece leggings, a 30 SPF shirt pretreated with mosquito repellent, a heat-retaining cap with visor, and a two-ounce Space blanket—in other words, a compact arsenal of techno-wear to enable her to handle every impossibility. I am not poking fun at Heidi, for as it turned out, she was the only one who was suitably prepared for mosquitoes with voracious appetites for Americans, and for skies that demonstrated with dramatic effect what might occur during a surprise flash flood.

When the rain first began to fall, soft as tears, our travelers had long since dispersed themselves like sheep on a sparse range. Each had gone off to stake his or her own unique experience. Roxanne had led the way uphill for Dwight and Heidi. Wyatt and Wendy sprinted down the shadier paths for a bit of smooching and pawing. Marlena and Esmé accepted Harry's invitation to search for wildlife and the fabled pine with limbs as gnarled as an old man's arthritic joints. Bennie and Vera wandered downward, taking the path of least resistance gravity-wise as they passionately discussed the building of the new Asian Art Museum and the various ways to blend innovation with tradition. Moff and Rupert jogged away, the younger lad soon being two turns ahead of his father, at which point he was seized with a desire to hoist his limber self up a steep face of rock, at the top of which was a grotto surrounded by a stone relief. He scrambled across scree, stepped over a low roped fence, and began to climb. At the bottom was a sign in Chinese that read: "Forbidden to Enter! Danger!"

Soon water was filling the rocky crevices of the canyon, and as the rain came down more ferociously, a distinctive wind-whirring and rock-tocking sound reverberated. It was like an orchestra of stone bells, the Chinese version of an aeolian harp. To hear it, you would think this was how the mountain had received its name; but in fact, the name came from a stony formation at the top that resembles a bell. It's quite prosaic. In any case, the sounds rang loud as a bell, loud enough to dampen the shouts of people to one another.

"Rupert!" Moff cried out. No answer.

"Which way?" Marlena shouted to Harry, who was peering up and then down the path. Her words fell to the floor of the canyon, unheard along with the cries of ten thousand others lost over the ages.

In short order, the paths had become too tricky to traverse. So everyone did what was most natural, what people over the last twelve centuries have done, and sought refuge in one of the sixteen grottoes and various temples that pocked the sides of Stone Bell Mountain.

Marlena, Esmé, and Harry were closest to the main temple grounds, whose original building, now gone, was constructed during the Nanzhao Kingdom, around the ninth century. The decorative pillars and tile roofs, which Harry could make out through the rainy haze, were from a remodeling job done during the Ching dynasty, only a hundred or so years old and repainted in more recent years after its near destruction during the Cultural Revolution. The three rain-soaked visitors scrambled up the zigzag path, and when they arrived at one of the temple buildings above a courtyard, they were stunned by what they saw from ancient times. As the rain poured down the awnings, it created a misty curtain, a scrim behind which stood a pretty, young woman in turbaned headdress and bright pink jacket singing to a young man who accompanied her on a two-stringed *erhu*, which had the versatility to sound like anything from a young woman moaning in love to a horse shrilling in fright. Our travelers stepped closer, but the singing couple remained oblivious of the intruders.

"Are they real?" Esmé asked.

Marlena said nothing. They must be ghosts stuck in time, forever reliving one moment that was dear to them, she thought.

The woman's singing rose, her voice warbling in unearthly surges. The man began to sing in response. Back and forth they went, with an incredible athleticism in their trilling vibrato. The man walked closer to the pretty woman, and at the end, she leaned into his chest, falling back like a viola returning to its protective case, and allowed him to wrap her in his arms.

"*Hullo!*" a female voice suddenly called out.

When Harry, Marlena, and Esmé turned, they saw a woman in a pink business suit standing under the eaves of another building, waving frantically. Behind her were two men, one with a video camera and the other holding a boom. They were, of course, the television crew that the old fellow at the entrance booth had mentioned in his instructions, the same ones that Miss Rong had failed to understand.

"Omigod! Are we in your way?" Marlena shouted back. "We are *so* sorry. We had no idea—"

The woman and her crew ducked from under their awning and ran toward them. The two costumed singers also came over, the man now smoking a cigarette.

"No problem, no worries," the woman said affably. "You are from UK? All three?"

"America, USA, all three," Harry answered. He pointed to Marlena, Esmé, then himself. "San Francisco."

"Very nice," the woman said. She translated for her crew and the singers. They nodded and talked among themselves, which worried Marlena. She, who had been raised in a Shanghainese family, understood about as much Mandarin as Miss Rong understood English, and it sounded to her as if the crew was upset that they had botched their shoot. Eventually, the pink-garbed woman spoke to them again in English. "We are documentary making for this region, from national television program, for awareness of Bai minority culture, as well the scenic beauty in Stone Bell Mountain, to show appreciating the tourists around the world. We like to ask you question. Is okay?"

Harry traded laughs with Marlena. "Sure. Absolutely delighted."

The cameraman positioned himself and motioned for Harry and Marlena to step more to the left and closer to the woman in pink. The soundman lofted the boom above them. Words were exchanged in Chinese, and the filming began with the woman speaking rapidly in Beijing-perfect Mandarin: "As you can see, Stone Bell Temple, with its rich culture, ancient historical grottoes, and fascinating landscape, deserves its world-renowned reputation. Tourists from many countries come, drawn by the enjoyable scenery and the educational prospects. These same tourists have a choice of visiting Paris, Rome, London, or Niagara Falls—but here, in beautiful Stone Bell Mountain, they have made their choice. Let us meet two of them, a prosperous family from San Francisco in America."

She switched to English: "Sir, lady, please to tell us what you think this place, Stone Bell Temple and Mountain."

"It's beautiful here," Marlena said, "even in the rain." She did not know whether to look at the camera or at the woman in pink, so she did both, glancing back and forth, which gave her a furtive appearance.

Harry assumed his television posture, a more erect back, chest forward, a steady and honest gaze at the camera: "This place is truly spectacular." He gestured to an elaborately painted beam. "Absolutely charming. We don't have anything like it back home. Nothing quite this old or, for that matter, so . . . so vibrant, so vibrantly red. The aesthetic is utterly, utterly Chinese, absolutely historical. Oh, and we can hardly wait to see the magnificent grottoes we've heard so much about, the female one." He looked back at the interviewer, gave a quick nod to indicate that he considered his delivery to have been an adequate take.

The woman switched back to Mandarin: "Even young children are so intrigued they beg their parents to come to Stone Bell Mountain." She gesticulated to the cameraman, and he immediately switched his direction toward Esmé. She was walking in the courtyard, which was decorated with bare crape myrtle trees and tubs of prunus flower bushes, their tiny pink buds in various stages of emergence. At the far end of the courtyard, an old woman sat on a stool with a baby on her lap, the mother and daughter, respectively, of the caretaker who lived on the temple grounds. Beside them was a dirty-white Shih Tzu, toothless and deaf. It reminded Esmé of the little puppy back at the hotel. As she approached, the dog jumped up, knocked over a low stool, and made a bluff charge at her, barking ferociously. Esmé shrieked.

"Little girlie," called the interviewer. "Please come back please, so we can ask you question why your parents bring you here."

Esmé glanced toward her mother questioningly, and Marlena nodded. When Esmé returned, the woman shoved her between her mother and Harry, then said: "You happy to be here with mother and father, come so far enjoy beautiful Stone Bell Temple. Yes?"

"He's not my dad," Esmé said peevishly. She scratched at an elbow. The itchy bumps left by mosquitoes made her even more irritated.

"Sorry. Can you say again?" the interviewer asked.

"I *said, she's* my mother, but he's *not* my dad."

"Oh! Sorry, sorry." The woman was now flustered. These Americans were always so frank. You never knew what kind of peculiar things they would say. They openly admitted to having unmarried sex, that their children were bastards.

The woman gathered her thoughts, reaching for a new angle, and began her interview again in English: "Just while ago, you enjoy the beautiful Bai minority folksinging, mountain girl call to her mountain boy. This traditional ballad happen every day for many thousand years. In your homeland you having Christmas ballad for celebrate two thousand years ago also until now. Is true or not true?"

Marlena had never thought of Christmas in that way. "True," she dutifully answered.

"Maybe since you already enjoy our traditional singing we can enjoy your same."

The camera zoomed in on Marlena, Esmé, and Harry, and the boom was lowered.

"What are we supposed to do?" Harry asked.

"I think they want us to sing," Marlena whispered.

"You're kidding."

The interviewer smiled and laughed. "Yes! Yes!" She began to clap. "Now you sing ballad."

Harry backed away. "Oh, no." He held up his hands. "No, no. Not possible." He pointed to his throat. "Very bad. See? Sore, inflamed, can't sing. Terrible pain. Possibly contagious. Sorry. Should not even be here." He stepped off to the side.

The interviewer cupped Marlena's mosquito-bitten elbow. "You. Please to sing us Christmas traditional song. You choose. Sing!"

"'Jingle Bells'?" Esmé piped up.

The boom swung toward Esmé. "'Jingo Bell,'" the woman repeated. "Yes! This is wonderful ballad. From Stone Bell to Jingo Bell. Please. Begin!"

"Come on, Mom," Esmé said. Marlena was horrified at what her daughter had wrought. Of all the times for Esmé to choose to be cooperative. Harry strode off, laughing and yelling back in encouragement, "Yes, sing! It'll be wonderful!"

The cameras rolled. The rain continued to play in the background, and Esmé's voice soared over her mother's squeaky one. Esmé loved to sing. She had a friend with a karaoke machine, and she sang better than all her friends. Just recently she had learned that you didn't have to sing the standard notes; you could do loops around them and land on the tune where and when you wanted. And if you felt the music deep in your gut, a natural vibrato came up. She knew how to do it as no one else she knew could. The pride she felt put a tickle in her throat until she had to sing to soothe it.

Marlena's and Esmé's singing grew fainter as Harry strode away. He took a path that led up, and he was soon in front of what he guessed was one of the famed grottoes with its life-sized figures. It reminded him of a nativity scene. The carved faces showed obvious signs of repair, and given the dim light, most of the finer features were difficult to see. Like many holy artifacts, these had been maimed during the Cultural Revolution, their noses and hands lopped off. Harry wondered what the Red Guards might have done to defile the Grotto of Female Genitalia. Where the devil was it, anyway? All those damn signs were in Chinese. What should he be looking for? In trying to imagine it, he pictured the luscious genitalia of Marlena, as she lay splayed on a secret hillside spot. A quickening surged in his groin, but it was not passion.

Bugger. He had to piss. He'd never make it back to that miserable loo. He looked back and could see Marlena and Esmé still performing their musical recital in the courtyard. The old woman had joined the small audience. She was holding the baby, making her clap her little hands in rhythm to another stanza of "Jingle Bells." Harry chuckled and continued walking along the path until he was out of view. In fact, he discovered he was at the end of the path. And there—how handy indeed—was a public urinal. This one was recessed in rock, about twenty inches wide, two feet in height, with a receptacle brimming with what looked like urine and cigarette ashes. (What that was actually was rainwater that had washed over joss-stick offerings.) The walls were wavy and smooth, leading Harry to think it had been worn down by centuries of men seeking the same relief. (Not so. That stone had been carved to resemble a vulva.) And portions of the loo, he noted, had been etched with graffiti. (The Chinese characters were in reality an engraving attributed to the Goddess of Female Genitalia, the progenitor of all life, the bearer of glad tidings to formerly barren women. "Open wide my convenient door," was how it translated into English, "so that I may receive good karma from everywhere.") Harry deposited his karma in one long, hissing stream. At last, his prostate was cooperating, what relief!

Off in the distance, the interviewer decided that it was best to get some shots of the Caucasian man so that she might reinforce the point that tourists came from everywhere. The TV crew walked up the path. From about fifty feet away, the cameraman trained his zoom lens on Harry, who was grinning ecstatically as he issued forth.

The cameraman in turn let go with a stream of invectives. He informed the others of what he had just witnessed. "Arrogant devils!" Together with the soundman and the male singer, he ran off in the direction of their holiest and now defiled shrine, shouting angrily. Marlena and Esmé followed, baffled and scared.

Harry was surprised to hear the commotion advancing his way. He peered about to see if the temple had caught fire. Were they about to wash away in a flash flood? What were the men so excited about? He walked toward the brouhaha. And then, to his astonishment, they had him circled: three men spitting, lunging, their faces twisted in rage. You didn't have to know Chinese to realize they were swearing a blue streak. Even the woman in the pink suit, while not as rabid as the men, wore a hostile expression. "Shame you! Shame you!" she cried.

Harry ducked the swing of the boom and hurried to Marlena. "What the devil did you and Esmé do?" The words fell out wrong, but that is what happens when you feel you are about to be massacred.

"What the hell did *you* do?" Marlena spat back. "They keep yelling something about urine. Did you pee on some shrine?"

He huffed. "Of course not. I used an outdoor urinal—" And just as he said that, he realized the probable and awful truth. "Oh, shit." He watched as the woman in ancient costume whipped out a mobile phone to tell the Bai minority chieftain what had just happened. How utterly amazing, Harry marveled, they get mobile phone reception way out here in the middle of hell.

The remainder of that momentous afternoon was a frantic attempt to herd the travelers into the bus so they could escape. Bai park rangers found Wendy and Wyatt half disrobed in another grotto. Rupert had to be rescued from a crumbling perch, and in the effort, damage was done to sensitive plant areas and the feet of a carved god. To keep dry, Dwight had kicked in the padlocked door of what he took to be an abandoned shed, and he, Roxanne, and Heidi entered and huddled inside. When park rangers discovered them in this off-limits temple, they shouted at them to get out. Hearing these unintelligible threats, Dwight and Roxanne picked up sticks and swung wildly, thinking the men were rogue thieves. Heidi screamed, certain she was about to be abducted and sold as a sex slave.

The old man at the tollbooth turned out to be the Bai chieftain. He shouted at Miss Rong and demanded a huge fine for all these unspeakable crimes. When he realized she didn't understand a whit of what he was saying, he switched to Mandarin and ranted at her until she began to cry, letting everyone see she had completely lost face. In the end, he said, each of the "American hooligans" had to pay "a severe price—one hundred renminbi, yes, you heard me right, one hundred!"

What a relief, Bennie thought, when Miss Rong told him. That was cheaper than a San Francisco parking ticket. Everyone was glad to fork over the money and be on the way. When the pile was handed over, the chieftain gesticulated and yelled again at Miss Rong. He held up the money and slapped it, pointed to the back of the bus, at the puzzled faces turned around looking at him, and slapped the money again. With each slap, Miss Rong jerked but kept her mouth pressed closed, her eyes tilted down. "Jeesh," Wendy said.

When Miss Rong finally got on the bus, her glasses looked steamed. She sat in the front seat, visibly trembling. She did not count heads or speak into the microphone to explain what they would be doing next.

On the bus ride back to the hotel, most of my friends were quiet, the only sound that of fingernails scratching skin. They had stopped at a roadside spot for the customary bathroom break, and a cloud of mosquitoes had descended on them, as if it were the Bai army chasing them away. Heidi passed out hydrocortisone cream. It was too late for the DEET.

Bennie was exhausted. His shoulders sagged. Was this an omen of things to come? Did they think it was *all* his fault for picking the tour guide? He was trying so hard to be perfect, doing things they were not even aware of! And look, there were no thanks, just complaints and blame and anger.

Dwight broke the silence. He remarked that Stone Bell Temple should have provided signs in other languages. How was he supposed to know it was a temple and not a chicken coop? Vera glared at him. "You still shouldn't assume you can break into places." She was angry with all the men except Bennie. They had exhibited the stupid male prerogative of ignoring the rules. Harry was beating himself up, feeling the fool, certain Marlena had a similar judgment of him. He had *shouted* at her, had accused her, when he had been the idiot who sent those TV folks into a tizzy. He sat at the back of the bus, having banished himself there. Marlena was also mulling over what Harry had said to her. She hated being yelled at by authority figures. Her father had done that, and it didn't make her feel cowed anymore, just livid.

Wendy was unabashed by what had happened. She leaned against Wyatt, giggling as she thought about being caught in flagrante. It was exciting, in a weird way. She told him so in a naughty voice. He nodded, keeping his eyes closed. What they had done was not cool in his mind. He had been on ecotours where he was the one who had to reel in tourists who stepped on native plants, or tried to sneak home a lizard to keep as a souvenir or to sell. It irked him when people didn't give a shit about the rules. He hated being guilty of the same.

Esmé sat with her mother, happily humming "Jingle Bells." She hoped those Bai people would still use the part with her singing.

When the bus arrived at the hotel, Miss Rong muttered a few terse words to the driver, who then went off, leaving her standing alone at the front of the passengers. She kept her eyes turned down. Slowly, haltingly, she told her charges she would not be with them tomorrow. The Bai chieftain had said he was going to report the trouble to the authorities at the head office of China Travel Services. Her local boss had already called her and said to report to him immediately. She would be fired, that was certain. But they should not feel sorry for her, no. This was her fault. She should have kept them together as a group, explained to them what they were allowed to see. That was her responsibility, her job. She was very sorry she did not understand how to work more effectively with such an "individualistic group with many opinions, all not agreeing." Since they were "so disagreeable," she should have made stronger decisions to prevent them from committing the "danger of broken rule." Her glasses were now spattered with tears, but she did not wipe them. She held her body rigid to keep from weeping aloud.

Though Miss Rong was incompetent, my friends were sad to think she might lose her job. That would be terrible. They looked at one another out of the corners of their eyes, unsure of what to say.

Before they could decide, Miss Rong took a deep, quavering breath to steady herself, picked up her plastic briefcase, and stepped off the bus.

My friends burst into talk.

"What a mess," Moff said.

"We ought to give her a nice farewell tip," Harry suggested. "Why don't we collect some money now?"

"How much?" Roxanne asked. "Two hundred renminbi?"

"Four," said Vera.

Harry raised his brows. "Four hundred? That's almost five thousand for all of us. Maybe it's too much. She'll think we're pitying her."

"But we do pity her," Vera said. "God knows they don't give people unemployment in China when they've been fired."

"I'll give more," Bennie said.

Everyone protested that offer.

Bennie added humbly, "Well, it was my fault for picking her."

And no one made any noises in denying that, he noticed, and then felt humiliated and rejected, which launched him into anxiety.

"If she gets fired, why don't we sign a petition of protest?" Wendy said.

Dwight sniffed. "Come on, this isn't Berkeley. Besides, she really is a pretty bad tour guide. . . ."

All of a sudden, Miss Rong was again standing before them. My friends hoped she had not heard their exchange. "I forgot tell you one more thing," she began.

Her former charges listened politely.

"One extra thing Bai minority chief tell me. Important I tell you."

Oh, shit. The chief probably wanted more money, Bennie thought. Twenty dollars each was too good to be true. They were going to be shaken down for thousands.

This time Miss Rong did not look down. Her hair now looked wild, a statically charged crown. She kept her gaze straight ahead, as if she could see the future through the back window of the bus. "Chief, he telling other tourist authorities don't letting you in . . . no cable car ride to Yak Meadow, no ancient music concert, no tourist traps. Because therefore you cannot enjoying no more beautiful things in Lijiang or in all Yunnan Province and China. . . ." Bennie had a sinking feeling. He saw the tour schedule crumbling, total chaos.

"He say for you bringing shame to Grotto of Female Things, everybody here you never have no more babies, no descendants, no future. . . ."

Dwight glanced at the mother-to-be of his children-to-be. Roxanne stared back.

Miss Rong's voice rose higher and sang out louder: "He say even you pay one million dollar, still not enough keep trouble away. . . . He say he tell all gods give these foreigners bad curse, bad karma, following them forever this life and next, this country, that country, never can stop."

Heidi's anxiety bells were ringing.

Miss Rong took a deep breath, and right before she left the bus, she said in a voice that sounded clearly victorious. "This I thought you must know."

At that moment, all twelve of my friends saw in their minds the water buffalo, knee deep in mud.

HOW HAPPINESS
FOUND THEM

At dinner, my twelve friends walked a few blocks into the old historic part of town, to Bountiful Valley Restaurant, which they had rejected only that morning. Now they were resigned to the menu I had called "A Taste of Winter Delicacies." No one was in the mood to search for alternatives that were either more "spontaneous" or more "authentic." They were just glad that their ill-omened trip to Stone Bell Temple had not yet infiltrated the word-of-mouth network of Lijiang. Not only did the restaurant send a message to the hotel that they could enjoy the same menu that evening, the owner had offered a bonus, "free surprises," he called them.

The first surprise was the restaurant itself. It was enchanting, not touristy at all. I knew this all along, of course. That was why I had chosen it. The building was charmingly cramped, a former dwelling whose outer courtyard had been converted into dining rooms facing the narrow canal, one of a watery lacework that ran through the streets of Lijiang. If you were to sit on the sill, you could have dipped your toes in the tranquil flow. The tables and chairs were old, marked with character in the way that has become popular with antiques in America nowadays, nothing refinished, no scratches or cigarette marks buffed out, the century-old bits of food now serving as grout in the cracks.

The beers arrived, somber toasts were called out:

"To better times ahead."

"Much better."

Dwight immediately suggested they vote in democratic fashion whether to leave Lijiang the next day so they might get an earlier start on Burma. When he called for the yea votes, the only holdouts were Bennie, Vera, and Esmé.

Bennie was understandably concerned about an early departure. If they left early, he would be the one scrambling to patch in a new itinerary. A day in the border town of Ruili and then three extra days in Burma—what would they do? But he said nothing in casting his nay, not wishing to come across as inadequate. He should have realized that the democratic process has no place on travel tours. Once you are a tour leader, absolute rule is the only way to go.

Vera tried to exercise her executive veto. She was used to working in an organization in which she was the top boss. As a born leader, she demanded consensus, and through her unilateral decisions, and her famous eye-locking gaze, she attained it. But here in China she was one of the masses. When the votes were called for, she appealed to the group's rationality. "Fiddle-dee-dee. I don't believe for a second that the chief has the clout to bar us from other places. Think about it. Is he able to get on the Internet and e-mail his cronies in a hundred places? Of course not."

"He had a cell phone," Moff reminded her.

"I doubt he's going to waste his precious cell phone minutes to complain about us. He was just spouting off—*not* that he didn't have every right to be infuriated." She cocked one eye and looked toward Harry, Dwight, Moff, and Rupert.

She then switched to sentimentality. "As you all recall, this tour was lovingly designed by my dear friend Bibi Chen, carefully put together as an educational and inspirational journey. If we leave now like scared little mice, we will miss out on some of the greatest adventures of our lives. We wouldn't get to feel the spray of the magnificent waterfalls at the bottom of Tiger Leaping Gorge. . . ."

Esmé's mouth rounded. They were supposed to go there?

"We would be forgoing a ride on a horse with Tibetan nationals in Yak Meadow. . . ."

That caught Roxanne's and Heidi's attention; they had each owned a pony when they were little girls.

Vera went on: "When in this lifetime will you have another chance to see an alpine meadow at seventeen thousand feet? Extremely rare." She nodded solemnly in agreement with herself. "As are those murals of Guan Yin in the sixteenth-century temple . . ."

Poor Vera, she almost had them convinced, until she mentioned the murals. Goddesses may have been Vera's niche in art history, but the mention of Guan Yin made others twitch with anxiety. Another temple? No, no more temples, please. Vera poked at the schedule, which she held up as if it were the Declaration of Independence. "This is what I signed up for. This is what I paid for. This is what I intend to do. I vote nay and I urge the rest of you to reconsider." She sat down.

Esmé also voted nay, with a slightly lifted hand.

Vera gestured to Esmé to get everybody's attention. "Another nay."

When asked to explain her vote, Esmé shrugged. She couldn't say. The truth was, she had fallen tragically in love. The Shih Tzu puppy had grown weak. When it tried to walk, it stumbled and fell. It would not eat the offerings of Chinese food given by the beauties. Esmé had also noted a lump protruding from its belly. The pup's caretakers seemed unconcerned by its worsening condition. The lump, they said, was nothing, and one of them pointed to her own chin to suggest that the problem was no more serious than a pimple. "No worries," they assured Esmé, thinking she was bargaining them down. "You pay less money. One hundred kwai okay."

"You don't understand. I can't take the puppy. I'm traveling."

"Take, take," they countered. "Eighty kwai."

Now, during the vote, Esmé could only sit grimly, chest tight to keep from crying. She could not explain any of this, especially not in front of Rupert, who rolled his eyes and groaned whenever someone referred to them collectively as "the two kids." He never said anything to her, even when forced to sit next to her, just kept his nose buried in his paperback. Besides, who among these grown-ups cared if a puppy died? "It's only a dog," they would say. "Some people have it even worse." She had heard that excuse so many times it made her puke. They weren't really concerned about people, just their stupid trip, whether they would get their money's worth in this dumb country or that dumb country. She couldn't talk to her mother about any of this. Her mother still called her "Wawa," a Chinese nickname for "baby." *Wawa,* the sound of a crying doll. She hated being called that. "Wawa, what color scarf should I wear?" her mother had said in a girly voice that morning. "Wawa, does my tummy stick out?" "Do you think I look better, Wawa, with my hair up or down?" *She* was the wawa, so goo-goo *stupid* over that *hairy*-armed *Hahr-ry* Bailley. Couldn't she see what a big phony he was?

Dwight asked if anyone had anything to add before they officially closed the vote. I was yelling as loudly as I could. *Stop! Stop! How can you possibly leave China early?* It was utterly mad. Had they known I was there, I could have shown them why it was ridiculous to even think of leaving. I had planned the itinerary carefully, explicitly, so that they might have a taste of the finest, so they could be like "dragonflies skimming the waters." Now they wouldn't even touch the surface.

The gnarled pine, I would have said, touch it. That is China. Horticulturalists from around the world have come to study it. Yet no one has ever been able to explain why it grows like a corkscrew, just as no one can adequately *explain* China. But like that tree, there it is, old, resilient, and oddly magnificent. Within that tree are the elements in nature that have inspired Chinese artists for centuries: gesture over geometry, subtlety over symmetry, constant flow over static form.

And the temples, walk in and touch them. That is China. Don't merely stare at those murals and statues. Fly up to the crossbeams, get down on your hands and knees, and press your head to the floor tiles. Hide behind that pillar and come eye to eye with its flecks of paint. Imagine that you are an interior decorator who is a thousand years in age. Start with a bit of Tibetan Buddhism, add a smidgen of Indian Buddhism, a dab of Han Buddhism, plus a dash each of animism and Taoism. A hodgepodge, you say? No, what is in those temples is an amalgam that is *pure* Chinese, a lovely shabby elegance, a glorious messy motley that makes China infinitely intriguing. Nothing is ever completely thrown away and replaced. If one period of influence falls out of favor, it is patched over. The old views still exist, one chipped layer beneath, ready to pop through with the slightest abrasion.

That is the Chinese aesthetic and also its spirit. Those are the traces that have affected all who have traveled along China's roads. But if you leave too soon, those subtleties will be lost on you. You will see only what the brochures promise you will see, the newly painted palaces. You will enter Burma thinking that when you cross the border, you leave China behind. And you could not be more wrong. You will still see the traces of tribal tenacity, the contradictory streaks of obedience and rebellion, not to mention the curses and charms.

But it was decided. "Nine votes yea, three votes nay," Dwight announced. "Let's raise another toast: To Burma!"

DINNER WAS SERVED, "A Taste of Winter Delicacies," with dishes I had sampled on a previous tour and selected as a sensual experience for the palate. Unfortunately, the restaurant owner made a few substitutions, since I was not there to make any objections.

Wendy was the first to admit that the roadside eatery that afternoon had been "kind of a mistake." If only she knew how huge. Nonetheless, I was greatly pleased to hear this admission come from her lips. A chastened group was a more honest one. And they raved about the fare I had chosen, or did until they encountered what the cook called "surprises" he had thrown in for free.

One was a roasted root with a crunchiness that the chef claimed the tourists would find as tasty and addictive as their American chips and English crisps. The roasted roots, however, had the unappetizing appearance of large fried larvae, also a regional favorite. But once the travelers were persuaded to try one, they devoured the snappy little appetizer with gusto, as they did a later dish, presented as the second surprise, which also resembled larva, and was. Then came another crunchy appetizer called "dragonfly," which they took to be poetic license and was not. "This one has more of a buttery flavor," Bennie said.

The third surprise was a spicy bean curd.

"I've eaten *ma-po* tofu all my life," Marlena said. "But this one tastes strange. I'm not quite sure I like it."

"It's almost lemony, and with a strong bite," Harry said.

"I don't care for it." Vera pushed her portion off to the side.

"It's not bad," Dwight said. "Grows on you, actually." He took seconds.

What they tasted was not the chili substitute often found in American-made Sichuan tofu. The Lijiang version was made of the berrylike pods of the prickly ash. The zing in the mouth derives from the numbing quality that the berries have on the mucosa. And the particular variety of the genus *Zanthoxylum* that my friends were eating was not only from Sichuan but also of the Himalayan region, where people eat it like jelly beans. It tends to have more heat factor, *ma*-ness, and also to cause an almost anesthesia-like paralysis of the gut, especially in those who are delicately inclined. That would be Dwight, I might add.

THE NEXT DAY, when the group assembled for breakfast, Bennie had an announcement: "By nothing short of a miracle, Miss Rong, as a final courtesy, was able to book flights for us today so that we can leave as soon as possible." In a few hours, they would leave for Lijiang airport and fly to Mangshi, which was only a couple of hours' drive from the Burma border. As Bennie knew, palm-greasing helps to speed things along. The night before, after the group had voted to leave Lijiang, he rang up Miss Rong and said he would give her two hundred U.S. dollars of his own money to use as she saw fit, no questions asked, if only she could help him out of this predicament. She in turn gave away a portion of that to the various expediters connected with hotels, airlines, and the office of tourism, who, in the age-old custom of *guanxi*-giving, showed their appreciation by granting almost a full refund on the much-shortened visit to Lijiang.

At ten in the morning, they boarded the flight, and as they ascended, so did their moods. They had escaped their troubles with nothing more than a few mosquito bites and the pinch of several thousand kwai.

Their new guide, Miss Kong, was there to meet them at the gate in

Mangshi. She was holding a sign: "Welcome Bibi Chen Group." I was delighted to see this, but it certainly took my friends aback. Bennie quickly introduced himself as the tour leader taking my place.

"Oh, Miss Bibi is not able to come?" Miss Kong inquired.

"Not able," Bennie confirmed, and hoped the others had not heard this exchange. If the tourism office here was unaware that the original organizer of this trip was dead, what else had they neglected to note?

The guide faced the group: "My name is Kong Xiang-lu. You may call me Xiao Kong or Miss Kong," she said. "Or if you prefer, my American nickname is Lulu. Again, nickname is Lulu. Can you say this?" She paused to hear the correct answer.

"Lulu," everyone mumbled.

"Sorry?" Lulu cupped her ear.

"Lulu!" they filled in with more enthusiasm.

"Very good. When you need something, you just shout Lulu." She said it again, in a singing voice: "Luuu-lu!"

Privately, as they walked toward the bus, Lulu told Bennie, "I saw report of your difficulties at Stone Bell Temple."

Bennie became flustered. "We didn't mean—that is, we had *no* idea . . ."

She held up her hand like the Buddha asking for meditative silence. "No idea, no worries." Bennie noted that everyone in China who spoke any English was saying that phrase, "No worries." Some Aussies must have come through, all of them solicitously murmuring "No worries" at every turn. Lost your luggage? No worries! Your room's crawling with fleas? No worries!

Bennie wanted to believe that Lulu's declaration of "No worries" was genuine, that she had solved all their problems. He had been hoping for a sign that their luck had turned, and by the minute he felt she was presenting it. She offered a clear plan, knew all the routines, and could speak the same dialect as the driver.

I, too, thought she was an ideal guide. She had an aura of assurance matched by competence. This is the best combination, much better than nervousness and incompetence, as in the last guide. The worst, I think, is complete confidence matched by complete incompetence. I have experienced it all too often, not just in tour guides, but in marketing consultants and art experts at auction houses. And you find it in plenty of world leaders. Yes, and they all lead you to the same place, trouble.

For Bennie, Lulu's no-worries and no-nonsense demeanor was as good as two prescription sedatives. Suddenly, devising a new schedule did not seem overwhelming. Her English was understandable, and that alone put her legions ahead of Miss Rong. Poor Miss Rong. He still felt guilty about that. Oh, well. In addition to being fluent in Mandarin, Lulu claimed to speak Jingpo, Dai, Cantonese, Shanghainese, Japanese, and Burmese. *"Meine Deutsche, ach,"* she went on in a self-deprecating manner full of good humor and mistakes, *"ist nicht sehr gute."* Her hair was cut into a short flip. Her glasses were modern, small cat's-eye frames with a hip retro fifties look. She wore a tan corduroy jacket, drab olive slacks, and a black turtleneck. She certainly appeared to be competent. She could have been a tour guide in Maine or Munich.

"The Chinese border town has very excellent hotel," Lulu went on. "That is where you stay tonight, in Ruili. But the town is quite small, just stopping-off place where tourists are eager to leave, so not too much for sightseeing. My suggestion is this, so listen: We stop at a Jingpo village along the way." Bennie nodded dumbly. "Later, we do a bicycle trip to a market, where selling the foods is very exciting to tourist who is seeing the first time. . . ." As Lulu ticked off various spur-of-the-moment activities, Bennie felt waves of relief. Lulu was doing an admirable job, God love her.

Lulu stood at the front of the bus, counting heads before she gave the takeoff signal to the bus driver, a man named Xiao Li. "You can call him Mr. Li," Lulu said. Lesser employees, Bennie noted, were accorded more respectful status. As the bus roared into gear, Lulu grabbed a microphone. "Good afternoon, good morning, ladies, gentlemen," her voice came out, loud and tinny. "You are awake? Eyes are open? Ready to learn more about Yunnan Province here in a beautiful southwest part of China? Okay?" She smiled, then beckoned her charges with a toss of her hand to answer.

"Okay," a few said.

Lulu shook her head ruefully. *"Okay?"* Lulu leaned forward, her hand cupping her ear, a now familiar cue.

"Okay!" the travelers shouted back.

"Very good. So enthusiastic. Today, you travel to Ruili, pronounce it 'Ray-LEE.' Can you say this?"

"RAY-lee!"

"Hey, your Chinese is pretty good. Okay. Ruili is Chinese border town, next to Muse in Myanmar. Pronounce it 'MOO-say.'" The hand flip.

"Moo-SAY!"

"Not so bad. In a next forty-five minutes, we are going to see a Jingpo village. For seeing the ordinary life, the ways of preparing food, or growing some vegetables. Is okay? What you think?" This was met with applause. "Agree, very good." She beamed at her attentive charges.

Lulu continued: "Does anyone know who are Jingpo people, what tribe Jingpo people are related? What tribe, what country? No? No one knows? Then today you will learn somethings new you never hear before, yes, somethings new. Jingpo is a same as Kachin in Burma, the Kachin people in Burma. Burma is a same as Myanmar, Myanmar is new name since 1989. Yes, Kachin people you may have hearing this or not, is very fierce tribe, yes, fierce tribe. You may know, reading this in a newspaper. Who is reading this? No one?"

My friends looked at one another. There were fierce tribes in Myanmar? Dwight seemed oddly interested in this fact. Roxanne had a headache. She wondered if her period was coming, hailing the dismal news, once again, that she was not pregnant. "I can't stand that microphone," she muttered. "Can someone tell her to turn it down, or even give us some silence instead of blabbing on and on?"

Lulu went on: "The story is this. The Kachin often make insurrection against the government, the military government. Other tribes in Myanmar do the same, not all, just some do. Karen people, I think they do. So if it is happening, the Myanmar government must stop this insurrection. Small civil war, until everything is quiet. But not here, no such problem. Here our government is not military. China is socialist, very peace-loving, all peoples, minorities, they are welcome and can do their own lifestyles, but also live as one people in one country. So here the Jingpo people are peaceful, no worries that you visit their village. They welcome you, really, they sincerely welcoming you. Okay?" She cupped her ear.

"Okay!" half the travelers shouted in unison.

"Okay, everyone agree. So now you learn somethings new. Here we have a tribe called Jingpo. Over there, Kachin. Language, the same. Business, the same. They do farming, living very simple life, have strong family relations all under one roof, from grandmother to little babies, yes, all under same roof. Soon you shall see. Very soon." She smiled confidently, clicked off the microphone, and began to pass out bottles of water.

"Finally!" Roxanne whispered loudly.

What a treasure, Bennie thought. Lulu was like a kindergarten teacher who could keep unruly children in order, clapping happily, and on their toes. He leaned his head against the window. If he could get a few winks, his mind would be able to function better. . . . So many details to attend to . . . He had to get them checked into the hotel . . . put together a to-do list before they entered Burma. Sleep beckoned. Mindlessness, senselessness. No worries, no worries, he heard the repeating voice of Lulu with her hypnotic calmness. . . .

"Mr. Bennie. Mr. Bennie?"

Lulu tapped his arm and Bennie's eyes flew open. She was looking at him brightly. "For your update, I have some F-Y-I to report. So far I have not secure necessary arrangements into Myanmar. We have no answer, not yet. . . ."

Bennie's heart began pounding like that of a mother who hears her baby's cry in the middle of the night.

"Of course, I am working very hard for getting it," she added.

"I don't understand," Bennie stammered. "We already have visas for Myanmar. Can't we just go in?"

"Visa is for coming in five days later. How you got this, I don't know. It is very unusual, to my knowledge. Also, this way into Myanmar is not so easy, with visa or not with visa. You are Americans. Usually Americans fly airplanes, go first to Yangon or Mandalay. Here at Ruili border, only Chinese and Burmese come in and out, no third-country national peoples."

Bennie began to sputter. "I still don't understand."

"No Americans enter overland, not in very long time. Maybe is not convenient for Myanmar customs to making the border pass to English-speaking tourists. The paperwork is already very difficult because so many peoples in China and Myanmar speaking different dialects. . . ."

Bennie had a hard time following this line of thought. What did different dialects have to do with their getting a border pass?

". . . That why I am thinking this is very unusual, you coming in this way."

"Then why are we *trying*?"

"I thinking Miss Bibi want start entry here on China side, drive overland into Muse on Myanmar side. That way, your journey can follow the history of Burma Road."

"Follow the history! But if we can't get in, we won't be following anything but our asses back to America!"

"Yes," Lulu said agreeably. "I thinking same things."

"Then why don't we just fly to Mandalay and start the trip there?"

She nodded slowly, her mouth pulling downward. It was apparent she had strong reservations there. "This morning, before you come, I change everything for you arrive early. Same cities, same hotels, just early date. No worries. But if we fly to Mandalay, skip other places, then I must be changing every city, every hotel. We are needing airplane and canceling the bus. Everything start over. I think is possible. We can ask a Golden Land Tour Company in Myanmar. But starting over means everything is slow."

Bennie could already see this was a bad idea. Too many opportunities for problems at every step. "Has anyone at least *tried* recently to come in overland?"

"Oh, yes. This morning, six backpackers were trying, both American and Canadian."

"And?"

"All turn back. But you be patient. I am trying somethings. No worries."

The blood vessels in Bennie's scalp rapidly constricted, then dilated, causing his heart to accelerate and boom. What the hell did this mean? Where was his Xanax? How was it that Lulu could wear a cheerful face when she had just presented him with such awful news? His tired mind was racing, crashing into dead ends. And would she please stop with the stupid "No worries" bit?

I must interject here. It's true that no Americans had come into Burma via Ruili in a quite a long time, in fact, many, many years. But I had arranged to be among the first. It was to be one of my proudest achievements on the trip. During my last reconnaissance trip, I had had an excellent tour guide, a young man who was with the Myanmar tourism office. He was very smart, and if I had a problem or needed to change anything, the first thing he said was not, "That can't be done," which is the knee-jerk attitude of so many, and not just in Myanmar. This young man would say, "Let me think how we might do that."

So when I said I wanted to bring a group and travel on the Burma Road from the Chinese border in Ruili and into Burma, he said that this would require special arrangements, because it might be the first time in a long time that this had been done. A few months before we were to start our tour, he wrote and said all the arrangements had been made. They had been complicated, but he had made contacts at the checkpoint, at the central tourism office in Yangon, with the tour company, with customs. The date, he said, was difficult to attain. But it was all confirmed for Christmas Day. Once in China, he would contact me at the hotel in Ruili, and he would be there to guide us through personally. I was so happy, I offered to give him a very special gift on Christmas Day, and he was excited and grateful to hear this.

But of course, neither Bennie nor Lulu knew of this. It was up to me to contact the tour guide again and make sure he could make new arrangements. How I would do that in my present state, well, it was very difficult to imagine.

HARRY HAD RESUMED SITTING next to Marlena, but the momentum between them was rapidly rolling backward. In front of them, Wendy and Wyatt snuggled and nuzzled each other happily. How sad, Harry thought, that he and Marlena were not similarly engaged. It was awkward for him to watch the young couple, see this contrast to him. It almost seemed they were flaunting their sexual intimacy. Marlena, meanwhile, resented their prolonged sessions of

French kissing. A little smooching was fine, but this was exhibition-ism. Who wanted to see their tongues damp-mopping each other's gums? The tongue-thrusting looked like a puppet show of a penile-vaginal encounter. Since these slurping antics were right in front of her, she had to work hard to ignore them. It was so embarrassing. She thought about asking them to stop, but then Harry might think she was a prude. Harry, in fact, was thinking of what he could say to begin a conversation with Marlena and reestablish their flirtation.

As Wendy and Wyatt worked themselves into a more fervent ses-sion, Harry unintentionally interrupted it by saying to Marlena, "Look at those huge birds! Those wings, how glorious!" He pointed out the window to circling birds. Heads turned, as did Wendy's and Wyatt's.

"Vultures," Wyatt said.

"Mm," Marlena said. "That's what they are, all right. We've cer-tainly seen a lot of them. Must be there's a carcass in the field." She was grateful that Harry thought to point out something that quickly snuffed out thoughts of sensual pleasure. "Chocolate or peanuts, anyone?" She began tossing out Halloween-sized bags of M&M's and trail mix. She had brought a huge duffel bag worth of snacks. Wyatt started popping chocolates, and Marlena hoped that his mouth, thus occupied, would not continue the lingual gymnastics.

Harry was mentally kicking himself. *Vultures!* What a sod he was. It was obvious Marlena thought so. Of all the stupid things to point out Of course they were vultures. He should have put on his bifocals. What happened to their spark, their frisson? Like an old married couple, they munched on their candies and stared wordlessly at the scenery with feigned interest and glazed eyes. The flat patches with different hues of green, a few low hills with clusters of trees. It all looked the same.

What they were actually seeing were fields of sugarcane with feathery tassels, thickets of tall bamboo, and twenty-foot-high small-needled pine trees. On the right was a hillside of tea bushes, a plot of carrots with white flowery heads. On the left were golden fields of rapeseed, and next to those, groves of rubber trees with leaves turned orange, red, and brown. Running alongside the road were the most vibrant bursts of life: fiery balls of lantana and scarlet hibiscus with their trumpet flowers open to hail a perfect afternoon. A perfect afternoon wasted on Harry and Marlena.

The bus turned up a bumpy dirt road, and all the nappers were jounced awake. Lulu conferred with the driver, and they came to an immediate agreement. It was time to disembark and walk the rest of the way to the village. The driver turned off the engine. "Bring your hat, sunglass, and water," Lulu ordered. "Also insect cream if you have. Many mosquitoes."

"Is there a restroom nearby?" Roxanne called out. Her camcorder was looped around her neck.

"Yes, yes, this way." Lulu gestured to the side of the road, to the tall vegetation. As people gathered their necessary belongings, tiny whimpers came from the back of the bus. Eyes turned toward Esmé, who appeared to be doubled over in pain.

"Wawa!" Marlena cried out. "Are you sick? What's the matter?" Light-headed with fear, Marlena ran toward the back of the bus, and the closer she drew, the more miserable Esmé appeared to be. Marlena leaned down to try to help her daughter sit up. A moment later, Marlena gasped: "Oh my God!"

The puppy whimpered again.

Harry ran toward them. Esmé began to howl, "I'm not leaving it! If you do, I'm staying here, too." Since the night before, Esmé knew the inevitable would happen. They would find out what she had done, and having kept her secret for so long, she had grown more anxious, and now she could not help but bawl. Surges of adolescent hormones contributed to a sense of doom.

Harry lifted a scarf that Esmé had fashioned by cutting up a

T-shirt. There in the crook of the hysterical girl's arm was a very lethargic-looking puppy. "Let me have a look-see," he said quietly.

"You can't have it!" Esmé blurted and blubbered. "If you try taking it I'll kill you, I swear I will—"

"Stop that!" Marlena scolded. In the past year, Esmé had said this a few times to both her and her ex-husband's new wife. Though Marlena knew it was just histrionics and empty threats, it pained her to hear her daughter use the word "kill" when there were teenagers who had acted upon such enraged thoughts.

Harry put his hand on Esmé's shoulder to calm her.

"Don't touch me!" she shrieked. "You can put your grimy hands on my mom but not on me. I'm underage, you know!"

Marlena flushed, and Harry did, too, with embarrassment and indignation. He looked up to see the others in the bus staring at him.

"Esmé, stop this right now," Marlena said.

Harry, remembering his training as an animal behaviorist, recovered his equanimity. With frightened dogs, shouting never helped matters. He made himself a symbol of calmness. "Of course no one is going to take away your puppy," he said in a soft voice. "I'm a veterinarian, and I can see what's the matter with him."

"No, you're not!" Esmé sobbed. "You play a stupid dog trainer on a TV show. You make them do stupid pet tricks."

"I'm also a veterinary doctor."

Esmé's sobs subsided into sniffles. "For real? You're not just an actor?" She eyed Harry, assessing whether to let go of her distrust.

"For real," Harry acknowledged, using this Americanism he normally despised. He began to talk to the puppy. "Hey, little wiggle-waggle, not feeling so well?" Harry opened the puppy's mouth and expertly peered at its gums, touching them lightly. He pinched up the skin on the puppy's back and let it fall back. "Gums are quite pale," he noted out loud. "See here? Slightly grayish. And see how the skin slowly drapes. Dehydration." He lifted the puppy and peered at its underside. "Mm. And it's a little lassie. . . . With a hernia in her umbilicus . . . About five weeks old, I reckon, likely not properly weaned."

"A lassie," Esmé said wondrously. Then: "Can you save her? Those girls in the hotel were just going to let her die. That's why I had to take her with me."

"Of course you did," Harry said.

"But darling," Marlena intervened, "the sad, sad thing is, we can't bring a dog with us, no matter how much—"

Harry put his palm up to indicate that her tack was going to backfire. He continued petting the pup as he spoke to Esmé. "She is a beauty." And then in tones of admiration: "How in the world did you get her past security and onto the plane?"

Esmé demonstrated by draping the triangled make-do scarf as a sling for her arm. She put a zippered sweatshirt over that. "It was easy," she said proudly. "I walked right through. She never made a peep."

Marlena looked at Harry, and for the first time since the debacle at the temple, their hearts and minds sought one another.

"What are we going to do?" Marlena mouthed.

Harry took charge. "Esmé, do you know when it last ate?"

"I tried to give her some eggs this morning. But she's not very hungry. She ate only a tiny bit, and when she burped, it came up. "

"Mm. How about her stools?"

"Stools?"

"Has she been making any poops?"

"Oh, that. She's peed, but no—you know, none of what you called the other. She's really well behaved. I think whatever it is has to do with that lump on her belly."

"Umbilical hernia," Harry said. "That's not necessarily serious or uncommon. Rather prevalent in toy breeds. Strangulation of the intestines could be a problem later, but most resolve in a few months' time, or if needed, it can be repaired with surgery." He knew he was saying more than was necessary, but he wanted Esmé to believe completely in his ability to help.

Esmé stroked the puppy's fur. "So what's wrong with her? Sometimes when she gets up, she runs really fast like she's crazy, then she falls over."

"Could be hypoglycemia." He hoped to God it was not parvo. "We need to get her rehydrated at the very least, and right away." He stood up and called to the others on the bus. "Would anyone by chance have a medicine dropper?"

A terribly long silence. And then a small voice asked, "I have an eyedropper, but would a sterile needle and syringe be better?" That was Heidi.

Harry was too surprised to answer at first, then blurted, "You must be joking. You have one?" And when Heidi's face reddened and fell with embarrassment, he revised himself quickly: "What I mean is, I didn't expect—"

"I brought it in case of accidents," he heard Heidi explain. "I read that you should never get a transfusion in a foreign country. AIDS is rampant in China and Burma, especially on the border."

"Of course. Brilliant."

"I also have tubing."

"Of course."

"And dextrose . . . in an IV solution."

"Wow!" Esmé said. "That's so cool."

Harry scratched his head. "That's . . . that's absolutely amazing. . . . I'm not sure if we should use them. After all, if we used your emergency supplies, they would not be usable later, if, well, you know, an accident did happen—"

"That's okay," Heidi said right away. "That's why I brought it, for any emergency, not just for me. I also have glucose tablets, if you want to try those instead."

Harry again couldn't help registering surprise.

"I'm hypoglycemic." Heidi raised her right wrist and displayed her MedicAlert bracelet.

Harry figured Heidi had what was often referred to in medical circles as "Marin County disease," a vague unhappiness that led people, women in particular, to complain of sudden weakness, shakiness, and hunger. Heidi had the medical knowledge and equipment of a hypochondriac. "Well, then," Harry said, "the eyedropper will do for now, if you would be willing—"

"Yes, yes." Heidi was in fact delighted. For once, her arsenal of remedies would come in handy. "I need to get into my suitcase first."

Heidi dug out her medical supplies, and the others scoured their hand luggage for items that might be useful: a wool cap for the puppy's bed. A facecloth as washable bedding. A pretty ribbon the puppy might wear once she was well and happily licking the faces of her saviors.

While Harry, Esmé, and Marlena tended to the sick puppy, the rest of the group followed Lulu out of the bus. Dwight went over to the side of the road and unzipped his fly.

It annoyed Vera that he was peeing within eyesight of her, that he assumed it was the responsibility of others to avert their eyes. The audacity. He controlled the group by acting as if he were the exception to every rule. He demanded alternatives when none should have been suggested. Grousing to herself, she trudged deeper into the tall grass to find her privacy. The brush closed in on her and she looked up at the clear sky, at its directionless blue. She was engulfed, disoriented, and she enjoyed the sensation, knowing she was not actually lost. She could still hear voices a few yards away. She lifted her dress, careful to bunch up the voluminous material so that she did not accidentally soil herself. How did the ladies of Victorian days manage to relieve themselves with those gigantic hoopskirts and petticoats?

In her wallet she carried a photo of a young black woman standing in front of painted scenery, solemnly staring at something off to the side. It was her future, Vera liked to think. Her hair was coiffed in the style of the times, wound and pinned, and she wore a high-collared black dress, an oval pendant at her throat, with a skirt that was smooth in front and in back as full as a Christmas tree. This was her great-grandmother, Eliza Hendricks. Vera often felt that woman in her soul; she had been a teacher at one of the first colleges for black women. Eliza had also published a book called *Freedom, Self-Reliance, and Responsibility*. For years, Vera had tried to find a copy. She had contacted hundreds of antiquarian book dealers. She imagined what Eliza Hendricks had written. As a result, Vera often thought about those subjects: freedom, self-reliance, and responsibility, what it meant then, what it meant now. She had hoped one day to write a book herself about the same themes and include anecdotes about her great-grandmother, if only she could glean more from public records. But in recent years, she felt frustration more than inspiration. What place do freedom and responsibility have when you're plagued with budget cuts, conniving upstarts, and competing charities? No one had vision anymore. It was all about marketing. She sighed. The trip to China and Burma was supposed to reinvigorate her, help her see the wild blue yonder once again. She looked up at the clouds. The village lay half a mile up a road thick with wild daisies growing eight or nine feet tall.

All at once, a hair-raising scream echoed down the road. "What the fuck was that?" Moff and Dwight said almost simultaneously. It was coming from the village up ahead. "A girl?" Moff guessed. Heidi pictured a girl being raised in the air by a tribal chief, about to be tossed over a cliff in a sacrificial ritual. Then came a whimper. A dog that was being hit with a shovel? A moment later, it was wheezing and braying. A donkey being whipped as it struggled to pull a load uphill? Next came what sounded like the blood-curdling cries of a woman. Someone was being beaten. What was going on?

Moff, Harry, Rupert, and Dwight sprinted up the road, crouching slightly in a protective posture. Roxanne, Wyatt, and Wendy followed. Adrenaline sharpened their eyesight, and heightened their hearing. They were on a mission.

"Come back!" Heidi shouted, a futile request.

"No worries," Lulu said. "That sound, it is only pig not people."

"My God, what's happening to it?"

"Getting ready for a dinner," Lulu answered. She drew a finger across her throat. "Zzz."

"Gross. People can be so mean and they don't even know it," Esmé said. She patted the puppy in the sling.

The group continued walking to the top of the hill. The screams had subsided into bleating. The pig's voice grew weaker, softer. Then it stopped. Heidi felt sick. Death had come.

At the fork in the path, they took the route that was more narrow, believing it would lead to something less seen and more special. To Bennie, the village looked like rural Appalachia. It was a cluster of small hills, winding up-and-down paths that would accommodate slim-hipped people walking in single file. Two or three houses clung to each hill, and around each compound were gardens and animal pens. Smoke from coal fires rose, as did gnats, muddying the air. Along the steeper inclines were steps fashioned out of a chunk of rock or a slim sheath of wood, just wide enough to accommodate a foot. Upright sticks had been pounded into the sides of the path to allow passersby to gain footing as they traversed this thoroughfare on rainy, muddy days.

They came to a pen that contained enormous pigs with coarse hair. As the visitors approached, the pigs wagged their tails and snorted. Outside the pen, pink piglets roamed freely like pet dogs, seeking handouts from barefooted girls of nine or ten, who carried in one arm their bare-bottomed siblings. "Run, run," Heidi whispered to the piglets. "You're doomed."

Upon seeing the foreigners approach, three boys engaged in mock battle, whacking at one another with their best replicas of swords. The two smaller boys used sugarcane stalks, but the biggest, a show-off, had chosen bamboo, which was sturdier and quickly reduced the sugarcane swords to limp green shreds. Whack! Whack! They were ancient tribesmen keeping the village safe from invaders. The biggest boy took a running leap onto the back of a water buffalo that was resting on the side of the road. He wrestled the horns of the implacable beast, then gave it a mighty kick in the side, before declaring for himself another victory. The other boys imitated him, getting a running start to vault themselves onto the buffalo and tumbling off its spine like gymnasts at a hillbilly Olympiad. Had the water buffalo been so inclined, it could have risen to its mighty hooves and easily trampled or gored the boys in a second. What had this buffalo done in a past life that he must now serve happily as trampoline and vaulting horse?

My friends continued until they had come full circle. "This way," Lulu said, and she walked ahead into the dirt courtyard from where the awful noises had emanated. The freshly killed pig lay on its side on a platform made of stone. Blood pooled from its neck, and some had already been collected in a large bowl, where it could congeal. A grill held a huge pile of kindling twigs. Two men were starting the process of cleaning the pig, knives and buckets at the ready. In a corner, young women were sorting baskets of greens. To the left was a mud-brick house. A man emerged from the lightless interior and walked with authority toward the visitors. He and Lulu exchanged greetings in Jingpo. "How's your grandmother this week?" she asked. "Much better, I hope."

After a few minutes, Lulu waved to my friends. "Come in, he is saying you are welcome to visit in courtyard, ask question, take photo. But he ask you please do not go into house. His grandmother is recently died and she is in there still. Today they get her ready for funeral feast."

"They're going to *eat* her?" Esmé whispered to her mother. Marlena shook her head.

"Good God!" Bennie said. "We shouldn't be here if they're in mourning."

"No, no, is okay," Lulu assured him. "She was very old, over one hundred and four years and sick for long, long time."

"A hundred and four?" Dwight interjected. "That's impossible."

"And why is that?" Vera said.

He shrugged. He should have let this one go, but he couldn't. "Look at the conditions here."

"I see them," Vera persisted. "It looks simple but peaceful, free of corporate stress and traffic jams."

"Traffic would be the least of their problems," Dwight said. "There's no sanitation, no heating. Half the people here don't have a tooth left in their skull. I doubt they have a stock of antibiotics on hand. And look at those kids. One has a cleft palate, the other has a lazy eye—"

"It's called amblyopia," Vera corrected. She knew about such things; her organization funded a Well Baby Clinic for inner-city mothers.

Dwight gave her a funny look. "It's also known as lazy eye."

"'Lazy' is a pejorative term."

Dwight laughed and shook his head. He had had "lazy eye" as a kid.

Lulu felt an argument brewing. "Come, come. Let's visit this family. It is good luck for you to come in. If you are in household where someone has died, this dead person will carry away all your bad luck when she goes to the next world." Had I also taken a load of bad luck with me? "This deed," Lulu said, "brings a household much good karma. So everyone is happy. Come, let us receive happiness."

All at once, Dwight looked stricken. A peculiar queasiness hit him and his stomach began to bloat, growing larger and larger by the second, as though some invisible force were growing, an alien, and now the creature was about to burst out through his stomach wall.

"Honey?" Roxanne said. "You look terrible. Are you sick?"

Dwight shook his head. "I'll be okay." His nausea doubled. The growing pressure turned into sharp kicks. His face turned the color of goose dung. He was not the sort who complained about pain. He had broken his leg once while skiing, and the sharp bone had protruded out of his skin. He had told jokes to the ski patrol guys who hauled him off the mountain.

This time he felt that he was about to die. Heart attack! Only thirty-one years old, and he was going to drop dead of a heart attack in a woebegotten village without a doctor and with no ambulance to get him out of there. His mind became confused, drunk with pain and the certainty that he was dying. He stumbled around, desperate for any remedy, deaf to his wife's anxious questions. Some mysterious force was going to kill him. The old dead woman—they said she was carrying away their bad luck, leaving behind only the good. He was the bad one, whom nobody liked. His eyes locked, trying to hold his system in a tenuous balance. He couldn't breathe, oh God, he couldn't breathe. What should he do now? No medicines here. The British vet with the dog. He would have something. Where the hell was he? He glanced to the left, at the darkened house and its open door. Ghost in there. He saw the men with their evisceration tools, staring at him; he was their next victim. He turned and saw his fellow travelers glaring at him. Vera hated him. He knew that. She wanted him dead. Even his wife looked as if she didn't care what happened to him. They had had an argument the night before. She had called him a self-centered asshole. She had hinted at divorce. He pushed his way past her and fell to the ground.

Within thirty-seven heaving seconds, Dwight's stomach emptied itself of its contents. It was the accumulation of three meals that had remained undigested, thanks to the *Zanthoxylum* berries of the previous night's dinner, which had anesthetized his gut into stasis. I shall not describe what those contents were, save to say they included many colorful things, which the piglets sought out and squabbled over and devoured.

A minute later, Dwight felt slightly less doomed. Death had passed him by. Five minutes later, he was able to stand up weakly. But he was a changed man. He felt defeated, all his bravado gone. Once again he was the boy who had been beaten up by the neighborhood kids, had the wind knocked out of him by a punch to his stomach, then another, and another.

"Dwight, honey?" Roxanne was asking quietly. "We're going back to the bus. Can you walk by yourself?"

He looked up and shook his head, unable to speak. "Can we get a cart?" he heard Vera asking someone.

"No worries, I ask right now," Lulu answered.

Vera added, "We can pay. Here. See if this is enough." This was her forte, taking charge in a crisis.

Lulu started shouting to the owners of the house, who shouted back cooperatively with numerous suggestions and, at first, refusals of any compensation. An honorary gift for the deceased? Oh, in that case, it would be too polite, too good to be true.

Soon a two-wheeled cart was brought over, pulled by the water buffalo that had allowed the sword-fighting boys to jump on its back. Dwight nearly wept with gratitude. Harry and Moff kindly helped lift him. Roxanne's face was drawn into motherly concern, and she stroked his brow. She still loved him. He wanted to weep. The wonder of love had never felt stronger.

As the foreigners left the village, the members of the household thanked their dead matriarch for bringing them such good luck: ten U.S. dollars, and for nothing more than taking the cart down to the end of the road. Happiness for all.

·5·

WE ALL DO
WHAT WE MUST

In border towns, everyone waits. So it is in Ruili. The fake-gem hustlers wait for the eager buyers of jade. The hoteliers shine the floors in anticipation of guests. The arms dealers and drug runners look for their contacts.

My friends were waiting for the border permit that would allow them to enter Myanmar via the northern end of the Burma Road. This was agony for Bennie, who felt responsible for getting them in. He would also be blamed if he did not. He was now eating sunflower seeds every minute of the day, as if each were a problem to be solved. He cracked the shells, looked at the gray bodies inside, and swallowed them like sedatives, wishing he could stop the overwhelming sense of dread and think clearly. In light of the news that no Westerners had recently entered Myanmar via the overland route, he had no idea how he would accomplish getting everyone in. Only a few months earlier, the road had been opened for passage to third-country nationals, but thus far no one had figured out the hellacious and antiquated process necessary to gather paperwork and stamps of approval from the proper authorities. When Bennie checked the group into the hotel in Ruili, he asked the manager whether they might stay longer, if necessary.

"No worries," said the manager. He looked at the list of twelve names Bennie had given him, along with the stack of passports, and compared it with his records. "And Miss Bibi Chen, she is not here?"

Bennie was blindsided to hear my name yet again. "She couldn't come . . . a last-minute problem . . . I'm the tour leader now. My travel agent *did* notify you."

The man frowned. "Notify me?"

"What I mean is, the office of tourism. It should say that in your records. It does, doesn't it? . . ."

"Yes, yes, I see that now. She had accident and is in hospital." He looked up with another frown. "Terrible news."

"Yes." (If only he knew how terrible.)

"Please give greetings to her."

"I will."

"And welcome to you. This your first time in Ruili?"

"Actually I've visited the area before," Bennie lied, "though not Ruili itself." He didn't know if it was detrimental to admit he was a neophyte.

"Excellent. May you have very good and happy stay with us."

Meanwhile, both Dwight and the Shih Tzu puppy had recovered sufficiently to be declared by Harry as having been "shooed away from death's door." Dwight's face was now the color of algae. As soon as he arrived at the hotel, he crawled into his twin bed, assisted by Roxanne, who brought him a glass of boiled water, as prescribed by Dr. Harry. He took small sips, trying hard not to regurgitate, then lay down, and as Roxanne urged him to relax, he faded from *sombre rêverie* to sound sleep.

Esmé's purloined puppy was also in reverie. Pup-pup lay on her back, blissfully stretching her legs whenever Esmé scratched her belly. Marlena was touched by how happy her daughter was. She remembered a time in her own childhood when she had begged her father to let her keep a kitten she had found. Without a word to her, he took it from her arms, handed it to a servant, and told her to drown it; the servant, however, simply put it outside, and Marlena secretly fed it scraps for months, until one day it did not show up. Esmé was so like her. She was now coaxing the puppy to eat a watery gruel of rice and chicken, ordered by Harry and obtained by Marlena from the hotel's kitchen staff. Marlena had reported that it was her daughter who was not feeling well and needed the special soup. A few American dollars convinced them of the veracity of this story. "Come on, Pup-pup," Esmé said, and held the eyedropper to the Shih Tzu's mouth, smacking her lips in further encouragement. Harry was most pleased in thinking they had become a family of sorts—for what was a family if not members of a crisis with a happy outcome?

At seven, everyone except Dwight and Esmé went to meet Lulu in the lobby. Before she went out, Marlena gave strict instructions to Esmé not to leave the room. As Lulu had already warned them, dogs were not allowed in any hotel. Moreover, Lulu had told them that people were not permitted to keep dogs in China unless they possessed a license, which cost thousands of yuan, and in any case, to apply for a license one must have a permanent residence. Though the rules were only casually enforced, from time to time the local government went on a purge and rounded up all dogs whose owners had disobeyed the rules. As to what happened to the dogs, well, she didn't want to say, except to caution, "Very bad, very bad result you don't want to know."

"You don't want to get caught," Marlena said, and Esmé replied in her blandest voice, "Tell me about it."

"Wawa, promise-promise me you won't leave the room. Promise?"

Esmé sighed heavily. "Quit it, Mom. I'm not a wawa anymore. I know what to do. You don't have to tell me." She kept her eyes focused on the puppy. "Come on, Pup-pup, eat something. It's good for you. . . ."

Marlena left reluctantly. In the lobby, Lulu roused her charges like a cheerleader. "Is everybody hungry?"

"Hungry," they said in unison, then made for the door.

As the bus took off, Lulu switched on the microphone. "I already telling you we call this town Ruili, yes, Ruili. But also is known as Shweli in Burmese, Shweli." Several people turned to their seatmates and said in a monotone, "Shweli."

"To Dai people, Ruili means 'foggy.'"

"Foggy," the passengers echoed mindlessly.

"But some say this can mean 'heavy mist' . . ."

"Mist."

". . . or 'fine drizzle.'"

"Jizzle," they said, imitating her pronunciation.

"This misty drizzle sometimes will fall in only one small location—one block, one building—but across street it is dry, not one wet spot. Very unusual, you agree?"

"Agree."

"Some local people make joke and say maybe this is urine from airplane passing by." She pointed upward.

And her guests looked at the sky, contemplating this possibility. In China, many notions previously thought to be impossible could not be so easily dismissed. Lulu laughed. "Joke! We only make joke."

Lulu instructed the driver to go through the "city center," to give the tourists a quick idea of what downtown Ruili had to offer. She did this only because it was part of the itinerary required by the government's efforts to infuse a little capital into local businesses. But Lulu had also seen the look of disappointment in many tourists' eyes once they reached central Ruili. Most had added the visit to their itinerary only so they might say they had stuck a toe into Myanmar. In fact, there was a white wooden post on the outskirts of the town where you could stand with one half of your body in China and the other half in Myanmar. You did not need special permission to do this. So without going into Myanmar, you could claim you had been there. This tourist spot was where Lulu had been called upon a hundred times to take a picture. Usually her clients stood in contorted poses, legs in China, head and shoulders in Myanmar, or a couple might divide up and face each other from their respective chosen country, and stare at each other with binoculars from six inches apart.

"Look at that," she would tell each busload of tourists, pointing to a small house nearby. "There one family lives, kitchen is in China, bedroom is in Myanmar. In this way, this family eats in one country, sleeps in other. I think this house been standing there for many centuries, yes, long time, before anyone decided where one country stops, the other starts."

Dwight looked at the surrounding landscape. He pictured it as it might have been more than a hundred years earlier, when his great-great-grandfather had come to this part of the world. Perhaps he, too, had entered Burma via the silk route and had passed this way station. Back then, it must have been a beautiful outpost of green mountains and rainforests, ambling waterways and profuse wildflowers, unmarred by barriers and signs.

I, too, could imagine it. By virtue of its geographical fates—the lucky juxtaposition of a river between two countries—this was a natural stopping point for thinking about what you were moving toward and what you were leaving behind. Fur traders, warriors, and refugees had come to this northern end of the trail. Which offered more opportunities, the Middle Kingdom or Old Mian?

And here the town still stood. The relics of ancient temples were overshadowed by a bland mix of high-rise hotels, one-story shops, and streets widened and developed so quickly that the surrounding land had been stripped of all signs of vegetation. Neon had replaced sunsets.

From the bus, my friends passed low buildings with long porches, where men, women, and children squatted on low stools. A pregnant Pekingese dog lay sprawled on a green plastic chair. Merchants beckoned to passersby to view their supplies of TVs, mattresses, stereos, rice cookers, and Lilliputian refrigerators. The shops were open at all hours, for who knew when the parvenus might have a notion to augment their status with goods of such high quality.

A few blocks later, my friends were passing the pink-light district, a lane of one-room open-air shops, each lit by a pink bulb and emblazoned with advertisements: "Karaoke, massage, $40, best lamb included."

Rupert looked up from his paperback. "What do they do with the lamb?" he asked coyly.

Lulu was embarrassed to say. "This is new expression," she tried to explain. "'Best lamb' . . . like saying, 'We must be careful.'"

"You mean they use condoms," Rupert said flatly, and Moff tried not to look surprised. Rupert attended a high school where students were encouraged to talk openly about safe sex. And though he acted unfazed by sex, he had yet to experience it. He had once groped a girl at a sleepover party where everyone was drunk.

"Very good," Lulu told Rupert. "Everyone in every country is concerning safety." As a government worker, she was not supposed to mention the high rate of AIDS in this town. In Ruili, opium slipped through the border like dirty water through a colander, and hence needle-borne illnesses passed back and forth between the two countries with similar ease. Anyone could see that addicts were plentiful among all those young women of the pink-lit "beauty parlors." I say "women," but perhaps it's best to describe them as girls. Many had been abducted from small villages at the age of twelve or thirteen and drugged into compliance. The lighting gave them a healthier glow, but one needed only to look at their meatless legs and arms to see that some were being eaten away by AIDS. A few sported short hairdos, having sold their locks to wig buyers. Quick kwai were always necessary when business was slow and the habit too strong. But you could cut your long hair only once.

When it came to vices, China could not stem the tide; it had to stanch it the way one daubs a bleeding artery. Prostitution was illegal, but in plain sight on nearly every block. In Ruili, there was more supply than demand. At most of the shops, two or three teenaged girls with bored faces sat on sectional sofas. They watched soap operas and game shows on television. The busier girls served drinks to their customers. The men, full of bluster, preferred to go in groups as if it were a competitive sport, each one having a go at the same girl. And in some shops there was only an empty storefront. The work took place behind the curtains, where there was a cot, a chair, a basin, and a single towel for washing up. Clothes-off was extra.

The bus turned a corner. "Over there," Lulu called out, and pointed to a shop where a man and a woman were seated at computers. "Internet café. Twelve kwai for forty-five minutes. Last chance. Once you go into Myanmar, no more Internet. Is not allow." Rupert made a mental note to return here.

The bus left town and went down darkened roads for several miles until it reached a restaurant consisting of two open-air pavilions, illuminated only by blue Christmas lights. Feast now, slim down later,

I would have advised my friends. The food in Myanmar can be terribly monotonous, no matter how luscious the surroundings. Some people have told me I am just biased with my Chinese palate.

The restaurant owner approached Lulu and Bennie. "How lucky you came tonight," he said in Chinese. "As you can see, we are not too busy right now." There were no other customers. "So we can make special things," he went on, "the kinds of foods that foreigners like."

What "foreigners like"! These were the very words I was most afraid to hear. Lulu merely smiled and translated to Bennie what the restaurant owner had said. Bennie did a most peculiar form of thanks—clasping both hands in front and bowing rapidly and stiffly, like a man in a movie, who is begging the king not to behead him. "Obsequious" is the word I am thinking of. The owner shot off a list of dishes made of cheap ingredients, topped off with plenty of Chinese beer. He scribbled the price on a scrap of paper and shoved that under Bennie's nose. I, too, looked. Was the food made of gold, carved of jade? Bennie performed the curious life-sparing bow again. "Wonderful, wonderful."

Looking out toward the darkening field, Wendy saw shapes moving. "What's that?"

"Brr," the owner said. This was his best English approximation of "Burmese."

"Birds," Lulu translated what she thought the owner was trying to say, and he nodded in gratitude. "Here in this part of China, many animals and birds, all year round. Those birds, we call egrets, have long neck, long leg."

Wendy and Wyatt squinted. "Oh, I see them," Wendy said. "See? There." She pointed them out for her lover, grabbing his hand under the table and placing it on her crotch. He nodded.

But the shadowy forms were not egrets. As the restaurant owner had tried to indicate, they were Burmese farmers, women to be exact, their backs hunched over, wearing bright pastel tops and thick flesh-colored stockings that protected them against leeches and the razor-edge stalks of sugarcane. They were working the fields, hacking the cane with long sharp knives. Whack, and off came the flowery lilac tops. With each slash they moved forward, six inches at a time. December and late spring were the two planting seasons, and winter the better of those two. The women now had only a short time to clear the harvest and get the fields ready.

Lulu finally saw that the shadows were people. She corrected herself. "Ah, sorry, these are not birds. Yes, now I see, they are probably Japanese people making secret ritual."

"Spies?"

"Oh no, ha, ha, not spies. They are Japanese tourists. In World War Two time, very famous battle happened here, very fierce, terrible. This is key location for Japanese and KMT, because this is major entryway to Burma, where they are also occupying."

Wendy was lost. "KMT?"

"Kuomintang army," Marlena explained.

"Right." Wendy nodded, though she had no idea with which side the Kuomintang army had been. She wrongly assumed they were the Communists instead of the Nationalists. You see how it is in American high schools: almost nothing is said about the Second World War in China, save for the American Flying Tigers, because that sounds romantic.

"Because many Japanese died here," Lulu went on, "they are coming here to make a pilgrimage. . . ."

Now I knew what Lulu was talking about. There was indeed a major battle, and the Japanese suffered a big loss. Many fell in these fields, and that's where they remained. Their relatives come to this site to honor their family members, to stand where they are likely still buried. They are not allowed to do this, however. They cannot openly honor a soldier who tried to kill Chinese people so that Japan could rule China. China has a long memory. But no one complains if they come at night and do this quietly. So it's a true story, but still Lulu was not right. They were not Japanese tourists, but sugarcane cutters, as the restaurant owner had said.

"The shadows in the field," Lulu said, "maybe they are wives, daughters, sons, even grandsons."

Or the dead soldiers themselves, Heidi imagined. *Ghosts in the field*.

"Cool," Rupert said. "How many were killed?"

"Thousands," Lulu guessed.

Heidi saw thousands of Japanese soldiers lying in the field, blood oozing into the dirt, turning it to reddish mud. And from this rich soil sprang ghosts like stalks of sugarcane. She stared at the hunched-over figures and imagined they were scavenging for bones and skulls as mementos. When the food arrived, she could only stare at the heaping platters.

Because the lighting was so poor, none of my friends could make out what was on the platters. They had to trust Lulu's explanation of what lay before them. "This is snow peas, mushrooms, some kind of meat, ah yes, beef, I think. . . . And this one, this is rice wrapped in a banana leaf. . . ." They tentatively began poking away, ladling food from the mounds onto their plates.

Heidi could still hear the pig screaming before it was slaughtered. She had decided right then to stop eating flesh of any kind. Now she wondered about the vegetables. Where had they been grown? Out there? Had blood leached into their roots? Had the bodies of soldiers served as the mulch? She had read in a gardening magazine that the degree of sweetness in vegetables depended a great deal on the mulch that was used. You could measure it on a Brix scale. The richer the soil, the higher the sugar content in what grew there. Incredible tomatoes, like the kind she bought at the Farmers Market on the weekends, had an advertised level of 13 to 18 on a Brix scale. Store-bought tomatoes, the farmers told her, were not even half that. And what about the vegetables in Ruili? Were they sweet? Didn't blood taste sickly-sweet?

HEIDI HAD SEEN pooled blood from a dead man, one of her house-mates. That was ten years back, when she was a freshman at UC Berkeley. The six of them lived in a ramshackle house in Oakland. The newest was a guy who had answered one of the "Roommate Wanted" signs pinned on the bulletin board at the Co-op grocery store and Cody's Books. He was a twenty-two-year-old guy from Akron, Ohio, nicknamed "Zoomer." She had enjoyed a few philo-sophical discussions with him late at night. One night, the house-mates went to a Pearl Jam concert, all except Zoomer. When the concert was over, some wanted to go to a bar. She elected to go home. She found the door unlocked when she got there, and this made her angry, because somebody or another was always careless about that. And when she walked farther into the living room, she was overcome by a terrible odor. It was not blood, but sweat, the es-sence of animal pain and fear. She did not remember seeing the body, calling the police, or their arrival, the investigation, the removal of the body. The next day, she saw only the pool of blood, the yellow tape at the front door, and she smelled him. How bizarre that his smell hung in the air after he had died. It was like a lingering message, as if he were still begging for his life. She saw in her mind's eye his last moments, the intruder's gun pointed at his face.

Heidi had known him for only a few months, so no one thought she could be too affected by his death. It was ghastly, everyone agreed, her finding the body like that. And she had every right to be freaked out for a while. But she seemed very calm when she told people what had happened. "I could tell he was already dead." She did not go into detail, and people dared not ask, although they were curious to know. Roxanne cried when Heidi told her what had happened. Because of their age difference, Roxanne had treated Heidi more like a distant niece. But this was the turning point that made them close as half sisters—as *sisters*. Roxanne had imagined that Heidi was nearly murdered as well. She urged her to confide in her, to let her know if she needed to get counseling or move to another house. She could even stay with her and Dwight, the younger guy she was about to marry. But Heidi said she was fine. She had been clear-eyed and matter-of-fact, surprising even herself. Heidi had always been sensitive, openly bursting into tears when teased or injured.

After the murder, she became secretive. She felt the murdered man had given her a sign that she would die soon, too. She forgot what the sign might have been. Nonetheless, she felt the dread. She was waiting for terror to manifest itself. She tried hard to control it. And in so doing, she began to prepare for all the terrible ways death might happen. She knew her precautions were useless. Death would come of its own accord, and she could not prevent it. Yet she still could not stop herself from trying, and she hated how she had become, conscious more of dying than of living.

Taking this trip to China was part of her effort to overcome her problems. She was determined to throw herself into many unknowns, face situations she'd ordinarily avoid. She believed she would be able to handle them, in part because she would be in a completely different country. The unknowns would prove to be nothing, and having survived them, she would be stronger and could return home practiced at pushing aside her phobia. China would be good for her, really, really good, she told herself.

THE MEAL HAD TURNED COLD. When the ever-popular American dessert of green-tea ice cream was brought out, the manager of the restaurant cued his wife and son, and they burst into singing "Merry Christmas," to the tune of "Happy Birthday."

On the way to the hotel, my friends hummed this new holiday concoction. Christmas was only days away, and who knew what the Chinese Santa would bring. Should they buy gifts for one another? The bus drove past the same pink-light girls waiting for customers, the storefronts were still manned by hopeful sellers, the pregnant Pekingese was still sleeping on the green plastic chair. If they did not get a border permit soon, these would be the sights they would see the next night, perhaps the next, and then for who knows how long after that.

Back at the hotel, Harry suggested to Marlena that they "take an evening stroll under the fair moonlight." There was no moonlight, but she agreed. She assumed Esmé was already asleep with her puppy. And so she and Harry headed down the dark street. Something was about to happen, she knew this, and was nervous in a pleasant way. As they walked, he offered his arm so she might steady herself. "The sidewalks have all sorts of *dangers* in the dark," he said. The way he said "dangers" made her shiver. She wanted to be swept away, drowned by incaution. And yet, before she went under, she wanted to grab on to a safety bar and pull herself up and out, before it was too late, before she fell and was beyond being saved.

As they walked in silence, Harry gathered himself, mustering the right balance of confidence and caring. It was so damn easy when he was in front of the camera. He didn't want to come across too forceful, too six-o'clock-news-ish. At last, he spoke in what he decided was just the right tone, one that was vaguely reminiscent of Cary Grant in those movies where he was baffled to find himself in love: "Marlena, dear?"

"Mmmm."

"I believe I'm becoming quite fond of you."

Marlena steadied her emotional equilibrium. Fond? What did he mean by "fond"? You can be fond of flowers, of fettuccine, of certain fashions. What did he mean by "fond"?

"It would be lovely to kiss you," he added. The debonair touch was becoming second nature to him now.

Marlena wondered to herself: Lovely? A sunset is lovely. A sunrise—and before she could equivocate with her emotions any further, he leapt at her mouth, and they both felt, despite the initial nervousness, that the experience was quite agreeable, wonderful, as a matter of fact, so natural, so much longing instantly fulfilled. Although soon, another kind of longing grew. Fondness turned into fondling, then more fondness, followed by more fondling, escalating minute by fervid minute, and all this took place on a featureless street in Ruili. Alas, they could not make love here, they both concluded.

"Let's go back to the hotel," Harry said.

"A hotel, how convenient," Marlena answered, and giggled. As they started to walk back, she had a sobering thought. "I should probably check on Esmé." Another minute passed. "Oh God, what will I tell her?"

"Why tell her anything?" Harry said, nibbling her neck.

"I wouldn't want her to worry if she doesn't see me there in the middle of the night."

"Then tell her you are going downstairs to have a drink."

Marlena was slightly annoyed by that suggestion. "She knows I don't drink. I'm hardly the type who goes to bars to pick up men." She had noticed that Harry sometimes drank an awful lot. She hoped he was not an alcoholic.

"You're not going to pick up men," Harry teased. "You've already picked *me*."

Marlena did not find this a romantic response. Did he think she was that easy? Was he suggesting this was merely casual sex, a one-night stand? "Listen, maybe we shouldn't do this. Not tonight."

"Oh, but we should. We already are, or could be. . . ." They reached the hotel. "See, here we are."

"No, really, Harry. It's late, and I need more time to prepare Esmé, you know, for the idea that you and I are more than just friends."

Idea? Harry sensed that their buoyant mood had rapidly deflated, as had certain body parts. He was disappointed, yes, but also irritated with himself for being overly eager, and yes, even a bit annoyed that Marlena so easily flip-flopped on having fun. It *was* late, and now that he was no longer charged with anticipation, he was tired. "All right. I'll leave you here. And *I* shall go to the bar to have that drink." He kissed her lightly on the forehead. "Good night, my midnight pumpkin." He turned and did not watch as she walked toward the elevator.

He had just received his scotch and water when Marlena raced into the bar, her eyes wide with fright. "She's not there! She's gone! The puppy, too." Her voice was weak and tight. "I told her not to leave, I warned her not to open the door. Oh, God. What are we going to do?"

"I would hope nothing," Harry replied. And before Marlena could lash into him for such a callous remark, he aimed his finger toward the other side of the lobby. There was Esmé, showing off the puppy to the room service staff, two of whom had come by her room earlier to deliver a thermos of hot water. As Marlena made her way over, Esmé saw her and came bounding toward her.

"Hey, Mom. Hi, Harry. Look what they made for Pup-pup. Rice and chicken! Just like Harry said she needed. And it's in this darling little teacup. Aren't they the greatest? They *love* her, Mom. We've been having the best time."

FROM DEEP SLEEP, Bennie picked up the phone.

"Miss Chen, please," the man's voice said.

"She's not here." Bennie looked at his watch. Shit. It was six in the morning. What idiot was calling at this hour?

"Have you any idea when she might return?" The voice sounded faintly British, though it definitely was not Harry Bailley.

"I don't know," Bennie mumbled. He did not have his wits about him. "Who's calling?" he finally thought to ask.

"This is Walter from Mandalay, Golden Land Tour . . ."

Bennie sat bolt upright. Mandalay!

". . . I have an appointment to meet Miss Bibi and her group this morning at the border crossing. I'm afraid the hotel is confused as to which room she has been assigned to. They directed me to your room. I apologize if there is a mistake, but are you Mr. Chen?"

Bennie was now wide-eyed, thinking in ten directions. Who was this guy? He grabbed his notes, the letter from the travel agency. Maung Wa Sao—that was their tour guide, not Walter. Walter must be an expediter, a contact. Did he play by the rules, or if not, could he be bribed? "Walter, I'm Bennie Trueba y Cela, the new tour leader. You must not have received the message in time. And evidently I did not receive a message from your end. I'm sorry. But yes! We're ready to meet you at the border. What time would you like us there?"

The line remained silent.

"Hello? Are you still there? Is this about our border permits?"

Finally Walter spoke. "I don't understand. Where is Miss Chen?"

"She was unable to come."

"Did she take ill last night?"

Bennie contemplated his choices, then decided honesty was the best route. "Actually, she died suddenly."

"Oh dear! She died yesterday?"

"A few weeks ago."

"That's not possible."

"I know. We were completely shocked ourselves. She was a dear friend."

"What I mean is, that's not possible because I spoke to her just yesterday."

It was now Bennie's turn to be thoroughly confused. "You spoke—"

"On the phone. She called and asked that I should change the date of your entry into Myanmar and meet her here today."

"She called about the border permits?"

"Yes. She gave specific instructions. Everything is approved. But we need to make sure your papers match. Oh, and now I will have to make a slight change and remove her name. For that, I'll need to make a phone call. . . ."

Bennie's confusion transformed into unquestioned joy. Obviously this Walter fellow had spoken to Lulu, or possibly someone in San Francisco. Bennie had sent a fax to the travel agent. Since everything had been referred to as the Bibi Chen group, Walter must have believed he was talking to the original tour leader. Well, it didn't matter now, did it? They had the permits! This was fantastic. Whoever did this was a genius! (I was pleased to hear such flattery.)

"Do you need anything else so you can add my name?" Bennie asked.

"No, it's all settled. We added your name when we received the fax. I had assumed you were an addition and not a substitution. So everything there is quite all right." Walter stopped and sighed. When he began again, he sounded quite distressed. "Mr. Bennie, I apologize for asking, this is most inappropriate, but did Miss Chen give you the Christmas present she brought for me?"

Flummoxed. Bennie thought fast. This was obviously some kind of under-the-table payment. How much money did the man want? He hoped the man didn't require it to be in Chinese money. "Miss Chen did mention the present," he ventured, trying to be tactful. "But tell me again specifically what she said she would give you. Was it in dollars?"

The man laughed slightly. "Oh no, not dollars. CD."

Certificate of deposit? Bennie was surprised at how sophisticated the bribes had to be in this wayward part of Asia. Don't panic, he told himself. You'll figure it out. He could call his broker back home. Then again, maybe this Walter guy would take more money instead of certificates. "And how much in CDs was it again?" Bennie squeezed his eyes shut in preparation for hearing the answer.

"Oh, this is most embarrassing to even mention," Walter said. "It's just that Miss Chen told me yesterday she would be bringing me a CD, and I was quite excited to hear that it would be the musical *Phantom of the Opera.*"

Bennie nearly wept. *Compact disc.*

"And I have brought her one with Burmese dance music, which I hope she will like, that is, that she would have liked, if indeed she has died."

"Ten CDs," Bennie suggested. "How does that sound?"

"Oh no, no! Really, that is far too many. *The Phantom* is quite enough, I think. That is what Miss Chen said she was bringing. Ten is, well, it is awfully considerate of you to even suggest it. Western music is terribly hard to come by."

"Ten it is," Bennie said firmly. "I insist. It is, after all, Christmas."

Walter said he would make the necessary phone call right away. He would meet Bennie at the border.

After they hung up, Bennie thrust his hands deep into his luggage to drag out the CDs he had brought. He flipped through a stack encased in vinyl sleeves: There it was: *The Phantom of the Opera.* What luck that he happened to have that exact one. And how about these? Diana Krall. Sarah Vaughan. Gladys Knight. He would cull a larger variety from the others, Dwight, Harry, Moff. They should contribute *something.* They got themselves into this fix. In fact, if Walter was delighted with ten, what would he do for twenty? He'd have the red carpet rolled out for them. A couple of CDs apiece, that's what Bennie would ask of his fellow travelers. Two each, or he'd present them with the choice of staying in unruly Ruili for another four days.

It was a lovely collection, I thought: from Bono to Albinoni, Nirvana to Willie Nelson, the disparate musical tastes of twelve Americans who cheerfully gave their best.

Let it now be known that I, too, had given my best. The night before, I had visited Walter late in the night when he was in the farthest shores of his sleep, for that was where I realized I could be found, in dreams, memory, and imagination. The sensory was no longer of any use to my existence. But I could exist in a free-floating consciousness not anchored to any reality. My consciousness could overlap his, now that it was so permeable. There I gave to him osmotically the memory that I had called with an urgent request. "Walter," I said, "you forgot to change the entry date to four days earlier, from the twenty-fifth to the twenty-first of December. We discussed this, remember?" He became upset, for he is a meticulous person who never neglects details. When he promised to attend to this change of dates, I sang to him "Wishing You Were Somehow Here Again" from *Phantom of the Opera*. He was immediately seized with longing for his father, who was imprisoned more than ten years ago by the military regime and never heard from again. Such beautiful music, the most touching words. Thereafter Walter would long to hear those same words over and over, the ones I borrowed from the CD that I found in Bennie's suitcase.

This dream did not fade as dreams naturally do. I swam with it back to the deepest part of his memory, to the subconscious recesses where anxious people become more anxious. And so, when Walter awakened the next morning, he had a sense of urgency. He hopped on his bicycle and went to the tourism office, then dashed to the government office to have the paperwork recorded and stamped. He then collected the driver so that they might make their way to Ruili posthaste.

THE ROAD TO MYANMAR is lined with Beheading Trees, so called because the more you cut them down, the faster and thicker they grow back. So it's been with rebels from various periods of China's history. Once they take root, you can't eradicate them completely.

Between the Beheading Trees were Eight Treasure Trees, whose pendulous leaves were large enough to cover the body of a child. And there were plenty of reckless children along the road who might soon need a death shroud. Three boys who appeared to be five or six danced atop the ten-foot-high loads of hay on the backs of mini-tractor trailers, their parents seated up front, seemingly unconcerned. To my friends in the bus, however, the children looked as if they were about to suffer brain damage. Mercifully, the boys appeared to have remarkable reflexes. They tumbled onto their bottoms, laughing gleefully, then stood back up on their stubby legs to prepare for the next tumble.

"Oh my God!" Wendy cried while continuing to snap pictures of each near disaster.

"I can't look," Bennie moaned.

"There should be a law," Marlena said.

Heidi stared ahead at the road for large ruts that would jostle the children to their deaths. Finally, the tractor trailer turned down a small lane and continued, the carefree children receding from my friends' view. The closer the bus drew to the border, the more colorful the world became. Burmese women walked about in flowery-colored skirts, their heads with turbanlike wrappings on top of which they balanced baskets of goods destined for the open market. On their cheeks, they had painted yellow patterns with a paste made from the bark of the thanaka tree. As with Shanghainese people, Burmese women prize pale skin. The paste supposedly affords sun-blocking properties. But I tried it on past tours and can tell you that the effect is quite drying. While it may shield the skin, it parches it to the appearance of cracked adobe. I cannot say it was flattering to my face. I looked like a dried-up clown doll.

Bennie had the CDs for Walter in a sack. Everything was falling into place. He would hand over the bribe and they would get the paperwork and be approved to enter. He hadn't told Lulu, for fear that what Walter was doing was on the side of illegality. Let her think that they got in on their own good luck. This morning she had said simply, "We must try. And if we are success, your Myanmar tour guide, Mr. Maung Wa Sao, will meet you at the crossing place."

At the Chinese border station, Lulu presented passports and documents to the uniformed police. Armed guards stood nearby. After ten minutes of inspecting and stamping and huffing with authority, the border police waved us on, and my friends waved back cheerfully, but no one returned their smiles. After a half a kilometer, the bus stopped in front of a large white gate.

"Soon you and I must say good-bye," Lulu said. "In a few minutes, your Burmese tour guide will meet you and take you over the border into Muse."

"I thought we already crossed," Moff said.

"You have left China," Lulu said. "But to leave one place is not the same as entering another. You are in Burma, but you have not crossed the official border. So you are in between."

It suddenly struck me that what Lulu had said described exactly how I felt. In between.

"Oh, great—we're in limbo," Rupert said.

Lulu nodded. "Yes, limbo. You do not yet know which way is coming, which is going. In China we are very use to this situation."

I wondered how long I would be in my own limbo. The Buddhists say a dead person stays three days around the body, then another forty-six before departing to the next incarnation. If that was the case, then I had yet another month or so to go. Not knowing the prospects, I feared them.

As if reading my thoughts, Marlena asked, "Where will you go after this?"

"Back to Mangshi airport," Lulu said. "Another group is coming." She looked at her watch.

"Does it ever get boring?" Roxanne asked. "Having to take care of people like us all the time—what a pain."

"Oh, no. You are very easy, no trouble. Not boring or pain."

"You're too kind," Bennie said. "What was your most difficult group?"

"No one is ever too much a difficulty," she said diplomatically. But then she sighed, looked down, and said, "Oh, maybe one time, it was more difficulties than the others. . . . Yes, that time, it was great difficulties." She forced a smile and went on: "I just took a big group to airport, we said good-bye, and I am leaving. A young Bai woman, she comes up very fast and right away is asking me, Hold my baby, sister, so I can grab my suitcase. She hurried away. Some minutes already are passing by, the baby is crying very softly, and I pulled the blanket and I am seeing this baby—oh, she is very new, and oh-oh, she has split lip, empty space from mouth to nose."

"Cleft palate," Vera whispered to Bennie.

"Two hours later, I knew this woman is not coming back, so I took this baby to my parents' house, decide what I should now be doing. In baby's blanket, we find money, hundred yuan, like ten dollars U.S., and also is note in simple writing, saying this baby girl is three days old. So we are not knowing what to do. We decide on keeping this baby. We make many plans, make clothes. And we know this baby will be needing the special surgery. But soon we are finding out she is not eligible because she is not registered to anybody. To register her,

I have to adopt. But to adopt, I must be thirty. At that time, I am only twenty-five."

My friends were absolutely silent.

"My parents also cannot adopt. Too old to qualify. So we are stuck, too young, too old. Even so, paper or no paper, we agree, we try to raise her ourself. But even we earn the money for the special surgery, she cannot have, because to hospital mind, she is not registered person. She is nobody. She does not exist. Then we know, with us, no future for her. She can never go school. She can never marry husband. In all situations, she is nobody. Because of this in-between situations, we finally decide it is better this baby is adopted by other people. Many American tourists already told me, Yes, yes, we want her, give her to us. But I decided, better she lives with people who look like her. That is why I gave her to a Japanese couple. So this experience, it is the time I had the most difficulties." She stopped, and nobody spoke.

"That is the saddest story I've heard in a long, long time," Marlena finally said.

"Sad only a short time," Lulu said. "Today she is six years old. Her face is so beautiful, mouth and nose already fixed, and no scar. Every year I see her. She is always calling me 'Auntie' in Japanese. Her parents are always calling me a good person."

"But for you to give her up . . ." Marlena sympathized.

"My thinking is this: Her original mother, she did what she must. I, her in-between mother, I did what I must. That Japanese couple, they also did what they must. One day, this little girl will grow up, and she will be doing what she must. So you see, we all do what we must."

At that moment, a slim young man with fine features boarded the bus. Lulu greeted him and exchanged documents. "Ladies, gentlemen, please to let me introduce Mr. Maung Wa Sao."

There he stood, a slight young man of twenty-six, in a collarless white shirt and dark slacks. He had shiny dark hair, conservatively cut. And his eyes were remarkable: lovely, kind-looking, intelligent, and wise.

He addressed his new charges: "Please, I prefer that you call me Walter."

SAVING FISH
FROM DROWNING

Crossing the border into Burma, one can spot the same pretty flowers seen from the bus window in China: yellow daisies and scarlet hibiscus, lantana growing as plentifully as weeds. Nothing had changed from one country to the next, or so it appeared to my friends.

But in fact all had suddenly become denser, wilder, devouring itself as nature does when it is neglected for a hundred years. That was the sense I had in crossing that border, as if I, like H. G. Wells in his time machine, possessed the same consciousness but had been plopped in the past. Moff and Harry immediately took to calling each other "Rudyard" and "George," after Kipling and Orwell, the chroniclers of old colonial Burmah. Like my friends, I, too, have found the literature of yesteryear intoxicating, engorged with the per-

fumes and pastiches of the exotic and languid life: Victorian para-
sols, stern pith helmets, and fever dreams of sex with the natives.

As for the more recent stories about Burma, how they pale. They
are mostly distressing reports. The stories go more or less like this:
Miss Burma is now married to a lunatic despot who has changed her
name to Mrs. Myanmar. She has gone to live in Oblivion, so no one
knows where she is. The husband is vile and beats his wife. The children have been abused as well, and now they bear scars and are
hiding in corners. Poor Miss Burma, the former beauty queen, she
would be gorgeous still if it weren't for the gaunt limbs, the missing
eye, the lips mumbling the same babble.

Naturally, we all have great sympathy, but who wants to read stories like that? Memoirs of sacrilege, torture, and abuse, one after
another—they are so difficult to read, without a speck of hope to lift
you, no redeeming denouements, only the inevitable descent into the
bottomless pits of humanity. When you reach the end of such stories,
you can't sigh deeply and say to yourself, "Oh my, how glad am I to
have read *that*." Don't tut-tut me. I *know* it's an utterly ugly sentiment, and I would never have admitted it in public while I was alive.
Nobody would, if they had any common sense. But tell me honestly,
who does read political books on horror-ridden regimes except
scholars of history and those studying that particular part of the
world? Others may claim they have, but more likely they skim the descriptions in *The New York Review of Books*, and then say that they
are informed, qualified to make judgments. How do I know? I've
done it. I just never saw the point in spending days and days reading
stories only to disturb myself with problems I was powerless to fix.

The truth is, I've always preferred the old fictions about any ancient land. I read to escape to a more interesting world, not to be
locked up in a sweltering prison and find myself vicariously standing
among people who are tortured beyond the limits of sanity. I have

loved works of fiction precisely for their illusions, for the author's sleight-of-hand in showing me the magic, what appeared in the right hand but not in the left, the funny monkeys chattering in the tree branches and not the poachers and their empty shell casings below. In Burma, despite the sad reports, it is still quite possible to enjoy what is just in the right hand: the art, first and foremost, the festivals and tribal clothing, the charming religiosity of taking your shoes off before stepping into a temple. That's what we visitors love, a rustic romanticism and antiquated prettiness, no electric power lines, telephone poles, or satellite television dishes to mar the view. Seek and you shall find your illusions through the magic of tourism.

Illusions, in fact, are practically sanctified in Burma, or rather, the notion that all is an illusion. That is what the Buddha taught after all, that the world is illusory, and since nearly ninety percent of the Burmese are Buddhist, I would say most live in a Land of Illusions. They are taught to shed their human desires like a snake its mortal coil, and once free they can achieve nibbana, nothingness, the ultimate goal for those who follow the old Pali scriptures, or even a military dictatorship. Granted, it's mostly only the monks who follow this Theravada Buddhism in its strictest sense, yet the illusions are still there and can disappear at any moment—people included, as we shall soon see.

Let me hasten to add that although I was raised a Buddhist during childhood, it was a Chinese kind of Buddhism, which is a bit of this, that, and the other—ancestor worship, a belief in ghosts, bad fate, all the frightful things. But it was not the Burmese version that desires nothing. With our kind of Buddhism, we desired everything—riches, fame, good luck at gambling, a large number of sons, good dishes to eat with rare ingredients and subtle flavors, and first place in anything and not just honorable mention. Certainly we desired to ascend to heaven, the topmost level in the wheel of life. O hear me now: If there is anyone listening with influence in these matters, please know that oblivion has never been high on my list of places to reside after death. Don't send me there!

Can you imagine anyone *wishing* to be obliterated for eternity if there were another choice besides hell? And who can honestly desire nothing—no aspirations for fame or fortune, no family jewels or great legacy to pass along to the next generation, not even a comfortable place to sit with your legs crossed for hours on end? Well, then, if you don't want anything, you'll certainly never get any bargains, and in my opinion, getting a good bargain is one of the happiest feelings a person can have.

All this talk of oblivion, of wanting nothing and becoming nobody, seems rather contradictory from a Buddhist sense. The Buddha did all this and he became so much a nobody that he became famous, the biggest nobody of them all. And he will never disappear, because fame has made him immortal. But I do admire him for his attitude and discipline. He was a good Indian son.

Not that all Indian families would want such a son—famous but desiring none of the rewards. Most of the Indians I know are Hindu, and they tell me Hinduism is an older religion that includes many of the precepts in Buddhism, and a lot to do with getting rid of illusions and desires and all that. But I must say, all the Hindus I know are vastly fond of their twenty-four-karat–gold jewelry. And they desire that their sons and daughters go to Oxford or Yale and become radiologists not beggar monks. They see to it that their daughters receive more than glass bangles at their weddings and their sons at least a Rolex and not the other watch that ends in an *x*. They want them to marry, if not within their caste or higher, then at least someone with a family home in a good area. It is not my opinion. I have seen it.

All I am saying is, no matter what the religious beliefs in a country, a certain degree of acquisitiveness is always there. And Buddhist though Burma may be, there is still plenty to acquire in the Golden

Land. Look here, the country is studded with six thousand stupas and elaborate pagodas! They're certainly ironic monuments for a religion based on ridding itself of worldly attachments. At almost every stupa, where they store relics of their dead holy ones, you can find a vendor who will sell you nibbana goods, a miniature pagoda, a hand-carved Buddha, or green lacquerware, that art of patient layering. You can get them at below half the asking price, which is practically nothing compared with what you would have paid back home. The trinkets are a means to different ends, one for the seller, one for the buyer. We all need to survive, we all need to remember.

But I am getting ahead of myself. As I was saying, we had only just arrived over the border into Burma, and what lay before us was what the magician prefers to hide in his left hand.

THE BUS HAD STOPPED next to a plain building that housed the customs-and-immigration checkpoint, a small shack made of plywood, painted mint green. The roof was corrugated tin, a remnant of missionary architecture, a thriftier style that contrasted with the former timber mansions built as colonial outposts in the hill stations. The method by which my friends had to make their presence officially known in Burma was also a throwback to a British age of convoluted rules and officialdom achieved with the flourish of a pen held by an unsmiling authority.

That authority would be the soldiers of Myanmar's government administration, the head honchos of the cabinet known as SLORC, which, I think, sounds like an evil opponent in a James Bond movie. The acronym stands for "State Law and Order Restoration Council," an entity put into place, as one can guess, when there was less in the way of law and order, which is precisely what happened when sixty-seven ethnic groups disagreed on how Burma should be governed, especially after the military overturned election results, claimed tribal territory as national land, and placed Aung San Suu Kyi under house arrest. SLORC also gave Burma its new name, Myanmar, and changed Rangoon into Yangon, the Irrawaddy into the Ayeyarwaddy. And thus practically no one in the Western world knows what those new names refer to.

It's true. Ask ten of your friends what and where Myanmar is, and I would wager nine would not know. But if you said Burma, they would say, "Oh, *Burma!*"—vaguely remembered in the way we say, "Oh, *Barbara*—how is she doing?" Like the Burmese dissenters who disappeared, the country formerly calling itself Burma is invisible to most of the Western world, an illusion. Well, I still call it Burma, so does the U.S. government. I've never been able to call it the other, even though more and more people do, like the newspapers and TV networks that have succumbed to the names, as if to say, "This is the new reality, now get over it." But to me, "Myanmar" sounds sneaky, Myanmar, like the twitchy *miao-miao* of a cat before it pounces on a trapped mouse.

A few years ago, with the help of a public relations firm, SLORC changed its own name in order to appear friendlier. As a matter of fact, it was an image-consulting company based in Washington, D.C.—yes, shameful, isn't it? State Peace and Development Council—SPDC—that's how they renamed themselves. But some find it too hard to say four syllables when one does nicely. "SLORC" rolls off the tongue more easily and sounds more fitting, suggesting a semantic and onomatopoetic accuracy. Some have noted that the sibilant-liquid combination is also the beginning of like-minded words: sly, slippery, slayers. They say it is impossible to keep up with shifting and shifty terminologies. And so SLORC is what they still call it.

Not so with people in Burma, and especially journalists. It does not behoove them to be out of fashion with terminology. Most of Asia has adapted to the new names. Meanwhile, some Westerners don't even know that there's a history to the names and that others must make a deliberate choice.

As for myself, I say Burma because it's been my habit for too long. I say SLORC because it is one syllable and easier to pronounce than S-P-D-C. I say Rangoon, because I'd have to think a second or two longer to remember the other. I am too old to change with the times.

But enough of this prattle, and back to the bus.

WALTER AND BENNIE disembarked and greeted the border police. The new driver, Kjau, or Mr. Joe, as my friends called him, stepped out to smoke a cheroot. The authorities at the customs-and-immigration shack treated Walter, a fellow Burmese, with suspicion. But customs people, no matter the country, are like that. There are never any jovial greetings of welcome and enjoy yourselves. Letter by letter, the names and addresses of each of our twelve visitors had to be compared with a set of approved documents, before being hand-written in an enormous ledger, and then hand-copied into an identical ledger. This was bureaucracy before computers, before carbon copies even. Dear God, this could take hours, Bennie realized.

Esmé placed Pup-pup in her baseball cap, where the sweet thing slept soundly, its tummy full of rice gruel. Marlena had a scarf at the ready, in case their new canine cargo needed to be hidden from the authorities. Actually, she needn't have worried. In Burma, dogs are not contraband, and there is no quarantine; however, getting them into hotels might be another matter. Harry sat beside Marlena, his right hand holding her left. It was a small gesture of affection, a symbol of attachment. He had won the privilege to touch her after dinner the night before.

"Marlena, dear, would you like a mint?" Harry now asked as the three of them sat like monkeys on a log in the back of the bus. In his younger years, this presentation of the mint was a cryptogram for wishing to engage in more kissing. Now he no longer had to speak in ridiculous codes. He could say what he meant. A mint was a mint. A kiss was a kiss. Yes indeed, he was well on his way to love, perfect understanding.

Marlena took the mint, hoping Harry would not try to act too amorous in front of her daughter. Esmé, meanwhile, threw sidelong glances at her mother holding Harry's hand. She wrinkled her nose, but this time it was not because she disapproved of Harry. He was her hero of sorts. But handholding, no matter who was doing it, was embarrassing. That woman Wendy had glanced back, Esmé noted, and seen what her mother and Harry were doing. Now she and her boyfriend were flashing knowing smiles at each other. What did they know that she did not? Had her mother and Harry done *it*? Whatever they did, the handholding stuff looked pathetic and possessive, not to mention that their palms were probably sweaty in this heat.

An hour later, Walter and Bennie returned from the checkpoint shack. Bennie spoke first: "We're provisionally approved, but we have to go to another town to record the paperwork line by line, and we'll need everyone's passports."

Groans emanated from the bus.

Walter held up his hand. "Once we reach this town, while I take care of these tedious details, you will be free to explore the town of Muse for an hour or so. There is a rather lively market, many shopkeepers with textiles and the like—"

"We'll be free to get off the bus?" Wendy said.

"Yes, it is quite all right. You can go about and wander. As Mr. Bennie said, you are all provisionally approved to enter. We simply need to copy the information about your itinerary and dot the *i*'s and cross the *t*'s, as you Americans say. But before you go, I suggest you change your money with me. I will give you the highest legal rate allowed, three hundred and eighty kyats per dollar. This is the same rate you would get in a bank. Without a doubt, you could do better on the black market. But it would also be doing worse, for if the police catch you, the consequences would be most regrettable, I can assure you."

"I wonder how much better," Wyatt whispered to Wendy.

In Muse, my twelve friends, flush with money, their pockets dangerously bulging with Burmese kyat notes, jumped off the bus and into the warm December sun. They walked toward the center of town and were soon engulfed in the everyday life of the marketplace: milling shoppers, open stalls of cloth, clothing, and plastic shoes, all in styles that suggested unwanted seconds from China. Around them moneychangers crouched on the ground, trying to catch their attention. Farther ahead, beckoning to them like the seventh heaven of bargains, was a gigantic tent that housed the food market.

As they made their way through the crowd, they remarked how different Burmese people seemed from Chinese. Here women smeared the yellow thanaka paste on their face as both sunscreen and beauty symbol. Atop their heads, they wore a length of cloth that had been swaddled into a turban. "It's almost tribal-looking," Roxanne said.

"That's because they *are* a tribe," Vera said. "It's in the notes Bibi prepared."

Wendy caught the eye of a Burmese woman who looked about her age. The woman was wearing a conical rattan hat with red piping. When she gazed downward, the hat obscured her face entirely. But when she looked up, her face conveyed desperation and anguish, or so Wendy thought. It was as if the woman wanted to say something to her, convey an urgent message. Sure enough, the woman started to step toward her, but then saw, on the shaded side of the street, two military policemen in their frog-green uniforms. The young woman blinked hard, turned, and scurried away. Was that sweat on her cheeks, or tears? What had the woman intended to say? Was it a warning? Wendy tugged on Wyatt's shirt. "I want to follow that woman."

"Why?"

"She wanted to tell me something. She needs help." The woman was now receding into the crowd, slipping away, disappearing. "Come on," Wendy said, and she maneuvered her way into the crowd, while the rest of the travelers pushed toward the food tent.

"Isn't it amazing?" Harry said aloud to Marlena. "We're just a few miles in and the national dress is completely different." He gestured to a man riding by on a bicycle. "I can't figure out how those chaps keep their skirts from falling off."

"The Scots wear skirts," Marlena said. "I also heard they wear no underwear."

"Did I ever you tell I'm half Scot?"

Marlena gave him a half-frown, half-smile. Esmé was nearby.

At an open-air stall, two women squatted atop reams of cloth, beckoning to the tourist ladies. As soon as Roxanne and Heidi glanced their way, the older of the women began quickly to unwind a bolt of cloth, brushing her fingertips across the weave. Vera went over immediately and admired the purple and deep burgundy, the intricate patterns in gold and silver. The younger seller tossed down more bolts to the older seller, who unwound them. "Pretty, yes, so pretty," Vera said, and nodded. "Pity-pity, so pity," the Burmese woman tried to repeat.

More and more bolts of cloth tumbled open, and Roxanne, who stood beside Vera, fingered a hand-loomed cotton gingham, deep blue with an iridescent sheen. "One thousand?" she said, reading a scrap of paper on which the seller had scribbled. She turned around and said: "Dwight, honey, how much is a thousand kyats?"

"Less than three dollars." He was standing five feet away, behind other women who were leaning in to inspect the wares.

"Wow. For one yard of cloth like this?" Roxanne said.

The woman tapped her hand and shook her head, then unfolded the cloth and extended it. "Two," she said, and held up two fingers.

"Oh, *two meters*. Even better." Roxanne draped the cloth over her legs. "I'd love to wear this as a sarong." She looked up at the seller, who had covered her mouth to laugh, as did the other women around the stall. She pointed to the bolt of blue check and shook her head, then picked up a bolt of pink with gold highlights. She pointed to the pink, then to Roxanne.

"No." Roxanne swept her hand to indicate the pink should be taken out of her sight. She patted the blue cloth and gave a satisfied smile.

The seller patted the same cloth, then pointed toward a man in a longyi passing by.

Heidi broke in: "She's saying that this color and pattern are what a man wears."

Hearing this, Dwight held up both hands. "No way." He strolled after Moff and Rupert.

Roxanne did not look up. "I know it's for a man, but I don't care. This is what I like." She smiled at the seller, pointed to several men in the marketplace to show that she understood. "Yes, I know, for a man." That done, the seller expertly measured off the standard length of cloth for a man's longyi. She asked Roxanne something in Burmese, and pantomimed clipping motions with two fingers, then placed her thumb on the cloth, as pinched fingers of her other hand hammered up and down. Yes, Roxanne indicated, using the same gestures: Cut it and sew it up. The bolt was tossed back to the younger seller, who disappeared behind the stall for a moment, then returned with the cloth properly prepared. The older seller called to a thin young man passing by. He ran over and at her behest was only too pleased to demonstrate the correct way that a man got dressed in the morning. He stepped into the voluminous tube of cloth, and with a pinch of the material in each hand, he pulled the excess taut at the sides and, in one rapid smooth movement, clapped his hands at dead center and instantly tied the ends into a knot so that the excess cloth protruded like a tongue. "Wow, it's like a magic trick," Roxanne said. She gestured for the man to do it again but more slowly. He repeated the movements, pausing only slightly between each step. Finished, he untied the cloth and slipped out of it, folded it precisely, and handed it to her.

Heidi thanked him with smiles and clasped hands. But as Roxanne started to step into the cloth, the seller tried to stop her, laughing and protesting.

"I know, I know," Roxanne told her. "I'm cross-dressing, lady, it's okay."

The seller shook her head and took another piece of cloth, this one a vivid yellow with an intricate pattern. She stepped into it and pulled the excess taut to one side, showing how the process for a woman was entirely different from what the man had just demonstrated. She then created with the bunching movements of one hand a series of folds, and tucked the top into the skirt waist.

"Hmm," Roxanne said, "I don't think I like that effect nearly as much as the knot in the middle. It doesn't look secure."

Heidi smiled at the seller. "Thank you. We see now. Different. Man's. Woman's. Very good." Through gritted teeth, she said to her sister: "You can try it on *after* we leave here."

The seller was pleased. She had prevented a valuable customer from making a social disgrace of herself. Roxanne and Heidi, along with Vera, continued to pore over the bolts of cloth, mining for gold. There were so many colors and patterns, each better than the last. But after a while, it was all too much. They were oversated and unsatisfied. It was like eating an excess of ice cream. Their senses were blunted, and all of the different bolts, at first so unusual, like exotic butterflies, had been rendered quite ordinary by their overloaded brains. In the end, Roxanne bought only the blue-checked cloth, feeling by then that she should have waited to see if she could find something nicer, and at a better price, elsewhere.

Wendy and Wyatt had gone looking for the mysterious woman and wound up in another corner of the market. Wyatt decided to take pictures. A group of boys with freshly shaved heads walked by, wearing the garb of acolyte monks, a single piece of cloth the color of deeply saturated orange-red chilies, which had been draped, tucked, and wound around their thin brown bodies. Their feet were bare, and they walked about as new beggars. One of them shyly held out a palm cupped into a begging bowl. Another boy slapped down his hand. The boys giggled. The monks were allowed to beg for their food, but only early in the morning. They went to the market before dawn with bowls and baskets, and shopkeepers and customers loaded them with rice, vegetables, pickled goods, peanuts, and noodles, all the while thanking them for allowing them this opportunity to increase their merit, merit being the good-deed bank account by which Buddhists improved their chances in future lives. These food supplies were taken back to the monastery, where the novices, ordained monks, and abbots lived, and a breakfast was made of the haul, a meal that had to last them the entire day.

But boys will be boys, and they were as curious as any to see what the foreigners would give if asked. Only a week before, they had been ordinary nine-year-olds, playing *chinlon* with their caneballs, swimming in the river, and taking care of their younger siblings. But the day had come when their parents consigned them to the local monastery to serve a voluntary course of time, from two weeks to several years, as all boys of Buddhist families did. Their heads were shaved during a family ceremony, their locks caught on a piece of white silk, and upon promising that they would obey the rules of Theravada Buddhism, they took off their clothes, donned the simple cloth of the monks, and became sons of the Buddha. This was their initiation into becoming human. A Burmese family once invited me to see this ceremony, and I found it quite moving, rather like the emotions I had when I watched a bris.

For poorer families, this was the only way in which their sons could receive an education. The well-to-do families collected their sons after two weeks, but the poorer boys stayed on longer, if they could. Through the monasteries, the boys learned to read the Pali scriptures, reciting them en masse under the watchful eyes of their elders, those who had chosen to remain in the monastery as ordained monks and abbots. And thus, they became both literate and devout, schooled in the piety of poverty. Being devout, as far as I could see, didn't rid the young monks of their love of mischief.

Wendy did not know any of this about the acolyte monks. She had not read the materials I had suggested in a reading list. "It's incredible that these poor kids are forced to become monks," she said to Wyatt. "I mean, what if they decide they want to have a sex life one day?"

"Check out those smiles," Wyatt said. He showed her the back of his digital camera. The monk boys crowded around to see as well. They pointed and hooted at their images.

Wyatt had not answered her question, she noticed. He did that a lot lately, giving non sequiturs in lieu of answers. Was he falling out of love? Or had he never been in love? Lately, what she felt when she was around him were twinges, pangs, aches, cracks, rips, and sudden hollows. His every response, or lack of one, hurt her. Maybe she was feeling this way just because she was hot, sticky, and cranky. She had left her sunscreen on the bus, and her freckled arms were growing pink. The sun burned hotter in this part of the world, and she worried what her face would look like in the half-hour before they could return to the bus. Her freckles would be the size of clown polka dots. What would Wyatt think of her when her face was sherbet pink and her nose was peeling like a bulb of garlic? He didn't have that problem. He may have been fair-headed, but his skin turned a delicious toasty brown from his frequent outdoor adventures. God, why did he have to be so gorgeous? She wanted to eat him up right this minute. Perhaps they could return to the bus early.

Just then, Wendy saw the woman in the hat who had caught her eye earlier. The woman spotted Wendy as well. She motioned discreetly for Wendy to come toward her. Wendy looked about. "Come on," she told Wyatt. "It's that woman who wanted to tell me something." She was certain she was on to important findings for Free to Speak International. Perhaps the woman knew the whereabouts of some people who had gone "missing." Wendy and Wyatt turned a corner and saw the woman up ahead, ducking into a doorway. They followed, and they, too, went into the doorway and at last saw the women squatting in the shadows.

"Mona Chen?" the woman said. She held up a big wad of Burmese kyats.

Wendy whispered back: "I'm not Mona, but I can still help you."

"She wants to change money," Wyatt said.

"What?"

"Mona Chen. Money change. See? She has money to exchange." Wyatt turned to the woman. "How much?"

"What are you doing?" Wendy exclaimed. "You could be jailed!"

"I'm just curious, that's all—"

By now two military policemen had walked by, backed up, and were staring at them.

"That," Wendy said, and pointed to the woman's conical hat. "How much for the hat?" She randomly pulled out a kyat note from her own wad. It was a hundred.

The woman nodded and took the note, then removed her hat and handed it to Wendy. The police moved on.

"They're gone," Wyatt said. "You can give back the hat."

"I want it. I need it, I really do. I'm getting burned out there. So how much did I pay for it? Too much?"

"About a quarter," Wyatt said. "A steal."

Wendy positioned the hat's rattan ring over her head, then tied the red ribbons under her chin. They walked out into the full sun, she now restored and refreshed. To Wendy, the hat was a shopping coup. She had saved them from being arrested by the police. And for twenty-five cents, she had a fashion accessory that bestowed on her an air that was cool and chic, like Audrey Hepburn or Grace Kelly in one of those movies from the fifties. Meanwhile, the locals were snickering among themselves. How funny to see the foreigner in a farmer's work hat, like a fish that has put on clothes.

Around the corner and down an alley, Moff and Rupert had found a shop that sold Western basketballs and badminton sets. As soon as they paid for one of each, Rupert began dribbling the basketball and Moff attempted to take it away. Shopkeepers and customers watched with grins on their faces. "Michael Jordan!" someone called out. Moff looked back. Michael Jordan? Even in this part of the world, they knew about him? Some boys with their longyis tucked up like short pants waved a hand, and when Rupert threw the ball their way, one of them caught it palm open. The boy expertly dribbled it down the lane before returning it to Rupert with a single bounce.

Another ball appeared, this one smaller, an airy globe of rattan. A boy in a brown longyi tossed it lightly and with an upturned heel kicked it to another boy. That boy let the ball bounce on his head and lobbed it toward Rupert, who instantly caught it on his knee and kept it bouncing there until he tossed it toward his father. Moff aimed his foot at the approaching missile, and it ricocheted in the wrong direction and fell to the ground. Rupert picked up the woven ball. "Cool," he said to Moff. "Like Hacky Sack but bouncier." He handed the caneball to its owner, the boy in the brown longyi. Moff held up a couple hundred kyat notes and pointed to the ball. The boy handed him the ball and solemnly took the two hundred kyats. "Cool," Rupert said again, and bounced the ball between his knees, moving forward in this manner as his father headed toward the peaked canopies of the produce market, the agreed-upon meeting point.

The tent was an emporium of colors: the golds and browns of turmeric, marigold, curry, and cumin; the reds of mangoes, chilies, and tomatoes; the greens of celery, long beans, coriander, and cucumbers. Young children fondly eyed trays of seaweed jelly artificially colored a vivid yellow. Their mothers watched as the vendors weighed their staples of rice, palm sugar, and dried rice noodles. The smells were both earthy and fermented. Moff saw Walter and Bennie standing at the entrance, both of them looking relaxed and pleased with themselves. The other travelers were already there waiting, too.

"Well?" Moff said to Bennie.

"Piece o' cake," he answered blithely, and snapped his fingers, as if it had never occurred to him that there might be a problem with the border crossing. He handed back passports. In truth, Bennie had worried so much that he had returned to the bus and stood next to Walter as papers were being examined and copied. Through the entire ordeal, his eyes were darting, his ears alert, and his sphincter muscles clenched in preparation for fight or flight.

"What I can't get over," Bennie now said, "is how Walter here can switch back and forth between perfect Burmese and excellent English. Have you noticed his English is better than mine? He's more American than I am." Bennie meant that Walter had a British accent, which in his mind sounded more high-class than his American midwestern one.

Walter was pleased by the flattery. "Oh, but being American has less to do with one's proficiency in English and more with the assumptions you hold dear and true—your inalienable rights, your pursuit of happiness. I, sad to say, don't possess those assumptions. I cannot undertake the pursuit."

"Well, you understand us," Bennie said. "So that makes you at least an honorary American."

"Why is it such an *honor*?" Wendy said peevishly. "Not everyone *wants* to be an American."

Although Bennie was annoyed, he laughed. Walter, ever the diplomat, said to Bennie, "Well, I'm flattered that you consider me to be one of your own."

On their way out, they passed a pile of shiny carp, the mouths of the fish still moving. "I thought this was a Buddhist country," Heidi said. "I thought they didn't kill animals." A few yards to the right was the bloody carnage of a dead pig. Heidi had glimpsed it and now would not look that way.

"The butchers and fishermen are usually not Buddhist," Walter said. "But even if they are, they approach their fishing with reverence. They scoop up the fish and bring them to shore. They say they are saving fish from drowning. Unfortunately . . ." He looked downward, like a penitent. ". . . the fish do not recover."

Saving fish from drowning? Dwight and Harry looked at each other and guffawed. Was he joking?

Heidi was unable to speak. Did these people actually believe they were doing a good deed? Why, they had no intention of saving anything! Look at those fish. They were gasping for oxygen, and the sellers who squatted nearby, smoking their cheroots, hardly possessed the caring demeanor of emergency doctors or hospice workers. "It's horrible," she said at last. "It's worse than if they just killed them outright rather than justifying it as an act of kindness."

"No worse than what we do in other countries," Dwight said.

"What are you talking about?" Moff said.

"Saving people for their own good," he replied. "Invading countries, having them suffer collateral damage, as we call it. Killing them as an unfortunate consequence of helping them. You know, like Vietnam, Bosnia."

"Those aren't the same thing," Bennie said. "And what are you suggesting, that we just stand around and do nothing when ethnic cleansing goes on?"

"Just saying we should be aware of the consequences. You can't have intentions without consequences. The question is, who pays for the consequences? Saving fish from drowning. Same thing. Who's saved? Who's not?"

"I'm sorry," Bennie huffed, "but that is *not* the same thing at all." The others were quiet. It wasn't that they agreed with Dwight, whom they hated to agree with, no matter what he said. But they could not entirely disagree. It was like a brain twister, one of those silhouettes that was a beautiful girl with a hat, then a crone with a crooked nose. It depended on how you viewed it.

"Oh God, what can we do?" Heidi said mournfully, still fixated on the fish. "Can't we say something? I want to buy all of them and throw them back in the water."

"Don't look at it," Moff told her.

"How can I not look?"

The fish continued to flop. Moff led Heidi away by the arm.

"Can fish drown?" Rupert asked once they had moved away from the fish stalls.

"Of course not," Bennie said. "They have gills, not lungs."

"Actually," Harry said, "they can indeed drown." All eyes except Heidi's turned toward him. "In humans who drown, the lungs fill with water, and because our lungs are incapable of filtering out usable oxygen, the person suffocates. That's the cause of death, lack of oxygen. We call it drowning, because it occurs in water or with some sort of liquid." He caught Marlena looking at him intently. He continued in his casual, confident manner.

"Fish, on the other hand, have gills that extract oxygen, but most fish have to keep moving about to bring in a lot of water to filter enough oxygen. If they were not able to move, say they were caught in a reef pocket at low tide, or stuck on a hook, they would eventually suffer from oxygen deprivation and suffocate. They drown." He saw that Marlena was staring at him, mesmerized, a look that said to him: You are so incredibly powerful and sexy. If there were a bed right here, I'd jump your bones. Actually, Marlena was wondering why he took so much pleasure in describing how fish die.

Heidi envisioned the panting fish they had just left. "If they can take oxygen from water, why can't their gills process it from air?"

Marlena gave Harry an expectant look. Harry gladly explained: "Their gills are like two silky-thin arches. They're suspended wide open in water, like double sails on a boat. Out of water, the arches collapse like a plastic baggie and press against each other, sealing them off so no air gets in. The fish suffocate."

Vera gave out a snort. "So there is absolutely no way someone can sincerely say they are saving fish from drowning."

And Harry replied: "No. They are drowning on land."

"Well, what about chickens?" Vera mused, gesturing toward a cage of chicks. "What benevolent action will do them in? Will they be receiving yoga lessons when their necks are accidentally broken?"

"It's no worse than what we do back home," Esmé said with sangfroid matter-of-factness. "We're just better at hiding it. I saw a program on TV. The pigs are all smashed together, then go through a chute, and they're all screaming, because they know what's going to happen. They do it to horses, too. That's what some dog foods are made of. Sometimes they're not even dead when they get chopped up."

Marlena stared at her daughter. Esmé seemed to have shed her innocence before her very eyes. How could her baby know these things? Marlena took her daughter's new strides in knowledge with maternal angst and sadness. She had loved those days when Esmé looked to her for protection and comfort, when it was expected that she, the mother, would shield her daughter from the ugliness of the world. Now she remembered a time, not too long before, when they had walked together through Chinatown, and Esmé had cried over the live fish after hearing the shopkeeper say they were "for eating not for petting." Esmé's hysterical reaction was not that different from the sentiments of the animal activists on the street who were passing out leaflets, encouraging people to boycott restaurants in Chinatown that killed fish and fowl on their premises to ensure the food was absolutely fresh. "The fish have their heads cut off *while they are still alive*," she once heard an animal rights protester complain. Marlena had shouted back, "All animals are alive before they are killed. How else do you propose to kill a fish? Let it die of old age?" She thought it ridiculous that people argued for saving a fish's life. But now she saw things through Esmé's eyes. It was awful to witness any creature in a fruitless struggle to stay alive.

"Ladies and gentlemen," Walter called. "You may return to the bus now, and those of you who still want to do a bit of shopping or sightseeing, please rendezvous back at the bus in fifteen minutes." My friends dispersed, Wendy to seek the shade of the bus, Moff and Rupert to wander the alleyways, and the others to find a photo opportunity to record that they had been in this town, whatever it was called.

Off in a corner of the marketplace, Bennie spotted an old woman with the sweetest expression. She was wearing a blue turban, which dwarfed her sun-parched face. He gestured to ask if he might do a quick sketch of her and her lovely display of mustard greens and turnips. She grinned shyly. He did the fast line drawing he used for cartoons, just enough sweeps to suggest the forms and features that captured the subject. Knowing what the features were—that was as much the artistry as executing the drawing. The weight of the turban on her small head, and now a big smile that nearly swallowed her chin. A bunch of loops for the turnips and mustard greens, and fainter squiggles for those in the back rows. After a minute or so, he showed the woman his sketch. "Oh my," she cried in a language he didn't understand, "you have turned me into someone else, much more beautiful. Thank you." She started to hand it back, and he stopped her.

"For you," he said.

She gave him another huge smile that engulfed her lower lip. Her small eyes sparkled. As he was about to step away, she grunted at him, then gestured to her vegetables for sale. "You like?" she asked in English. Bennie nodded, to be polite. She gestured that he should choose something. Bennie raised a hand and shook his head politely. She insisted. He was dismayed that she was now asking him to buy her goods. Finally, still smiling, she snorted and dumped a handful of fermented turnips into a small pink bag, then twirled it and tied off the top, so that, with the air caught inside, it resembled a plump pink bladder. She held this up for him to take.

What the hell. How much could it cost? He offered her a few bills, the equivalent of thirty cents, which was a fantastically huge sum for a bag of fermented turnips, but she looked insulted and firmly pushed his hand away. He finally came to understand: *Oh*, a gift. A gift! She gave a firm nod. He gave her a gift, and she was giving him a gift. Wow! He was overwhelmed. This was the true kindness of strangers. *This* was a *National Geographic* moment: two people, vastly different, separated by language and culture and a whole lot else, yet giving and giving back the best they had to offer, their own humanity, their cartoons, their pickles. He gratefully accepted the pink plastic bag with its soggy lump, this beautiful token of universal friendship. It was incredible, so warming to the heart. He would keep it forever—or until disaster struck, which would be only a few hours later.

THE BUS ROLLED FORWARD, its wheels now in contact with the Burma Road, a rough-coated two-lane thoroughfare shared by Brahmin cattle of both the wandering variety and the kind manacled to carts. My friends looked at the new scenery. The hills were covered with smaller mounds that jutted out like carbuncles. In the fields stood shacks on stilts, the walls made of woven rattan, the roofs of thatched grass. The more prosperous homes had the benefit of blindingly shiny corrugated tin roofs. On this warm winter afternoon, the windows were blocked by shutters, sun-bleached and monsoon-washed such that they evoked a history-rich, distressed style greatly admired by Roxanne. Marlena, for her part, thought the buildings were so surrealistically gorgeous they achieved a reverse trompe l'oeil effect, a deception of the senses that made it seem the shutters were not real but painted on.

"Look at all those Christmas plants," Esmé said. "There's like a thousand dollars' worth right there." Poinsettias, interlaced with bougainvillea, spread along the base of banyan trees, harmonizing with the ubiquitous bushes of panpuia and their lilac-tinted pom-poms.

"They're not native," Moff said. "Poinsettia here is actually an interloper, an ornamental native to Mexico." Heidi asked if the seeds were blown all this distance. "The early ones probably came by boat," Moff said. "But as gifts from diplomats of another century. Nice ecosystem here for any kind of plant."

When the bus had gone a mile or two, Walter spoke again. "You are to be congratulated," he told the passengers. "You are probably the first Westerners to travel this section of the road coming in from China. Last year the road was not passable, and it would have taken me three weeks to go from Mandalay to Ruili. This year, the work is completed, and the journey takes only twelve hours."

Walter did not tell them that the road had been rebuilt by one of Burma's tribes, which I shall not name here, but whose résumé includes such feats in past years as headhunting, and in more modern times gunrunning and heroin commerce. At one time, they were powerful insurgents against the military regime. The tribe had fought hard and well, and the military government finally sought a truce so that they might negotiate like reasonable despots of the world. By and by, the tribe signed off to a cease-fire in exchange for a nod to build a business empire, unobstructed by the government and unfettered by competition. The Burma Road and its tollbooths, the major airlines, and some of the hotels my friends would be staying in were under the control of this entrepreneurial tribe. In the corporate world of Myanmar, hostile takeovers mean something different from what they do in the United States.

Shortly after his announcement, Walter asked the driver to pull into a small dirt road off the highway.

"Bathroom break," Wyatt said, "just in time." Others agreed.

"This is not a rest stop," Walter said diplomatically. "If you can be patient, we will make another stop further up the road. The reason I brought you here is so that you can see one of our traditions followed by nearly all, without regard to religion or tribe." He got out of the bus and, followed by the others, walked up to what looked like a bamboo birdfeeder, decorated with Christmas tinsel, placed in the cranny of a tree. "This is a small shrine for a Nat. . . ." He went on to explain that Nats were believed to be the spirits of nature—the lake, the trees, the mountains, the snakes and birds. They were numberless. But thirty-seven had been designated official Nats, most of them historical people associated with myths or real tales of heroism. Some were martyrs, people who had been betrayed or had suffered a premature and frightful death. One had died of diarrhea and was reputed to inflict that on those who displeased him. Regardless of their origins, they were easily disturbed, given to making a fuss when they were not treated with respect. My friends made jokes about odious people they knew who would make good Nats.

There were also local Nats in villages, and household Nats that lived in shrines in family homes. People gave them gifts, food and drink. They were everywhere, as were bad luck and the need to find reasons for it.

"What does a Nat look like?" Esmé asked.

"Ah, yes. They can be of many forms," Walter said. "At festivals that are held for them, you can see statues, large and small, created to represent them—a figure on a white horse, or a man who looks like a monk, royal people dressed in the clothing of yesteryear. And some, like the spirits of nature, are invisible."

"Are they like ghosts?" Esmé asked.

"There is some similarity," Walter replied. "You might see them, you might not. But as I understand it, you Americans hire people to remove ghosts, or 'bust' them, as I believe you say. Your ghosts are only people or possibly animals. And you don't create shrines or give offerings to keep them happy. This particular shrine is for this tree. There were many accidents on the old road, until people realized a Nat was here. After the shrine was placed here, no accidents have happened."

"So they're everything and everywhere," Esmé concluded.

Walter tilted his head slightly to indicate it was a possibility.

"So what else do Nats supposedly do when riled?" Vera asked.

"It could be anything," Walter answered, "some mischief, at the very least. A valuable object might be broken or snatched. Illness. And there can be greater calamities, even catastrophes to entire villages. Whatever the misfortune, people might then believe that they weren't dutiful in propitiating a Nat. But please don't think that all Nats are bad. If you've honored them well, they might be inclined to help you. One of the tourists I guided last year likened them to your concept of mothers-in-law."

"Do you believe in Nats?" Marlena asked.

Walter turned and smiled. "Educated people generally don't. But it's tradition to give an offering. Like presents under your Christmas tree from Santa Claus." He did not tell them that he had a shrine in his family home, a beautiful one, tended to, and supplied with daily offerings. He now walked up to the tree shrine and, with his back to the tourists, carefully tucked a packet of sunflower seeds inside. A flicker of apprehension ran over his face.

He turned back to them. "If anyone else cares to make an offering—please." And he gestured that they could step forward. Mr. Joe stepped forward and took a fresh cigarette from a pack and placed this on the shrine's little balcony.

"As you can see," Walter said, "our Nats love to smoke, as well as to drink, everything from palm toddy to Johnnie Walker Black."

Esmé walked up and solemnly stuffed a mini-bag of M&M's inside the shrine. Heidi gave a packet of daily vitamins, and Wyatt a postcard. Bennie jokingly whispered to Marlena and Harry that they ought to give it Valium or an antidepressant, and all three chuckled. Vera came forward and stuffed in an American dollar. She believed one should honor another country's traditions, and her offering would show that at least one American had. The rest of them offered nothing. The rest of them didn't think you had to show respect to something that obviously did not exist.

THE ROAD HAD BEGUN to wind and twist, and soon gave way to hairpin turns. Only Walter was awake. He glanced back at the passengers behind him. Heads lolled left and right, up and down in rhythm with the bumps and bounces of the bus. The jiggling heads looked as if their owners were performing the puppet dance of the dead. He stared out the window.

Cloud shadows passed over bushy hills, leaving dark bruises on the bright green slopes. The Nats lived in nature, in trees and stumps, fields, and rocks. Beneath this visible surface was an earlier stratum of beliefs, the molten core and shifting plates belonging to animism.

Some of those animistic beliefs came from China more than a thousand years ago, when sprites and demons headed south, as my friends were doing now. The peripatetic Nats clung like burrs to the robes of persecuted tribes and defeated armies taking a back road into Burma. Were bad-tempered hitchhikers now riding on the tailpipe of the bus, sitting on the bumper? Nats have always been tied to disaster. They were the coincidence of accidents. And they grew with a never-ending supply of tragedy and death. No religion would eject them, not Buddhist or Baptist, not Methodist or Mormon.

Walter faced forward in the bus. While he appeared calm to his charges, he was, in fact, troubled by what Bennie had told him in their morning phone conversation. It is impossible that Miss Chen is dead, Walter thought. *I talked to her just yesterday.* He tried to rationalize and recalculate how he had known ahead of time to change the documents for an earlier entrance into Burma. Had her death been gruesome? (It was.) Had she been angry that the tour continued without her? (No, I was with them.)

Walter heard Bennie mumble. He had partially opened his eyes to check his watch. "Mr. Bennie," Walter said softly, and Bennie turned to acknowledge him. "I beg your pardon, but could I trouble you to tell me how Miss Bibi Chen died?"

Bennie bit his lips as the vision of my body sprang into his mind. "Nobody really knows," he said. "Some say that she was murdered. She was found with her windpipe slashed. She either bled to death or suffocated."

"Oh, dear." Walter's heart raced. For certain, Miss Bibi was a disturbed spirit.

"It was horrible, a total nightmare for all of us. We almost canceled the trip."

"I see. . . . Was Miss Bibi of any particular religion?"

"Religion? I don't think so. . . . To be honest, I don't really know. Isn't that awful? I knew her really well, but religion wasn't something we ever talked about. I would have to guess that she wasn't devout about anything in particular. You know how it is. I'm a lapsed Baptist on my mother's side. Are you familiar with them?"

"Quite. Many a Baptist missionary has come through Burma. They were successful in recruiting many converts, particularly the hill-tribe people."

"No kidding. Is that how you learned your English?"

"I grew up with English spoken in the home, along with Burmese. It was part of our inheritance."

"How do you *inherit* English?"

"My family has spoken English for generations. My great-great-grandparents worked for the British Raj, and later generations of my family found employment with missionaries, but English was already their public parlance."

"Well, you speak it beautifully."

"You're too kind. And thank you for answering my questions about Miss Bibi. I appreciate your frank answers on this difficult subject. And now I won't interrupt your rest any longer."

"No problem. If you have any other questions, fire away." Bennie settled back and closed his eyes.

Walter stared out the window. He mused: In the last five generations of his family, all had had reasons to use English as part of their work. And at least one person in each generation before his had died as a consequence. English was their inheritance, the purveyor of opportunities. But it was also their curse.

WALTER'S GREAT-GREAT-GRANDFATHER had learned English as a lad when he did chores for a British teacher who ran a one-room school for colonial boys in Mandalay. As he went about sweeping in the courtyard, he listened to the voices of the teacher and his pupils floating out the windows. Later, he would trace the words written on the chalkboard before washing it clean. He was adept at learning, and the teacher recognized this, and eventually allowed him to sit at the back of the classroom. His English grew to be as beautiful as that of his employer's children, with the right amount of crispness at the ends of words and roundness within. When he was twenty-seven, he was recruited as an interpreter for the British Raj. His command of the languages did not win him alliances with other tribes, however. In one remote outpost, neither the British nor the Burman presence was tolerated, and one day a hail of wild gunfire spattered trees and bushes, birds and monkeys, and Walter's great-great-grandfather. It was amazing that no one else was killed.

As compensation for the interpreter's death, his son was sent to study at a secular school for native boys, run by British educators. Thirty years later, this same boy, now grown, returned to that school as its first Burmese headmaster. While the academics were first-rate, the headmaster was just as proud that the school's cricket team was undefeated among other native schools. One day, the team was invited to play against its British counterpart. The foreigners sat on the shaded side, in seats under awnings. The Burmese were seated in the sun. It was an especially hot day, and when the Burmese team won, the headmaster cried out, "Huzzah! Huzzah!" and then collapsed and died. Likely it was heatstroke, but that is not how the story of Walter's great-grandfather was told. By the evidence of his last words, he died of English joy.

The son of the headmaster also found work in education. He taught in schools established by the missionaries who had flocked to Burma once the Japanese were run out. Through the mission school, he met a Burmese nurse with bright shining eyes who worked at the surgery. She, too, spoke impeccable English, having been raised since toddlerhood under the guardianship of a British couple, whose automobile accelerated for no apparent reason, then struck and killed her parents, who had been their devoted servants. One day, the nurse and three missionaries rode out to a village where there was a malaria outbreak among the new American teachers. On the way, their car ran off the road and overturned in a ravine. The nurse, Walter's grandmother, was the only one killed—taken, some said, by the Nats of her parents. How else would one explain this third death by automobile in the family?

The nurse left behind her husband, three sons, and a daughter. Walter's father was the oldest. He went on to become a journalist and a university professor. Walter remembered that his father, who was a stickler for grammar, had a favorite saying, which clarified the proper use of "good" and "well": "While it is good to speak well, it is better to speak the truth." Walter's father had valued the truth more than his own life. In 1989, he was arrested after he joined students and other teachers in protesting the military. The fact that he spoke English was enough to convict him as a spy. Walter's father was arrested and taken away, and a year later, a man who had been released from prison told Walter's family that their father had died after a beating that collapsed his lungs.

Sixteen-year-old Walter, his sisters, and their widowed mother went to live with the children's grandfather. It became a divided household. The grandfather now believed that English had been the cause of these tragic deaths in the family—his own dear wife's, for one. Why hadn't he recognized the pattern sooner? He forbade his daughter-in-law and grandchildren to speak English. The novels by Thomas Hardy and Jane Austen and all the other works by troublemongers were cast out, and Nat shrines replaced them on the bookshelves.

Walter's mother, however, refused to give up English. She had not received it effortlessly as an inheritance. As a girl, she had struggled to learn the difficult twists of the tongue, and had passed one examination after another in the European code. By listening to her husband speak, she had improved her pronunciation, so that it was no longer like that of those students with the pidgin diction of their native teachers. Her mastery of the language was a blissful expression of the spirit to her, like playing a musical instrument. And her most intimate and private memories of her husband were in that language. What books and periodicals her husband's father had not hacked to pieces, she locked away for safekeeping. On special occasions she took them out and read the stale news of magazines many years old, savoring them sparingly, as she did the waxy bonbons given to her one Christmas by a visiting professor from an American university, before it was illegal to let foreigners in one's house.

For the past ten years, Walter's grandfather and mother had refused to talk to each other, except through Walter. He spoke Burmese to his grandfather and English to his mother. There had been no better preparation for him in his career as tour guide, a career that required him to be adept at managing the misunderstandings of two people who spoke separate languages, while circumnavigating the same place at the same time.

But now and then, Walter wondered about his family's curse by the English language. Was he next? How would it happen? And when?

THE BUS HAD STOPPED. Slowly, my friends roused themselves and straightened their cramped necks. Walter stood up: "This is not a photo opportunity, I'm afraid. We are at another checkpoint. We will be here for half an hour or so. For your safety and security, please remain on the bus."

Safety? Security? The mention of those words caused my friends to feel unsafe and insecure.

Walter gathered his packet of passports, then stepped off the bus and headed for a booth. Outside, rifle-toting solders in camouflage were opening car trunks, removing boxes and suitcases tied to the roofs. Clothes lay strewn about, picked through by the soldiers.

Boxes containing foodstuffs were opened. Some soldiers poked at a foam sofa that had been compressed and covered in plastic tarp, then wound in string, and strapped atop a station wagon. A flick of a knife, and the strings were cut, the tarp sliced through. The sofa was excised like a tumor, and freed from its confines, it expanded until it seemed impossible that it had ever been in such a small package. The passengers—three men and a woman—looked nervous and unhappy. An old woman approached the station wagon, offering eggs as snacks for sale. The occupants did not look at her. The sofa cushions were unzipped, and hands shot in and brushed back and forth. The soldiers ordered the people out of the car. As they scrambled to obey, one soldier barked that they were to stay with the car, not move away. The soldiers leaned into the car and patted the seats, the floor pads. They lifted out the backseats and ran their hands up the back cushion. They violently pried open the side panels on the doors. The passengers looked as though they were on the verge of either breaking down or running for their lives.

And then, all at once, they were told to get back in. One of the soldiers grunted, and the driver hurried to start the engine. In a few seconds, the car was gone, heading toward China. Now my friends could see a sign posted on the side of the checkpoint, written in Chinese, Burmese, Thai, and English: "The penalty for smuggling drugs is death."

This made some of my friends wonder whether they had inadvertently brought in any illegal substances. The polar fleece vest, Wyatt remembered, and sat up. Had he searched all the pockets, the secret ones as well? Was there a forgotten marijuana joint in one of them?

Bennie thought of a bottle into which he had thrown prescription pills of all kinds, in case of emergencies; some of the pills were Darvocet. Was that related to heroin? Did that count as drug smuggling, a reason to line him up against a dusty wall and fill him with bullets?

Heidi had a similar fear. She was tallying up the items that might be considered drug-related: the syringes, the multiple bottles of pills, and the tubing, the kind used by heroin addicts to pump up their veins. What else did she have? She wondered how she would be able to survive in a prison, let alone face imminent death alone.

It crossed Vera's mind that some of her compatriots might have been less circumspect about the safety of others. Moff, for example, that so-called bamboo grower, had been a bit too keen to see the open markets where drug dealing was done. She stared hard at him. He was reading a book. She pictured him still reading, as they stood shackled in the dock in a closed courtroom, listening to unknown charges read aloud in Burmese.

Moff pretended to read, but kept an eye out for what was happening. Best not see too much. He had heard that the soldiers could be easily corrupted. Perhaps they were not searching for contraband at all, but stuffing their own blocks of heroin into tight spaces. Their contact on the China side of the border, another corrupt worker, would find it and send payment back in another car that had been duly "searched."

Esmé threw her mother's scarf over Pup-pup. Marlena squeezed her daughter's hand, and reflexively, she also squeezed her left hand, which held Harry's. Harry squeezed back. He was not overly worried. Tonight was the night, he was thinking. Esmé would have healthy little Pup-pup to sleep with, and he would have Marlena to play with. He reached into his pocket with his free hand, extracted a mint, and popped it into his mouth.

Walter returned to the bus. "Ladies and gentlemen, we have been given permission to proceed." By then, several members of the group had developed upset stomach, which they thought was the result of high stress from waiting at the checkpoint. But in fact, unbeknownst to them, *Shigella bacillus* had finally multiplied in sufficient numbers to besiege and scour the linings of their bowels. This was the souvenir of the now forgotten meal served at a restaurant on the way to Stone Bell Temple.

Our travelers went ever deeper into Burma. The fields now resembled crazy quilts, with irregularly shaped plots and borders that never managed to run a straight line. The fields had been passed down in families, and their original boundaries had been marked by the natural growth of bushes. In those colorful fields stood haystacks shaped like stupas. Along streambeds, graceful ladies leaned over huge buckets and splashed themselves as part of their twice-a-day bathing ritual. Tiny children perched on water buffaloes, having already mastered perfect balance on a furry hump.

Dusk was approaching, as marked by the smell of smoke. Fires for the evening meal were being lit. A haze rose from each household and hovered over the land like a blanket of benediction. My friends turned and saw that the banks of the hills were the color of chilies, sharp tastes that brought tears to the eyes. Soon this deepened to blood red, and then the sun dipped past the end of the fields, the land and sky turned black, save for a slice of moon, a colander of stars, and the golden smoke of cooking fires.

·7·

THE JACARANDAS

T he overhead lights of the bus came on, a feeble green, casting a
pickled pallor upon the faces of my fellow travelers.

On the last leg, during the climb up the Burma Road into
Lashio, the exhaust system on the bus had malfunctioned, and toxic
fumes were sucked through the air-conditioning; my friends were
made stupid with headache and nausea. Walter noted that even the
noisiest ones—Wendy, Moff, Bennie, and Vera—had quieted into a
daze. Then Mr. Joe, the usually morose driver, cried out that he had
seen a Nat riding toward him on a white horse. Walter ordered that
they pull over for fresh air. All the men tumbled off the bus, searching for privacy in the pitch-dark night and unknown vegetation. The
women preferred to wait until they arrived at the hotel, which Walter
promised was only a half-hour away. It was actually forty-five minutes, but he knew that would have sounded unbearably long.

For once, Harry did not need to use a loo. But he, too, left the bus, to clear his head. He and Marlena were suddenly at odds with each other, and he could not fathom why. In his mind, he had simply tried to show a bit of affection—this was in the way of rubbing her rump—and she had recoiled, as if he had been trying to sodomize her in front of her dozing daughter. She shot him a look, a castrating look. His ex-wife used to aim such a look at him frequently toward the end of their marriage, and he was an expert at interpreting it. It meant: "Not if you were the last sperm bank on earth." Yet the night before, Marlena had been as passionate as he had been, he was certain of it. There was absolutely no reluctance there. She had reciprocated on the sidewalk of Ruili, providing fully fifty percent of their physics of frottage. Why this sudden turnabout?

The look Marlena gave him was actually one of mortifying distress. She, along with several others on the bus, was starting to feel the cramping effects of dysentery as it prepared to make its inexorable descent. How could she tell him, especially in front of Esmé, the reason that their ardor needed to be put on hold? Even if Esmé were not there, of all things to put a damper on romance, not this. Dear God, the agony, the inconvenience.

Rupert, Moff, and Bennie hurried off with feeble flashlights in search of a spot where they might have solid footing. Here, I averted my eyes. I would like to point out, however, the highly unfortunate coincidence that what an American takes to be an ideal outdoor toilet is what some Nats—perhaps the one who died of intestinal malaise—consider to be home sweet holy home, in this case, a small grove of jacaranda trees, still leafy in winter but missing their magnificent mane of lilac-colored blossoms. Cross-culturally, mistakes were made, unintentional to be sure, and nothing would have come of it had Rupert not yelled out: "Daa-ad! Dad! Do you have toilet paper?" He cursed, pulled out the paperback from his jacket pocket, and reluctantly ripped out pages he had already read. "Never mind!" he yelled again.

Thus shaken from a drinking game, two Nats in the form of military police jumped to their feet. Earlier they had left their guard posts and sneaked into the field, so that they might smoke cheroots and get drunk on palm toddy. The soused men shouted in Burmese with the prerogative of those on guard. "What the fuck's going on out there?"

Walter, hearing their curses, had no desire to discern whether they were farmers or spirits. He summoned the rest-stop takers to re-board quickly. Trousers were yanked up, dark figures hobbled toward the vehicle while tugging on their zippers. But Harry, happy wanderer and slow pisser, was oblivious of all of it. He was farther down the road, gazing at brilliant pinpricks of stars, when he heard the commotion. He glanced back and saw the others mounting the bus. Time to walk back. He assumed the same leisurely pace that had taken him there. A second later, the bus engine started, and the rear brake lights glowed red. What's their big hurry? Harry began to walk a bit faster. A sharp pain shot through his right knee. He bent down and clutched where it throbbed. Old ski injury, the onset of arthritis. Drat, he was getting old. Well, no use aggravating it further. He slowed to a walk again, deciding he would simply have to apologize for the delay once he reached his companions. But instead, when he was some twenty feet away, much to his astonishment, the bus pulled off.

"Hey there!" he shouted while hobbling forward. The bus belched black fumes, and in reeling from this noxious assault, Harry leapt to the right and fell into a shallow ditch, landing on his left shoulder and in a manner not conducive to proper arm rotation. A few moments later, he climbed out, coughing and swearing. Was this a joke? Surely, it had to be, and a wretched one at that. He rubbed his shoulder. He'd be lucky if he had not torn his rotator cuff. All right, ha, ha, ha. Any moment now, they would stop and turn back. They had better do it quick. He waited a bit more. Come on. He imagined hearing the hiss of the bus door opening. "Get your bum in here," he expected Moff to say. And Harry would launch himself at his chum's torso in a fury of mock punches. But his expectations of reprising the jokes of their youth dwindled, as the red brake lights of the bus grew smaller and dimmer, then disappeared completely, as did the blackened road before him.

"Damn!" Harry said. "Now what?" And as if in answer, two drunken policemen in green fatigues rushed from the fields with torchlights and rifles trained at his face.

WALTER HAD NEVER MADE a mistake like that. He was usually fastidious about ensuring that all passengers were accounted for. Before Mr. Joe drove off, Walter had turned on the garish overhead light to perform the count. The eyes of the nauseated throbbed, and they groaned and covered their faces with their hands. "One, two . . ." He counted off Bennie and Vera, then Dwight and his grumpy wife, Roxanne. Five was the pretty lady, Heidi, who had a cautious manner, much like his girlfriend in Yangon. "Six, seven," would be Moff and his son, then came the mother and daughter with the small puppy. . . . Walter paused. Did he just count seven? He was also suffering a bit. He had a frontal headache brought on from inhaling carbon monoxide from the bus exhaust, and this impaired him. Thus, as he made his way back up the right side of the bus, he included in the count a rattan conical hat balanced atop a backpack, the same hat Wendy had purchased for a hundred kyats in the alley. In bad light, the hat and backpack looked like the head and shoulders of a passenger who had nodded off. ". . . Eight, nine, ten, eleven, twelve," Walter counted. "All here, off we go."

Actually, before I tell you what happened to Harry, there is also the matter of Marlena to report. She should have been the first to note that Harry was missing. But as you now know, she was concentrating on her stomach cramps, counting the seconds each lasted, as if she were doing Lamaze birthing exercises. In any case, she did not feel like explaining her troubles to Harry, who had left with a cold frown.

She assumed it was a cold frown, when in fact it was merely genuine English puzzlement. Completely understandable on her part, I might add. I've always found that the English, as opposed to the Americans, or even the Welsh and Irish, have a severely reduced range of expressions. Pleasure, pain, bemusement—they are signaled by only the slightest changes in facial musculature, practically indecipherable for those who are accustomed to uninhibited expressions of emotions. And people say the Chinese are inscrutable.

But back to the point: When Harry did not resume his place by her side, Marlena concluded he was demonstrating his displeasure with her. She resented that kind of behavior in people, especially men. The disapproving look of the patriarch galled her, pressed all the neurotransmitters to the area of her brain that controlled survival and defense. In fact, the more she thought about it, the more she fumed, convinced now that Harry had the exact same attitude that her father and ex-husband had too often expressed, the withholding of emotions combined with a critical mashing together of the eyebrows.

A few rows up, Bennie had his eyebrows contorted into a frown of pure misery. He hoped he could restrain himself until the bus reached the hotel. He leaned forward and placed his forehead on the padded back of the seat in front of him. As he did so, his right knee came to rest against an inflated pink plastic bag he had stuck in the mesh magazine rack. Inside was the gift of humanity from the wizened woman in the marketplace, a quarter-pound of fermented spicy turnips sloshing about in their juice.

But now some three hours had passed, the last half-hour in cold, sweating pain. Bennie had forgotten about humanity and pickles. His mind was devoted fully to the perturbations of his bowels. Another cramp shot through his intestines, and he rode the waves by pressing down harder on his knee, which in turn placed an equivalent pressure on the pink bag. It burst with an audible pop, and the fermented turnips and pungent juice splashed on the floor, sending into the confined bus cabin a smell not unlike that of the entrails of a rat floating in a sewer. That is how the others would have described it, had they not already been gagging and vomiting.

As for myself, I have always been fond of pickled turnips. They are excellent in all manner of home-style dishes, a welcome bit of crunch in a bowl of morning rice porridge, which had once been my fond custom.

IT WAS NOT until their arrival at the hotel that Harry was missed. Walter began to collect passports. Eleven? Why were there only eleven? He glanced about, trying to match faces to passports. Mr. Joe was busy unloading luggage from the hold, and the passengers were pointing out the pieces that belonged to them. All the men had canvas duffels, though one of Bennie's bags was a fake Gucci in leatherette. The women had a preference for expandable wheelies, decorated with bright bunches of yarn that would make a surreptitious luggage thief look elsewhere. Heidi was passing out antibiotics from her bountiful supply.

"Two pills a day for three days," she said. "If it's the usual kind of mild dysentery, you'll find relief by morning. Be sure to drink plenty of boiled water." Moff, Rupert, Marlena, and Bennie nodded weakly, accepting the pills like dying Catholics getting their final holy wafers.

Ah, Harry! That's who it was, Walter decided. Harry Bailley had not yet given him his passport.

"Has anyone seen Harry?" Walter asked.

The travelers were annoyed. They didn't want anything to delay their getting settled in their rooms. They assumed Harry had sprinted off to take a leak in the dark. "Harry!" Moff called out. "Harry, you bastard, get your arse over here!" They all cast their eyes about, expecting to see him jump out of the bushes.

To their left was a gigantic neon sign that said "Golden Land Guesthouse." Below was another neon graphic, a menorah. My friends were so exhausted by illness and travel they did not even notice this odd decorative touch. The guesthouse was a two-story colonial affair that might have provided genteel hospitality in an earlier time. It had the requisite rickety staircase, shabby, with threadbare stained red carpet. The innkeepers were an ethnic Chinese couple who claimed to be Jews. They boasted that they were descended from the lost tribes who wandered into this part of Asia from Mediterranea more than a thousand years earlier, some of whom migrated farther north to Kaifeng. They even possessed a Haggadah written in both Chinese and Hebrew.

Let me hasten to add that the fact that the owners were Chinese did not figure into why I chose the guesthouse. There simply were no other choices to speak of, that is, none with private bathrooms. The privacy that these bathrooms afforded, however, was more visual than real. The walls were flimsy pressboard, the punch-through kind you find on the Hollywood sets of cowboy westerns with saloon fights. A person sneezing or producing other involuntary body emissions would send the walls rattling to near collapse, and the corporeal sounds would echo one floor up and down, as well as to the ends of each hall.

It was in these reverberating echo chambers that my friends sought refuge. Walter managed to register them all as guests, despite Harry's continuing and now worrisome absence. Actually, only Walter was concerned. The others assumed Harry was chasing after an exotic bird, or sitting at the bar, having an exotic cocktail. But Walter had seen Wendy climb out with the strings of her ridiculous conical hat clutched in her fingers. That's when he said to himself, *Number twelve*.

What had led him to make such a mistake? As soon as the question formed in his mind, he knew. Miss Chen, the Nat. Trouble was starting already. The sickness, the missing passenger.

Don't be ridiculous, I shouted, but to no avail. I wasn't a Nat. Or was I? Insane people often don't know they are insane. Did I not know I was a Nat? I would have to find a way to prove I was not.

The sun had set. The temperature was sixty-five degrees. "Ladies and gentlemen," Walter said, "please adjust your watches back to seven. We are ninety minutes different from China." My friends were too sick to do so.

"Those who wish to eat," Walter said, "should meet in the dining hall at eight. That is one hour from now. When you have finished your meal, those among you who are brave souls may wish to stop in the lounge, where you can sing with the locals. I hear they have quite a good karaoke system."

Walter left them and met Mr. Joe back at the bus, where he had told him to wait. The driver had a cloth soaked in lime juice covering the lower part of his face. He had spent the last twenty minutes furiously cleaning the bus of vomit and stinks, and had left all of the windows open.

Walter announced that they were going back to where they had made a rest stop. "Do you think you can recognize the place?"

The driver nervously ran his fingers through his hair. "Yes, yes, of course. Forty-five minutes, that way." And he jerked his head toward the pitch-black road.

Walter was thinking that Harry might have fallen. Perhaps he was drunk. With past tour groups, there had been troublesome clients like that. He might also be sick like the others, too weak to walk.

"Slow down when we near the place," Walter said. "He could be lying along the road."

With tremendous bravery, the driver started the engine. He would find the exact spot, all right. It was where the Nat had come riding toward him on a white horse, near the clump of jacarandas. No doubt about it, the Nat had snatched Harry. They would be lucky if they found him at all. And if they did and tried to take him from the Nat, there would be trouble to pay. Before he put the bus in gear, Mr. Joe leaned over to Walter's side and opened the glove compartment, where he kept his emergency supplies. Inside was a small dollhouse-like structure, heavily carved, with an elaborate roof whose eaves curved up like my Persian slippers. It was a miniature Nat shrine. He made an offering of a cigarette, pushing it into a tiny door.

FORTY-FIVE MINUTES AWAY, Harry was trying to explain to the two military-garbed policemen why he was alone, wandering on a deserted stretch of the Burma Road at night. The younger one had his rifle pointed toward him. "ID," the older and stouter one demanded, using one of the few English terms he knew. The muzzle of his rifle moved slightly, like a sniffing wild dog.

Harry fumbled at his pocket. Was it good or bad to show an American passport? He had read once that in certain countries, it was a badge of honor. In others, it was an invitation to be shot. In those cases, pamphlets had warned, when asked for your nationality, say Canadian and smile jovially.

Perhaps he should explain that he was born in England. "British, British," he could say. "UK." It was the truth. But then, he realized, many Burmese had bad feelings about the British colonialists of yesteryear. The police might view his British origins as reason to pummel him into mincemeat, and then they'd continue the beating for his being American as well. All right, then, forget mentioning the British birthplace. He was sweating though the air was cool. What had he read about the military police? There were stories about people who protested against the government and were then made to disappear. What did they do to foreigners who crossed them? What were those human rights groups always making a noise about?

The younger, taller policeman grabbed the passport from Harry and looked at the blue front with gold letters, then inspected the photo. Then both policemen eyed Harry critically. The photo had been taken seven years before, when his hair was still dark and his jowl line more taut. The shorter policeman shook his head and grunted what sounded to Harry like a pronouncement that they should kill the foreigner and be done with it. Actually, he was cursing his colleague for leaving the liquor bottle in the pitch-black field. The younger policeman flipped though the pages, examining the various entry and exit stamps, to England, to the United States, to France with a new fling, to Bali with another, to Canada to ski at Whistler, to Bermuda to give a talk to a wealthy dog-fanciers' club, to England again, which was when his mum, a difficult woman who had hated every woman he had ever dated, was diagnosed with cancer. She refused all treatment, saying she wanted to go with dignity. After that, he made a trip to Australia and New Zealand for his doggie seminars. Then it was England, England, guilt-laden England, the last not for his mother's funeral but for her birthday, celebrated with the knowledge that there was no more evidence of the cancer. It was a bloody miracle. In fact, it was never cancer but only swollen lymph nodes, and she had just assumed it was the worst possible thing, because that was the kind of luck she had always had, she said. Harry had prepared himself for her death so well that he even made promises of all kinds to her, knowing he would never have to keep them. Now she was calling in the chips, reminding him that he had said he had always wanted to take her on a safari in Africa and do a special on wild dogs for his show with her providing commentary! Let's do it, she said. Good Lord! And now, perhaps there would be no African special to worry about. There would be no Harry after this. He pictured his mum weeping, saying she always had such bad luck, the bad luck to have had a son who was killed in Burma in a stupid misunderstanding about a passport.

The older policeman finally found the stamp for Myanmar immigration, punched at Muse just that morning. He showed it to his partner. They seemed to relax their grips on their rifles. The muzzle went down, and Harry wanted to cry with relief. He heard the older one utter a question. In doing his best at universal communication, Harry began to pantomime walking along the road, minding his own business, then the bus making *v-v-v-rroom* sounds. He sprinted in place, grabbed his knee, pointed to the ditch, and rubbed his shoulder. The policemen growled at each other in Burmese: "This foreign fool must be drunker than we are."

"Where were you going?" the taller policeman asked Harry in Burmese, which, of course, Harry did not understand. The stouter man snapped open a map and ordered Harry to point to his destination. What Harry saw looked like a treasure map for underground ants, a maze of trickling syrupy paths leading to seismographic tracings. Even if he had been able to read the map, he realized now he had no idea where the group was headed. That was the beauty of tour groups, wasn't it? You did not have to do a whit of planning. You went without any of the responsibilities of the trip: none of the transfers, the bookings, the hotels, the distances between them, or the time it would take to reach the next one. Of course, before he left San Francisco, he had reviewed the itinerary simply to see what delights awaited him. But who could remember the names of cities in a language he couldn't pronounce? Mandalay, that was the only place he recalled he would visit.

"Look," Harry said, trying again. "The guide is named Walter.

Waaahlll-tuh. And the bus says 'Golden Land Tour.' I was walking and fell, see? Boom!" He pointed to the ditch again, then to his shoulder and the red dirt smudged on his crisp white shirt. "And the bus, it went: *Vrrrooom!*" He stood on one foot, as if hailing a taxi. Wait, wait, stop, stop." He placed his hand over his brow, watching the imaginary bus disappear into oblivion, leaving him in this terrible predicament. He huffed and said, "Off they went. Bye-bye, shitheads."

"Shithead?" the younger man said, and started to laugh. He mumbled something to his partner, and they guffawed like madmen.

Harry recognized his cue. Years of studying animal behavior came into play. Observation. Analysis. Hypothesis: They recognized the American expletive. Like all young men, they loved these words. Of course they did. A love of cusswords was part of the chromosomal makeup of the male brain, no matter what race. Now all Harry needed to do was positively reinforce any glimmer of desired social behavior stemming from that response, and keep it coming.

When the men stopped chortling, Harry nodded and pointed down the highway. "Shitheads went that way. Me, here." He shook his head. "And they took off and left me here." With you two dickheads, he added to himself.

Five minutes later, Harry was walking with the young policemen to their command post, a small shack at the intersection of two roads. Since passage beyond checkpoints stopped at six p.m., there was no traffic to monitor. Once there, Harry had to rev himself up again to do the expletive routine with the new audience, two senior policemen. After much conviviality, Harry brought out a wad of bills and asked if it was possible to hire a car.

"Taxi?" he asked, with feigned innocence, as if one could summon a taxi in the middle of nowhere. "Taxi go zoom-zoom, down this road." "Taxi" was a word the men understood, as was Harry's leaving the booty on the table. They pointed to their police car outside.

They pointed to Harry, then to the two of them, and nodded. They spoke magnanimously in Burmese about ensuring Harry's safe return. The map was laid on the table near the money. They burst into rapid discussion about a careful plan of action that resembled a military deployment: "We take this route, you see, heading due south from latitude . . . Hey, what's our latitude?"

As Harry leaned forward to see, he saw the money palmed by the man in charge. The discussions became more animated: "To judge by the foreigner's clothes, he's probably staying at the best, the Golden Land Guesthouse. In any case, we'll do a recon on that and investigate."

As one man refolded the map, another offered Harry a cheroot to smoke along the way, and although Harry did not smoke, he deemed it unwise to refuse and thus compromise the level of camaraderie achieved so far. Ten minutes later, a small white police car was blazing down the road with its light spinning, sending fear into the hearts of all who heard its siren.

One of the fearful was the bus driver. He saw the police car approaching. It was white, white like the horse that the Nat rides on, bad luck. What calamity had happened? Was it before him or behind him? The police car flew by.

Twenty seconds later, Mr. Joe saw a flashing light in his rearview mirror. Walter looked back. The police car was right on their tail, like a butt-sniffing dog. Mr. Joe looked at Walter, and Walter, whose heart was pounding in his neck, forced himself to act calm and told him to pull over. As the bus eased to a stop, Walter gathered his composure, swept his hand into his pocket, extricated his identity card with the grace of one who had done it thousands of times, and then stepped out. Mr. Joe opened his glove compartment and tossed in three more cigarettes to the Nat shrine.

"Shitheads!" he heard Harry cry fondly as he leapt out of the backseat of the police car. Harry was pointing to them, grinning like a madman. The police, who moments before were laughing, now resumed their demeanor of morose rectitude. One held out his hand and twitched his fingers ever so slightly to command that Walter place his identity card in his palm. Walter also handed him documents, including the manifest with Harry's name. The policeman gave everything a stern going-over. He threw down the stack of documents and said in gruff tones: "Why do you let your customers wander around on their own? This is against the rules for tourism."

Walter did what he learned was best when dealing with the police. "Yes," he said. "A mistake."

"What if this foreigner had wandered into a restricted zone? Very bad business."

"Yes," Walter answered. "We're fortunate he didn't."

The police snorted. "The next time, you may not meet people as forgiving."

Once on board the bus, Harry waved merrily to his police comrades from the window as Mr. Joe pulled around to head back to Lashio. When they were a safe distance away, Harry hooted in victory.

Walter turned around to face Harry. "I apologize for leaving you behind. It was all such a rush, you see. . . ."

"No need to explain." Harry said merrily. He was still exhilarated, high on adrenaline. He had done it! He had used his expertise and fast reflexes to save his skin. It was amazing, when he thought about it. There they were, ready to fire, their fingers taut on the triggers, and he had deftly analyzed the situation, sent out calming signals, interpreted correctly when their hackles were no longer raised. It worked. Incredibly, it worked. Not since the early days of his career had he felt such excitement. Bing, bing, bing, it had all fallen into place. He sighed. That's what he had been missing in his work these past few years—the risks, the highs that come from taking a huge chance and then succeeding beyond your wildest imagination. He had to recover that sensation, give up the old routine that had grown so comfortable, predictable, lucrative, and dull.

Harry took in a big breath of resolve. And then he sniffed. "Good God, what's that smell? It's hideous."

Walter turned around again. "Some of the others have taken ill, I'm afraid. I suspect it's a touch of traveler's malady. We've done our best to make them comfortable."

"Who?" Harry asked. "Who's ill?"

"Mr. Moff and his boy. Mr. Bennie as well, and Miss Marlena. But her daughter is fine, not at all sick."

Marlena! Poor girl, no wonder she snapped at him. She was feeling dreadful. Well, then! The explanation cheered him. The situation between them was not as bad as he thought. So, what could he do to make her feel better? All the usual methods—the florist, big cozy hydrangeas, bubble bath ingredients—were clearly unavailable. A cup of tea with honey, perhaps? Offers of a massage. Suddenly he knew. The endorphins still surging through his brain allowed the miraculous answer to come wafting over him.

Words. He knew the power of words. He merely had to select the right ones that she needed to hear precisely this instant. If it succeeded with a bunch of bloodthirsty soldiers, it would be easy as pie with Marlena.

"Marlena, darling," he would say. "I'm back for you." He pictured her face, slightly feverish, damp with sensuality. Should he act doctorly, knowledgeable and assuring? Or should he take the role of lover, pledging that love was the antidote to whatever ailed her? Harry could be truly awful at romance when he tried.

Luckily, he lost all thought of Marlena as he gawked at the hotel. "What's a bloody menorah doing in a place like this?" Once shown to his room, he could hear through the thin walls that Marlena was in no condition whatsoever to have a visit from him, doctorly or amorous. Poor girl, she sounded wretched. So did the person in the room on the other side. It was like a symphony for the plague, all tubas, bassoons, and a repetitive refrain of squeaky flutes.

At midnight, Marlena finally ceased her visits to the bathroom. But then, one floor below, a rowdy group of Burmese men took over. They were smoking and shouting, stamping their feet and clanking bottles. The fumes of cheroots and cheap liquor rose to the rooms above. Marlena pounded the floor and shouted: "Shut up!" After a while, Harry spoke to her through the paper-thin wall. "Marlena, dearest, try to rest. I'll take care of this."

He went downstairs and knocked on the door of the offending group. A red-eyed man answered, his upper body weaving in circles as if he had just been punched. Fetid alcohol blasted from his slack mouth. Harry saw there were five men. They were gambling. Their blood alcohol must have been pure palm toddy, their brains saturated. What could he say that would possibly bring these men to reason?

A few minutes later, Harry was back in his room. He could hear the drunken men trying to be quiet as they exited downstairs. They tripped on a lamp cord, broke a windowpane, cleared their throats of mucus with motorcycle-throttle intensity, and lobbed spittle onto whatever stood in their way. In their hands were a total of fifty American dollars, their surprise winnings, courtesy of Harry Bailley.

They were not leaving as a favor to Harry. He had suggested only that they be quiet. On their own accord, they decided to sneak out before they had to pay their hotel and liquor bill. It was a very bad decision on their part. Theft in the military-run Myanmar is a serious matter. You would be extremely lucky to get away with it, foolish to try. And weaving down the road does not improve your chances of avoiding bad luck.

Ten miles down the road, they ran their car into a shallow ditch to avoid a Nat on a white horse. It sprang into the middle of the road from a clump of jacaranda trees.

Shortly after that, two military policemen, one tall, one stout, arrived with rifles aimed at the men's heads. "It was a Nat," the men kept saying. The police examined documents, confiscated fifty American dollars, two hotel blankets and five towels, and pushed the hotel thieves onto a truck bed. The truck sped away, taking them down a black ribbon of road that soon disappeared.

·8·

It Was Not Just
a Card Trick

The waters of Inle Lake are blue and so shallow you can see the bottom on a cloudless day. This is where ladies bathe their newborn babies. This is where the dead float with their eyes toward the sky. This was where my friends came the morning of Christmas Eve.

They were relieved to have left Lashio, where they had spent time recovering from illness. To their delight, Walter had found an opening at a resort on Inle Lake. There they could bide their time in luxury until they picked up on their original itinerary in Burma. A bus from Helo airport brought them to the busy dock in Nyaung Shwe Town. While waiting for their luggage to be unloaded, Rupert tucked his paperback under his arm, fetched out his newly acquired caneball, and shuttled it back and forth between his knees. When he tired of this, he bounced the basketball, leaping up and pretending he was aiming for a hoop. Next, restless as usual, he fished out from his backpack a deck of cards, which he shuffled in midair, creating a flapping-pigeon sound.

A circle of people formed and grew by the second. "Pick a card, any card," Rupert told Dwight and Roxanne. The locals watched closely as Roxanne reached in and pulled out the king of clubs. "Show everyone your card," Rupert said. "You know what it is? . . . Good, don't forget it. We're going to put it back in the deck. Now pick another card, any of them. . . . Good, the two of diamonds . . . Show it to everyone. . . . That one, put it behind your back. . . . You have it there, right? You're sure? Okay, we're going to shuffle the cards." The cards flew with the beating of wings.

"Things are not always what they seem." Rupert intoned. *"And what you choose is not always what you get. Others may choose for you."* The timbre of his voice had changed completely. It was deeper, more resonant, that of a much older man. He had been reading a classic tome for magicians, *The Expert at the Card Table*, and he knew that with illusions, the skill is in the hands, the eye, and the showmanship.

Rupert held the deck facedown and with one sweep fanned the cards out in an arc.

"In magical lands, magic can happen. But only if we believe." He looked at Roxanne with a face that was no longer that of a boy but that of someone many years older, a knowledgeable man of the ages. His eyes were fixed on hers, not breaking away for even a second. *"And if we believe, the impossible can happen. What we wish to have will manifest. What we wish to hide turns invisible. . . ."* The way he spoke gave her an eerie feeling, but she passed it off as too much sun.

"I believe," Rupert said, like a boy again. "Do you?"

Roxanne laughed. "Sure," she said, and rolled her eyes at Dwight standing next to her.

"Touch one," Rupert said. She did so, a card near the middle. Rupert flipped it. "Is this your card?"

"No," Dwight answered for Roxanne.

"Are you sure?" Rupert said.

"Wrong card," Dwight said. "You're busted."

Roxanne was staring at the card and shaking her head. "I don't believe it," she said. Dwight looked. It was the two of diamonds. She whipped out the card that she had held behind her back. *The king of clubs*. People roared. Dwight grabbed the card and felt it.

Three boatmen had been in the crowd, watching. They saw the young man manifest the card. He could make things invisible and make them come back. And he had the Black Book. They knew that book, the Important Writings that the Older Brother had lost, and thereby caused their downfall. They had been waiting for a hundred years to get it back. And finally he had come, the young man with the cards. He was the Reincarnated One, the Younger White Brother, Lord of Nats.

The boatmen quietly discussed the matter. The Younger White Brother gave no indication he had seen them. They would approach him soon. And what about the others he was with? Were they his retinue? A few moments later, they approached Walter with a fare low enough to beat out other boatmen who had water taxis waiting to be filled with tourists.

At first, I was confused. So many thoughts and so much excitement was exchanged among these boatmen. Reincarnated One? I have received many new minds since my change, but I don't yet possess the Mind of Eternity. I sensed only this. They believed Rupert was a deity who could save them. He could manifest miracles. He could make troubles disappear. Soon, three longboats carrying my twelve colleagues, their guide, and excessive amounts of luggage sliced through the waters of Inle Lake. I was the invisible bowsprit on the lead boat. The ride would have been idyllic if not for the chill air and the rat-a-tat drone of the outboard motors. But my friends were happy, their teeth gritted against the wind.

The pilot in the lead boat was a handsome young man in a checked longyi the colors of assorted mushrooms. He was the one who had led the discussion on the dock, insisting what they must do. He was called Black Spot by his friends and family, a nickname given for the birthmark on his hand. As in China, such nicknames were meant to be unflattering, a ruse to discourage the gods from snatching babies away. But in Burma one could get stuck with a new nickname to reflect a change in circumstances or reputation. Black Spot's two companions, Fishbones, who was rather skinny, and Salt, who had a salty tongue for being a gossip, piloted the other two longboats.

Black Spot sat at the rear, one hand on the rudder. He squinted, thinking of the sick child he had left at home. Only three years old, and already she could see the goodness in people. He pictured her dark eyes, bright and darting as they had been before the sudden, frightening change. Her body had begun to shake, as if to get rid of the intruder ghost. Then she stared upward as the dead do, seeing nothing. And her mouth, out of that came the babble of someone tortured.

He had to leave her while she was still sick. The twin gods had told him to return to the town. Salt and Fishbones assured him many times: She will get better, of course she will. The twin gods' grandmother had thrown the chicken bones, examined the feathers, and spilled the rice. She had told Black Spot that it was his own mother, confused by her green death, who had wandered in the night and come to the little girl's bed mat by mistake. She had lain in her soul and gone to sleep. She meant no harm. She loved Black Spot's daughter like nothing else in the world. Don't worry, Salt and Fishbones said, the shaman has tied your daughter's wrists and bound her to earth. He has done a ceremony to remove your mother's green ghost. And your wife has been giving your daughter the leaf tincture, putting it under her tongue and on the moist parts of her inner cheeks. Every hour she does this. So you see, everything has been done.

Black Spot's little daughter was at home with his wife in the forested high hills, in A Place with No Name. In the winter months, he visited only when the rains fell or when trouble brought the military and closed off the area to tourists. Then no planes came to Helo airport bearing visitors to Inle Lake. There were no customers to fill the water taxis and take to the far side. At times like this, Black Spot and his fellow boatmen went to see his cousin Grease, who worked in a shop repairing tourist buses.

"Hey, brother, can you take me up the hill?" Black Spot would ask, and Grease never denied him, for he knew Black Spot would bring supplies for his family as well—fermented shrimp paste, noodles, peanuts, a hundred spices, the foodstuffs that a jungle did not yield. Black Spot would also bring whatever equipment he and his fellow boatmen and their secret supporters had managed to obtain through cooperative theft. Grease would choose a vehicle that had been repaired, and they would drive east, away from the lake, down a scarce-used road that took them to a secret opening in what seemed to be impenetrable thickets. Here they wound their way up into an area with the taller trees of the rainforest, until the canopy above allowed only meager slices of sunlight. At the edge of a sinkhole, they stopped. The depression ran up and down a cleft in the mountain, created by the collapse of karst roofs covering an ancient river deep in the earth. Grease would stop the vehicle, and Black Spot would jump out, ready to cross the chasm to No Name Place.

None of the people of Nyaung Shwe Town knew that this was the true home of the three boatmen and the mechanic. The people in the lowlands referred to anyone who lived up there as "people of the jungle." They might have been isolated tribes, bandits, or the pitiful remnants of insurgents, about whom it was difficult to speak, except with a quiet sigh of relief that you were not among them.

Tomorrow, Black Spot and his tribal brothers would return home, perhaps for good, because today the course of life had changed. The Younger White Brother was here, and as he had promised during his last visit on earth, he would save them. He could manifest weapons. He could make the tribe invisible. They would then leave No Name Place, walk openly without being shot, until they reached a patch of land, the promised land, just big enough to grow the food they needed. There they would live in peace, and no outsiders would cause them trouble, and they would cause no troubles to them. Their only desire was to live peaceably among themselves, in harmony with the land, the water, and the Nats, who would be pleased by how much the tribe respected them. It could all happen, thanks to the return of the Younger White Brother.

THE AIR AT THE DOCK had been warm, but as the three boats sped over the cool lake, the passengers began to feel chilled. At the front of my boat, where the prow narrowed, Moff's ponytail whipped wildly and smacked Dwight's face. Harry and Marlena snuggled against each other, Harry's jacket draped over their chests and bent knees. Rupert sat toward the rear with Walter, and although he was cold, he resisted putting on the windbreaker his dad had handed him. He faced the wind like a god, not knowing that was what he would soon become. On the other passenger boat, Esmé and Bennie huddled together, with Pup-pup bundled between them. Wyatt and Wendy held the conical hat in front of themselves like a shield.

At times, the three boats appeared to be racing against one another. "Ahoy!" Vera shouted as her boat accelerated, and when her friends turned to look from their boat, she snapped a photo. What a good idea. Others reached into bags to pull out cameras. Beyond them, on the banks of the river, children waved next to their hunched-over mothers, who were washing clothes in the shallows.

Walter leaned toward the boatman to give directions in Burmese: "Take the detour through the market." Unbeknownst to Walter and the others, Black Spot actually spoke a fair amount of English, but he always found it to his advantage to pretend he knew none and to eavesdrop on conversations. Never show a weapon before you need to use it. His father had taught him that. Bitter words to recall, for his father had had no weapons when he needed them. Neither had Walter's. . . .

BLACK SPOT HAD GROWN UP a sharp and curious child, and he learned his English by absorbing it from the tourists who said and did the same things every day. The same questions and requests, disappointments and complaints, photos and bargains, appetites and illnesses, thank-yous and good-byes. They spoke only to the guide. No one ever expected a child to understand.

He had grown up among tourists. Unlike the Karen tribes who stayed in the hills, his family was Pwo Karen; he had spent his early life on the plains. His family lived in a town about seventy miles from Nyaung Shwe, and they were comfortably situated although not well-to-do. His father and uncles did not farm, as most Karen people did. They were in the transportation business: the transportation of tourists in longboats and the repair of tourist buses. Their women sold shawls and shoulder bags woven with their special knot. They found it easier to take their chances with the whims of tourists rather than those of monsoons.

Life was good until the purges came. After that, there was nothing to do except flee into the jungle, high up, where it was so thick only wild things grew. When the purges stopped, Black Spot and his friends and cousin went quietly to the town of Nyaung Shwe, where they were not known. They procured black-market identity cards of dead people with good reputations. After that they lived two ways: in the open life of the dead, and in the hidden life of the living.

THE NOSES of the longboats pointed left, toward a canal leading to a clump of teak buildings on stilts above the water, their roofs steep-pitched with rusty corrugated tin.

"We are headed toward a small settlement, one of two hundred along Inle Lake," Walter explained. "We won't be stopping here, but I wanted you to have a quick look-see at what you might find in this area, these hamlets tucked away in small channels. Unless you've lived here all your life like our boatmen, it's rather easy to become confused and lost. The lake is shallow, and the hyacinth grows by the acre each week and shifts around like landmasses. It's been quite a problem for these farmers and fishermen. As their livelihoods are choked off, they depend more and more on tourism, an industry that is, I'm afraid, not very dependable, subject to changes of weather, politics, and such."

Bennie took this comment as a personal challenge not to disappoint the natives. "We'll buy lots," he promised.

When the boats drew closer to the settlement, the pilots eased up on the outboards until the noise fell to a soft clicking. Side by side, the two passenger boats edged water gardens bright with tomatoes and glided under wooden walkways, and were soon upon a floating market, where dozens of canoes laden with food and trinkets sped toward the tourist boats like hockey players after the puck. The canoes, ten to twelve feet long, had shallow hulls of hand-carved light-weight wood. The vendors crouched at one end, overseeing their stocks of woven bags, low-quality jade necklaces, bolts of cloth, and crudely rendered wooden Buddhas. Each vendor beseeched my friends to look his way. Onshore were the vendors who sold more practical goods to the local people: yellow melons, long-stalked greens, tomatoes, golden and red spices, clay pots of pickles and shrimp paste. The colors of the women's sarongs were those of a happy people—pink, turquoise, orange. The men squatted in their dark-colored longyis, the ever-present cheroots clenched between their teeth.

"What's with them?" Moff said. On the dock were a dozen soldiers in camo-gear with AK-47 rifles slung over their shoulders. Heidi immediately felt nervous. She was not the only one. It was an ominous sight. The group noticed that the locals paid no attention to the soldiers, as if they were as invisible as I was. Or were the local people watching as cats do?

"They are soldiers," Walter said. "Nothing to be concerned about. I can assure you there has not been any trouble with insurgents in quite some time. This area—much of southern Shan State, actually— was once known as a red zone, a hot spot for rebel warfare, and no tourists were allowed then. Now it's been downgraded to white, which means all is perfectly safe. The insurgents have fled high into the hills. There aren't many left, and those who are hiding are harmless. They're afraid to come out."

For good reason, Black Spot said to himself.

"Then why all the rifles?" Moff asked.

Walter laughed slightly. "To remind people to pay their taxes. That's what everyone fears now, new taxes."

"What are insurgents?" Esmé asked Marlena in the nearby boat.

I noticed that Black Spot was listening intently, his eyes darting toward the daughter, then the mother.

"Rebels," Marlena explained. "People against the government."

"Is that good or bad?"

Marlena hesitated. She had read sympathetic reports of rebels who were fighting for democracy. They claimed that their family members had been slaughtered, the daughters raped, the sons enslaved, their homes burned. But what could she say so she would not alarm her daughter?

Esmé read her mother's face. "Oh, I know. It *depends*." She sniffed knowingly. "With everything, it depends." She stroked the puppy in her lap. "Except you, Puppy-luppy. You're always good."

"Hey, Walter," Wendy called loudly. "So what do you feel about the military dictatorship?"

Walter knew questions like this were inevitable. The tourists, Americans especially, wanted to know where he stood on political issues, whether he was adversely affected, and if he supported "The Lady"—he was not supposed to say her name out loud, but he did from time to time when he was with tourists. In former days, anyone who said her name with praise could be taken away, as his father had been. After The Lady won the Nobel Peace Prize, the camera flashes shone on Burma. The world asked, Where is Myanmar? For once, a few people knew. Walter nurtured a secret hope that Aung San Suu Kyi and her supporters in other countries could actually drive out the regime. But the years went by, and sometimes the junta released her from house arrest only to put her back soon after. They made overtures to talk about a transition to democracy. And everyone would be heartened that the bully had finally softened. But then they would say: Talks of democracy? What talks are those? It was a sport, that's what Walter finally realized. Let the democracy lovers score a point, then take it back. Let them have another point, then take it back. Let them think they are in the game, and watch them spin in circles. He now knew there would be no change. The children born after 1989 would never know a country named Burma, would never know a government other than SLORC. His future children would grow up with an obeisance to fear. Or would they sense there was another kind of life that they could be living? Was there an innate knowledge that would tell them that?

He looked at Wendy and took a deep breath. "The poor," Walter began, measuring each word, "especially those who are not well educated, feel things are better now than in years past. What I mean is, while Myanmar is among the poorest countries in the world, the situation is, shall we say, more stable, or so the people feel. You see, they don't want any more trouble. And perhaps they are grateful that the government has given them little gifts from time to time. At one school near here, an important military officer bought the head teacher a tape player. That was enough to make people happy. And we now have paved roads from one end of the country to the other. To most people, this is great and good progress, something they can see and touch. And there is also less bloodshed, because the rebels, most of them, have been contained—"

"You mean killed," Wendy inserted.

Walter did not flinch. "Some died, some are in prison, others have gone to Thailand or are in hiding."

"And how do you see it?" Harry asked. "Is Myanmar better off than old Burma?"

"There are many factors. . . ."

"It depends," Esmé said.

Walter nodded. "Let me think how to put this. . . ." He thought about his father, the journalist and university professor who had been taken away and presumably killed. He considered his job, a desirable one that supported his grandfather and his mother, who never spoke to each other. He thought about his sisters, who needed a clear record to attend university. Yet he was a man of morals who despised the regime for what had happened to his father. He would never accept it. On occasion, he met secretly with former schoolmates whose families had suffered similar fates, and they talked of small personal rebellions, and what would happen to their country if no one ever again spoke out in opposition. He had once wanted to study to become a journalist, but was told that such studies would lead only to a degree in death—death of the mind if not the body. You could not write about any bad news, so what was left to write?

The girl was correct. It depends. But how could he tell these Americans that? They were here so briefly. They would never be affected. What would they gain by his telling the truth? What did he risk losing if he did? And as he gazed out on the lake, he saw a way to answer.

"Look there." He pointed. "There—the man standing in the boat."

The travelers craned their necks and uttered cries of delight upon seeing one of the famous Intha fishermen of Inle Lake. My friends retrieved their cameras, making ripping sounds as they pulled open the Velcroed cases. They cooed happily as they looked through the viewfinders.

Walter continued: "See how he stands on one leg while the other is curled around a paddle? This allows him to glide as he uses his hands to fish. It seems impossible. Yet he does this effortlessly."

"Niche adaptation!" Roxanne and Dwight simultaneously called to each other from their separate boats.

"I'd fall into the lake," Bennie said.

Walter went on: "That, in essence, is how my friends and I sometimes feel. We have adapted so that we can effect this one-legged stance and not fall over. We can dream of fish and propel ourselves forward, but sometimes our nets are empty, our rowing leg tires, and we are just drifting with the current, along with the weeds. . . ."

My friends had already forgotten the question. They were contorting their heads so that they were best positioned for capturing this oddly beautiful scene. Only Black Spot heard Walter's answer.

FLOATING ISLAND RESORT was only a year old, modeled after its competition, the highly successful Golden Island Cottages and its sister hotels. It was the subsidiary of a large tribe, which had agreed to a cease-fire with the Myanmar military junta in exchange for a stake in the hospitality industry. This latest resort had the additional advantage of Western management and expertise in comfort, decor, and service, or so the brochures proclaimed.

This management came in the robust form of a Swiss German expatriate named Heinrich Glick, who knew what amenities appealed to foreign tastes. As the longboats drew to the dock, uniformed boys in matching green-checked longyis welcomed the passengers and speedily unloaded their luggage. Names were called out, cottage numbers quickly assigned, and the designated bellhops grabbed keys attached to small floats. The bellhops earned their keep solely from the generous tips that Western tourists gave, and each tried to outdo the others in carrying the greatest amount of luggage.

Heinrich appeared on the dock. When I first met him years ago, he had been a handsome man, with thick, wavy blond locks combed back, a smooth voice, a sophisticated air, and a Teutonic jawline. Now he was portly, with a pouchlike neck, thin legs, sparse hair, pink peekaboo scalp, and Windex-blue eyes rimmed in red. He wore a collarless white shirt of loose-weave linen over yellow washed-silk trousers.

"Welcome, welcome," he saluted his guests. "Welcome to paradise. You've had a pleasant trip, I trust. A bit brisk, *ja? Brrrrr.* All right, then, go admire your rooms, and after you are settled in, please join me in the Great Hall for a toast with bubbles." He gestured behind him, toward a tall wooden building with many windows. He looked at his watch. "Let us say noon-ish, with scrumptious lunch to follow. Run along now and freshen up." He shooed them away with his hands as if they were a flock of pigeons. "Ta-ta! See you soon."

My friends and their bellhops scattered toward the various oiled teak walkways that fanned out from the dock like the legs of an insect. Cries of delight echoed as they approached their accommodations: "This is more like it." "Just like tiki huts." "How cute is that?" The bungalows were indeed rustically charming.

Bennie stepped into his. The interior was of pleated rattan, the floors covered with hemp mats, the low twin beds adorned with simple white linens and enveloped by gauzy mosquito netting. Oh, he loved that last touch, so tropically romantic, reminiscent of former nights of sweaty tangled limbs. On the walls were painted renditions of celestial creatures and carvings on bone, the sort of mass-produced native art that passed as chicly primitive. The bathroom was a nice surprise, spacious and free of mildew, the floor covered with a plain white tile, and the shower built a step lower and separated by a half-wall.

In Heidi's room, the bellhop opened the windows. They lacked screens, and nearby were coils of insecticidal incense and pots of citronella, all signs that alerted her to the fact that the stagnant waters beneath the walkways were mosquito breeding grounds. One door over, Marlena and Esmé were all oohs and ahs over the views of the lake, marveling that this place truly was paradise, a Shangri-La.

Harry was even more pleased than the others. His bungalow was at the far end of pier five, and its secluded location made for a perfect love nest. Oh, look. The resort had thoughtfully provided lemon-scented candles, a romantic touch. He went outside to the small porch. It held a couple of teak chairs with adjustable reclining backs—fantastic, ideal for lying together to do a bit of moon gazing and set the mood for an exquisite night of lovemaking.

Marlena and Esmé had stepped out of their bungalow just two piers away from him. A porter who looked to be about the size of Esmé had arrived, dragging two mammoth suitcases, a duffel slung from each shoulder. Harry waved to catch Marlena's eye, and she eagerly waved back. They were like two lovebirds flapping their wings. The message was clear: Tonight was the night.

A half-hour later in the Great Hall, Heinrich poured champagne into plastic tumblers. "To pleasure and beauty, to new friends and lasting memories," he said warmly. Soon he would bestow on them pet names—Our Great Leader, Our Lovely Lady, Our Nature Lover, Our Scientist, Our Doctor, Our Resident Genius, Our Roving Photographer, and the like—the same stock descriptions he assigned to all guests to make them feel special. He never remembered actual names.

Heinrich had managed a five-star beach resort in Thailand for a number of years—I went there twice myself—but then it was discovered that three tourists over the previous six months had died not of misadventure, heart attack, and drowning, respectively, as the death certificates had indicated, but of jellyfish stings. The place was closed down after the demise of the third victim, the son of an American congresswoman. After that, Heinrich surfaced in some directorial capacity for a luxury hotel in Mandalay. I ran into him there, and he acted as if I were his long-lost friend. He called me "Our Dear Art Professor." And then he wrote down the name of a restaurant he described as the "utmost." His moist palm encircled my elbow, rubbing it as he might a lover's, as he told me in confidential tones that he would inform the maître d' that my companions and I were coming. "How many of you are there? Six? Perfect! The best table with the best view shall be reserved, and I shall join you and would be honored to have you as my guests."

How could we refuse? How bad could a free lunch be? We went. He was unctuous and jovial as we perused the menu. He called out the specialties we should order, and to hell with the bloody cost, it was his treat. By the second course, he was blustery and loudly sentimental about Grindelwald, his birthplace, it seemed. He began singing a Swiss German yodeling song, "Mei Biber Hendel," that sounded like a chicken clucking. A table full of Thai businessmen seated nearby cast sideways glances and made "tut-tut" comments in low voices. The end was signaled by his head lowering until his forehead rested on the table, and that was where it remained until waiters arrived and lifted him by his armpits, then dragged him to his waiting car and driver. The waiter and maître d' shrugged regretfully when I informed them that Mr. Glick had said he would pay. Thus, I was stuck with the bill, a rather costly one, given the number of people, and the quantity and caliber of alcohol that he ordered for all and which he largely consumed. But at the hotel the next day, Heinrich apologized profusely for his "sudden illness" and hasty departure. He said he would make up for the lunch bill by deducting an equivalent amount from our hotel charges. "How much was it?" he asked, and I rounded the number down a bit and he rounded it up with a sweep of his pen. In this manner, he ingratiated himself to his clients, dined lavishly free of charge, and pilfered from his employer.

As you can see, he was a slippery charmer and a thoroughly dishonest man. He once told me he had managed the Mandarin Oriental in Hong Kong, a claim I found hard to believe, given that he knew not a whit of Cantonese. "What's good to eat there?" I asked, baiting him. And he said, "Sweet-and-sour pork," the favorite of those who know nothing of Chinese food and are unwilling to try anything else. So I knew he was full of poppycock, and it was maddening that he showed absolutely no shame about his lies. He never lost the gleaming smile.

Some of the other tour leaders told me he was not really a hotelier at all. He worked for the CIA, they said. He was one of their best operatives. The accent was faked, the Swiss nationality a sham. He was an American, Henry Glick, from Los Angeles, the land of actors. In the early days, when he first came to Asia, he listed his occupation as "waste management consultant." On other visas, he said he was a "water purification engineer." "Waste" was code for CIA targets, don't you see, people they wanted to get rid of. "Purification" was code for filtering information through sources. For a spy, a position in the hospitality industry was ideal, since in this capacity, or rather as the incapacitated host, he wined and dined all sorts of government officials in Thailand, China, and Burma, and gave off the impression he was merely a bumbling drunkard, too soused to be of any threat as they spoke of under-the-table deals when he was under the table himself.

All this I heard. But I found it too incredible. If I knew of the story, then wouldn't the people he was supposedly spying on have caught wind of it as well? He would have been ousted by the Myanmar government long before now. No, no, he could not possibly be a spy. Besides, I had smelled the alcohol on his breath. How do you fake that? I watched him drink the "bubbles" until he nearly burst of carbonated blood. Then again, he had to be up to something to have managed all these years to hang on to a job. Granted, his career had taken him to the backwaters of Asia. For a hotel executive, this was clearly a demotion.

Strangely enough, only Esmé detected early on that Heinrich was a phony. The child was innocent yet astute beyond her years, as I had been when I was her age. She saw how easily her mother was duped into liking him. "Our Ravishing Beauty," he called her. Harry became "Our English Gentleman," and a bit later, when someone informed Heinrich that Harry had a popular television show on dogs, he dubbed Harry "Our Famous TV Star," which pleased him a great deal.

Heinrich, however, was not skilled at beguiling children. He smiled too broadly and spoke as many adults do to infants. "Is your tummy hungry?" Esmé watched him suspiciously and saw the pattern: how he always had some excuse to touch the women lightly on their arms, press a palm on the men's backs, compliment each person in private with, "You look like a seasoned traveler, different from the others, a person who seeks more deeply when in another's land. Am I right?"

Esmé was carrying Pup-pup in a nylon sack. A light scarf was draped over the top, and the puppy was content to curl up in this improvised womb, that is, until she needed to relieve herself and tried to climb out. Then she let forth a yelp. When Heinrich glanced toward Esmé, she pretended to sneeze. The pup squeaked again, and again Esmé pretended to sneeze. She headed for the restroom, where she pulled out a few pages of the teen fashion magazine she had brought, and laid these on the tile floor. She put Pup-pup on top and urged her to "go potty," and soon enough the puppy squatted and the pages darkened. Pup-pup was very smart for being just a baby.

When Esmé returned, Heinrich greeted her with glazed eyes: "Ah, so Our Little Pipsqueak has come back to the fold." She gave him her best blank face, then hurried to find her mother seated at a table. Lunch was about to be served, *tout compris*, except for the wine and beer, and, as they would learn later, the overpriced "welcome" champagne they had downed with their gracious host.

Over lunch, Heinrich joked that they had better not gripe about the food and service here. "'Tis all owned by a formerly fierce tribe that once settled disagreements by having you over for a *tête-à-tête* and carrying off your *tête*. What's more, they receive protection from their friends, the SLORC soldiers. So you see, your satisfaction is guaranteed, no complaints. Ha, ha, ha."

"No complaints here," Bennie said. "Food's great."

"What do you mean, protection?" Moff said. "Like the Mafia kind?"

Heinrich looked around as if to check that no one among his staff was listening. "Not exactly." He rubbed his fingers, the sign for filthy lucre. "If you help others, you receive merit, a bit of good karma. Oh, come now, don't act so surprised. It's a tradition in other countries, yours as well." He clapped Moff on the shoulder. "Isn't it so, my friend? *Ja?*" He laughed uproariously at his own comments. Then he added, "Actually, yes, everyone has become quite friendly, quite, quite. When business is good, relations are good. The past is old business—*fffttt!*—forgotten, time to move ahead to the future." He paused and reconsidered. "Well. Of course nothing is ever completely forgotten, unless you're dead, but we can *selectively* ignore, can't we? He cupped his hand near his mouth, then silently formed the syllables: "Be si-lent."

As I said, he was a slippery man. Wait another minute and he would have changed his position another one hundred eighty degrees, then another, until you had gone in a circle, and all by his reporting differing, vague innuendoes. Even now, I felt I did not understand some essential aspects of this man. I couldn't. He had thrown a barrier up. Or had I? In Buddhism it is said you must have complete compassion to have complete understanding. I, on the other hand, wished that the slick Mr. Glick would fall face-first into the water. I don't suppose that would qualify me as compassionate. Suffice it to say, I did not know at the time all there was to know about Heinrich Glick.

AT ONE-FIFTEEN, my friends walked down to the dock, where the three boatmen were huddled and talking excitedly. When they saw their passengers, they quickly hopped into the longboats to assist them as they boarded. Heinrich waved to his guests. "Dinner is seven-ish. Ta-ta!"

"It's annoying that he uses that British affectation so much," Bennie said. "Ta-ta! Ta-ta! It's such a colonial throwback."

"It's actually a Burmese expression," Walter said. "The British conscripted it along with other things."

"Really?" Bennie thought about this. Ta-ta. The sound of it now seemed more genteel, less arrogant. He sounded it out, feeling the tip of his tongue dance behind his upper teeth. Ta-ta. It was lovely, as a matter of fact.

"This afternoon," Walter said, "we're going to a village that is holding a fair for the hundredth anniversary of one of its stupas, those dome-shaped shrines you've seen. There will be a big food market, plenty of games and competitions, gambling as well, though

I warn you, no one wins. And the children from the local school are going to perform onstage. Each class has practiced for months. A special arrangement—I believe you call them skits in the States. Not to worry, it is quite all right to take photos."

The fact that Walter said not to worry made Wendy wonder whether she should. Each time she had seen the military police, she had become afraid, thinking that her secret mission was evident on her guilty-looking face, and they might spot her as an American insurgent. There was no way she would try to talk to anyone with those creeps around. Not that anyone could speak English, anyway.

She whispered to Wyatt that she was sleepy and that maybe they should stay behind and take a "nice long nap" together. "I have some Nō-Dōz," he offered. Wendy felt rebuffed. This was his answer to her offering of love and wanton lust?

The two longboats motored into the lake, cut to the right, and soon wove in and out of clumps of hyacinth and floating vegetable gardens. A small river appeared and they took this tranquil route past a shrubby shoreline, where women drew buckets of water and poured them over their children.

I have long held the opinion that the Burmese are among the cleanest people in the world. While they may live in conditions that are impossible to keep spotless, they bathe themselves twice a day, often by the river or lake, for there are no private baths for most. The women wade in with their sarongs, the men in their longyis. The younger children are not fettered by clothes. Bathing is a beautiful necessity, a moment of peace, a cleansing of body and spirit. And afterward, the bather is able to remain cooled through the heat of the day and is dry by the time the cooking fires are lit.

Contrast this to the Tibetans. They bathe once a year and make a big ceremony about it. Then again, the weather there is not conducive to more frequent dousing. I admit to having let my usual habits slide when I was there, in places with inadequate heat and sometimes no running water.

And just so you don't think I am being prejudiced, let me be the first to say the Chinese are also less than fastidious, unless they are well-off and can afford modern conveniences. I am speaking, of course, of the rural Chinese in China, the China under Communism. Cleanliness among comrades has become less valued than saving water. I have observed the greasy hair, matted into whorls and cowlicks formed during sleep. And the clothes—heavens!—they are impregnated with months of fried cooking smells. Theirs is the smell of pragmatism, of getting things done, with cleanliness being a luxury.

Don't misunderstand me. I am not obsessive about cleanliness, not like the Japanese, who soak in a deep tub of near-boiling water. I never did care for that alternative, to be scaldingly clean, your skin sloughing off in your own soup, the rest of you bleached to the bone. Why, even their toilets are equipped to spray your bottom with warm water and then dry it with wafts of air, so that you might never have to touch that part of your anatomy again. This strikes me as abnormally antiseptic.

And while I'm on the topic, I can't say that cleanliness is renowned among the British I have known. Since recorded time, the Chinese and Burmese have made unkind asides about them. Theirs is a spit-and-polish kind of clean, a shiny shoe, a scrubbed face, while parts unseen are left untended.

The French are so-so, in my estimation, though I don't have a tremendous amount of experience here, since they are a people not known to willingly mingle with others who do not speak their language perfectly. But you do have to wonder why they invented so many perfumes.

Whereas many Germans, despite their tendency toward neatness, emit a mustiness that is overpoweringly strong, the men especially, and they don't seem to notice. Take Heinrich, for example. He had a very strong odor, a mix of alcohol and calculated mistruths, I think. All his indiscretions rose from his pores.

As for Americans, they are a composite of all the smells, good and bad. And they, too, are inordinately fond of their various deodorants, aftershave lotions, perfumes, and room fresheners. Things that stink, they cover up. Even if they don't stink, they cover up the smell and make it unnatural. But I don't think it's cultural as much as target marketing.

This is only my opinion.

A SHORELINE AND DOCK came into view. The longboats cut their motors and drifted in, and a dozen hands reached over to help pull the boats close to the pier so the passengers could disembark.

"You are about to encounter many interesting things to buy," Walter said. "Bargaining is completely expected. But let me offer this rule of thumb: Set in your mind what you wish to pay, then name a price that is half that, and work up to it during the bargaining."

As soon as their feet touched ground, peddlers ran up to them. "Lucky money, you give me lucky money," they all shouted. In their palms were tiny jade animals.

"They believe the first sale of the day brings them lucky money," Walter explained.

Bennie cast a doubtful look. "How could we be their first sale of the day? It's nearly two in the afternoon." No wonder he was hungry. He rummaged in his backpack for a Snickers bar.

"You very well may be," Walter replied. "I don't believe they are lying."

"Why not?" Dwight said.

"That is not the nature of Burmese people. It would not serve them well."

"It's the karma thing," Heidi said.

"Yes, exactly, karma. If you buy their goods, they receive luck and you receive merit."

Vera considered this, and then gave in to the "lucky money" plea of a young woman. She bought a little jade frog. She held it up to the sun, then tucked it into the pocket of her caftan. Was the frog symbolic of something? Was it an astrology sign, a virtue? What could it mean, an animal that was green and warty, that waited all day to eat a fly? She laughed. It would be a reminder, she told herself, to be more patient when things didn't go the way she expected. Had she known what awaited her, she would have bought a dozen.

Moments later, we were among clusters of folks who were walking along the riverbank, making their way from other villages. We passed contests with girls skipping rope, boys in a three-legged race, and younger children running backward. A loudspeaker called encouragement and announced the winners. Three students, the top in their school, also went up to the stage to receive colorful certificates. To celebrate the contest winners, twenty boys and girls, all of them heavily made-up with eyeliner and bright red lipstick, lined up in neat rows and sang to a karaoke tape of the Supremes' "Baby Love."

Soon my friends had entered a bazaar crowded with stalls. Giant woks bubbled with oil, fried dough bobbing to the top. Baskets were heaped with vegetable-filled rolls. In one corner, a craps game was under way, observed by red-eyed men in dusty jackets and trousers. One man rolled a pair of gigantic foam dice. The men stood and stared, then sat down and pushed more money forward, fervently hoping that their luck would change with the next roll.

I hovered about, watching my friends meander into the market, pursuing their own idiosyncrasies. Rupert soon took off in his own direction and may not have heard his father call out that he should meet at the pier in an hour. Marlena set about buying little snacks that she thought Esmé and Harry would enjoy. Esmé carried Pup-pup in her pouch and fed her bits of roasted meat. Harry watched a hustler break a brick over a worthless piece of blue glass; he then gladly forked over the equivalent of fifty dollars so he might surprise Marlena later that night with this proclaimed "genuine sapphire." Vera, whose kindhearted face and bejeweled fingers had become legend in the market, continued to attract sellers with trinkets calling to her to give them "lucky money." Heidi looked at herbal remedies for bites of all kinds. "Bzzzzz," she said to a merchant who did not understand her request for an insecticide. She made a loopy dive with one finger toward her arm. "Bzzzzz," she repeated. Ah, yes, yes, the merchant understood at last. Next she made a two-pronged head with her fingers, which she demonstrated as leaping at her leg, "Hssssss." Snakebite remedy, she inquired. Ah, yes, yes.

Bennie stood as inconspicuously as a foreigner could, which is to say not at all, while he sketched the cooks and their kettles. A dozen people crowded around to see what he was drawing, murmuring admiration. Dwight had on headphones and was deaf to the natural din of the bazaar, preferring instead to listen to Stevie Ray Vaughan on his CD player as he followed Roxanne, who aimed her camcorder at thirty-second segments of life. She held out a digital microphone in one hand so that she might also capture the musically inflected voices, the obligato of commerce.

Off in the distance, Wendy and Wyatt saw a shady path leading into a forest of bamboo, and strolled hand in hand. Wendy had not yet recovered from her perceived rejection by Wyatt, but she pretended that all was fine. She chatted and flirted, yet she had a sick pang of fear in her chest. She was looking for proof that he felt equally warm toward her, which was—well, it was hard to say, exactly, except that she knew he felt none of the uncertainty that she did. He was perfectly at ease with their being together, as he had been, she imagined, with every woman. Why was *he* not concerned whether he felt more for her than she for him? Why didn't *he* worry over whether he had given more than she had? Did he feel no risk of emotion? When her eyes began to sting with tears, she pretended a lash had caught under the lid, and she rubbed at her eye. He, in turn, raised her face to his, to see if he could help extract the offender. To see such concern from him filled her with even more desperation, and she wrapped her arms around him. He instinctively did what she craved. He kissed her, clutching her buttocks. And in joy, she blurted the forbidden words: "I love you."

To his credit, Wyatt continued to kiss Wendy, covering her mouth so that she did not utter anything more along these lines. He had been expecting her to say this, afraid she would. He liked Wendy a lot. She was fun most of the time, except when she was analyzing everything he said with those searching eyes. He didn't want to hurt her feelings. Also, they had another two weeks to go on this trip. Keep it steady. Keep it fun.

Wyatt and Wendy did not realize that a troop of young boy monks was watching them. Look at those two foreigners, they whispered, and giggled. The man and lady were leaning against a tree and pushing up against each other. He was clutching her big bottom and putting their clothes into unholy disarray. The boys imitated the couple by sticking out their tongues and wriggling them like snakes. The others shook their hips, then jerked them back and forth. Loud laughter shot out.

Wendy and Wyatt broke apart and looked at the shrieking children up the path. The boys ran off like squirrels, and then slowly, one by one, came out from behind the bamboo, eyes alert should they chance upon a disapproving elder monk. Wendy liked risky sex out in the open, but not in front of little boys.

"Let's give them the pens," Wyatt said. That had been his idea back in San Francisco, to give pens and not candy or money to children who begged. Walter had approved of his plan, but suggested that he give the pens to teachers, who would then distribute them to students. But Wyatt forgot that detail, for in front of him was a cool bunch of boys in cinnabar-colored robes. "Look at those faces," he said to Wendy. "They're *amazing*."

Wendy would have described them as unwashed. The boys had dirt on their cheeks, goo in their noses, and greenish chunks in the corners of their eyes. Quite a few of them had sores on their lips. Wyatt turned on his digital camera and took a young monk's photo. He showed the boys the still frame on the back. The boys pointed to one another, laughed, and exclaimed in their own language, "Look how ugly you look!" "No, look how ugly *you* look!"

The two lovers continued their walk into the forest. It was dark and cool in here. They passed blackened circles on the ground. What is that, they wondered aloud, before seeing a group of men farther ahead. One was stirring the coals of an improvised barbecue, the hairy leg of a pig roasting, hoof and all. As they drew closer, they saw two men standing, one wearing a wooden yoke from which a pair of car batteries dangled on a rope. What in the world were those for? The man looked as if he were pretending to be an electrified ox. Wendy and Wyatt smiled as they passed them; the men seemed embarrassed and looked away.

Wendy and Wyatt did not recognize them, the pilots of the longboats, Black Spot and Salt, who had taken them across the shallow waters of Inle Lake. To most tourists, the people of Burma were indistinguishable beyond male and female, young and old, attractive and not. I am not being critical. It is just an observation. I am the same way with most people, regardless of nationality. But after tomorrow, my friends would come to recognize these men all too well.

·9·

NO TRACE

It was Christmas Eve. At nine-thirty, Marlena listened to her daughter's sonorous rhythms and then tiptoed into the bathroom. She quickly ran a razor over her legs and massaged an ambergris-scented lotion on them. She removed her sturdy underwear, hoping the humidity would erase the panty line on her skin, then donned a long gauzy cotton sheath the color of tangerine sherbet. With pounding heart, as if she were the daughter and not the mother, she eased past Esmé's bed and out the door, and slipped down the plankway toward Harry's bungalow.

Now here they were together at last, Harry and Marlena, lying beneath the mosquito netting, their naked bodies lit by the golden glow of a citronella candle. Marlena's eyes were pressed shut, and her mind and body were in an unequal battle between maintaining control and losing it utterly and completely. Harry was tracing small circles on her neck, her shoulders, her breasts, kissing each spot, then feeding on her mouth before continuing the trail downward. Warmth spread over Marlena's face. It surprised her. Such passion, such heat, such . . . *smoke?*

Suddenly Harry yelped, flung himself off the bed and yanked Marlena to the floor with him. The conical mosquito netting, having floated onto the burning candle, was now like a snowy Christmas tree aflame, the fine white mesh turning into a blackened web of dancing tendrils and lattices. Marlena scrambled to her feet and flung open the door, shouting, "Fire! Fire!" She was about to run out, when she remembered she was naked, and stood paralyzed in the doorway looking back at the brightly burning room.

"We have to get out!" she cried. But Harry had transformed into heroic mode: he grabbed a piece of cloth on the floor, doused it with a bottle of water from the nightstand, and flogged at the flames licking the ceiling. Seconds later, after an eternity had passed, Harry put down the wet rag. "It's out," he announced wearily. Marlena turned on the light. The charred wisps of netting floated like a scorched ghost.

Under the fluorescent blueness and amid blackened debris, Harry and Marlena had to confront the various concave and convex slopes of their nakedness. This time it was without the forgiving glow of lust and candlelight, and soon, without privacy as well. What was this? Shouts of men, footsteps pounding the plankway! Harry and Marlena frantically sought their clothes, so recently abandoned on the floor with happy tosses. Harry managed to locate his trousers and was struggling to get one leg in, while Marlena found only a soggy wad of blackened orange gauze, and realized all at once that this was the pathetic remnant of her sheath, which had been used to put out the fire in more ways than one. She moaned, and at that moment four Burmese men with fire extinguishers rushed in, and Marlena sprang into the bathroom with a shriek exactly one second too late.

Though the fire was out, the men doused the smoldering ceiling and charred netting for good measure, each one taking a turn, discharging streams of white powder that exploded against the ash in clouds of gray fallout. Soon Rupert loped in, followed by Moff, Dwight, Roxanne, and Vera. Only Bennie, his CPAP mask affixed to his face, heard nothing. Across the water, the others called out, "What's happening?" "Is everything all right?" Marlena donned one of Harry's shirts and a pair of boxer shorts. As she walked back into the bedroom, she saw a mournful face: Esmé was standing in the doorway.

Soon after, Harry watched Marlena leave with her daughter. She was too distraught to speak, and waved away his questions, his apologies. The tattered netting had been hauled away, the ruined bedding stripped, and now he was alone. The damp bare mattress before him reminded Harry of a shameful time in his childhood. "What were you possibly thinking?" both his mother and Marlena had shrieked. A headache began to pound in his temples.

He could not sleep, so he sat on the edge of the undamaged twin bed, punching the pillow and cursing, "Sod's law, bloody sod's law!" If anything could go wrong, it would. He pictured Marlena's face, how ashamed she looked with an inadequate towel wrapped around her hunched-over body, pleading with her daughter to go back to their bungalow and wait. Esmé had remained in the doorway, wordless and inscrutable.

An hour later, Harry finished the last of a bottle of champagne he had bought at Heinrich's exorbitant price; it had been intended to toast the start of his and Marlena's love affair. He put down the empty bottle and rummaged in his carry-on case for the liter of duty-free liquor he had bought on the airplane. There it was, Johnnie Walker Black, his fine Scottish friend for the lonely night. Outside, an Intha fisherman, obviously soused to the bones, began bellowing with operatic strength, and in the arena created by the lake and the semicircle of floating cottages, his serenade boomed and reverberated for a captive audience. To Harry, the tune sounded like a wail to the universe. It was awful, he mused, well suited to the occasion.

THE NIGHT BEFORE, Walter had assured them that the early wake-up call would be worth it. "A sunrise on Christmas Day," he had said, "is the best present you can give yourselves. We'll go in two of the longboats to a beautiful spot on the lake. Dress warmly and do wear sturdy shoes, no flip-flops. We'll be doing a bit of walking. After the sunrise, we'll visit various factories making paper, woven cloth, and cheroots. Bring a camera and a mid-morning snack. If you're not on the boats by six-fifteen, I will assume you preferred to sleep in, in which case we'll meet you in the Great Hall for lunch."

At five-thirty in the morning, everyone but Harry rose for an early breakfast. As for Harry, after listening to the drunken fisherman most of the night, he had finally drifted off to sleep at four. With so much alcohol in his bloodstream, his sedated brain kept him somnolent until nearly noon, at which time he awoke with a terrific hangover.

In another corner of the resort, Heinrich was also awakening. He often kept late hours. He took a brisk shower, dressed in his woven silk trousers and shirt, and padded over in slapping sandals to the dining hall to greet his guests for lunch. What a surprise to see the hall was empty except for the Famous TV Star. "Aren't they back yet?" he asked.

"Apparently not," Harry said, and sipped his coffee.

"And you stayed behind?"

"Apparently so."

Heinrich went into his office to meet with three of his staff and organize for the day. He glanced at the schedule Walter had given him. The sunrise viewing and morning shopping was supposed to last only a few hours, with a return by ten or ten-thirty and lunch at noon. Perhaps they had opted to do more Christmas shopping.

The staff told him of the previous night's fire. They spoke to him in Burmese. No, no one was hurt, they said.

"Anyone jump in the lake?"

The men laughed. Not this time, but the man sure was hopping scared. They said it was the cottage of the moping TV star in the dining room. The damage wasn't bad. Workmen were just now replacing the ruined sections of rattan on the ceiling. The bed would dry out on its own. Should they put up another netting?

Heinrich scratched his head. He had meant to buy the fireproofed netting, but the son of one of the head honchos had insisted that Heinrich take a brand of his tribe's own making, an older style that was illegal in other countries. This was the third fire at the resort. "Put up a net but remove the candles," Heinrich said.

There was also a lady in the TV star's room, the staff told Heinrich, a naked woman. They chuckled to themselves. "Which one?" Heinrich asked in Burmese. The Chinese lady, they said. He nodded, affirming Harry's good taste.

"Also sorry to report, boss, we've had another theft."

Heinrich sighed. "What now?"

"The bicycle generator." This was what they used to power up twelve-volt car batteries during the frequent electrical failures. "They left behind the bicycle this time."

"Wasn't the shed locked as I instructed?"

"The lock was beheaded. Cut clean."

"What about the guard dogs?"

"Still in the pen, but chewing on fresh bones."

Heinrich counted the items already stolen over the last six months: a small television, the satellite dish for illegally receiving international channels, a bicycle, a hand-crank flashlight, some large Toyo twelve-volt batteries, a box of ginger-flavored sunflower seeds, and now the bicycle generator.

"Go into town and see if the generator is for sale on the black market. If so, notify the police and report back to me." But Heinrich knew it was unlikely that the generator would ever be found. Still, it was best to follow proper procedures. He would simply charge the Famous TV Star two hundred U.S. dollars for fire damage that could be repaired for less than ten. With the remaining cash, he would buy a new generator, perhaps a fuel generator this time, now that he had a good black-market source for buying petrol without government rationing coupons.

As with any problem, you simply had to be more creative.

THERE IS A FAMOUS Chinese sentiment about finding the outer edges of beauty. My father once recited it to me: "Go to the edge of the lake and watch the mist rise." At six-thirty, my friends had been at that edge. At dawn, the mist rose like the lake's breath, and the vaporous mountains behind faded in layers of lighter and lighter gray, mauve, and blue until the farthest reaches merged with the milky sky.

The motors of the longboats had been cut. All was quiet. The mountains reflected in the lake waters caused my friends to reflect upon their busy lives. What serenity had eluded them until now?

"I feel like the noise of the world has stopped," whispered Marlena. But then secretly she wondered what had happened to Harry. Had he lain awake most of the night, as she had? She glanced at Esmé, who still refused to look at her, despite the fact that Marlena had offered to let her have forbidden things for breakfast, coffee cake, doughnuts, a Coke. Throughout, Esmé had remained silent.

She was embarrassed by her mother and Harry. They looked so *stupid*. They wrecked the little house. They nearly got themselves killed. Everybody saw and was talking about it. She had done things far less stupid than that, and her mother had been mad and wouldn't talk to her. "I just can't deal with this," she would tell Esmé, and then not look at her for hours. It had made her stomach ache. Well, now her mother could see what that felt like.

"Man, this is so worth it," Wyatt said. Wendy nodded, silent for once.

Heidi had not felt stillness like this since the murder. The water buoyed her, and the mist took her worries away. She realized, after a while, that she had not thought about bad things, like the boat tipping . . . No, she put it out of her mind, and turned her face toward the mountains.

Here the lessons of Buddhism seemed true, Vera thought. Life was merely an illusion you must release. As she grew older, she was aware of her changing position on mortality. In her youth, the topic of death was philosophical, in her thirties it was unbearable, and in her forties unavoidable. In her fifties, she had dealt with it in more rational terms, arranging her last testament, itemizing assets and heirlooms, spelling out the organ donation, detailing the exact words for her living will. Now, in her sixties, she was back to being philosophical. Death was not a loss of life, but the culmination of a series of releases. It was devolving into less and less. You had to release yourself from vanity, desire, ambition, suffering, and frustration—all the accoutrements of the I, the ego. And if you did, you would disappear, leave no trace, like the mist at dawn over the lake, evaporating into nothingness, into nibbana.

I was appalled at the idea. Evaporate? Would that happen to me? I wanted to expand, to fill the void, to reclaim all that I had wasted. I wanted to fill the silence with all the words I had not yet spoken.

THE PAPERMAKER WAS the first to report to the military police that he had seen the missing tourists. "You saw them before or after they disappeared?" the police asked.

"Must have been *before*," answered the papermaker. "Otherwise, how could I be telling you I saw them?" Go on, they said. They were standing in the papermaker's yard, in front of his house, a six-poled, one-room affair. The tourists had been his customers, he explained. He went over to a bucket and picked it up. They had watched him as he lifted it and poured a batter of mulberry leaf mash onto a wood-framed silk screen. And then he had taken this wooden trowel—see how it's the same width as the frame, and see how it spreads the slime thinly and evenly over the screen? Then, he said, he took bits of flower petals and ferns. The police watched him sprinkle them onto the silk screen in captive flourishes. The pretty little girl with the dog liked that very much, the papermaker said. He went to another frame, which had already dried, and peeled off a sheet of rough-hewn paper, the kind that sold for ten dollars in American stationery stores. Can you believe it? Ten dollars! That's what they told him anyway, though he charged these customers only a hundred kyats.

The little girl picked up a sheet of paper, and as soon as she did, the Chinese lady, who must have been her mother, offered to buy it for her. The little girl said nothing, would not even look at her, as if her mother were invisible. Then the girl spotted the sun umbrellas, made of the same flowery paper, popular items with tourists. The Chinese lady again wanted to buy one for her daughter, simply be-cause the girl had looked at it! And after the mother paid, the daugh-ter smiled—although not at her—and this filled the woman with joy. I tell you, American children are so easy to please, the papermaker said to the police, because they have so many desires to choose from.

The cheroot maker also said the Americans had come by. He knew they were Americans because none of them smoked, and they ad-mired the lacquered containers more than the dozen cheroots they held. They had politely watched his girls making the cheroots. The police now paused to admire a particularly lovely girl with a sweet face and large cat eyes. She took a flat, disc-shaped cheroot leaf and expertly rolled the blend of tobacco and woody root together with a filter made of layers of cornhusks. The cheroot maker appeared to think hard as he went on: A tall man with long hair bought a dozen, to qualify for the free container. And when he lit one to smoke, the black lady was very upset, as was a pretty young woman who turned on a small whirring machine around her neck. Something seemed very peculiar about those foreigners, the cheroot maker concluded.

Several women at the silk-weaving factory confirmed that they, too, had seen the foreigners. All the women who worked on the first floor of the rickety wooden building were old, and their job was to spin thread out of silk. The black lady and a woman with pinkish hair, they said, were very curious and asked odd questions. They asked about their work hours. "Whenever there was daylight," the thread spinners had answered, "dawn to dusk, every day." And their wages? "Two or three hundred kyats a day"—less than an American dollar. And what happened to them if they were sick or injured? How much were they paid? "Of course there's no pay for days not worked," they had told her. Wasn't that a strange question to ask! The policemen nodded.

The second floor was much noisier, and the women here were young, some just girls, for they were the weavers and had to be energetic to operate the looms. The weaving women reported that the black lady was astounded by their skill, more so than most tourists, who seemed to think their bodies were merely extensions of machines. The police now watched a young woman move her feet rapidly over the outer then the inner pedals of the loom, her arched soles flexed and dancing. Meanwhile her hands operated at another rhythm to jerk a string with the exact degree of force needed to send a wooden threader flying from left to right, right to left. This required enormous concentration and coordination, the old weaving woman said, and as everyone knew, no man possessed the ability to stay eye-sharp for such a long time. It was a patient woman's work, the ability for hands and feet to think independently, for the mind to remain focused through the same movements, thread after thread. Between daybreak and light's end, each woman created a full yard of intricately patterned silk that would sell for the fixed price of ten U.S. dollars. That was how they helped their company make a very good profit, they said. Yes, they enjoyed their work, they told the American black lady. Very, very much. Constancy is its own satisfaction, said one of the older ladies, the predictability of days, the serenity of seeing the same loom and spools, the same co-workers beside me, the same wooden walls and high roof, with only occasional rain tapping the roof, like the thrumming fingers of a god, which was a small but welcome intrusion.

We saw the tourists the whole time, up to the moment they were leaving, one of the weaving women told the police. But in the next moment, they were gone, with just the strong smell of them left behind. Snatched by Nats, that's what I think.

HERE IS how it actually happened.

At nine-thirty in the morning, my friends had finished visiting the weaving mill. They were standing on the jetty, ready to climb into the longboats. "Our next stop," Walter said, "is my Christmas surprise to you. We may have to walk in just a little ways, but I think you will enjoy it enormously."

Everyone liked the sound of those words: Christmas surprise. What a delightful combination of syllables. Black Spot and Salt also heard how easily they agreed to such a simple invitation. A surprise could be anything, could it not?

What Walter had in mind, in fact, was a visit to a local school where young children had practiced singing a Burmese rendition of "Rudolph the Red-Nosed Reindeer." He and the teacher had agreed months before that it would be a joyous event for the schoolchildren and foreigners alike. He would bring whatever groups came in December, and he would also suggest that they make a small donation to the school's book fund. Even though the schools did not officially celebrate Christmas, it was their duty to help win over more tourists as part of the "Visit Myanmar" campaign to change foreign perception of their country. The past two groups Walter had led said it was a highlight of their trip, one that had touched their hearts. Walter hoped this group would like it as well.

As my friends waited on the jetty, they had no idea that this humble pageantry was the Christmas surprise, and thus they were impatient to be on their way and see what source of awe or amusement awaited them. But as usual, they were delayed, waiting this time for Rupert.

"You should buy him a watch," Vera said sharply to Moff.

"He's got a watch," Moff replied.

"Then one with a timer and an alarm."

"It's got two timers."

Stepping off his boat, Black Spot offered to help Walter find the boy. Walter could go in one direction, he in the other, and both would return in fifteen minutes. A good plan. Off they went.

Happily, next to every dock and jetty there are vendors with trinkets to see, lacquerware to buy, and folk art to admire. The goods were laid out on cardboard tables, and the vendors urged the tourists to examine the excellent quality—see, touch, buy! Bennie and the women bargained in earnest, while Moff, Wyatt, and Dwight stood at the end of the dock and lit up cheroots, commenting that they tasted like a cross between a cigarette and a joint. Esmé dipped into the treats her mother had brought and found a bag of teriyaki turkey jerky she could share with Pup-pup.

Within ten minutes, they saw that the boatman in the brown longyi had returned with Rupert. The miscreant confessed he had been demonstrating a card trick to some local men.

"What did I tell you about everyone sticking together?" Moff said. "You can't just go off and do what you want."

"They begged me to show them," Rupert explained. "Honest." Moff gave the usual lecture about one's responsibility to the universe, how it was rude to keep anyone waiting, let alone eleven people.

"Ten," Rupert said. "Harry's not here."

"What about Walter?" Moff said.

Yes, what about Walter? Fifteen minutes went by, then a half-hour, and still he had not returned. Salt, the round-faced friend of Black Spot, gesticulated to the tourists that he would go in the direction Walter had taken, to see what the delay was. After five minutes, he returned with a big smile. He and Black Spot had a quick exchange in their dialect. "Okay, okay, no worries," Black Spot told the tourists. He gestured to his boat and motioned them to step in. And then, pointing to some vague place on the other side of the lake, he said, "We are going there."

"Hey," Esmé said. "He speaks English. Did anyone notice? He speaks English!" No one paid much attention to Esmé. They assumed that everyone spoke some amount of English.

"What the hell is Walter doing *there*?" Dwight said aloud.

Black Spot smiled enigmatically. "Christmas surprise," he said, recalling Walter's words. The words were like magic. Their secret helper had told them that the boy would never come willingly. And Black Spot had worried over how he would persuade the Younger White Brother that this was his calling. But then their helper gave him a useful tip: The boy would not go unless everyone else went with him. And see how easy it was. They did not even know what the surprise was, yet they were willing to go find it.

Marlena told her daughter, "Walter must be getting things ready." Esmé still wasn't looking at her, except by accident.

"We are hurrying now," Black Spot said. He motioned to them to make their way posthaste onto the boats. A few minutes later, the two boats were speeding across the lake, the cool breeze soothing throats that had so recently been swollen with the irritation of delays and cheroot smoke. I sat at the prow of one boat, trying to warn them to go back.

We drifted among islands of hyacinth, into one narrow inlet after another. The canal turned and twisted like a waterlogged hedge maze. After innumerable detours, the boats floated toward a makeshift ramp constructed of reeds latched together and set atop treadless truck tires.

"Are we sure this is steady?" Heidi said as she stood to climb out.

"Very safe," Black Spot answered.

Moff sprang out first and extended his hand to help the others. In single file, they walked through a slim cut in the thick reedy banks. The air had warmed, and the mosquitoes were stirred to action by their footfalls. Hands slapped at legs, and Heidi brought out a small pump bottle of one hundred percent DEET, which everyone gratefully partook of. Vera, who had on thick-soled sandals, sprayed her feet, and unbeknownst to her, the repellent dissolved her coral nail polish, which she then smeared on her opposite foot, which she also did not notice.

A little ways in was a one-lane dirt road, where a truck bulged over the sides. "That must be at least fifty years old," Bennie said. Two young men waved. They seemed to be acquainted with Black Spot and Salt, who walked over to them and began chatting energetically. And in fact, they did know each other, for the truck driver was Grease, Black Spot's cousin, and the other man was Fishbones, the thin man who had piloted the longboat with the luggage the day before. My friends noted that all four men were behaving rather oddly, throwing nervous looks toward them. Ah, the travelers surmised among themselves, they were doing their best not to give away wily Walter's Christmas surprise.

Rupert pointed to Grease, and said to Moff: "Hey, that's the guy who asked me back there to show him my card trick. What's he doing here?"

"Can't be the same guy," Moff said.

"Why not?"

"Because that guy was there, and this guy is here."

"Well, we were there, and now we're here."

Rupert waved his arm back and forth in the truck driver's direction. When Grease saw him, he waved back tentatively.

"See?" Moff said. "Not the same guy."

Black Spot returned to the tourists. "Now we are climbing into the truck, we are going to a very special place. Up there. Very nice people." He pointed toward the mountain.

"Cool," Wyatt said. "I love to see how people really live."

"Me, too," Vera agreed. "Real life."

"Is that where we're having lunch?" Rupert said.

"Yes, we are fooding there," Black Spot said. "Very special lunch we are making for you."

My friends peered in. The truck's sides were made of broad timber planks, and over the top was suspended a dark rubberized tarp to provide, they supposed, protection from sun and rain. Both sides of the truck bed were lined with wicker benches, dented in spots, and in the middle of the floor were two monstrous twelve-volt batteries, a funny long contraption into which one of the batteries was set, and baskets and knotted-rope slings of food supplies.

"There aren't any seat belts," Heidi observed.

"There aren't any *seats*!" Vera grumped with a disparaging look at the low benches.

"We're probably not going that far," Wyatt said.

"I'm sure Bibi wouldn't have picked something that wasn't both interesting and safe," Vera said. Heidi was standing at the back of the truck, and she listened intently to assess what she was getting herself into. Moff got in ahead of her, then pulled her up, appreciating the way her breasts rose and fell with a nice little jiggle. Meanwhile, Black Spot and Fishbones quickly lugged the longboats out of the water and tucked them into the brush. A moment later, there was no evidence of the boats. The two men climbed into the cab with Salt and Grease, and off the truck went, brushing past overgrown shrubs and snapping off branches that were in the way. In the truck bed, the travelers jounced and yelped over each bump. They had all grabbed on to the side slats to brace themselves. Because of the large, dark tarp, they could see only from the rear: the wake of dust, the dense green of untamed ferns and colorful flora.

About a half-mile later, the driver shifted down, and with groaning gears and churning engine, the ancient truck began a laborious winding ascent up the mountain. My friends lurched and tilted like bowling pins about to keel over. Roxanne clutched the side and stood, trying to get a shot of everyone being jostled about like cattle. She joked about the "*ultra-deluxe* bus" that was taking them to a "Christmas surprise."

Wendy shouted back with her own commentary: "This better be good!"

Half an hour went by, forty-five minutes. A most curious thing should be noted here: My friends never considered that this journey might possibly be dangerous. Instead, the unorthodox truck and the difficulty and roughness of the passage further convinced them that the surprise must indeed be worth the trouble, and extremely rare, that is, unavailable to most tourists. They liked adventures off the beaten track, especially the males, all except Bennie. This was exactly what they had been hoping for, instead of endless shops and factories. With each arduous mile their expectations grew. As they shared bottles of water and candy bars, they mused over the possibilities. An ancient city buried in the jungle, the Machu Picchu of Myanmar! Or perhaps a village filled with those "giraffe-necked" women who were so famous in these parts. Or it could be a Shangri-La of such magnificence and splendor that nothing like it had ever been seen, even in the movies.

The only complaint was from Roxanne, who lamented, "I wish I could see where the hell we're going so I could film this stuff."

At last the truck came to an idle. The passengers stuck their heads out. The trees were much taller here, and the canopy was so dense that only thin slants of light fell in. The road continued upward to the left, but my friends saw two of the men jump from the truck's cab and approach a mattress-thick wall of brush and tangles along the mountainside. The taller one gave a shout, and together they grasped handholds of vines, which, with a grunt, they slowly lifted. The moving vegetation revealed itself to be a gate of greenery, strands and branches of bushes, ferns, bamboo, and vines, lashed together onto a lightweight frame. This was placed all the way to the side, so that my friends, some of whom had climbed down from the truck bed, could now see an opening, a leafy archway leading to an unknown world, what seemed as fantastical to them as the entry into Alice's Wonderland. The men in the cab gave a shout for everyone to climb back into the truck. The travelers hoisted themselves in, the truck reversed, and with a gunning of the engine, it aimed its nose toward the opening. It seemed impossible that it could fit through, but the vegetation gave way with scrapes and snaps, and the truck squeezed through the resistant portal like a newborn bursting its mother's perineum.

They had entered a green-veined new world, a vibrant, single-hued world of wildlife that quivered and breathed. Everywhere the travelers looked, it was choked with creepers, vines, and liana hanging, winding, and snaking their way through, making it seem that the jungle ended only a few feet in front of them. It was disorienting to see so much green. The tree trunks were mossy and bedecked with epiphytes: ferns, bromeliads, and tiny pale orchids took root in the soil-rich nooks and crannies of trees. Birds called warning. Somewhere in the distance, a branch creaked with the weight of an unknown creature, possibly a monkey. With small intakes of breath, my friends registered their astonishment.

"Amazing." "Heavenly." "Surreal." It was their unanimous opinion that Walter—and I, posthumously—had done a superb job in taking them to such a spectacular haven for their Christmas gift. Lunch no doubt was in those baskets and would be served picnic style. But where *was* Walter, anyway?

"Where's Walter?" Moff asked.

Black Spot pointed ahead to an opening through a web of green. "We are just going up this way." By now, Grease and Fishbones had finished replacing the leafy gate. From here on, Black Spot said, they would walk. Walk? My friends were puzzled. What more besides *this* was there to see? What could be farther ahead? Well, obviously, something even better. Without questioning their new leader, they began to trudge through the tricky undergrowth, stepping where Black Spot had slashed out a path.

Bennie wiped his brow. "Walter said we'd be doing a bit of walking—talk about understatement."

Like good little schoolchildren, they followed Black Spot into the rainforest. They did not even know his name. Yet they went blindly, willingly, going closer and closer to a tribe that had been waiting for them for more than a hundred years.

· *10* ·

No Name Place

Poor Harry. He lay on a wooden chaise longue on the deck outside his newly repaired cottage. He was more peeved than worried that Marlena and the others had not yet returned. It was Christmas Day, for God's sake, and here he was alone, mired in boredom, while they were gallivanting about like elves, getting red-nosed on Burmese beers—and, oh yes indeed, no doubt telling jokes about last night's fire. Wherever they were, he groused, it was damn inconsiderate of them not to ring him with news of their whereabouts. Though, come to think of it, was there even telephone service in a remote resort like this?

Harry wondered whether he should ask, and I reinforced this thought with a surge of urgency. He jumped to his feet, and I applauded. Off he went to find Heinrich. But from dock to dock, he encountered only the help. "Telly-phone," he overenunciated, and shaped his hand into the universal sign for a handset, but this received only shrugs and downcast looks of regret. His headache from last night's binge began to throb more intensely. How in hell did he get talked into coming to a country that didn't allow cell phones?

Back at the bungalow, so as not to be consumed with frustration and self-pity, Harry turned his attention to profit-making work. He had brought with him the rough draft of his book-in-progress, *Come. Sit. Stay.* It was meant to be a collection of light commentary and anecdotes on the interactions between humans and dogs, a mix of topics relating to human and canine personalities—*not* the sort of book he would have chosen to write, mind you. But an editor had come to him with the idea after he had won his third Emmy. There was a good market for it, she said, along with a bit of dosh—enough, he calculated, to cover the down payment on a ski chalet at Squaw Valley, and it was all his, provided he turned the manuscript in within the year. Flush with Emmy pride at the time, Harry had responded, "Easily done." Now he judged he was insane to have agreed to such an impossible schedule. He read the notes from his editor, suggestions that she said might serve as a springboard: "What happens when you place a calm Lab with a restless person? Or an anxious border collie with a relaxed person? How about an assertive terrier with an indecisive person? Who affects whom? Could some combinations be therapeutic?"

What idiocy. The misguided dear was barking up the proverbial wrong tree. He paused to think how to set things in a proper frame of reference. . . . Perhaps something to do with personality and adaptability in different species . . . He began jotting notes: Explain the science behind that, ergo, the paleoanthropology of hominid Erectus before and now. Yes! Add the biology of species diversification— some basic Darwinian analogies to make the whole thing have an impressive foundation. Brilliant. Roxanne wasn't the only one who knew a thing or two about Darwin. What else could he say to set himself apart from that barmpot on the other channel who also called himself an animal behaviorist?

Harry created two columns, "Humans" and "Dogs." Under "Humans," he wrote: "Social hierarchies & birth order issues; evolved language yielding shared social intelligence; public conscience, morals, ethics; goal-setting; the ability to discern and judge; therefore, a need for meaning." Under "Dogs," he put down: "Social hierarchies beginning in blind neonate stage; changeable temperament (and personality!!) in puppyhood; four-month window for hardwiring social behaviors via environment; operant learning modalities; food-motivated; seek-to-please submissive traits . . ." The columns weren't exactly equivalent, he considered. Still, it was a bit of all right, an excellent premise: species differentiation in a social adaptability framework.

He pictured himself expounding on these points with his ideal reader—Marlena, yes, why not? He imagined her look of total adoration in listening to them, the synergy of them upon her open mind, how they would transform her, sending tingles into her heart, then ripples into her sexual organs, creating massive, massive . . . *boredom.* My God, this was all rubbish.

He pictured Marlena's face once again—how unreadable and distant it had looked the night before. What bloody good was human adaptability if people weren't willing to change? Wasn't that why no penal system really worked to prevent crime, why people went to psychiatrists for years without any intentions of overcoming their obsessions and depressions? Humans had this extraordinary fondness for their own peccadilloes. That's why you couldn't change a Republican into a Democrat and vice versa, why there were so many divorces, lawsuits, and wars. Because people refused to adapt and accommodate to others even for their own good! Precisely so! When it came to their own needs, humans, and women especially, were more territorial about their bloody psyches—their so-called *needs*—than dogs were over their raw meaty bones.

That was the core problem with every woman he had ever loved. Oh, in the beginning, to be sure, she appeared to be amazingly flexible, telling him that it did not matter what restaurant or movie they went to. But later, once she moved in—guess what, she hated sushi, *loathed* it, didn't he ever *notice*? And while she was always late to every engagement, she wanted him to phone if *he* was going to be delayed by even a minute. "What good is a fucking cell phone," the last one fumed, "if you never turn it on?" Criminy, none of them knew anything about encouraging behavior, only about criticizing it. It was all about *her*, her needs, her perceptions. If she *felt* he was insensitive, ipso facto he was. If he argued he was not, ipse dixit, the proof was in his *protesting* about it. What's more, the woman *always* had to come first, no matter how busy he was with his television show. Everything became a proving ground for what was most important—to her. With the last one he dated, he could not go skiing for a weekend with Moff without its becoming a "negative statement" about the relationship. *Whose* negative statement?

With respect to turnarounds, his ex-wife was practically a multiple personality. His kitchen, for example—as his newly bedded girlfriend, she had loved it to pieces, adored it, had openly gushed and admired it for its original 1920s fixtures, as well as that gorgeous gem of a stove that looked almost exactly like an O'Keefe & Merritt, which would have been worth thousands had it been authentic. As newly wedded wife, she began hectoring him about *her* kitchen, its defects and disasters. Oh no, she could not possibly be content with what she derided as "a splash of paint here and there." She would not hear of refacing the cabinets; the kitchen had to be gutted, top to bottom. She wanted custom cabinetry, a La Cornue range with burners hot enough to weld trucks together, a butcher-block island with a pre-tarnished copper sink, a rubbed marble top that looked as if Italians had been kneading dough on it since the Renaissance. Then there was the matter of the floor. No, she did not think the 1950s linoleum floor was friendly and fun or full of interesting history. She said it looked like "rivers of barf." "I beg your pardon," he had said. "*Barf?* What sort of Americanism is that?" She went on to say she wanted the floor to be limestone tiles embedded with tiny fossilized sea creatures. He had joked, "Pray tell, what for? So they can mingle with dropped fusilli in a sea of spilled pesto sauce?" It was the wrong thing to say. Then again, *everything* was the wrong thing. With the amount of money spent on the kitchen, they could have dined at Chez Panisse every night for *years*. And in fact, they nearly did, since the dear wife rarely cooked.

He imagined Marlena seeing his kitchen for the first time. "Charming," she would no doubt utter, "quite charming." She would run her manicured fingers along the marble, wiggling her lovely arse up onto the cool counter and lying down with a come-hither look. The remodeled kitchen might have some advantages. It had had them with other women he had dated, though he had promptly discovered it was not advisable to make love on a cool, narrow counter. Perhaps it was best to imagine Marlena leaning against it, washing dishes, her backside facing him. That was nice, very nice.

Despite what had happened the night before, she was still good for sexual daydreams. His last girlfriend said it was abnormal and disgusting that he thought about sex every hour and with every woman he met. It must have been madness and too many martinis that led to his confessing that. He wouldn't make that mistake with Marlena. No relationship needed to be *that* honest. Keep some of the mystery, better for romance that way. At least the divinely mature Marlena would have no issues about popping out more babies. Talk of babies killed the lovey-dovey factor. Yet with the younger lady friends, the need to replicate themselves seemed to raise its ugly head at inopportune times, usually once they had finished making love and when he was two seconds from becoming happily unconscious. This was despite the fact that he had culled only those women who said that having babies ranked well below seeing all the continents of the world. He had asked specifically: Which would you rather have, an eructing baby or a trip to Antarctica? They all opted for the ice floe. But about three months into the affair, four at the maximum, the girlfriend would tease about having a "baby version" of Harry. They each used that *exact* imagery. Peculiar, wasn't it? They loved him so much they wanted to *miniaturize* him, then watch him grow from itsy-bitsy babyhood to handsome young man, ready to change the world.

He fell for it—once—and as soon as she crossed the threshold as Mrs. Bailley, the campaign started for him to change. She demanded that he drink less, exercise more, stop telling the same jokes that "weren't funny the first time 'round," and please curb his damn patronizing behavior. What behavior was that? And she would enumerate. What! She wanted him to stop being *himself*?

Harry was so perturbed remembering this that now he could not think of anything positive between him and Marlena. After all, he barely knew her. . . . But then he paused to reconsider. What is life without intimacy with another? What good was success if you could not share it with a beloved? Something felt right about Marlena. He no longer wanted an underling, he wanted an equal. What a surprising notion. What's more, she was different from the rest. He knew human nature, and she was more secure, more content, and also more independent, not to mention financially secure. She would not look to him to fulfill her completely. She was already complete, save for the fun and jolly of being with him.

Granted, she was a bit standoffish at times, but in a way that made wooing her even more delicious. Her reticence was her mystery, he reasoned, a lovely conundrum, and he was the privileged man who would be allowed to unravel the complex and private package, to view her naked soul. And she would know this was the lure and the promise. Yes, he was now prepared to show her who he was, the insecurities, the loneliness, the occasional rash decision leading to shame—everything but the part about his thinking about sex all the time. All in all, he was not a complicated person. If anything, his greatest fault was being too hopeful. Disappointment had quashed him, but he always sprang back.

He hoped Marlena wouldn't be the same as the others. He pictured her teasing him about last night's fiasco, giggling like a schoolgirl, saying it would make for fond memories in the years to come. He sighed happily.

But next he remembered her chiding his feeble attempts to douse the flames with her dress. How could he have known that slip of cloth was an expensive designer sheath? My God, she acted barking mad over that orange scrap. She didn't yell; it was worse. She had stared at him with an implacable Asian face, unreadable, unreachable, unadaptable, like a cat's. No wonder he liked dogs. When things went wrong, they were the best creatures to have around, forgiving, nonstop jolly, all let's go play, waggy-wag, woofy-woof, scratch my belly, please. A sure thing, no insidious neuroses that might creep out and claw him on the nose.

When Harry awoke from a nap in the late afternoon, he was still alone except for the resort staff idling about. Perhaps the tour group had pushed on, to take in more museums, pagodas, and monasteries. Not that he cared to poke around in such places, but he felt Walter should have at least warned him that he would miss out on a whole day's activities (and without Marlena!) if he did not join them at that ungodly hour for a sunrise cruise. He glanced at his watch. They should be returning for dinner any minute now. "Back so soon?" he would say in his most nonchalant voice, belying how tetchy he truly felt.

It was not until the dinner hour that Harry finally saw Heinrich sauntering in. Harry ran up to the resort director to inquire what the group's actual plans had been for the day. Heinrich looked at his watch and surveyed the dining hall, as if this were the first time he had noticed it was empty. "Tst, tst," he said. "The guide said he would have them here for dinner."

"Well, where are they?"

"Ah yes, where, indeed? It's the habit of people on holiday to be late," Heinrich said in an offhand way. But I could sense that his eyes were evasive, his back rigid and his shoulders tight. It seemed to me he was not conveying the true concern he felt. He leaned over a table and straightened silverware that was already perfectly aligned. "Have patience, and please, *do* have your dinner. We're serving an excellent prawn dish tonight. Pity if no one tasted it."

Harry skipped dinner and had four bottles of Burmese beer, which he drank while pacing the dock, scanning the dimming landscape, the darkening lake. The busboys, now dressed as waiters, stood at attention in the bar, hands clasped behind their backs. When Heinrich strolled up for his fifth whiskey sour, Harry cornered him.

"We must talk."

"Oh dear, still fretting, I see." Heinrich tapped his cigarette on an enameled bowl, then sat back heavily in a rattan chair, inhaled deeply, and surveyed the night.

Harry remained standing. "Look, I'm beginning to think they've gotten themselves into some sort of trouble."

Heinrich gave forth a small cough and a laugh. "Oh, I doubt that very much." His tone was clearly dishonest, and I could still feel his tension, his duplicity. He was hoping that he would not have to report this to the authorities, at least not yet. But why? He was protecting his hide, I sensed that much. The particulars remained obscure to me.

He waved his cigarette in circles as he thought of what to say to

Harry. "Well, perhaps they're having a very small trouble." He made a pinching gesture with his thumb and forefinger. "Small. Could be a problem with the motors, or maybe they've been waylaid by a military blockade across the lake. It's happened before. Bombastic figure arrives from the capital, wants to take a boat ride out to see his pretty little mistress. So the police cease all other passage—for the sake of security, they say, but everyone knows it's really to impress the hell out of the lady. I believe your American presidents do the same when touching down at public airports. Nearly the whole city shuts down. Am I right? So you see, that sort of thing is common everywhere. Damned annoying, but nothing we can do about it."

"Nonetheless," Harry said, "we must notify the authorities to be on the lookout for them."

Heinrich grunted. "Have the military police *pursue* your friends? Is that it? Not wise, no, not wise at all. Has it ever occurred to you that this is precisely the sort of thing that could really get them into trouble?"

"Look, have you got a telephone?"

"To be honest, the wiring for our telephones went down in the last monsoon—bloody dreadful rain we had in the summer—and we haven't gotten around to rewiring. Hard to get the parts out here. But it helps to give the aura of a secluded resort, don't you agree?" He winked at Harry.

"No *telephone*?" Harry retracted his head like a repulsed tortoise. Heinrich's answer sounded suspicious. "How the hell do you ever get bookings if you never answer the telephone?"

Heinrich gave a placid smile. "It's all booked by the tourism agency in Yangon. Assigned, you might say. We get a weekly update, sent to us by a messenger. Your group was a last-minute fill-in, as you know. Luckily, we had room."

Harry was incredulous. "So you've done without a phone for all these months?"

"Well, for emergencies, I do have my own satellite phone, of course."

"Brilliant. We can use that to call around to people in the area."

"My dear man, I hardly know everyone. The lake is fourteen miles long. And it would be frightfully expensive to use a satellite phone to ring up various people on the off chance . . . Well, it's hardly an emergency, is it? Ringing up the neighbors might raise an unnecessary alarm." Heinrich saw that Harry was not to be dissuaded. How much could it possibly cost to make a few social phone calls? He would soon lance Harry for two hundred dollars to cover the damage to his cottage. Why not simply make it two hundred fifty? Heinrich rubbed his chin. "I suppose I could ring my colleagues at the Golden Island Cottages, a few other places as well. How would that be?"

"Excellent! Thanks so much."

"Not at all." Heinrich walked to his lodgings behind the Great Hall. A few minutes later, he returned with marching steps and an angry frown. "The satellite phone's been *stolen*." He slammed the heel of his hand on the table, making a busboy jump. "This is too much! The generator was one thing, but this—they've gone too far!"

"Who's gone too far?" Harry said. "Does this have anything to do with—"

Heinrich waved impatiently and barked orders in Burmese to a couple of men who had peered from the kitchen. They nodded and went running out of the building. Then he turned back to Harry. "We've been having trouble with thefts—not the belongings of our guests, never fear—but our equipment is disappearing like sand out of an hourglass. And now my own satellite phone—Lord, I paid a fortune in Swiss francs." There was no more arguing over what to do. They would have to wait until morning, at which time they could dispatch a boat and a search party for the missing guests.

During the long night, Harry stayed awake, waiting for his replacement sentry to report for duty. At last the man glided up, late but ready to serve—the drunken fisherman, who let go with a wail that sounded to Harry as if it could knock the starry teeth from the heavenly firmament. To the strains of that caterwaul, Harry closed his eyes and fell into dreams that Marlena had come back to him, only now he was a tree and she was a monkey. It was I who planted this image in the slippery banks of his brain, where dreams oozed and fell out. Harry felt Marlena crawl up his trunk and curl against him, pressing her breasts to his back. And then she dug in her fingernails to hang on, dug until they pierced him in the heart. But he could bear the pain. The pain was necessary. Love made it so.

WHEN I LAST reported on our intrepid and hungry travelers, they were tramping over vine and brush to reach No Name Place, where they believed their designated Christmas lunch spot lay. As they navigated the forest, they passed by many No Name Things, creatures they failed to see. Instead, they were dumbly occupied with where to place their feet while sidestepping fallen trees and matted vines. They twisted their upper bodies to avoid prickly branches and fronds that might contain insects that were genetically designed, Heidi believed, to implant them with encephalitis and jungle fever.

But I could see the details of the world they passed through. Now that I had the gifts of the Buddha, I could flow unimpeded by safety concerns, and the hidden forms of life revealed themselves: a harmless snake with iridescent stripes, myriad fungi, flowering parasites of colors and shapes that suggested sexual turgidity—a wealth of waxy flora and moist fauna endemic to this hidden spot of the earth, as yet undiscovered by humans, or at least those who assigned taxonomic labels. I realized then that we miss so much of life while we are part of it. We fail to see ninety-nine percent of the glories of nature, for to do so would require vision that is simultaneously telescopic and microscopic.

My friends pressed ahead, accompanied by the orchestral sounds of snapping twigs, whistling birds, and the nasal buzz of a male tree frog broadcasting his desire to hop onto a female. Bennie was breathing heavily. Every now and then he tripped. His face was splotchy pink with exertion and rosacea. In an adventure travel guide, he groused to himself, this trek would have been rated as "extremely difficult, experts only," five out of five hiking staffs to warn people off. But to that I say bosh. It was not that challenging, and Vera was proof of that. Had it been more arduous, she simply would have stopped walking and announced, "You go on ahead and send me a postcard when you're recovering in intensive care." That was what she said when we were climbing the path to Taktsang monastery in Bhutan a few years back. Several times she said that, then refused to go beyond the coffeehouse. But here she trudged on with the rest. It was odd, however, that she was reciting French: *"Je tombe de la montagne, tu tombes de la montagne . . ."*

For nearly an hour, the group stumbled forward. When they came upon another fallen teak tree, Bennie yelled to the Burmese men ahead, "Hey, guys! Can we stop for a rest?"

Black Spot and Grease turned around. "No worries," Black Spot called back, using that same vacuous promise that had followed us from China. He and Grease held a private powwow. "You go ahead and let everyone know we are coming," Black Spot told his cousin. A few moments later, Grease raced ahead, while Black Spot returned to the travelers, who were now in various positions of repose on the large fallen tree with its enormous network of roots. Underneath it were small crushed trees, their branches rising at angles like broken arms.

"My goodness," Bennie said to Black Spot in sarcastic syrupy tones. "You've certainly taken us on a fun little death march."

"Thank you," Black Spot said.

"When will we reach this place?" Vera asked.

"Soon," Black Spot answered. "We are walking just a little more this way."

"Soon," Vera said with a sigh, and fanned herself with her scarf. "That's what he said an hour ago." She turned to Black Spot again. "Excuse me, but what *is* your name?"

"You can calling me Black Spot."

Esmé slumped with a heavy sigh onto a boulder and arranged her face with the weariest of expressions. Pup-pup yelped in sympathy, jumped out of the scarf sling, and licked her young caretaker's hand. Esmé let go of the paper umbrella they had bought that morning, and it rolled off to her side. Because she had silently insisted on bringing it, she could not complain. Normally, Marlena would have reproached her and made her carry the object of her impetuous desire until she admitted she was wrong. But this time, Marlena reached over and grabbed the umbrella. It was pure folly to have bought it, and they should have left the cumbersome thing in the truck, but Esmé had said: "We need a parasol in case it's all hot, and Pup-pup needs some shade." *Parasol?* Where had Esmé learned such an archaic word? Well, the important thing was that Esmé was finally talking to her again. If she was still upset, it was hard to tell from her mood, which was alternately tired and impatient, then playful and silly with the dog. Still, Marlena worried. What had Esmé actually seen? Had she seen *everything*?

Marlena felt a drop on the top of her head. The humidity made the branches above them laden with dampness, and they were sweating as heavily as Bennie. She tipped the parasol over her head. High above in the canopy, a monkey flew from branch to branch, sending down droplets that drummed on the taut oiled paper. "Hey, Mom," Esmé declared with evident pride. "Good thing we bought that umbrella."

"You're absolutely right, Wawa." Marlena nodded, happy that Esmé was happy. More drops fell on the umbrella. They reminded Marlena of Harry's attempt to put out the fire. She thought of the water-soaked dress he had used to flog at the flames, the gray driblets falling on the bed and floor. She pictured Harry standing naked and bewildered, trying to discern the significance of the charred mosquito netting as if it were a Calder mobile in a museum. He seemed so lost and little-boyish. Then she pictured his face, the way he had looked at her before the fire, the raw lust in his eyes and open mouth. She shivered and giggled. "Mommy!" she heard Esmé call. "Do we have anything to eat? I'm starved." In an instant, a frisson of motherly propriety washed over her. She dug into her bag for her supply of candy bars and dried fruit.

Esmé picked through the selection, then said, "Can Pup-pup and I have the parasol back? We have drips, too."

Wyatt had sprawled out lengthwise on a log. Wendy was picking out bits of twigs and leaves from her lover's thick, wavy hair. She traced his nose, blew flirtatiously on his eyelids, which made him laugh and wave her away. "Stop," he said. She blew again. "Stop," he repeated. *"Please."* She needed his constant attention, the evidence that he adored her as much as she adored him, and she persisted because he had not yet said the actual word "love." She blew again. To see it from Wyatt's side, this childish play was suffocating. He wished Wendy would just enjoy the moment rather than work at it. He had found her so much more fun to be with when he first met her and she was so easygoing and did not demand attention but drew it naturally.

Rupert with his flexible young knees sat in a hunch-and-crouch pose in imitation of the natives. He spotted a mammoth tree and wished he could sneak off and climb it. But his father had sternly warned him that he was to stay with the group. He fished his paperback out of his pack and began to read.

Vera used the edge of her scarf to dab at her face. She had been mulling over ideas for an invigorating speech to her staff on self-reliance, that old-fashioned word from the days of her great-grandmother. Or maybe she would write a book on the subject. This trip, she imagined herself writing, was the springboard for the book. "For there I was, a woman of sixty, lacking the lung capacity to climb what amounted to a hundred-storied building. And while I could have asked for help physically, I had to rely on myself mentally. It was as much about mental endurance . . . ." She paused to think whether this was true. She was abeam with moisture, and the tip of a fern had inserted itself in her springy cap of hair, so that she looked jaunty and beautiful, like a huntress.

The others were leaning against fallen trees. The creaking and crunching of vegetation had stopped, the heavy breathing had slowed to restful, and silence descended as heavy as thunderclouds. High above there was the occasional *whoop-whoop* of a monkey—or was it something more dangerous?

"What kind of wild animals are out here?" Wendy asked, looking into the dense foliage.

Dwight made a boogey-man laugh. "Bwaaaaah! Lions and tigers and bears, oh my."

"Actually," Moff said in a droll tone, "there *are* tigers and bears in Burma."

Heads turned. "You're joking," Wendy said.

Heidi added: "It was mentioned in the materials Bibi put together. There was a whole section on flora and fauna."

Moff began to enumerate the animals: "A small barking deer, tapirs the size of donkeys, gibbons and elephants, of course, oh, and a flying fox, rhinos, and the usual assortment of parrots and peafowl, nasty biting insects, nastier leeches, even nastier spitting cobras, a deadly poisonous krait, kills you in an hour by paralyzing your muscles—not to mention what the bear and the tiger would do once you're unable to run away."

Bennie spoke up. "I'm sure the tour company vetted this area and can guarantee we're in a safe place."

Cautious eyes darted about toward dark edges of the forest. Since Lijiang, they had not considered Bennie's opinions to be that informed. Moving slowly, they lifted their feet, inspected the backs of their legs for blood-sucking, poisonous creatures. "That's why I wear permethrin-sprayed clothing and hundred percent DEET," Heidi said.

"You sound like a commercial," Moff joked.

"And that's why I'm carrying this," Heidi added. She held up her improvised walking stick, a long slim branch.

Dwight snickered. "You think *that's* going to keep you from getting attacked by a tiger?"

"A snake," she said. "I plant it ahead of where I walk. See?" She turned over a leafy covering. A beetle slick with moisture scurried away. "And that way if there's a snake or something, it'll attack the stick first or crawl off."

The others began rummaging around the forest floor for an appropriately sized stick; Dwight did as well. Thus equipped, they were soon on their way. Every few minutes screeches or curse words pierced the air, signaling that one of them had found a gruesome creature attached to a pant leg. Black Spot would come over and flick the offender off.

"What's this place we're going?" Bennie asked. "Is it a village?"

"Not a village, smaller."

"Smaller than a village," Bennie mused. "Okay. Hamlet, settlement, outskirts . . . private estate, enclave, gated community . . . micrometropolis, compound, jail . . ."

Vera laughed at Bennie's list.

"It is a place," Black Spot said. "We are calling No Name Place."

"And how much longer till we get to this No Name Place?" Bennie asked.

"Very close," Black Spot promised.

And Bennie heaved a big sigh. "We've heard that before."

A few minutes later, they stopped and Black Spot pointed toward what appeared to be a creek bed running through the cleft of the mountain. "Just over this," he said. But as they drew closer, they realized it was a chasm that ran up and down as far as they could see, about twenty feet wide, and frighteningly deep—a dizzying labyrinth of twists and turns that spiraled downward in such a way as to make it impossible to know what dead bottom was. It looked as if the earth's core had cracked and split the mountain.

"Could be a sinkhole," Roxanne said. "We saw one in the Galápagos. Six hundred feet deep, that was the guess. No one knew for sure, since everyone who went down to investigate never came back up."

"Thanks for telling us that," said Bennie.

Bisecting this abyss was a flimsy-looking bridge made of bamboo slats held together with a network of ropes. The ends were lashed to large tree trunks. It did not convey a sense of architectural competence or engineering rigor. I would say it looked rather like a wooden clothes rack sitting on top of a place mat. Evidently my friends thought so, too.

"They expect us to go over that?" Heidi squeaked.

"It doesn't look sturdy," Vera agreed.

"I can do it!" Esmé chirped, twirling her reclaimed parasol.

"You stay right here," Marlena snapped, and grabbed her daughter's arm.

Fishbones scrambled to the middle and jumped up and down to show the tourists that the bridge was safe and strong. He loped easily to the other side, covering the twenty feet in a matter of seconds, then returned halfway and extended his hand.

"It must be safe," Bennie said to the group. "I bet these places have to pass strict safety standards to be designated a tourism site."

Moff peered into the ravine, at its great yawning mouth of rocks and scrubby brush. He picked up a stone the size of his fist and tossed it in. It hit a ledge, bounced and fell another fifty feet before smashing into another outcropping a hundred feet below. The sound of the object careening downward continued long after they lost sight of it. "I'll be the human sacrifice," Moff said. "Just be sure to get some video, so that if I'm killed, you'll have evidence to sue whoever made this thing." Roxanne aimed her camcorder. "Think of this as Tarzan's amazing adventures," he said. He took several deep breaths, gritted his teeth, and slowly angled forward. When the bridge dipped in the middle, he let go with an elongated warbling shout—*"whoa-OH-ohhh"*—that matched the somersault in his stomach. As soon as he regained his balance, he walked steadily forward; then he called out to Rupert to come next. If his ex-wife could see what they were doing, he would be in jail for child endangerment. "Hang on to the sides," he advised. "Steady as you go, as smoothly as you can, and adjust your body to the ups and downs, rather than reacting and pushing against it."

"You mean, don't do what you did," Rupert said. The group watched him stride smoothly forward, hands free like a tightrope walker. "Man, that was cool," he said when he reached the other side. Black Spot, Salt, and Fishbones noticed how cool.

One by one, the rest traversed the short distance, some slowly, some quickly, others with much coaxing, or with Black Spot leading them forward. Roxanne was the last to cross. She had already handed the camera to Black Spot, who gave it to Dwight, so he could document her rite of passage. Once all were safely on solid ground, they were awash in self-congratulations, gloating and giving instant replays of their own ten seconds of peril, until Heidi reminded them: "We have to go back over after lunch." Their elation thus doused, they moved onward.

Still behind them, on the other side of the bridge, were the three young men with their machetes and supplies. Balanced over their shoulders were thick bamboo poles from which hung big twelve-volt batteries, a generator frame, the jackets of their guests, and assorted food supplies. One by one, these men deftly went across, and then lowered their loads to the ground. With practiced expertise, one of them began to unwind the knots that tethered the bridge to its tree anchors, while the other two unwound a rope that was off to the side, curled around the trunk of another tree to create a winch. This was the long tail of the bridge. Carefully now, the men lowered the bridge while relaxing the long rope. Down it went, until the bridge hung like a useless ladder on the opposite side. They swung and jostled the tail end of the rope still attached to the bridge until it blended with the lianas of the winding gorge and disappeared. The free end was lashed to the root of a tree that had fallen over, decades before. Ferns hid it completely.

From this vantage point, the people of No Name Place could see the bridge. But no one approaching their secret home from the other side would know a bridge had ever been there. And that was how they kept themselves cut off, hidden in a secret world no one knew existed, they hoped. For the past year, the bridge had been brought up every other week, when they needed supplies and felt there was no risk that soldiers were in the area. If the soldiers discovered the bridge, the Karen people would run toward the deep jaws of the mountain and jump in. Better that than to be caught, tortured, and killed. And if they weren't able to kill themselves first, if they were caught by the soldiers, they would gouge out their own eyes so they could not watch the soldiers rape their sisters and daughters, or cut the throats of their mothers and fathers. The soldiers, they remembered, liked to smile when they held the knife to make someone rise or lower, as if they were puppet masters pulling the strings of a marionette to retell one of the old Jataka tales of the Burmans.

They feared the soldiers most during the monsoons. The rain beat down the thatches over the tribe's small verandahs, and they lived in mud and picked off leeches every few minutes. During that season they hung bamboo-lattice hammocks in the trees where they sat and slept. It was then that the SLORC soldiers came. They could approach a whole settlement from behind and catch them on the wrong side of a raging stream, unable to escape except into the water. The soldiers, some of them boys of only twelve or thirteen, would stand on the shore, aim their rifles, and laugh when they hit a target and its arms stopped flailing. Sometimes they would toss in a grenade that exploded and sent lifeless bodies and fish floating to the top and then swirling in eddies like lily pads. A few of the people at No Name Place had lost their entire families this way. It was a miracle and a misery that the Great God had spared them.

But this was the dry season. This was when the hunter soldiers were lazy, getting ready for the good times of Independence Day. The numbers of soldiers had been fewer at this season the year before, but there was no sure pattern to anything that SLORC did.

Black Spot ran ahead of my friends, as they wearily plodded onward. Another hundred yards lay in front of them before they reached No Name Place.

Earlier, while they had rested by the fallen log, Grease had sprinted up the mountain and into the camp to announce that the Younger White Brother and his retinue were coming. The inhabitants of No Name Place stood still. This was the miracle they had prayed for. For three years, they had given offerings that this might come to pass.

"This is true?" an old grandmother finally said.

"Kill one of the chickens," Grease said. "They're expecting a feast."

And then the tribe members ran in different directions. There was barely enough time to ready themselves. Women pulled out their best clothes, black boxy jackets woven with checkerboards of red and gold diamonds. The old women dug out of the ground the last of their silver bangles. Some ladies covered their chests with a profusion of ropy necklaces made of glass beads from the old traders and Chinese beads that had been in their families for hundreds of years. Others had only plastic.

Grease heard Black Spot's whistle, a signal that he had crossed the bridge. He returned the call with two shrill blasts. Half a minute later, Black Spot rushed in and his friends surrounded him. They spoke rapidly in the Karen language, unable to contain their happy disbelief. "You got so many to come!" one man said. "God is great!" said another. "Which one is the Younger White Brother?" And Black Spot replied that it was clear, if they used their eyes. They looked at their approaching saviors, my friends, lifting one heavy foot after the other, all of them exhausted, except for Rupert, who could have run circles around them, and was now striding forward, yelling, "Come on! We're almost there."

A thin little girl of three ran forward and grabbed Black Spot by his legs. He lifted her in the air and examined her face, before concluding that her laughter and smiles were signs that she was well, the malaria gone. He set her atop his shoulders and walked farther into the camp. Black Spot's wife watched this, but did not smile. With every reunion, she would think, Will we remember this as the last?

Black Spot was the headman of this small tribe of people, the survivors of other villages. He guided them toward consensus by providing them with sound reasoning to solve squabbles. He often reminded them of their tradition to remain unified. Like all Karen, they stuck together, no matter what.

My friends entered the encampment and were instantly surrounded by a dozen tribal people who pushed and jumped to get a glimpse. They heard the natives uttering a pretty garble of sounds. Some of the old women had their hands clasped and were bowing rapidly. "It's like we're rock stars or something," Rupert said.

Bennie saw that some of the men had slung their arms around Black Spot and were offering him a cheroot. Others jumped on the backs of Salt and Fishbones and hooted. "These people sure are friendly with those guys," Bennie remarked. "Walter must take people up here a lot." My compatriots were disappointed to think that the formerly "rare opportunity" might be a common tourist destination.

"What tribe are they?" Vera asked Black Spot.

"They are Karen," he said. "All good people. The Karen are the original people of Burma. Before there are Bamar or others tribe coming to Burma, the Karen people are already here."

"Kah-REN," Roxanne repeated.

"You like Karen people?" Black Spot asked with a grin.

"They're great," she said, and this was followed by a chorus from my friends, affirming the same opinion about a people they as yet knew little about.

"Good. Because I am Karen, too." Black Spot pointed to the other boatmen. "They are Karen, too. Same. Our families are living here in No Name Place."

"No wonder you knew the way up here so well," Bennie said.

"Yes, yes," Black Spot said. "Now you are knowing this."

A few of my friends suspected that Walter and Black Spot had a deal going on under the table. But if they did, what did it matter? This was an interesting place.

With a throng of Karen people trailing behind them, my friends came into a larger clearing, an area about fifty feet in diameter. Above, the sky was barely visible through the overlapping tree canopies. The campsite was partially covered with mats. Close to the center was a stove made of stacked rocks, with a maw for feeding wood. Flanking that were teak logs used as tables, on top of which were assorted bowls of food. The surprise Christmas lunch. Fantastic.

They glanced about. At the edges were rounded huts the size of children's tree houses. Upon closer inspection, my friends saw that they *were* tree houses, each the hollow of a tree base just large enough for one or two people. The walls were formed of the long skeletal roots, their spacings woven with palm thatch. The roofs were low, and bound with interlaced vines and runners. Other tree huts and various small shelters lay beyond the perimeter.

"It's so *unchanged*," Wendy whispered to Wyatt. "Like the twentieth century forgot to come here."

"You like?" Black Spot said. He was bursting with pride.

The camp now massed with its residents—I counted fifty-three— many of the older ones wearing turbans and red-and-black smocks. My friends saw crackly-faced grandmothers and smooth-cheeked girls, curious boys, and men with red betel-nut juice staining their teeth, making it seem as if their gums were bleeding from an ulcerating disease. The people cried in the Karen language, "Our leader has come! We'll be saved!" My friends smiled at this welcome, and said, "Thanks! Good to be here."

Three children ran over to get a closer view—foreigners in their jungle home! They stood in awe. Their young faces were solemn and watchful, and as soon as Moff and Wyatt crouched down, they shrieked and ran off. "Hullo!" Wyatt called after them. "What's your name?" Girls in white sackcloth dresses stood at a safe distance, avoiding eye contact. When the white man was not looking at them, they gradually moved closer with shy smiles. One of the boys ran close to Moff, the tallest of the foreigners, and in that universal game of dare, he slapped the back of Moff's knee and darted off with a high-pitched shout before the ogre could strike him down. When another boy did the same, Moff let out a groan and pretended to nearly topple over, much to the delight of the children.

Two more children appeared, a boy and girl, who looked to be seven or eight. They had coppery brown hair, and both were dressed in cleaner and more elaborately embroidered clothes. The boy had a long white chemise, the girl a Western christening dress with lace edging. Vera noted with dismay that they were smoking cheroots.

They were actually twins, and according to the tribe's beliefs, they were divinities. They boldly pushed past the others, grabbed Rupert by his hands, and led him toward their grandmother, who was tending a pot on the rock hearth. The old woman scolded the children as she saw them approach. "Don't drag him around like that. Hold his hands with respect." When Rupert was before her, she shyly averted her eyes and offered Rupert a stump to sit on, which he refused. He shook loose from his admirers and walked about the camp.

Marlena observed that except for the twins and older people, few wore the distinctive costumes seen at most dance and cultural spectacles. Could this be an authentic tribe and not one designer-garbed to look ethnic? The head wraps on the men and women were clearly functional and not decorative. They looked like dirty Turkish towels wound without regard to fashion. And the women and girls in sarongs had chosen loud plaids and cheap flowery designs. The men were clothed in raggedy pajama bottoms and dirty tank tops that hung to their knees. One wore a T-shirt that said "MIT Media Lab" on the front, and on the back, "Demo or Die." Who left *that* behind? Only a few had rubber flip-flops, leading Marlena to recall childhood warnings to never let your bare feet touch dirt lest tiny worms pierce them, crawl up the insides of your legs, into your stomach, ever upward until they lodged in your brain.

Moff stepped closer to the tree houses. Finally realizing what they were, he became excited and called Heidi over. He pointed out the vast roots. "They're mature strangler figs. I've seen them in South America, but these are absolutely huge."

"Strangler," Heidi said, and shuddered.

"See up there?" And Moff explained how the seeds had taken hold high in the scummy crannies of host trees. Aerial roots spread downward and girdled the host tree, and as the host grew, the vascular roots thickened in a deadly embrace. "Kind of like a marriage I was once in," Moff said. The host tree was choked to death, he went on to say, then decomposed, thanks to armies of insects, fungi, and bacteria, leaving behind a skeletal trunk. "The result," Moff said, "is this hollow, a cozy bungalow for rodents, reptiles, bats, and apparently, the denizens of the rainforest." He looked up and whistled. "I love this. I've written a few articles about rainforest canopies. My goal is to get something published in *Weird Plant Morphology* one day."

From another part of the small camp came shouts of jubilation. The tribe was watching Rupert taking whacks at timber bamboo with a machete that Black Spot had given him. With each swing, the tribe cheered. Black Spot said in Karen: "You see his strength. This is another sign that he is the Younger White Brother."

"What other signs did you see?" a middle-aged man asked.

And Black Spot answered: "The book and the Nat cards. He manifested the same Lord of Nats. He then made him disappear and jump out in another place." More people came into the crowd to catch a glimpse of the Reincarnated One. "Is it really him?" the jungle people asked among themselves.

A young woman said, "You can tell he is the one by the eyebrows, thick and at a slant, those of a cautious man."

"He looks like a TV star," said another woman, and giggled.

"Is that book the Lost Important Writings?" a man called out.

This time, Black Spot explained, the Younger White Brother chose to bring a black book and not a white one. It was similar to the one the Older Brother lost, but this was called *Misery*, titled like the old Lamentations. Black Spot could read only a little, but from what he saw, he believed it concerned their sufferings over the last hundred years. That would make these the New Important Writings.

"But what did you see him do?" a one-legged man asked. "What did the sign look like?"

"They were at the dock in Nyaung Shwe Town," Black Spot reported, "and the Younger Brother easily drew a crowd to him, as only leaders can. He spoke with great authority and called upon people to believe in his magic." Just then Rupert walked by, and Black Spot said to him in English, "Please, sir." He made the fanning motion of a deck of cards. "You can showing us the disappearing of things?"

Rupert shrugged. "I guess." He slipped the deck out of his pocket and began to shuffle in midair, sending the cards leaping.

The tribe broke into grateful cries. At last, they would grow strong again. No more eating rotted fruit from the Tree of Trial. To the Karen, it did seem fate had led Rupert here. He had the deck of cards, the Important Writings, the slanted eyebrows. For years this splinter tribe had been seeking signs. They had studied every foreigner who arrived at the dock in Nyaung Shwe, where a young man had arrived more than a hundred years earlier, the Younger White Brother. Just as likely, the tribe could have seen other signs—a young man with sandy hair wearing a white coat and a straw hat. Or these: a gilded cane, a carefully clipped moustache, a small wormlike scar below the left eye. Equally convincing: any sleight-of-hand, particularly the ability to change a person's hat without his realizing it, or to open a book and make it seem as if God were blowing the pages. These people, now so desperate for any kind of hope, saw what they wished to see, the signs, the promise. Don't we all see them? We wait for signs that we will be saved, or protected from future harm, or endowed with unusual good luck. And often, we find them.

The people of No Name Place created a receiving line and beckoned the visitors to go through. "Use your right hand," Bennie advised. "In some countries the left is considered untouchable." My friends did as Bennie suggested, but their hosts used both their hands to clasp each visitor's right. They shook hands up and down, gently. *"Dah ler ah gay, dah ler ah gay,"* the people of the jungle murmured, and followed this with a slight bow. Marlena was surprised to feel the roughness of their skin, even on the young children. Their hands had been toughened by calluses and cuts. One man, she was shocked to learn, had only two bony fingers on one hand, and he gripped her hard, as if to take away three of hers as replacements.

Rupert was standing next to Marlena, and as they made their way through the receiving line, she noted something peculiar: With Rupert, the Karen looked down, covered their mouths, and bowed extra low. Perhaps it was a custom accorded to men alone. But she saw that Moff and Dwight received only the slight bows shown to her, and the Karen had no problem looking at them straight in the eye. Who knew what the customs and taboos were here?

A few girls spotted the little dog Esmé held tightly to her chest. They pointed and sang out: "Woo-woo! Woo-woo!" Everyone laughed, except Esmé. A few kids reached to pet the dog, their eyes seeking permission. "Just the head," Esmé instructed firmly and with a watchful eye. "Right here. Gentle." And the little dog licked each child's hand like a benediction.

Roxanne motioned to Black Spot to come over. She held up her camcorder. "Do they mind? It's okay?"

"Please," he said, and swept his hand back to suggest an invitation that she take it all in.

She did a panorama, rotating to include three hundred sixty degrees, narrating where they were and how welcoming the Karen tribe was. She saw Dwight. "Honey, stand over by those women behind you," she directed. He knew the ploy. Instead of capturing him, she would film the natives in natural poses. But as soon as she pressed the record button, the old ladies looked up at the camcorder and waved. "What hams," Roxanne said. She waved back. "We've come to this beautiful place . . ." she now narrated for the video.

Wyatt and Wendy were talking to two young women. Wendy pointed to herself.

"America," she said, and then pointed to Wyatt: "America." The women repeated, "Merraga, Merraga." Black Spot uttered in their dialect: "They come from the United States." One of the young women shot back, "We knew that. They're telling us their name. Both are called the same."

"They're so friendly," Wyatt said, and let two boys look at the photo captured on his digital camera. The rest of my friends were similarly engaged in meeting the inhabitants, making the most of this cultural activity. Bennie tried to buy a few items that looked interesting—a bamboo cup, a wooden bowl—but when he inquired about the price, intending to double whatever was asked, the owners insisted he take them for free. "They're so generous, which counts twice as much because they're poor," he told Vera.

The greatest attention, of course, was heaped on Rupert. The crowd surrounded him and moved him toward a long carved plank that was laden with a banquet—a banquet, that is, by the standards of a tribal people bedeviled by years of hardship. Black Spot gave out the invitation: "Please, we inviting you—eat, sir."

To my friends, the jungle repast looked ill conceived, one dish after another, what Moff called "mystery meats," grayish-greenish substances, some shiny, some slimy, none of it looking palatable. But as they would soon discern, the food was actually quite delicious. There were seasonal weeds, sticky rice, and the leaves of woodland trees and shrubs. There were also, in beautiful small bowls carved out of tree knots, tubers and seeds, buds and stems, small growths that were as delicious as pistachios and almonds, fungi of all kinds, gathered from the base of trees, left to dry, and then stored for occasions like these. The main platters held nascent reeds. And at the other end of the long narrow table were bowls with roots, sliced fermented eggs, roasted larvae, and a prized chicken. The dishes had been colored and flavored with whatever dry goods were stocked in the primordial kitchen: colorful ingredients of shrimp powder and turmeric, coarse chili and curry, garlic chips in place of fresh, preserved vegetables, as well as paprika, salt, and sugar. Next to the chicken, the most prized dish was the talapaw, a vegetable soup prepared by the twins' grandmother, who knew just the right amount of spices and peppers to pinch with her fingers and mix into the crushed rice, fish sauce, and green beans, ingredients that Black Spot had brought her after his last foray into town. To bind all these many flavors, a big pot of rice was set in the middle of the table.

The twins' grandmother signaled Rupert to be the first to fill his bowl. "Yum," he said in flat voice. "I'll just dig right in." After his first bite, his eyebrows rose. After his second, he announced, "Not bad." The young women around him kept their faces down, but beamed and giggled as he nodded, and gave a thumbs-up. Two young boys mimicked the gesture.

Marlena leaned over and said to Moff: "I think Rupert has found some female admirers."

When lunch was over, Roxanne held up her camcorder and captured the happy occasion. Bennie stood next to the pecked-at banquet table. He waved and called: "Hi, Mom! We love it here! Good food, too. Yummy-yum." Marlena tried to think of something to say about the strangler figs. "Our new home . . ." she quipped, and gestured toward the tangle of vines. "The rent is supercheap. Comes with expansive backyard and lots of trees. We're moving in." Rupert was caught showing the tribe yet another card trick. He looked up at the camera and grinned. "The way things are going I may never leave this place. . . ."

All at once, a child's high voice cried out, and everyone fell silent. All heads turned toward the coppery-haired boy with a smoky cheroot hanging from his mouth. He was standing on an upturned stump and looked wild. He was rocking forward and back. His twin sister mounted the stump next to his, and she, too, began to sway. Staring blankly, the boy seemed to be in a trance, moving his upper body in cadence to his keening. The people of the jungle fell to their knees, shut their eyes and clasped their hands, and began to pray. The twins' grandmother stood and began to speak.

"Christmas entertainment's starting," Moff announced. "Must be the manger scene."

My friends glanced about. Who were these people? They could not fathom what the twins were doing, yet they certainly looked odd. But as I had found more and more often, with the proper attitude, the Mind of Others—and a bit of eavesdropping on private conversations—many truths are knowable.

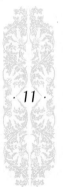

They All
Stuck Together

The boy was praying, not to a Buddhist deity, as one might expect, but to the Christian God, the Great God, and his emissary, the Younger White Brother, Lord of Nats. This was a renegade ethnic tribe who had no orthodox religion but had accommodated a pantheon over the past century. And so they believed in Nats and witches and green ghosts as both mischief makers and deliverers of disasters. They worshipped the Lord of Land and Water: O Lord, we're sorry we had to chop down the saplings, but please don't let our soil and crops wash away to the bottom. They had given thanks to the Crop Grandmother in the days when they had fields: We pray to you to give us good rain, good rice, no chewing insects, and not too many sticky weeds.

And they believed in the Younger White Brother, who had been part of their mythology for hundreds of years. They had once had an elegantly written language, and not the chicken scratch that some now used. Their stories were contained in three books of Important Writings. Those writings held their strength, their protection from ill forces. The books were supposed to be safeguarded by two divine but absentminded brothers, who lost them by placing them where they were eaten by wild animals or burned by a cooking fire. As prophesied, one day the Younger White Brother would bring back another copy of the Important Writings and restore their tribe's power.

As you can imagine, missionaries over the years found a willing flock, who readily accepted Jesus and were keen to learn the Bible. The tribe mistook each of the pastors who arrived over the years as the Younger White Brother. As with the Buddha, the tribe gave offerings to the Great God to receive merit, and this gave the missionaries merit and made them happy. The tribe loved consensus and mutual respect. When a pastor died—as many did, from malaria, typhoid, or dysentery—the tribe waited patiently for him to return as a Reincarnated One. In 1892, the one who would be the most influential of the Younger White Brothers arrived among the Karen.

He was born in England, an ordinary boy, named Edgar Seraphineas Andrews, his odd middle name chosen by his mother, who thought she had passed from life while giving birth to him but was then miraculously returned to vital shores by a large-winged angel, who pried her neck from Death's cold grip. That was the Seraph. The rest of his name came from his father, Edgar Phineas Andrews. They were not a titled family but a rich one. In former years, the elder Andrews had been noted for his charm, his prodigious conversational skills, and his generosity. Aided by his wife, Matilda, he used to invite battalions of guests to join him for weeks of witty parties, in which the visitors were required to dress in the funny costumes native to whichever of the colonies had been chosen for the evening's theme. But in later years, his perceived charm dwindled along with his bank account. Duped in a speculation scheme, he suffered a devastating reversal. There were no more costume balls filled with laughter, no laughter, for that matter, for there were no servants to attend to the preparation, upkeep, and disposal of laughter. No manservant or valet, no cook or scullery maid, no gardener or groomsman. Matilda Andrews fell into a perpetual state of mortification and remained in her rooms talking to the wives of dignitaries in her mirrors. Young Seraphineas kept to himself and read books—books on magic, which he perceived to be the fine art of conjuring money out of rich fools. He practiced many of his illusions on his father, a willing subject, as he had already proven all too well.

In 1882, Phineas Andrews was invited to Rangoon by an old and loyal friend, a captain with the Raj, who beckoned him to witness the courage of the soldiers who served Her Majesty in the wild jungles of Burma. At first glance, Phineas became enamored of Burma and her verandahs and lazy days, her palanquins and polite deference to the British. In Burma, he started a small export business in feather fans, the feathers plucked from the marvelous array of birds found in this tropical land. In short order, his business included other exotic luxuries: elephant-leg stools, stuffed-monkey lamps, tiger-skin rugs, and drums fashioned out of the bowls of two human skulls, which produced a sound like no other. Many items remained unsold, but the profit margins were high enough to make Phineas a wealthy man again. In that small society, the Andrews family was soon elevated to the equivalent of high pooh-bahs. They had twenty servants—they could have had a hundred, if they liked—and lived in a house with so many rooms and gardens that most of them had no particular purpose.

Phineas was not a bad sort, merely dissipated and ineffectual. But the youngest of his three sons was "a friend of evil," as some he tricked would later describe him. Whatever charm his father had possessed for entertaining, Seraphineas used without hesitation for ill gain. Whereas the father could convince his costumed guests that he was the Sheik of Araby, the son could convince a tribe of thousands that he was the Lord Almighty of Nats.

Having spent a good part of his boyhood in Burma, Seraphineas Andrews was adept at debauchery in two cultures. He took to bedding loose ladies and seducing laced-up ones, smoking opium and drinking absinthe. In Mandalay, he learned from watching illusionists of all nations and stripes, and soon began to defraud even the savviest gamblers. He found opportunity in the thousandth of a second between movements, and he knew the power of psychological diversion and verbal smokescreen. What his father had lost through speculation he could more than make up through manipulation. The supply of gullible people in the world was delightfully endless.

Seraphineas Andrews made it his habit to discern quickly what religious, mystical, or superstitious beliefs people held. Their illusions, he found, made for interesting twists in his illusions. He might thump a Bible to ask God to deliver the right card into the victim's hand. He might cause watches to disappear from men's pockets, and reappear in the palm of the Buddha. The more people believed, the more they could be fooled.

One day, he was performing his usual repertory of tricks, a deck of cards in one hand, the Bible in another. He set the Bible down, opened to Psalms, and as he shuffled and exhorted God to manifest Himself to the unbelievers, an exhalation of his breath caused a few pages to rise and turn. He had not intended to do this, but instantly, a dozen new believers felt the hand of God seizing their necks.

From then on, Seraphineas Andrews practiced and perfected a trick he called the Breath of God. At first he could turn a single thin page of the Bible from a distance of one foot. He increased this to two feet, then learned to shoot his breath from the side of his mouth without any sign that he was puffing his cheeks or rotating his lips. In time, he could converse and between words aim his breath backward five feet and ripple the pages from Old Testament to New.

He had discovered that changing a person's beliefs was intoxicating, far more satisfying than performing tricks that only induced a temporary bewilderment. For a while, he was able to convince a number of young ladies that God had commanded them to grant him intimate favors, which they could give freely, for God, they would see, restored their purity as soon as the gift was given. He progressed to cheating grieving widows out of their bank holdings in exchange for a reunion with their deceased husbands. The husbands bade greetings and adieu with the rippling pages. He later had a retinue of young men to carry out his orders, from robbing banks to stabbing to death a man who threatened to expose him as an impostor. When friends of the dead man began to investigate, the crooked finger of fate pointed at Seraphineas Andrews and he ran into the Burmese jungle.

Seraphineas Andrews knew of the myth of the Younger White Brother. How convenient that he was supposed to be white. Andrews set up an impromptu church on a busy market day. He opened a traveling table and placed a short stack of twelve cards on one side and the open Bible on the other. "Within your villages," he intoned, "you have many Nats, who want to do you mischief and harm." He fanned out the cards with a single tap of his finger. "I have captured their likenesses here." The crowd peered at the faces: the Lord of Spades, the Lady of Spades, the Son of the Lord of Spades . . . He then called upon the Heavenly Father and Lord Jesus to recognize him as the Younger White Brother who had come to deliver these souls from evil. "Show me a sign that I am the one chosen to lead the Lord's Army." He looked upward. The pages stirred and stood upright for a moment, then rapidly flapped forward.

There was another sign that Seraphineas Andrews often used. He would select the most blustery man from the crowd and ask him to pick a card from a full deck of fifty-two, which was always the king of clubs, one of the colorful cards that represented a Nat. Next he was told to pick another card, and invariably it was the two of diamonds. He was then told to hide that card—behind his back, in his turban, under his shoe, wherever he liked. Seraphineas would then slip the two of diamonds into the cards and shuffle the deck, tap the top card, and ask the man to turn it over. Without fail, the Nat card that the man had hidden would be there, and the one he retrieved from its hiding place would be the two of diamonds. Seraphineas Andrews would ask the crowd: "Do you now believe that I am the Lord of Nats, ruler over all Nats?" And the open pages of the Bible would fly forward, calling forth the answer.

The Lord of Nats soon had a fast-growing flock. His followers were called the Lord's Army, and this subgroup of Karen constituted both his cherished children and his soldiers in battle. His doctrines contained the precise combination of elements that would keep an oppressed people under absolute control: fear of oblivion, strict laws of obedience, harsh punishment for doubt, rituals with feasting, the manifestation of miracles, and the promise of immortality in a Kingdom of Everlasting Rice Fields. In a few years, Seraphineas Andrews's flock grew to thousands, bolstered by the numerous "children of the Lord of Nats," the hundred or so conceived by Seraphineas Andrews and his two dozen perpetually virgin wives.

If any good can be said of Seraphineas Andrews, it is the schools and clinics he built. He allowed his daughters and eventually all girls to attend school so that they could read and write and do sums. The instruction was motley, a collision of English and Burmese, but one can't quibble with the good of an educated mind in any language, even if it's pidgin.

There is one other mystery associated with Seraphineas, which has never been settled to any degree of certainty. It involves a book, wittily written in an acerbic voice, that was published in the United States under the name S. W. Erdnase, and entitled *Artifice, Ruse, and Subterfuge at the Card Table*—the work of an obviously cultured mind. No one has ever determined the identity of S. W. Erdnase. Some, however, point out that "S. W. Erdnase" is "E. S. Andrews" backward.

Through trick or book royalties, Seraphineas had money to buy goods in America, and a friend would ship these to Burma. Every year the crates arrived, with schoolbooks, blackboards, and medicines, as well as replenishments of favorite foods. There were also white dresses with rickrack for his virgin brides and the latest fashions for his wardrobe, all in a creamy ivory: French-tailored shirts, morning jackets and waistcoats, cravats, and a Panama hat. The kidskin boots were always lacquer black. The walking stick was ebony and gold, with an inlaid ivory handle.

One day, while on a picnic with several of his favorite wives and sons, he walked into the jungle and did not return to his half-eaten meal. At first, no one worried too much. The Lord of Nats had the power of invisibility. He had often disappeared when soldiers of the British Raj came to arrest him for swindling and murder. He had given some of his invisible powers to his children as well. But this time, too many hours passed, the hours turning into days, then weeks, then months. No trace of him was ever found, not a scrap of clothing, shoe, bone, or tooth. The Important Writings were also gone. In later years, when it was time for myths to be enlarged, several of his followers recalled that they had seen him flying with white bird-angels to the Land Beyond the Last Valley—to the Kingdom of Death, where he would conquer its ruler. But he would return, the faithful said, never fear, for it was written in the book of Important Writings. And when he did return, they would recognize him by the three Holy Signs, whatever those turned out to be.

Although many missionaries had come and gone since, it was Seraphineas Andrews's influence that prevailed with this Karen splinter tribe. His followers continued to be known as the "Lord's Army," but his actual descendants were few, for most of them had been killed over the periods of upheaval. The rusty-headed twins were two who remained, from the lineage of the Lord of Nats and his Most-Most Favorite Concubine. She was much higher in status than the Most Favorite Concubine, and somewhat lower than the Most-Most Favored Wife. This was according to the twin's grandmother, who was not from the paternal side, and so not of the divine lineage. But she was the one who named the boy "Loot" and the girl "Bootie," English words meaning "goods of great value taken in war." She kept them from being that, as she now testified to the tribe and the Younger White Brother.

"EVERYONE RECOGNIZED Loot and Bootie as divinities," the grandmother recounted. "There were three signs. . . ."

The first was their double healthy birth when times were bad—they were the long starving days, for sure. But the moment those two came into the world, a big juicy bird fell from the sky—glutted drunk on fermented fruit—and landed head side down and feet side up, right in the cooking fire. All we had to do was pull it out, brush off the ashes, and put it in the pot.

No tears, that was the second sign. The twins never cried. Why a divinity has no need to cry, I don't know. But they never did. Not when they were babies. Not when they were hungry. Not when they fell down and broke a nose or a toe. Not when their father and mother died. This would be very strange for anybody else, but not when you are a divinity.

But the greatest proof came the day the soldiers chased us into the river. It was three years ago, when we still lived in the southern end of Karen State, to the south of where we are now, before we came back to the home of the Younger White Brother. In those days, we lived among the flat fields. Down there they were building the big oil pipeline to Thailand, and many villages were burned down to make room for that. My husband was the headman and he told them that the SLORC army would not only burn our homes but also force us to work on the pipeline. We knew what happened to people who did that. They starved. They were beaten. They got sick and died. So we made a plan. We wouldn't go, that was the plan. We would take our best things high in the mountain and deep in the jungle—our cooking utensils, our farming tools. We would leave a few junky things just to fool them into thinking we would come back.

We flatland farmers went to live in the jungle like the hill tribes. We lived by a big stream, and we learned how to swim the slow green waters. We bathed there every day, and it was never deep. We had made another plan. If the soldiers came, we would jump in the river to escape. But the day the soldiers came, the stream was running like a crazy spitting demon. It was the monsoon season. Still, we ran for the water as the soldiers ran for us. I grabbed Loot and Bootie—and the river grabbed us, and there was no time to think what was up and what was down as we tumbled along.

Some of the villagers were thrashing, some were paddling, and I was holding the edge of a bamboo pallet, that's what Loot and Bootie were sitting on. How we got this pallet, I didn't ask myself at the time, never did until just now, and now I am telling you that the Great God gave it to Loot and Bootie, since there was no reason He'd give it to me.

So on this pallet, Loot and Bootie were riding, and I was hanging on to just a small edge, a pinch, careful not to tip them over. I saw our whole village moving down the river as one, and I had a vision—or maybe it was a memory—it was everyone in the threshing field on the first day of harvest, which wasn't so long ago and was also coming up soon. In that field, we thrashed as well, moving through waves of ripened grass. We moved as one, for we were the field, we were the grass, that's how I remembered it. And here we were again—our entire village, our headman, my family people, and the dear old faces of girls who had pounded the rice with me since the days we wore our littlest white smocks. Now they were pounding the white water to keep their heads afloat.

Those old girls and I saw the green soldiers running along the banks of the river. Oh, they were mad that we had escaped. We had jumped into the river and ruined their fun. They'd have to wait another day, wouldn't they? The old girls and I had a fine laugh about that. Their eyes were crinkled into smiles, and over each old face was a beautiful shiny veil of water, poured from the top of her head, running over her eyes, then falling into the cup of her happy mouth. With these bright veils, my old sisters wore young faces again, like the first time we wore our singing shawls. It was for an old-old elder's funeral. We walked 'round and 'round the body, pretending to mourn, and shook the shawl fringes to sound the bells. And the young men went 'round and 'round the other way, to catch our smiles and count how many they caught. How glad we were that the old-old elder finally had the good sense to die.

And quick as that, the years swam by, and there we were in the crazy water, over fifty years old, the age of our dead elder. And the young men were now running along the banks in their ugly green uniforms. We saw them tip the noses of their rifles at us. Why were they doing that? And each nose made a little sneeze, like this, up and down, up and down, but no sounds. No crack, no hiss, just one watery veil turning red, then the other, and me wondering, Why no sounds? No *boof-boof.* My sisters were shuddering, trying to keep their spirits in their bodies, and I was trying to grab them to hang on, but then with one great heave, they went limp, just like that.

When my senses came back, I saw that the twins and their pallet were gone. I pushed my poor old sisters away to see if Loot and Bootie were underneath. The soldiers still had their rifles aimed toward us. All around me, the villagers were pounding the water, but not to get away. They were hurrying to shore. Maybe my husband told them to do this. Everyone listens to the headman and doesn't argue. Maybe he said, We'll work the pipeline and make another plan later. Whatever he said, I saw them climbing the banks. They were sticking together, because that's how we are. And I would have done that, too, but I had to find Loot and Bootie first. The Great God told me I had to do this.

So I stayed in the water by the Great God's will and against my own. Only one soldier tipped his rifle nose at me, but he was very young, and instead of a little sneeze, his rifle made a big one, so he couldn't shoot anything but the sky. I saw our village was already on fire. The thatch of the houses was burning, the rice sheds, too, black smoke rising. I saw my family and the other villagers crawling on knees and hands toward the soldiers. My husband, my daughter, her husband, my other daughter, the four sons of my rice-pounding sister, her husband, who was still looking back to see where she was. I saw some of them fall flat onto their faces. I thought they had been kicked. One by one, they fell. One by one, I shouted, Ai! One by one, I was leaving them. And even if I had tried to swim back, the stream was too fast, and it carried me away, like an empty boat.

I was going to tip myself over and fall to the bottom of the river. But then I heard them, Loot and Bootie. They were laughing like the tinkling bells of a singing shawl. They were still on the pallet, spinning in an eddy. After I reached them and checked them twice for holes, I cried and cried for I was so happy, and then I cried and cried again for I was so sad.

That was the day I knew Loot and Bootie had the power to both resist bullets and disappear. That's why the soldiers never saw them. That's why they're still here. They're divinities, descended from the Younger White Brother, who also knew how to disappear. Of course, Loot and Bootie are still children and quite naughty at that, so mostly they disappear when I don't want them to. But now that the Younger White Brother has come, he can teach them how to disappear properly. It's time they learned.

Why am I still here? I have no divine powers. No such thing for me. I think the Great God kept me so I can watch over Loot and Bootie, and that is what I do, my eyes never leave them.

He also wanted me to live so I could tell this story. If I didn't tell it, who would? And then who would know? I'm past the age when most are gone, so that's proof, too, of the Great God's will. He told me to bear witness of what I know—just the important parts, and not about the old girls and how pretty they looked. But that's what I remember, too, that and no sounds. Why no sounds?

The important part I am supposed to tell is everything I didn't see, what happened after the river took me away. I now know this: Some they shot as soon as they came ashore. And others, they tied their hands behind them, poured hot chilies in their eyes, and covered their heads with plastic bags, then left them in the sun. They pounded many with rifles and our own threshing tools. To the rest, who wept, they shouted, Where are your rifles hidden? Who is the leader of the Karen army? They took one man and cut off both hands and all his toes. They dangled the babies to make the fathers talk. But we did not show them the rifles. No one did. How could we? We had no rifles. So a soldier showed a man his rifle and shot him dead. They shot all the men who were still living. I cannot tell you what they did to the babies. Those words won't come out of my throat. As for the women and girls, even the ones who were only nine or ten, the soldiers kept them for two days. They raped them, the old ones, too, it didn't matter how young or old, six men to one girl, all night, all day. The screams never stopped for those two days. The soldiers called them pigs, they pierced them like pigs, told them they screamed like pigs and bled like pigs. With those who tried to fight them off, they cut off their breasts. Some of the girls died from bleeding. As for the ones who lived, when they were all used up, the soldiers shot them. All but one girl. She prayed and prayed for a way to live, even while the soldiers were using her. And the Great God answered her prayers. While the soldiers were using her she fainted, and they threw her off into a corner. When she revived, she saw they were busy with another girl, so she crawled away and ran into the jungle. Many days later, she found another village and told what had happened. When she finished, she started again. She could not stop talking. She could not stop crying or shaking. The tears kept pouring, like a monsoon cloud, until she used up all the water in her body and died.

I wasn't there to see any of this, but I am supposed to tell these things. And if there isn't time to say all my testimony, then the important part to know is that we three are alive, Loot and Bootie and myself, and one hundred and five people from my village are dead. That's the only reason the Great God didn't let me stick together with them, so I can be here today, so I can tell you these things, so you can remember it, so we can write it down, now that the Younger White Brother has brought back the Important Writings.

As soon as the old grandmother finished her testimony, the twin boy Loot sang out in his native tongue: "Dear Great God and Older Brother Jesus, today Ye deliver us from evil. Ye deliverest Your messenger, the Younger White Brother, Lord of Nats. Ye deliver a warrior for victory. Ye bring Your troops, strong men and women! Count them! Ye deliver food, excellent food for nourishing our bodies, food so we can face Your enemies and fight with bodies that cannot be pierced by bullets or knives or arrows. Make us invisible. Give us victory against the SLORC army. We also pray for the Nats, keep them peaceful. We pray for our brothers and sisters who died a green death after they were baptized in the stream. For Yours is the kingdom and the power . . ."

To my friends, it sounded like rap music.

Bootie broke in, and her prayer was in a liturgical English of sorts: "Dear Heavy Fazzer, Great God and Bo-Cheesus, we pray Dine Lord of Nats safe us fum gheen dess. Not let us die in bud and bosom of life like our fazzer and muzzer before us, our bruzzers and sissers before us, our aunties and unkies before us, our cuzzins and fends before us. Potect us so we not falling into hands of enenies or new Nats dat die gheen dess. When our fends and enenies be dead, keep dem in Dine grafess. Keep us safe."

The two children closed their eyes and appeared to drift off to sleep while standing.

"What the hell was that about?" Dwight whispered to Roxanne. "It almost sounded like English. Did you understand any of it?" Roxanne shook her head, then added, "Nothing beyond Great God and Cheez Whiz."

The residents of No Name Place then passed around a wooden plate with seeds, first to the twins, then to the rest, and each partook of one seed, downing it like a communion wafer. My friends politely ate one each as well.

When the ritual was done, the twins' grandmother approached Rupert with a long sacklike tunic made of a royal-blue cloth woven with a zigzag pattern. She bowed and mumbled to him in Karen to accept this humble gift symbolizing his faithfulness in returning. The girls nearby giggled with hands cupped over their mouths. "You teks," she told Rupert.

Rupert held up empty hands and shrugged. "I don't have any money," he said. He was *not* about to bargain for a dress. When the grandmother insisted once again that he take the gift, Rupert pulled his pockets inside out. "See? No money. I swear." He had only the deck of cards he had been given on the flight to China. He held them up as proof that he had nothing valuable.

All at once, the people in front of him fell to the ground and prostrated themselves.

"For God's sake," Moff said to his son. "They're begging you. It's a Christmas present. Just be polite and take it."

"*You* take it," said Rupert, and as Moff started to reach for the cloth, Bootie cried out, "No, no, he teks." She walked up to Rupert. Moff whispered fiercely through clenched teeth that Rupert should simply accept the damn dress and be done with it. And once Rupert took the unwanted gift, the people rose to their feet, and the twins sidled up to him.

Loot tapped the hand holding the cards and pantomimed a fanned deck.

Rupert grinned. "Man, everyone in Burma likes to see card tricks." He happily shuffled the deck, drawing the cards up with one hand and letting them slide into place. He held the deck in front of Loot. "All right, pick a card, any card." And the twin divinities were delighted to hear this start of the ritual, the identical words that had been uttered more than a hundred years before by their founding father, the con artist Seraphineas Andrews. In short order, the twins shrieked joyfully as their sign appeared, the Lord of Clubs, the avenger of all evil.

Three other children aligned themselves near the center of the camp and began to sing a cappella. The tune sounded almost like a church hymn, but much sadder, Vera thought, and it had that Asian tonality, as if the harmonic thirds had shifted to fifths. She and the other Americans stood quietly, appreciating the heartfelt performance. With the second refrain, two men joined in, one beating a bronze drum decorated with detailed frogs, the other blowing a buffalo horn. My friends gave Black Spot the thumbs-up. "What tribe are you again?" Bennie asked him. "I want to tell my people in America that we visited you."

Black Spot responded in his accented English, "We are ethnic Karen people, but we are also calling the Lord's Army."

"I'm sorry. What was the last thing you said?" Bennie leaned in to hear above the chanting songs.

"The Lord's Army," Black Spot repeated.

"What did he say?" Vera asked.

Bennie shrugged. "It sounded like 'the Lajamee.'"

"There is a subtribe that begins with *l*," Heidi said. "Bibi wrote about it. It's in the folder back at the hotel. The La-something. Must be the Lajamee."

Wendy added, "You can tell they're a tribe because of the black and red colors on the older people—and that thing wrapped around their heads, the terry-cloth turban. That's a dead giveaway of something."

It was now three o'clock, my friends noticed. Dwight cursed: "Damn you, Walter, wherever you are, we're going back down and you better have a good reason why you weren't here." Black Spot heard their plans to leave and turned to Grease and Salt. They needed to quickly remind the Reincarnated One who he was. The three men went to the small huts beyond the clearing to ask those residents to come out.

Roxanne had taken out her camcorder and was now instructing the group to mill about so she could get some last shots of the twins, the strangler fig huts, as well as the more colorful members of the "Lajamee" tribe. As she panned the camp, she suddenly stopped. What was *that*? A skinned animal? She zoomed in closer. It was the stump of a leg! And its owner had a face that was even more disfigured. My other friends turned, and they, too, murmured disbelief. What in God's name had happened to these people? There were two men, two women, and a pretty girl no older than ten. Each was missing a foot, or an arm, or the lower part of a leg, the limb ending abruptly in a coral cluster of blasted flesh. Why were they so horribly mutilated? Had they been in a bus accident?

Roxanne faced Black Spot. "What happened to them?" she said quietly, and aimed the camcorder at him.

"Three of them are once working for SLORC army," Black Spot said, "walking to find land mines. They are going in front of soldiers, go right, go left. When the mine is exploding, no more danger, and then soldiers they very happy. Now path is safe for walking." He glanced quickly at Rupert.

Rupert was stunned. "They had a job stepping on land mines?"

"Karen people not having choice." Black Spot gestured toward the wounded. "That man, he both lucky and no. He now living, yes, but wife, sister, brother, they not living. The soldiers are shooting him in the head and body. But he not dying. That girl, she not dying." Roxanne directed the camera toward the unlucky man. He bore a quarter-sized dark indentation in his cheek, and his shoulders were laced with pale scars. The pretty girl had an arm that bent at an odd angle, and on her shoulder was a keloid that looked like a meaty-red tumor. Despite their mutilation, these five people smiled at the camera and waved. *"Dah blu, dah blu,"* they sang. Roxanne was in tears by the time she turned off the camcorder. Several others were as well, and Black Spot felt great hope rising that they would help the tribe.

When my friends were out of earshot of Black Spot, Wendy said, "A friend told me the Burmese military does stuff like this." She was referring to Gutman. "He's with a human rights group, so he knows all about these atrocities, horrible, horrible things. That's why he said tourists should boycott coming here unless they're coming as witnesses."

"I feel awful," Bennie said, instantly filled with guilt.

"We all do." Vera placed her hand on Bennie's shoulder. "We wouldn't be human if we didn't."

Marlena muttered: "I was the one who said we shouldn't come to Burma."

"Well, we're here," Dwight replied grimly. "So there's nothing we can do about that now, is there?"

"But we *should* do something," Heidi said. My friends nodded, thinking in silence. What could they do? What can anyone do in view of such cruelty? They felt uselessly sympathetic.

"It's kind of weird that Bibi had us come here as one of our activities," Wyatt said.

I was a sputtering ball of indignation until I heard Vera: "Bibi didn't put this on the original itinerary. Inle Lake got patched in— remember?—because some people voted to leave China early."

Heidi sighed. "I just wish Bibi had told us more about the military here, the bad stuff. I mean, I sort of knew about it, but I thought it was a long time ago."

They went on talking softly among themselves, thinking how to deal with their moral discomfort. If only they had known more. If only someone had warned them. If only they knew that lives were at stake. If, if, if. You see how it was, In their minds *I* should have provided the information, the arguments, the reasons why it was all right to visit or not. But how could I have been responsible for their morals? They should have taken the initiative to learn more on their own.

And yet, I admit I was shocked as well to see the people of No Name Place. I had not encountered anything like this when I was alive, never in all my previous trips to Burma. But when I was alive, I was not looking for tragedy. I was looking for bargains, the best places to eat, for pagodas that were not overrun with tourists, for the loveliest scenes to photograph.

"Maybe tourism is the only way that they can make money," Heidi reasoned.

"We should definitely support their economy," Bennie said. He promised to buy a lot of souvenirs.

"I've done guiding on a number of ecotourism trips," Wyatt said, "where the clients pay a lot of extra money to plant trees or to do research on endangered species. Maybe they can do something like that here. Get people to come and help them set up ways to become self-sufficient."

"We could each give them some money when we leave," Esmé said. "We can tell them it's for the children." My friends accepted this idea as the obvious way to be of immediate help and lessen their discomfort.

"A hundred each?" Roxanne said. "I have enough to cover all of us. You can pay me back later." Everyone nodded. This was the same solution they used for many situations. I am not criticizing. Most likely I would have done the same. Give money. What more can a person do? Roxanne picked up her camcorder and did one final pan, resting longer on the maimed, the young children, the old ladies with their smiling faces. Wyatt put his arm around a man missing the lower part of his leg. The two men grinned at each other as if they were great friends.

"We've come to this beautiful place," Roxanne narrated, "and we've learned that within beauty, there is tragedy. The people here have suffered terribly under the military regime . . . it's heartbreaking. . . ." She spoke of the forced labor, the explosions of land mines. She concluded with a promise to help. "We can't just give them sympathy or a token bit of help. We want to help in a bigger way, a substantial way that can make a difference." She was speaking, of course, about their generous contribution.

They decided to give the money to the twins' grandmother. She seemed to be the one who bossed people around the most. They had a little ceremony to thank her for the tribe's hospitality. They spoke slowly in English, bowed to express gratitude, made a thumbs-up sign for the food, gestured around at the wonders of this dark, dank settlement. They put on sad faces, as if reluctant to leave such wonderful people.

Then Roxanne stepped forward and took the grandmother's tiny, rough, clawlike hands and pressed the money into them. The old woman looked at the wad, appeared shocked and insulted, pushed it back into Roxanne's hands, and kept a palm upraised as if fending off a demon. They had expected she would. Marlena had already advised that the Chinese had to dramatically refuse three times, and maybe they had a similar custom here. On the fourth offer, after Black Spot muttered to the grandmother to take the money, she snapped at him, saying the money was useless out here, and if anyone was caught with it by SLORC soldiers, it would buy nothing but a grave. Black Spot told her to take it and hand it to Grease, who would put it in Roxanne's satchel when the Americans were not looking. So the old woman smiled at my friends, bowed and bowed, kissed the money and held it toward heaven for the Great God to see. She shrieked thanks as if deliriously grateful.

Warmed that they had done the right thing, my friends picked up their packs and turned to leave. "We better head back," Moff said to Black Spot. Several members of his tribe cried to him, "Why does the Younger White Brother want to leave us?" Black Spot quietly told them not to make too much noise about this. It takes time for a Reincarnated One to recognize who he is, even if he has shown the three signs. It was true for other holy people, true even for Loot and Bootie. But once a Reincarnated One knows who he is, he will slowly regain his senses and his powers, and fulfill the promises he made. The tribe was soothed to hear mention of this. They all knew the promise of the Younger White Brother. He would make them invisible, with bodies that no bullets could pierce. They would take back their lands. They would live in peace, and no one would ever try to harm them again, because if they did, the Younger White Brother would unleash on them all the Nats.

Black Spot and his cohorts discussed how to handle this latest situation. They had been lucky in getting the boy and his followers here. Perhaps they needed a little bad luck to keep them. They had no choice. They had to delay the boy as long as they could. Say good-bye to them, Black Spot instructed the tribe, wave to the foreigners just like they are doing.

My friends left, with Black Spot, Grease, Fishbones, and Salt following behind. Vera complimented the tribe, knowing Black Spot would hear and report this flattery to his people: Really nice folks, so generous and sincere. Others piled it on: That place was the greatest. And those strangler trees—have you seen anything so bizarrely beautiful? What a wonderful surprise. They were so glad they came. And lunch was unusual yet tasty. It was good to try something new. But now they were looking forward to hot showers. Of course, there was still that wobbly bridge to get across. The second time would be easy. Just take a deep breath.

When my friends arrived where they had crossed, they were puzzled. Where was the bridge? They must have come down the wrong way. They were about to ask Black Spot for guidance when Rupert shouted: "Dad, look!" He pointed at the barely visible bridge, dangling by limp ropes on the other side.

Bennie gasped. "Oh my God, it's fallen down!" He rushed to Black Spot. "The bridge!" He gestured madly. "It's broken. How are we going to get out of here?"

Black Spot looked at the dangling bridge. He yelled to his comrades, telling them to act surprised. He did not want their guests to become alarmed, thinking they were held against their will. He simply wanted them to remain as their guests. Moff called over to Black Spot: "What's another way out of here? We need to get down before dark." He pointed to the dimming sky.

Black Spot shook his head. "No other way," he said.

Dwight broke in: "Maybe the ravine is less deep up ahead, and we can climb down into it and then up." Again Black Spot shook his head.

"Oh man, this is bad," Bennie moaned. "This is so bad."

Dwight shouted at the top of his lungs. "Christ! Walter, you fuck! Why aren't you here to deal with this?"

Vera noticed that the men from the tribe looked ashamed that their guests were unhappy, so she tried to calm the group. She was skilled at dealing with crises. "If the Lajamee people can't get us out soon, I'm sure Walter will send for help once he gets here. Maybe that's what he's already done. He came and saw the bridge was gone and went back down. The best thing we can do is stay put."

There were sounds of agreement, acknowledgment that this was reasonable logic, the probable truth. Help was on its way, they now believed. And so, with the exception of Dwight, they agreed to retreat to No Name Place and bide their time there. As they walked back into the camp, the people of the Lord's Army greeted them with hands clasped in prayer. Thanks be to the Great God. Black Spot told them to give their guests the best of everything.

Dusk came, Walter did not. Another hour rolled by, then another. Except for firelight, the camp was pitch black. The inhabitants of No Name Place slashed bamboo and sharp palm leaves to weave stools for their honored guests. Black Spot had told them that foreigners did not like to sit on mats. Grease and Fishbones brought a pile of clothes and set them down. They pointed to them: "Take, take."

"Hey, that's my polar fleece," Rupert said, and he pulled out an orange jacket. The others dug through the pile and found the clothing they had brought to wear during the chilly morning ride that now seemed so long ago.

"I thought we left these in the truck," Marlena said.

"Those porters must have brought everything along with them," Vera replied.

"Thank goodness they did," Marlena said. "It's a lot cooler up here than down there." She tossed Esmé a purple parka and shimmied into her own black one.

"I wish we were in a hotel with a *real* bathroom," Esmé said. Earlier in the afternoon, most of them had visited the latrine, situated a discreet distance from camp. A palm thatch screen, about five feet high, provided the scantiest of privacy, and behind it was a trough of rushing water, flanked by two long boards on which the user could balance. Instead of toilet paper, a bucket of water with a ladle stood off to the side.

Marlena put her arm around Esmé. She watched an old woman stoking the fire in the rock hearth. What a long night this would be. Her thoughts drifted to Harry. What was he doing now? Was he worried about where she was? Was he even thinking about her? She pictured his face again, not the one that was lustful or embarrassed. She was seeing the sheer wonder in his eyes when she first lay down on the bed with him. Tomorrow, she thought, but no candles, no mosquito netting this time.

"Think of this like summer camp," Marlena consoled her daughter. "Or a sleepover."

"I never had a sleepover like *this*." Esmé was feeding Pup-pup scraps of chicken.

Others were having similar thoughts. Would their beds be hard as a rock? Would there even be beds? What kind of people were the Lajamees, really? Moff and Wyatt exchanged stories of the travails of past backpacking trips: A thunderstorm in a leaky tent. Bears that got their food. Getting lost after smoking pot. Moff said they'd probably look back on this night as one of the more memorable parts of the trip.

A strange sound arose. Sirens? Could it possibly be . . . police cars sent out *here*? Off to the side, my friends saw a glow of intensely bright light. It flickered. They rose and approached this mysterious illumination, and there they beheld rows of people watching—good Lord, of all the amazing things one might find in a jungle—a television set! A news channel was on, and a female voice was reporting on a gigantic fire in a nightclub in China.

"A TV!" Wendy exclaimed. "How funny is that? And it's in English." More news reports followed. My friends were transfixed.

"Global News Network," a man's deep voice announced after a few minutes. "Making news in how we report the news."

It was good old GNN!

My friends moved closer to see. Those were the familiar faces of news anchors beaming back at them. Instantly they felt comforted. They were closer to civilization than they thought. But then one of the twins aimed the remote and switched from the news to a program that featured people wandering through a jungle. The crowd whooped and cheered.

A woman in outback duds held a mike in guerrilla reporting style. "Will Bettina eat the leeches?" she asked in an Australian accent. "Stay tuned and find out on the next episode of *Darwin's Fittest*!"

"How the hell are they getting reception out here?" Dwight asked.

"Here's your answer." Wyatt pointed to some snaky cords leading from the television set to a car battery. Another cord ran along the ground and up a tree.

"Must be a satellite dish above the tree canopy," Moff said. "Man, that's a lot of tree trunk to cover." He kneeled and tapped a loop of rope that circled the tree trunk. "And here's how they climb it. They get inside the lasso and leap like frogs."

"But where did they get the satellite dish?" Bennie asked. "It's not like you can order this stuff and have it delivered up here."

Rupert inspected the battery more closely. "Didn't that come in the back of the truck with us?"

Two young Karen women rushed to offer Rupert a stool made of rattan that was taller than the others. He would have sat on it, too, if Moff had not given him a look that strongly suggested he let Vera have the seat. Soon additional improvised seating was made available to the other guests—stumps and more low stools, which they placed near the television.

"We're back!" the Aussie woman chortled. "*Darwin's Fittest*, number one among kiwis and wombats."

"Numbah one! Numbah one!" the children chanted.

The Aussie woman leaned close to the camera so that her nose looked like a frog with dark holes for eyes. "And now we'll see which of our survivors will be brave, and which will face hunger and *starvation*." Suspenseful music rose, bass fiddles sawed away.

"You'd think the people here were watching this show to get pointers," Roxanne joked. And in fact, they were. The tribe had fantasized that they might one day have a TV show. They were fitter than these survivors. If they had a show, everyone would admire them. And then SLORC would be too ashamed to kill a tribe that was number one.

When the show ended, the jungle hosts led their guests to their accommodations. They were given greenish-colored blankets, woven from the fibers of young bamboo, the panels stitched together with heavy thread. Rupert, Wyatt, and Wendy broke into grins when they learned that they would be staying in the strangler tree "bungalows." Bennie noticed right away that the floor was a platform of rattan raised six inches above the ground, and atop that was a springy bed made of layers of small bamboo strips, which, as he discovered upon lying on his back and then his side, was amazingly comfortable.

Heidi used her headlamp to inspect the interior of her room for the night. The sinewy root walls were smooth and clean, devoid of the dreaded four: mold, bats, spiders, and muck. She took out her Space blanket and wrapped it around herself; it would reflect and retain up to eighty percent of her body heat, or so it was advertised. While she was putting the Lajamee blanket over that, an old woman poked her head in. She hurried over to Heidi, threw off the blanket, turned it the other way, and pointed to the fringe, gesturing that it must always be at the bottom, never near the face—that was a big no-no. Heidi was amused that the woman was such a stickler for details. That should hardly matter out here.

When Heidi was settled in, Marlena borrowed her headlamp, saying that Esmé was scared of the dark. Actually, Esmé was already asleep.

"Don't put the blanket fringe near your face," Heidi warned. "The fashion cops will get you. And you can keep the headlamp. I have another one that's smaller."

Marlena aimed the light at the interior of the tree she shared with her daughter. The more gnarled portions looked like arthritic gnomes in agony, a bas relief created as a Lamaist version of an *Ars Moriendi*.

And so they settled in for their first night, what they believed would be the only one. Moff told Rupert to sleep with his shoes on, in case he had to get up in the middle of the night. Esmé had Puppup tucked under her arm. Bennie lay wide awake for hours, worried because he was without his medications and the CPAP machine.

Marlena was trying to remember whether snakes were attracted to body heat at night. But soon these thoughts gave way to reptilian fantasies about Harry. She pictured his undulating tongue, snaking along her neck, her breasts, her belly. Suddenly, she had pangs of longing, of sadness, of fear that the two of them had missed their opportunity. She knew what was meant by "star-crossed lovers." The black sky was filled with a billion stars, and some of them made an eternal pattern for each destined set of lovers, a constellation for them, which thus far she had failed to see. She had been too busy looking down at the ground, searching for pitfalls. She fretted over the years already gone by without great passion, the possibility that what she had had with her ex-husband—those meager moments of rapture, which she preferred to forget—would be all that she could lay claim to as an approximation of ecstatic love for the rest of her life. How sad that would be! And with those thoughts, she drifted into fretful sleep.

Hours later, she jolted awake with a pounding heart. She had dreamed she was a monkey living in a tree. She was crawling up its trunk to get away from dangerous creatures below, but soon she tired and dug in her fingernails. Were all trees this warm? When she placed her face against the trunk, she saw that it was Harry, and soon she and the tree began to make love. But in doing so, she let go of her grip and fell, jerking herself awake.

Why had she dreamed that she was a monkey and Harry a tree? And why had she dug in her fingernails so deep? Was she too clingy? Before she could ponder any further, she saw that someone was moving outside. It was not yet dawn. Were people making breakfast already? The figure was hunched over, eating furiously while glancing about. The figure froze, eyes fixed on Marlena's. She was confused, for it was as if her simian dream-self had escaped and was just ten feet away, a hoolock gibbon with a white-rimmed eye mask, stuffing its mouth with the candy bars left out by the new intruders at No Name Place.

IN THE MORNING, over coffee, Harry and Heinrich were discussing who should be sent out with the search party, when a huge clatter and whine broke the air. A longboat with four military policemen came swooping up with an impressive backwash. Most boats slowed to a soft putter well before they reached the resort. But these men were beyond such rules, because they had made them.

They jumped onto the dock, and with important strides went directly to Heinrich and spoke rapidly in Burmese. Harry strained to understand what they were saying from the tone of voice, gestures, and reactions. Heinrich seemed astonished, and the police looked stern. Heinrich pointed out toward the lake. The police pointed in a slightly different direction. More exchanges, and Heinrich shook his head vehemently. The police pointed to Harry, and Heinrich made a dismissive motion.

"What is it?" Harry's heart was racing. "Did they find them?"

Heinrich excused himself with the police and turned to Harry. "They found the guide, the young fellow named Maung Wa Sao."

"Walter?"

"Yes. Walter, exactly. He was lying inside a pagoda on the other side of the lake. Some monks found him early this morning."

"Good Lord! He's been killed?"

"Calm down, my friend. It seems he was climbing about inside the pagoda and a bit of holy carving crumbled and fell on his head. Knocked him out cold. Those pagodas—*ach!*—they're all in a terrible state of disrepair, and even a thousand Burmese receiving merit for their donations wouldn't be enough to fix them up properly. It's a wonder the entire structure didn't fall in a dusty heap on top of him. Anyway, the poor fellow's in hospital now, a bit dehydrated, a nasty bump on the head, but otherwise doing perfectly fine."

Harry exhaled in relief. So that's what had happened. "And the others are with him?"

"Well, that's the thing. They're not, I'm afraid to say, and they haven't been seen. What's more, this fellow Walter can't tell where they've gone."

Harry's heart quickened again. "Can't tell? Why not?"

"Can't remember. Not a thing . . ."

"I thought you said he was perfectly fine."

"Well, he's not terribly injured. But his mind—" Heinrich tapped his temple. "He can't recall his name or his occupation, not the foggiest notion, and certainly not a clue as to what he was doing just before the accident. That's why the police are here. Checking to see if your group had returned."

"Well, they must have gone to get help," Harry surmised. He used a professional tone that suggested authority, to quell his own panic. He pictured Marlena taking charge. She was nurturing in that way. They had gone off to find a village, yes, that was it, and a doctor, aspirin. . . . But then Harry thought again. Why wouldn't someone have stayed with Walter? Not all of them would have needed to go. This did not make sense. "We must ask the police to do a search and find them immediately."

Heinrich spoke in a low, even voice: "Patience, my friend."

"Patience, my foot!"

Heinrich raised his hand as both benediction and warning. "Do you really want the military involved? They're already asking why your friends are missing yet you are here."

"Good God, they can't possibly think I've had anything to do with this! That's outrageous."

"I won't second-guess what they might think, outrageous or not. In the meantime, the best thing you and I can do, my friend, is to act calm, to not make any sort of fuss or demand. And now I'm going to my office to get everyone's passports from the safe. The police have asked for them. I suggest you use this opportunity to view the beauty of the lake. Let me handle this. . . ."

It is amazing, isn't it, how easily people hand over the reins to those who presume power. Against their own intuition, they allow themselves to trust those who they feel should not be trusted. I include myself as one who once did this. But then again, I was only a child, whereas Harry was a grown man with a doctorate in behavioral psychology. He dutifully went to the edge of the water. Gazing out, he tried to imagine where Marlena and the others were. The mist on the lake had long evaporated, yet he could see nothing but the uncertain future.

·12·

DARWIN'S FITTEST

The only thing certain in times of great uncertainty is that people will behave with great strength or weakness, and with very little else in between. I know from experience. In fact, I am reminded all too clearly of a time when my family faced mortal danger and a perilous future. I tell it to you now as example of how one incident can be instructive for life.

It was 1949, and we were leaving our family home in Shanghai on the eve of the Communist takeover. I have already mentioned what madness it was, determining what to take and arranging for our passage. There was room for only our family, so we weren't able to take any of our servants with us, which was terribly sad for all of us, but we also realized we were shockingly ignorant as to how to manage on our own. Cook and my brothers' nursemaid wailed unceasingly to have lost their place in the world. Others—the least industrious of our servants, I noted—were already making plans to become powerful proletarians under the new regime, and in trying their hand at being blowhards, they let it be known to our faces that they were eager to be rid of us, "the bourgeois parasites of China," as they called us. A rather nasty farewell.

But the one servant I most vividly remember that night was the gatekeeper, Luo. He, his father, and his grandfather had all been with our family.

Tradition or not, Luo was a disagreeable sort who liked to gamble and sleep and visit certain teahouses, pastimes that led to his disappearance at regular intervals. My stepmother also said he was disrespectful to her, but then again, she said that of nearly everyone, especially me.

During those last hours, we were confused, every one of us. My father was mumbling to himself, unable to decide which of his books to take, and in the end he took none of them. My brothers acted bored to mask their terror. My stepmother, as I have already told, had a tantrum. As for myself, well, it is hard to be objective about oneself, but I would say that I moved as if in a trance, without emotions. Only the gatekeeper seemed to keep his wits about him. You can imagine our surprise when in those frantic hours of our leaving, this gatekeeper worked kindly and efficiently to get us packed and supplied with foodstuffs for our perilous journey. In what appeared to be a last-minute fit of loyalty, he had comforting words for everyone, expressions of concern, assurances that the gods would protect us, and so on and so forth. Oh, how we had misjudged him! He was also the only one who cleverly thought to take our family's jewels, gold, and foreign monies from the inadequate sacks that we had secreted in our luggage, and to sew the valuables into my dolls, the linings of our jackets, and the hems of our skirts and trousers so they would not be found. In my coat lining I had my mother's jade hairpin, which I had stolen from Sweet Ma's dresser.

It was not thieves that concerned us, but the Kuomintang, for under pain of being deemed unpatriotic and then shot, we had been ordered to turn in all gold bars and any foreign monies for the new currency. We had exchanged a bit for show, but kept most of our gold and U.S. dollars. Good thing, too, for the new currency soon became worthless. Now we were trying to leave with evidence of unpatriotic wealth, and that could turn into an instant death sentence. What a good man Gatekeeper Luo was for helping us evade detection and begin our new life with comfort.

But our worst fears came to be, and we were stopped at the first checkpoint on our way to the waterfront. Kuomintang police surrounded our automobile and said they had to perform a search. They flung open our valises and steamer trunks, and we silently praised our gatekeeper to the heavens for his wisdom in removing our valuables. They returned our luggage to the trunk. And then they felt along the cuffs and lining of our clothing, pulled and yanked at the hems. All at once, one of them shouted he had found something, and as the police slashed at our clothes, I began trembling so hard my teeth were tap-dancing. My brothers looked like senseless, bloodless ghosts. My father gazed at us with farewell eyes. The police held up what they had found in my coat. I held my breath.

And then I heard the police laughing. Only then did we learn the truth—how the gatekeeper had saved our lives, although clearly he had not intended to. He had substituted lead weights for the gold, cut-up pages of Father's books for the currency, and gravel for the loose diamonds. Upon realizing we had been both tricked and saved, I was so overjoyed my legs shook and collapsed, and I fell into a happy heap. It was one of the few times I have lost my senses.

As I said before, in moments of great danger, many people show their deficiencies. They turn stupid with trust, as did we, or they turn stupid with greed, as did the gatekeeper. Six months later, a cousin who still lived on Rue Massenet wrote us that Luo had been shot for being too rich. We were neither happy nor sad to hear that. It was simply the new order, and you had to adjust your fate accordingly.

It was a lesson my friends would soon learn as well.

THE NEXT MORNING, Marlena was the last to rise. Her vision of the hoolock gibbon the night before had left her heart pounding, her nerves frayed. She felt she was sweeping thick clouds from her mind, as she tried to make sense of a conversation between Bennie and Vera. ". . . It was a centipede, not a millipede," she heard Vera say. They continued their exchange of insect stories.

Upon entering the clearing, Marlena saw no evidence of the previous night's simian gourmand, but there was this bizarre sight: a man from the tribe riding a stationary bicycle, pedaling as diligently as one might in a fitness center.

Heidi had slept later than the others as well. When coming back from the jungle latrine, she too noticed the Lajamee riding the bike. As she drew closer, she saw that the bicycle was attached to the contraption with the battery, what had been used to power the television.

"Get a load of that," Moff said from behind, causing her to jump. He nodded in greeting to the bicyclist and stepped up closer to inspect. "Lookie here. Stationary axle. It holds the back of the frame in place, so the rear wheel can spin against the rollers and create friction. You got your flywheel, your centrifugal clutch, basic but competent, and this, a common series-wound motor. Nifty. Haven't seen one of those since seventh-grade science class. Follow the connection wire to the twelve-volt car battery. Spare battery off to the side." He walked to the front of the bike. "Cool." The man on the bicycle smiled to hear these admiring tones.

"Why don't they hook it directly to the TV," Heidi said, "and pedal as long as they want to watch?"

"Bad idea," Moff said. "Any increase in speed and friction and you'd blow up the TV's electronic innards. TVs are fussy that way. Recharging the battery is a much better idea, batteries being more tolerant of variation. Besides, you can power up all kinds of things with a car battery as a storage source—TV, lights, radios."

"How do you know these things?" she said, and smiled.

He shrugged but was secretly flattered. "I'm a farm boy, a simple rube." I noticed that his eyes intentionally locked on hers, lingering until Heidi gave out an embarrassed giggle. It was the man on the bicycle who broke the spell. He slid off the seat and invited Moff to take his place. "Missed going to the gym last night," Moff told Heidi as he got on. "Might as well get a workout this morning." And he began pumping heartily, as men do when they are surging with machismo.

In the middle of the clearing and toward the front of the camp, a fire crackled in the rock pit, and a pot of broth simmered atop a metal plate fashioned out of a wrecked car door. Close by, on a platter, were a heap of cooked rice and a smaller pile of forest vegetation. This was to be breakfast. Esmé and Rupert stood watching hungrily with unwashed faces. The cooks, an older woman and two pretty, young ones, smiled at them and said in their own dialect: "Yes, yes, we know you're hungry. Almost ready now."

"Know what?" Esmé said to Rupert with cool reserve. "My mom and I saw a monkey last night. It was huge." She held her arms above her head and stood on tiptoes to make herself as tall as possible.

"No way," said Rupert.

"*Way*-ay," Esmé retorted, and shrank back to earth. She had not actually seen the monkey herself, but when her mother had described it to her a few minutes before, she had such a sense of horror and fascination knowing it had been close to her that she felt she had experienced it firsthand.

"Well, I saw a bat last night," Rupert said. He had not actually seen a bat, but he heard a fluttery sound that made him think one was hovering about.

"No way," said Esmé.

The rest of my friends were meandering about, taking care of morning rituals, lining up for breakfast. Their clothes were rumpled, their hair mashed into peaks and dells. The cooks passed out wooden bowls of rice, with gravy made of ground rice, peas, peanut powder, dried shrimp, chili, and lemongrass that Black Spot had just brought. First served were the esteemed guests, while the residents of No Name Place queued up behind them. Several of the younger women giggled when they saw Rupert, then looked away when he turned. An elderly woman grabbed his elbow and tried to lead him to a seat that was cut into a fallen log. Rupert shook his head and broke from her clutches, saying through clenched teeth, "This is getting really annoying." In truth, he was pleased and embarrassed by the attention.

Bennie assumed his role as tour leader. While the rest ate their breakfast, he walked over to Black Spot. "We need your help," he said, "so we can leave this morning as soon as possible."

Black Spot shook his head. "You cannot be leaving."

"You don't understand," Bennie said. "We can't stay any longer. Now that it's daylight, we need to make our way down, even if our guide isn't here."

Black Spot was apologetic. "Bridge is not fixed. We cannot be leaving. So you cannot be leaving. This is same problem for you, me, everybody."

Bennie launched into a convoluted and hopeless conversation over who might fix the bridge and what they might try now that it was daytime. Black Spot kept shaking his head, and Bennie wanted to grab him by the shoulders and shake his whole body. He was so passive. He had no initiative. Hell, if there was a TV here, there had to be a way out of here.

"Can you make a new bridge? Who made the other one?"

If the tribe had needed a new bridge, they could have created one in a few hours. But Black Spot only shook his head. "No way making this."

"Did anyone go down yet to see if Walter's come back? You know, our guide Walter?"

Black Spot looked uncomfortable, for he was going to suggest what was untrue. "I think he not coming. Bridge go down. Guide . . . I think guide go down, too. . . ."

Bennie clutched his chest. "God! No! Oh God! Oh God! Shit! . . ." When he could catch his breath, he said weakly, "Did you look?"

Black Spot nodded and said in a flat voice: "We looking. Nothing we can do." Which in a way was true, if you have seen nothing.

Bennie returned to my other friends. "Do you know what the boatman just told me?" he said in a shaky voice. They looked up. "Walter's dead."

For the next couple of hours, they mourned Walter. Heidi murmured, "He made one mistake but otherwise he was so dependable." Marlena used the words "sweet and gallant." Moff said that he was "articulate and damn smart." Bennie observed that Walter was a hero, because he took the plunge for them.

Dwight and Wyatt did not know what to say about grief, so they returned to the chasm to picture exactly what had happened. This time they looked more carefully. They estimated the trajectory a body would take if it fell from the middle versus the end of the bridge. They scanned the ledges and the rocky funnel below. They applied Pythagorean geometry to their tragic calculations, and having seen evidence of blood, they pinpointed "the spot," a sharp slab of rock with dark splotches of rust-colored lichen.

Wyatt concluded: "One bounce, and you wouldn't know what after that."

Dwight appended: "Let's hope so."

The men returned with their field report. Walter was one or two steps away from reaching the other side and—Dwight snapped his fingers—it must have been just like that. A fraction of a second later, it's over. That's how it happens. You barely have time to be surprised.

Bennie thought about the surprise. The more the group talked, the more his mind became a horror show of—not Walter—but himself, plummeting, screaming, grabbing on to eternity, and then feeling one great thud, and life sucked out by a giant vacuum cleaner. It made his muscles ache. All this talk was making him ill. He went to sit on a log by himself. Every now and then, he sighed heavily, scratched at his unshaven face, and slapped at mosquitoes. He berated himself. Their current troubles were his fault. To what degree, he could not assess. He was the tour leader, and that was the awful and unchangeable fact. How was he going to get them out of this disaster? He stared out, his eyes and mind blank with exhaustion. Without his CPAP machine, he had slept poorly. He was in worse trouble for not having his medications, the ones for depression, high blood pressure, anxiety, and most dire of all, seizures.

Until that moment, I had not known he had seizures. Then again, Bennie had not told anyone. And why should he, he thought to himself. The seizures were mostly under control. Besides, he reasoned, people had such uninformed notions about seizures, as if everyone who had them fell to the ground with convulsions. Most of his took the form of odd distortions—he'd smell the phantom odor of a putrefying mouse, or see lightning raining down in his room, or feel the room spinning on a turntable, and sense a spiritual elation. Those episodes were simple partial seizures, and they hardly counted, he often told himself, since they were so brief, lasting only a minute or two, and for the most part, they were rather enjoyable, like an acid trip without the acid.

But every now and then, he had another kind, a complex partial seizure. It started with a peculiar feeling that rose like waves pushing up his throat, and this filled him with morbid dread and nausea. Next, he flew like a roller coaster, propelled forward and tilted on his side, until he zoomed out of the reaches of his consciousness. Sometimes people told him later that he had taken on a zombie stare and had repeatedly fiddled with his shirt buttons, while murmuring, "I'm sorry, I'm sorry." Hearing these reports, Bennie would flush and say, "Oh, I'm sorry."

More recently, the roller-coaster ride had become prelude to a grand mal. That usually happened when he was tired or had inadvertently missed a dose. Since the dosage had been increased, he had not had a really bad seizure in more than a year. He would be fine off his medications for a day or two. This thought took him back to his original dilemma. How would they get out? What if they were stuck for two more days? Don't stress out, he reminded himself; that's what always triggered his seizures. He wondered if this tribe—the Jalamees or Lajamees, whatever they were called—might possibly have coffee. Coffee beans grew in the mountains, didn't they? If he did not have his daily ration, he would have an intractable headache by noon. Now, *that* would be stressful.

Heidi sat down next to Bennie on the log. "How's it going?" For her, the night had passed without incident. She had loved the cocoon of her thatched shelter, the sounds of the jungle, the novel idea that she was experiencing an adventure rather than a catastrophe. She had slept soundly, coated in bug repellent and her Space blanket, proof that she had handled the newness of everything well. No one was more amazed than she. Here she was in the jungle, and there was no *imagining* danger, no fearing it would reveal its hideous self. Danger was a given in a place without locks, lights, hot water, or fire alarms, in a habitat teeming with poisonous creatures. And the others—look at them—their haggard faces, their eyes darting about. They now felt as she had these past ten years, always on guard, in anticipation of unknown danger, confused, and fearful of what might befall them, while she had been prepared. She felt—what was the sensation?— free. Yes, she was free, out of an invisible prison. It was like the days before the murder, when she could go anywhere and do anything without a thought to risks and consequences. It was exhilarating. But would it last? In any case, she reasoned, she should continue to be prudent. No use letting herself get so giddy that she turned stupid. She reached into her pack and took out a bottle of antibacterial hand lotion and doused both palms.

"What's the plan?" she said as she saw Vera coming over.

"The plan is to make one," Vera answered.

Within the hour, they group had discussed two courses of action. The first was to cut their way down the rainforest, staying along the crevasse as much as possible, until they reached another village. They would borrow a machete and take the boatmen, since they needed to get back down as much as anybody. Perhaps one of the Lajamees might also accompany them, since they were knowledgeable about the jungle. This sounded reasonable, until Roxanne brought up tales of people in the Galápagos who were lost and tried to make their way out in a similar manner, only to be found thirty or forty years later with scrawled notes tied to their shoes, the rest of them a scattering of bleached bones. Wyatt added that an adventure magazine had recently run a story about two guys who had gotten lost in Peru and survived. Of course, they were expert mountain climbers and had had pitons, and knew how to rappel with ropes.

The group settled on trying to signal for help as their first course of action. At least with that, they weren't risking their lives. They simply had to use their intelligence. They emptied their rucksacks on a mat in the clearing. Heidi's, of course, held the most possibilities. She had a headlamp with possibly ten to twenty hours of light left. Marlena had the other, and there were extra batteries as well. Amazing. They could aim the lamps up at night when planes flew overhead. The Space blanket would be excellent for creating a flash that people in rescue helicopters could see. But how would they spot aircraft overhead when they could barely see the sky? And why would the pilots think it was they who were signaling and not insurgents shooting? They settled on lighting fires day and night at the campsite and stoking them to create billows of smoke.

The group went to Black Spot to ask him to enlist the tribe's help in finding more rocks and fuel, certain they would be grateful for American ingenuity. But instead of exuberance, Black Spot looked resigned. He had to tell them now. "They cannot be helping you. When the soldiers are finding you, they are finding the Karen people, too," he said. "Then they killing us."

Oh no, my friends assured them, no one would blame the tribe for the tourists' getting lost. It was the bridge that fell down. That was plain to see. And when they were found, the group would be sure to say right away that the tribe had helped them and were wonderful hosts. Maybe they would even get a bonus from the tour operator. "Tell them that," they urged Black Spot.

"They are not believing that," Black Spot said. He again tried to explain to his guests that there was a reason these people lived in No Name Place. They had come here to hide. To the SLORC soldiers, they were like goats, animals to be hunted and slaughtered. They would keep hunting them until a SLORC leader's dream had come true: that the only Karen you could see in Burma was stuffed and in the glass case of a museum.

"That's a terrible thing to say," Roxanne agreed, while thinking that the tribe, like many other uneducated folks, had taken things so literally. "But it's an empty threat. They couldn't possibly do that."

Black Spot put his hand over his chest. "This here empty," he said. "We all empty." Sweat poured down his face. "If the soldiers then finding us in No Name Place, we already dead people. We better be jumping into big hole in the earth." He paused, and then decided to tell them why he had brought them there. "We cannot helping you leave No Name Place. We bringing you here to help us."

"And we would," Vera said, "if we could get out of here—"

"This boy," Black Spot interrupted, and looked toward Rupert, "he can helping us. He can making us invisible. He can disappearing us. Then SLORC cannot finding us." Black Spot added a version of what Rupert had been heard to say with his card tricks: "Now you seeing, now you not."

My friends looked at one another. Moff broke the news: "It was a magic trick. He can't really make anything disappear."

"How you know?" Black Spot said.

"He's my son," Moff said.

Black replied: "He also Younger White Brother to Karen people."

My friends decided it was no use arguing with the boatman. They would have to find their own way out.

THAT EVENING, Rupert was the first to shiver. Moff felt his son's forehead and whispered in a hoarse voice verging on panic: "Malaria." Others would follow over the next few days—Wendy, Wyatt, Dwight, Roxanne, Bennie, and Esmé—knocked down one by one with bone-racking chills and delirium-inducing fever. Those who had not yet taken sick were occupied with tending their compatriots and frantically warding off buzzing mosquitoes they now viewed as mortal enemies.

But it was not these female mosquitoes that infected them with the *Plasmodium* parasites. It takes at least a week for the parasites to incubate before bursting from the liver. Seven days earlier, they were in China. Seven days earlier, they were being cursed by the Bai minority chief at Stone Bell Mountain. As Miss Rong had told them before she left, the chief had promised that from here on out, trouble would follow them wherever they went and for the rest of their days. And even before she informed them, he had already made good on his word, for at the very next rest stop after visiting the grottoes, the moment my friends stepped off the bus, a cloud of mosquitoes followed and feasted on promised flesh.

Throughout the night, the tribe walked past Rupert and listened to his nonsense pleas for help. They were doubly concerned. How could the Younger White Brother be so sick? How could he make them invulnerable to death when he was now slipping from the edges of life? Before they could carry on with more of this talk, the grandmother of Loot and Bootie scolded the doubters and disbelievers. Don't you remember what happened to us, when Loot and Bootie and I swam the River of Death? Through trial with death, you discover your power. Through trial, you shed your mortal flesh, layer after layer, until you become who you are supposed to be. If you die, you were mortal all along. But if you survive, you are a god. So don't go speaking your doubts so loudly. This god might waken and arise, and if he hears your fickle and fomenting talk, he'll put you in a place with no pretty maidens, just barren rice fields. When all of us are ready to leave, he'll make you stay right here in No Name Place.

Two women brought jugs of cool water and soaked cloths in them. They placed these on the crown of Younger White Brother's head and under his neck where the hot pulse runs. And then the twins' grandmother tried to feed him a tonic, but Vera ordered her to stop. She examined the bowl and sniffed the strong odor of bitter herbs and alcohol.

The twins' grandmother made everything perfectly clear. It is very good, all pure, I cooked and fermented it myself. This tea comes from the leaves of a bush that grows in the forest. The first time we ate those leaves it was only because we had no food. And do you know what? Those who were sick grew well. And those who were well never got sick.

Of course, Vera understood not a word. She shook her head and put the bowl out of reach. The women tried to persuade her, but she stood firm. "No voodoo medicine." And so the ladies of the jungle sighed and took back the bowl with the special tea that could save a life. Never mind, the twins' grandmother said. They would wait until the black lady fell asleep. And if she continues to interfere, put some of that other kind of leaf in her food, and then each night she will sleep a little more.

It must be done. If they die here, their green ghosts will be stuck in these trees. And then we'll be stuck trying to get them out.

·13·

OF PARTICULAR CONCERN

Harry, who was decisive by nature, now wavered. He wanted to leave Floating Island Resort to look for Marlena, yet he did not dare leave for fear he would miss her return. He did not know whether to trust Heinrich, and yet there was no one else to turn to—no one else who spoke English, for that matter. He pictured Marlena lying, like Walter, unconscious in a crumbling temple, then saw her at a much classier resort throwing back her head with a laugh, as she told a horde of handsome men: "Harry's an ass. Serves him right that we left him marooned at that horrid place."

Harry walked around in circles, trying to use logic and common sense. On the second day after his friends had disappeared, the twenty-seventh, he had managed to get a boat ride to Golden Princess Resort so that he might find someone who knew how to make a telephone call to the U.S. Embassy in Rangoon. He finally located an

American expatriate, but the man was not encouraging. "Tricky business," he said. He explained that anyone from the Embassy had to have permission from the junta to travel outside Rangoon. So if an American fell into trouble, the Embassy staff would be stymied for God knows how long. Christmas week was also a bad time to get anything done promptly. The Embassy might not even be open. That was probably why they didn't answer when he called. "Tough luck," the man said. "The U.S. calls Burma 'a country of particular concern.' That's overly diplomatic, in my opinion."

In the afternoon, another group of pleasure-seekers arrived at Floating Island. They were Germans from a middle-class suburb of Frankfurt, and Heinrich spoke to them in their common language. Harry was soused, sitting on a stool at the tiki bar on the verandah, eyeing the newcomers with a glum expression. When Heinrich brought them over for the obligatory toast with "bubbles," he introduced Harry as "a TV star in America and now in our midst." "*Weltberühmt,*" he concluded— yes, so world-famous that the Germans had not the slightest idea who Harry was except an example of another American infatuated with his *fünfzehn Minuten* of fame. Heinrich explained that the others in Harry's group had pressed on to do a few daylong tours, while he had remained behind because of illness. "*Nicht ansteckend,*" Heinrich assured them, then leaned over and mouthed to Harry, "I explained you were ill but not contagious." This was Heinrich's subtle way of letting Harry know he had been discreet about his hangover.

Harry nodded at the Germans and smiled, then said in English: "That's correct. Food poisoning is not contagious. Not to worry."

"Dear God!" Heinrich sputtered. "Whatever are you saying? It was *not* food poisoning. The idea! We have never had such problems."

"It *was* food poisoning," Harry repeated. He was drunk and being horribly naughty. "But don't worry. I've nearly recovered." This exchange caught the ear of a few of the English-speaking Germans, and they translated for the others.

"Perhaps you had a tummyache," Heinrich grumbled, "because you have been so nervous."

Harry agreed: "Having my cottage nearly burn down the other night did not help matters."

Heinrich laughed with hearty falseness, and then said a few jolly words to the new guests, "*Ein berauschter und abgeschmackter Witz,*" to inform them that Harry was just a drunken fool. By now half of the new guests had folded their own brows into frowns, and the others were asking for more details. Even if the American was only joking, what kind of drunken madman had they been saddled with at what was supposed to be a first-class resort? Heinrich excused himself and departed to sort out passports and dinner arrangements.

Harry went up to the German who had done most of the translating. "Where in Burma are you coming from, may I ask?"

"From Mandalay," the man said evenly. "Very interesting city. Beautiful and very many histories."

"Did you happen to see a group of Americans, eleven of them, by any chance?" And here Harry paused to think how best to describe them, by their most distinguishing characteristics. "A very pretty Chinese lady and her daughter, twelve years old. And a black lady, quite tall, who wears long stripey caftans and walks like an African queen. Also there was a teenage boy, looking rather Asian, which he is by half, and the others, well, sort of what typical Americans look like . . . tall, wearing baseball caps. Have you seen them? Yes?"

The man translated briskly for his group. "He is asking if we have seen Chinese tourists, women and children, American in style." And they all returned the same answer: No.

"Thought not," Harry said. He was quiet for a moment, then said to the designated interpreter, "Would you be so kind as to ask your friends to be on the lookout for my friends? If you happen to run into them while you're sightseeing today or tomorrow . . . Well, you see, they've been missing since Christmas morning. All eleven of them."

"Eleven?" the man repeated. "What do you mean, this 'missing'?"

"The fact is, no one's seen them, haven't heard from them either. Anyway, you're on holiday, and I didn't meant to trouble you. But if you could be good enough to spread the word, I'd be most obliged."

"Certainly," the man said. "Eleven Americans," and he gave a decisive nod, a look that was meant to evince both sympathy and solid expectation that all would turn out well. "We will spread."

And indeed they did. They spread the news like a virus. As the days went by, it led to rampant speculation, assumption, conclusion, then panic all around. "Have you heard? Eleven Americans have disappeared, and the military police are trying to cover it up. Why hasn't our embassy issued a travelers' warning?"

You could not visit a pagoda without hearing the anxious buzz. At Floating Island Resort, the arriving tourists were understandably nervous. They would have left if their guides had found new accommodations elsewhere. At the tiki bar, an American businessman said this was probably the sinister handiwork of the military. A French couple countered that perhaps the missing tourists had done something forbidden by the government—passed out pro-democracy pamphlets, or held demonstrations to release Aung San Suu Kyi. You simply can't do things like that and not expect consequences. Burma is *not* America. If you don't know what you're doing, leave well enough alone. That's the problem, the French woman said knowingly to her husband, these Americans want to touch, touch, touch everything they are told not to, from fruit in the market to what is forbidden in other countries.

Meanwhile, the Shan people around Inle Lake believed that angry Nats had taken the eleven Americans. No doubt the Americans had offended a few if not many. Of all the Westerners, the Americans tended to eat the biggest feasts. Yet they didn't think to give feasts to the Nats. A Nat certainly would be offended by that. And many Western tourists had no respect. When they thought no one was looking, they did not remove their expensive running shoes before stepping into holy areas. They believed that if no one saw them, no wrong was committed. Even the ladies disregarded what was sacred and went into areas of monasteries where only men were allowed.

Western news bureaus stationed in Asia caught wind of the story, but no one had any solid information, only hearsay. How could they get to the American at the resort? And what about the tour guide in the hospital? They needed sources, access, interviews, material that was "authenticated." But from whom would they get these things? No Burmese journalist would dare work with them. And as Western journalists, they couldn't waltz in with camera equipment and sound booms in tow. Many had tried to do so surreptitiously—an interview with Aung San Suu Kyi was a journalist's prize—but most were caught, interrogated for days, strip-searched, deported, and their equipment confiscated. Obtaining information was as risky as smuggling drugs, the result being either rich reward or utter ruin. Yet there were always covert sources, a few expatriates, or journalists on tourist visas who brought no fancy equipment and used their eyes and ears.

By New Year's Day, one hundred thirty international newswires had run stories about the eleven tourists missing in either "Burma" or "Myanmar." The phones at the U.S. Embassy rang nonstop, and the consular staff had to be careful what they said, since they had to work with the Burmese government to leave Rangoon and investigate. By January 2nd, the top brass at the New York headquarters of Global News Network knew they had a winner worthy of more airtime. Viewers, they concluded via focus groups, were riveted by the mystery of the missing, two of them being innocent children, the romantic angle of Burma, and an obvious villain in the form of a military regime. There was also Harry Bailley, whom middle-aged women found attractive, and whom viewers under eighteen, their most important demographic, liked "a lot" because of his love for disobedient dogs. GNN executives called this "sexy news," and they were determined to do whatever necessary to get the scoop, to conjure whatever drama and dirt they could to beat out the competition and improve their ratings.

By the time Harry's tale of woe had made the rounds at all the resort hotels in Burma and Thailand, a young, wavy-haired tourist from London named Garrett Wyeth arrived at Floating Island Resort. He was an independent videographer for low-cost adventure travel shows, and he wanted to break into serious documentaries. He had come to Burma with a modest, tourist-type camcorder to gather footage for a documentary that he was calling *Oppressed and Suppressed*. He hoped to sell the edited footage to Channel Four, which several years earlier had funded a story, *The Dying Rooms*, in which Western reporters posing as charity workers revealed how orphan girls in China were being systematically killed. That program had inspired him. It was brilliant what those disguised reporters had done—infiltrated the system, duped those cretins into talking openly about all kinds of problems. The hidden cameras captured it all, amazing footage of terrible scenes, gory-awful. It was a huge success piece, creating splashy waves of international outrage and condemnation of China. Huzzah for the journalists! Prizes all around. Of course, some deedah always has to go and make a bloody ding-dong over "negative consequences." What controversy doesn't have them? So China slammed shut the doors to its orphanages for a while. No more adoptions, cleft palate surgeries, or pretty new blankets. That lasted for—what?—a year at most. Sometimes you have to accept a few scrapes to clinch the race. Then everybody wins. In any case, *his* story would have nothing to do with dying babies, and it would yield, he was sure, all *good* consequences, absolutely, and at the same time, it would secure his credentials as a hard-hitting journalist who could do *real* stories. How freaking brilliant was that?

In Harry Bailley, Garrett saw an unanticipated but lucrative opportunity. He would persuade his fellow countryman—and Harry *was* British by birth—to give an "excloo." He would go to Channel Four and present this tantalizing tidbit, a taste of things to come. And if they turned their noses up, he would then sell the piece to the first network that offered him top whack. Global News Network was a possibility, not his first choice, however, because it teetered on the sleazy side of journalism, but when it came to scoops and scandals, the people there knew how to stack the banknotes and fan them in your face. Ah, the smell of success. This bit with Harry Bailley could be worth a quick thousand quid or two. And if the tourists died—well, let's not go there.

"I don't know if that's a prudent idea," Harry said when Garrett first approached him. He was confused and tired, having slept only in snatches the entire week. "I don't want to make things worse for my friends. The military government here, well, they seem rather strict on how one does things. The fellow who runs this place thinks it safer to remain mum."

Garrett realized that Harry had no idea what had already been broadcast on international news. Floating Island Resort was an information wasteland—no satellite TV, no BBC, CNN, or GNN, nothing but two Myanmar government-run channels forecasting good weather. He had to play this close to his vest, so Harry would not get too confused as to what to do and whom to turn to. "Listen, my friend," Garrett said, "you're right to think of your friends as top of the list. But that bloke Herr Heinrich is just watching his own back. He doesn't want to scare away the customers. Can you trust what he says? Bloody no. He's a blag artist, first-rate. What you know in your heart and your gut is what's right. It trumps all else."

"But the military—"

"Bah! You aren't cowed by them, are you? You're an American! You can do what you bloody want. Freedom of speech! It's your right, and pardon my being blunt, it's your responsibility."

By freedom, Garrett, of course, was referring to *American* civil rights, not international law, as he led a befuddled Harry to think. The truth is, Harry had as much right to express his views freely as did any Burmese citizen, which is to say, none at all.

"Your words will reach *millions and millions*," Garrett told him, "and that's precisely the pressure you want—for those shitheads to know everybody's watching, and for the U.S. Embassy to feel the heat to do more to find your friends."

"I see your point," Harry replied. "But still—well, I just don't know. . . ."

"All right," Garrett said patiently, "I know you're also wondering, 'Say, how am I going to keep my own skin out of the fryer—'"

Harry broke in. "That's not it at all."

"So let me ask you this," Garrett said. "Who's the biggest opponent of the Burmese military? Right, that woman Aung San Suu Kyi. She's been telling them to bugger off, in a manner of speaking, for the past ten years. And what do they do? They don't lock her up and throw away the key. They confine her to her house. Why? Because they know the world is watching. That's the difference. It's column inches, airtime. The media makes it happen." He held up his thumb in conspiratorial agreement with himself, then added in a low voice: "*That's how news determines what happens in the world!*" He nudged Harry. "But it starts with you."

Harry nodded, nearly convinced. "All I want is to do best by my friends."

"Believe me. This is the very, very best you can do. And you needn't say anything unflattering about the military government. You simply explain in a factual and completely unbiased way that you want your friends back. Honest and heroic."

"No harm in that," Harry agreed.

Garrett recorded while his girlfriend, Elsbeth, conducted the interview. She was a lanky blonde who would have been beautiful had she not had misshapen teeth further marred by tea, nicotine, and the British tradition of dental care. They were in Harry's bungalow, where no one could see them. "Dr. Bailley," she began. "Would you care to tell us what happened the morning of December twenty-fifth?"

Harry sighed noisily and stared out the window to his right. "I was sick that day. Food poisoning . . ." As he conveyed the story, Harry reminded himself never to smile or appear overly friendly with the camera. Nothing worse than seeing a grinning newscaster reporting on tragedy. When he finished he looked wistful, slightly hopeful. It was not simply playacting.

Elsbeth turned sideways toward Garrett. "Is it enough?"

"Ask about the others. Get him to describe them for the viewers," Garrett said. There had already been some pieces broadcast showing photos and giving backgrounds, but Garrett wanted the personal touch, how these people really were, according to one heartbroken man. "Yeah," he told Elsbeth, "the personal touch. Let's make them cry their eyes out and want to see the poor souls saved."

Harry overheard Garrett's instructions. Yes, of course! That was the point, wasn't it? He needed to help get them rescued. As Garrett said, the media could make this happen. A wonderful opportunity— far better than photos on milk cartons. He assumed the thoughtful look, looking slightly away, envisioning the perfect combination of words to create an outpouring of sympathy. Thank God for his expertise as a television personality. Come on, work the camera, bring up the emotions, keep the buggers from pushing the remote buttons. And then out rolled "The Voice," as his producer called it, as smooth as thirty-year scotch. "We're all very good friends, you see, from San Francisco or thereabouts." He played with his hands, the sensitive man abstracted by worry. He looked back up at the camera. "In fact, one of them is my oldest, dearest friend from childhood, Mark Moffett. He runs one of the largest and most successful plantations specializing in landscape-architectural plants. Bamboo, mostly. Sterling reputation, and what a heart of gold." He snorted a wry, wistful laugh. "Always wears safari shorts, no matter the season. He once ascended Everest, and I'd wager he was wearing those safari shorts then as well." He laughed sadly, the way one does when giving humorous anecdotes during a eulogy. "His son, Rupert, well, what a good all-around lad he is. Makes friends easily with other kids from other lands, plays basketball, shows them magic tricks—he's quite talented at that and attracts quite a crowd. . . ."

And so Harry went on to describe his compatriots with broad superlatives, inflating their moral character, providing instant makeovers in their appearance, adjusting their age downward and their fortitude upward. They were well educated but down-to-earth; deeply in love and happily married; brave and adventurous but not careless; altruistic and considerate, with never a concern about their own comforts; naive people who loved native people. . . .

Harry saved the best for the last. Again, he fiddled with his hands, rubbing them, finding it difficult to speak of heartbreak. "There's also a very, very special lady, Marlena Chu. She's amazing, truly, a purveyor of fine art—de Kooning, Hockney, Diebenkorn, Kline, Twombly—I'm an ignoramus when it comes to modern art, but I've heard those painters are rather good." Bosh. Harry was making up the list. He'd always memorized the names of artists, poets, musicians, and the presidents of various African nations, knowing that knowledge came in handy at the various parties and important functions he attended. His best shot was reciting "The Dying Light," a poem about a soldier who finds the light dimming at dusk as his final moments dwindle. Almost without exception, it caused women to become teary-eyed and want to wrap their arms around him, as if to safeguard him from death, loneliness, and beauty of thought without an appreciative ear.

"You were close to her?" Elsbeth prompted.

"Yes. We're very, very—" His voice broke, and Elsbeth patted his hand. He took a deep breath and continued bravely in a whisper: "I'm devastated. I should have been on that boat ride with her."

Harry's emotion was true, for the most part, but his delivery was laughably clichéd. Elsbeth and Garrett gave no indication that they thought so.

"How old is she?" Elsbeth asked gently.

"She's—" Harry began, but realized he had no idea what the answer was. He punted and gave forth a little laugh. "Well, if this is going to be televised, she would hardly want me to reveal her age. But I will say this: Like a lot of Asian women, she looks not a day over twenty-nine. Oh, and she has a daughter, a girl of twelve, standing about this high. Esmé. Terrific kid. She's quite precocious, fearless, and dear. Has a little white dog, too, a puppy, about six or seven weeks old, a Shih Tzu, with a herniated umbilicus. I'm a veterinary doctor, you see, so I notice such things. By the way, have you seen my show, *The Fido Files*? No? We're actually negotiating for UK programming. Oops, you better edit out that last comment, since it's not a done deal. But dogs are my love, besides Marlena, and if I had the means, I'd arrange for a team of trained search-and-rescue dogs to be sent on the next plane. . . ."

ON THE NINTH DAY of my friends' prolonged stay at No Name Place, a GNN report came out with this: "Eleven Americans, two of them children, have been missing for a week in Burma, the country that the military regime renamed Myanmar just before it overturned a landslide democratic election in 1990. The Americans were on a carefree holiday when they went for a boat ride from which they never returned." Photos of the missing came up, replaced by an image of stern gun-toting soldiers.

"Since the military coup, Burma has been plagued by civil unrest and has often been cited for human rights violations. A GNN exclusive last year reported on the systematic rape of ethnic women by the military. Equally horrific abuses occur in unseen areas of the country—from the abduction of men, women, and children who are then forced to carry loads for the military until they die of exhaustion, to the outright razing of entire villages suspected of hiding supporters of the National League for Democracy." Footage of boy monks and smiling girls appeared.

"This is the atmosphere in which the missing Americans find themselves. The Burmese military and U.S. Embassy officials in Rangoon say they have no leads. But some speculate the tourists may have been imprisoned for unknown offenses to the regime. One of the missing is suspected of being an activist and supporter of Nobel Peace Prize winner Aung San Suu Kyi, the popular leader of the National League for Democracy, who is now under house arrest. In the meantime, tourists in Burma are leaving the country as fast as they can. One man, however, remains optimistic that the Americans will be found—Dr. Harry Bailley of the popular TV show *The Fido Files*. He is a member of the tour group whose other members are missing. Because of illness on that fateful day, Dr. Bailley stayed behind, while his friends left for a sunrise boat ride just before dawn on Christmas Day. GNN spoke with him firsthand in an exclusive report filmed at an undisclosed location in Burma. Coming up next on *World Hot Spots with GNN*—making news in how we report the news."

IN THE ANTIPODEAN WORLD of San Francisco, Mary Ellen Brookhyser Feingold Fong was awakened one morning by a telephone call from someone with the U.S. State Department, informing her that her daughter, Wendy, was missing.

Thinking the male voice was Wendy's landlord, Mary Ellen said, "She's not missing. She's in Burma. But if she's behind on her rent, I'm happy to handle it." It had happened before.

The man with the State Department explained once again who he was, and twice more, Mary Ellen's mind refused to budge from the notion that Wendy was not missing, she was merely irresponsible, for to give up this illogic meant accepting a reality that was beyond her comprehension.

In Mayville, North Dakota, Wyatt's mother, Dot Fletcher, received a similarly confusing call. She, too, was certain that her son was on yet another expedition in an area without adequate communication. It happened all the time. He would be in the middle of the Indian Ocean, the engines out and the boat stuck in the doldrums. Or he might be trekking in eastern Bhutan, seven or eight days' hiking distance from the nearest phone. He was not missing. He was simply not reachable by phone. And in that respect, she was correct.

And so the calls continued to be made: To Moff's ex-wife, since she was Rupert's mother. To Marlena's ex, since he was Esmé's father. To Heidi and Roxanne's mélange of parents and stepparents. To Bennie's mother, though not to Bennie's life partner, Timothy, since he was not officially listed as next of kin. The calls came at odd hours, when the recipients were sure to be at home, when even the first ring heralded disquiet, and even before GNN made its broadcast of breaking news. My friends' families watched in shock as a smarmy man with a British accent spoke of their loved ones in terms normally reserved for eulogies. As Garrett watched the story in his suite at the second-best hotel in Bangkok, he regretted that he had not asked for more than fifteen thousand U.S. dollars.

By seven a.m. Pacific Standard Time on this day, the various next of kin were anxiously watching GNN for the third time. The same story ran every hour, with the smallest of added details heralded as "breaking news." GNN pulled researchers and camera crews off other projects and gave them a laundry list of what to find and whom to talk to. For visuals, they dug up from their archives file footage on both the military coup and travel to exotic locales. They used snippets from home movies taken by tourists who had left Burma early and were arriving in waves at the Bangkok airport. In the States, network staffers had uncovered additional morsels of viewer interest. One of the missing was an heiress, they reported, the daughter of the PVC-pipe king. A photo was shown of Wendy Brookhyser, taken years before at a debutante ball. Roxanne was seen accepting an award, looking smart and shiny-faced with perspiration. There was a still of Marlena and an eight-year-old Esmé hugging at Disneyland, next to a waving Mickey Mouse. Heidi was caught sitting on a friend's porch steps, eating an ice cream bar. Even an old clip from *The Fido Files* constituted "fast-breaking news."

Throughout the day, more scraps of news poured in. There was evidence, GNN reported, that one member had once been arrested for possession of marijuana. This was Moff, who had indeed been busted some twenty-two years prior, and was charged with a misdemeanor, fined, and given probation. On GNN, he was shown standing against a wall of bamboo, wearing his standard-issue safari hat, shorts, and wraparound shades. In this context, he looked like a drug runner proudly displaying his wares. This news item abutted another segment, cobbled together by a resourceful GNN producer, on Burma's Golden Triangle and its colorful history as "the heroin capital of the world." While the piece did not explicitly say that Moff had any ties to the heroin growers, the juxtaposition implied one.

I saw it all on Heinrich's television. He had hooked it up to a satellite dish newly purchased on the black market, which replaced the one that had disappeared recently. I must confess, I found it *un peu amusant* that my friends were subject to bad reporting and unflattering photos, just as I had been when the newspapers reported my mysterious death.

The worst of the news hounds, in my opinion, was Philip Gutman of Free to Speak International. That megalomaniac contacted GNN and dangled bait in front of them, and they bit. With a flapping, fleshy mouth, he vociferously denied the rumors. "Not true, not true, none of the missing are spies." He then cleverly praised those who did serve as peacemaking watchdogs, particularly in countries, such as Burma, with atrocious human rights records, and he was proud that a member of Free to Speak was among the missing. He added in dramatic fashion that "this person has now joined the tens of thousands of people now missing in Burma," and he hoped his friend would not wind up like the rest of them—with an "unspeakable fate." Naturally, this led to a flurry of guesses as to who this activist was, and the curious and concerned were not simply the international viewers of GNN, my friends' families, and the U.S. government, but the military regime of Myanmar as well. Who was this troublemaker, they wanted to know. And on whose watch had this person slipped in? The punishment for spies in Myanmar was similar to that for people who were caught smuggling drugs: death.

Wendy may have been an immature nitwit, but that did not mean she deserved to have her head lopped off simply because her former housemate seized any opportunity to promote his cause. I don't take issue with people who work to improve human rights, not at all. It's admirable and essential. But Gutman's entire proviso was geared to garner headlines. He favored the news-catching denunciations, demonstrations, and demands. He never negotiated quietly behind the scenes like some other activists. Gutman would sit on stories of abuse until it was most advantageous for getting the biggest headlines, usually around the time he had scheduled a fund-raising campaign. Alas, in every community that proposes to do good, there are always a few who do good mostly for themselves.

By the evening news hour, GNN knew they had on their lucky hands the news sensation of the week in the United States—one that beat out the pre–Super Bowl hoopla, the sex scandal involving a congressman and his biggest campaign contributor, the movie star who had been arrested for pedophilia. The scoop was the heart-rending, suspenseful story of missing Americans, innocent and beautiful, successful and well respected, rich and envied, outspoken and outrageous, and with just enough hints of impropriety to tantalize. GNN put up a call-in poll asking viewers to vote: Were the tourists at fault for their disappearance, entirely, somewhat, or not at all? A comforting eighty-seven percent believed the tourists were innocent victims. What should America's response be: do nothing, offer a reward, send in the troops? A shocking seventy-three percent voted to invade Burma, and a fair number of posts on the GNN message board said, "Nuke 'em." The U.S. government vehemently denied that it had any intention of doing either. GNN gave the green light to increase coverage and airtime.

The GNN bureau chief in Bangkok coordinated with headquarters in New York on interviews. At the Bangkok airport, reporters from GNN and other media outlets swarmed the tourists arriving from Mandalay and Rangoon. Had they been frightened? Did they leave early? Would they ever go back?

The people from New York and Rio de Janeiro gave wearied and disgusted looks, as they pushed past the newshounds. But a few travelers were easily stopped, because they were from cities like Indianapolis, Indiana, or Manchester, England, where it was considered rude not to acknowledge someone who asked you a question. Those from Los Angeles also willingly stepped before the camera, since that was their civil right. "It was so hard to spend time in a country," a woman from Studio City commented, "where eleven people wind up dead." She was reminded that no one was confirmed deceased, so she added, "Well, it still gets to you."

"Were you scared?" a reporter shouted to a couple emerging from a set of doors.

"This one was," said a sunburned man, in a flat tone, and he jerked his thumb toward the woman behind him. "She went hysterical." The woman gave him a smile of annoyance. She turned to the reporter and said, her stony smile still affixed, "To be honest, I was more concerned we'd get stuck if they shut down the airports." Her response—plus that gritted smile meant for her husband—was replayed each hour, making it seem to millions of people that she was a coldhearted bitch.

In Mayville, the citizens held a candlelight vigil and bake sale for Wyatt's family. They raised funds for Mrs. Fletcher, and the deputy sheriff she was dating, to go to Burma to search for her only son. The lesson plan in elementary schools across the country now included a geography lesson on where Burma was located in the world, and that lesson was broadcast nationally as well, since another poll had revealed than ninety-six percent of Americans had no idea where either Myanmar or Burma was. In San Francisco, Mary Ellen Brookhyser Feingold Fong was in touch with the mayor and "the three Georges"—one of them a political bigwig with connections to the State Department, another a filmmaker, and the third a billionaire humanitarian with a private jet. The staff of *The Fido Files* selected the very best of their shows to rerun, including a popular segment on training search-and-rescue dogs using scent detection and trailing, coupled with simple techniques ordinary pet owners could use to teach their own couch-potato dogs—boxer, beagle, or bichon frise, it didn't matter what breed—to sniff out a child playing hide-and-seek. Even before the end of that broadcast day, plans had been made to fly to Burma via private jet the following people: Mary Ellen Brookhyser Feingold Fong; Mrs. Dorothea Fletcher and her deputy boyfriend, Gustav Larsen; and Saskia Hawley of Golden Gate Search-and-Rescue Dogs, a former gal pal of Harry's.

On the plane, Saskia Hawley reflected on the past she had once shared with Harry Bailley. She still felt a fondness for him. What did he feel for her? Like all his former lovers, she was petite, thin, and, as Harry had once put it, "emotionally demanding." "Cute" was also how Harry described her, a term she despised since it connoted someone less than equal. "Don't call me cute," she repeatedly demanded. "But you are, darling," Harry would answer. "What could be wrong with that?"

As Saskia now recalled, Harry did have his endearing qualities. He was loyal, for one thing, just like a dog. With other women, he looked, but he didn't touch, and in that sense, he had never betrayed her, not like the last guy, the dickhead. When she was in trouble or distress of any kind, Harry came to her aid, no matter the hour. And there was the bedtime factor. He was plain fun between the sheets. In retrospect, he was a lot more desirable and cohabitable than the other lovers who had come and gone since she and Harry called it quits six years back. The term they actually used was "cooling period." They never stated it as final. Could she ever take up with him again? No, no, no, no, she protested a bit too much.

Saskia had chosen to bring two dogs with arguably the highest-caliber noses in the business. There was Lush, a loose-tongued, smiley-mouthed, black-and-white border collie bitch. She had earned her stripes as a FEMA Urban Search and Rescue dog, beginning with the Oklahoma City bombing. Lush was also experienced as a cadaver dog, but Saskia did not reveal that to the other passengers on the plane. She wanted to convey that she was just as optimistic as they were. Officially, this was still a rescue, not yet a recovery. But Saskia was a realist; experience had forced that down her throat. And if the tourists were dead, God forbid, the scent might be apparent to a dog even years after the fact, especially if the decaying materials had leached into tree roots. Saskia's team had been involved in two murder cases in which the corpse was dug up, one next to a pine, the other next to a gingko. As with all of Lush's finds, the dog had circled and sniffed, then gone back to the source with the strongest scent and done a decisive sit as signal that she had found the object that would lead to her reward, a game of fetch with a gummy tennis ball. The first time Lush alerted Saskia to a tree, the other search team members guffawed. Saskia then told them to dig next to the tree, at the spot most hidden from view of those approaching. Sure enough, they unearthed the bones, and after Saskia explained why dogs pick up the scent on the trunk, the other searchers exclaimed, "Good Lord! A blood-sucking, carnivorous tree." But there was a troubling fact about cadaver dogs in Burma. The dogs would be in a constant frenzy, for an excessive number of bodies would have been secretly put in the ground. Lush was in danger of working her nose raw.

The other canine member of Saskia's team was Topper, a black Lab, who was a wilderness-rescue dog. Being a Labrador, he was also a big galoot who loved to do water work. There might be a need for that, too, to judge from what the consular officials said of the disappearance. Saskia wondered how deep the lake was, and just as important, how cold, and thus how well refrigerated the bodies might be. That would help in staving off decomposition and aid the dogs in searching for a smaller target rather than a dispersed one.

So these four people and two dogs flew to Bangkok. There they would find out whether they would be allowed entry by the military government of Myanmar. Would they be granted expedited visas— or any visas at all? To help them in this regard, one of Mary Ellen's Georges, the political bigwig, had exerted his influence in the State Department. It was hoped she and her entourage could pass as ordinary tourists, albeit rich ones with their own private plane, and thus be issued the last-minute visas. Whether they got them would depend on whether the Myanmar regime was unaware of their connection with those who were missing. And that was possible, staffers felt, since GNN was not broadcast in Myanmar—or more correctly, was not *allowed* to be broadcast. The broadcast ban extended to all foreign programs. The approved news was reported on the two government-run channels, and the stories on both had to first pass muster with the Information Ministry. One of the old generals set the guidelines for all the news that was fit to report, and the Press Scrutiny Board ensured that these were followed to the letter. Among the prohibitions: no bad weather forecasts, or news of economic downturns, or depictions of dead civilians. None of that was good for morale. And if Aung San Suu Kyi was mentioned at all, the words "evil tool of foreign interests" had better appear next to the name. Words like "democracy," "education," and "corruption" triggered close scrutiny. So a story about eleven missing and possibly dead tourists was not likely to see headlines in the regime-controlled newspapers, television programs, or radio broadcasts.

Don't be mistaken. This did not mean the Information Ministry and their Office of Strategic Studies in the Defense Ministry had no inkling who the relatives of the missing were. The generals, the directors, and their subordinates had already reviewed tapes of GNN's stories of the missing. The ministry was in charge of finding such stories—anything that reported on the country, whether in a good or a bad light. They tuned to the Voice of America and BBC Radio, which had escaped their control and which many bad-intentioned people listened to surreptitiously. They also had a satellite dish that pulled international reception from abroad. And their Press Scrutiny Board gleaned every television program from unfriendly and powerful countries for any mention of Myanmar. Often it was the nephew or niece of some highly placed official who had the cushy job of watching *The Simpsons*, sitcoms like *Sex and the City*, and the reality program *Darwin's Fittest*, which many of them enjoyed as well. The more rigorous review of news broadcasts went to those with critical minds. Names of the guilty were thus collected and placed on appropriate lists for banned entry, expulsion, and if appropriate, future "enlightenment."

The busiest news year had been when the Dead General's daughter won the Nobel Peace Prize. What a lot of negative stories that had caused. A constant bombardment! A disaster! Those Swedes were always handing out peace prizes just to foment trouble. In private thought, the ministers in charge of propaganda and patriotism recalled that they had not handled the "situation" in the best possible way. They had closed ranks and swiftly stopped any displays of support for The Lady. And that only added to the world's dislike of them. It was now very important how they dealt with this latest challenge.

The Office of Strategic Studies was particularly perturbed and wanted answers fast. The country's "Visit Myanmar" campaign, launched several years earlier, had never soared to the heights that had been predicted, and was now in utter shambles. Hotel cancellations were flooding the lines, and the already dismal twenty-five-to-thirty-percent occupancy rate plummeted. The airlines reported that planes were empty flying into Mandalay and Yangon, but were bulging on the way out. As if that was not enough to bear, leaders from ASEAN—Thailand, Vietnam, Malaysia, and especially Japan—had called the cabinet office to say it was advisable that Myanmar clear up this delicate matter speedily and certainly before the next ASEAN summit meeting. They were like a family in ASEAN, and this could be a family embarrassment. Had it been a mistake to admit Myanmar into ASEAN? Should trade with Myanmar be curtailed, and development aid suspended?

The Office of Strategic Studies met at all levels to discuss how to deal with this "temporary situation."

And luckily for Harry, the unexpected happened. At the risk of sounding self-congratulatory, I admit that I had something to do with it. I visited a few people in the Land of Sleep. I had discovered that I could enter dreams quite easily with those who were predisposed to magic. As Rupert had said on the dock when showing his card tricks, magic could happen, but you had to believe. Even in the higher echelons of the Myanmar government, many believed in Nats, ghosts, and signs. My idea was quite ordinary, anyone could have thought of it, so I am not suggesting that I be accorded credit for what followed, not in the slightest, or at least, not all of it. I simply wanted the tyrants to feel that it was a good thing to safeguard the tourists and also those harboring them. Garrett had put it best: *The world is watching.*

Suffice it to say that several Myanmar ministers suddenly came up with the same, rather startling suggestion, one that was highly unorthodox to their usual way of doing things: Why not use this free media attention to showcase our country's beauty, its wonders, and its friendly people—yes, even its caring and friendly government?

The generals were taken aback, but ten seconds later, each in turn said, Why indeed not!

Now that the concept was enthusiastically embraced, a little preparation would be needed, of course, to spruce up and make sure the image was carried off with perfection. For one thing, as the ASEAN leaders had suggested, they might release a few hundred prisoners—or even a thousand, one general said, why not be magnanimous?—to emphasize that no people were jailed for political reasons, only detained for their own good. The Lady, for instance—let us speak openly of her—though she may be popular with a small and sentimental portion of our people, she is clearly not in favor with most of our happy citizens, who praise the tremendous progress we have made in the last decade. We fear for the safety of our little sister—yes, that's excellent, call her "sister"—for we know there are those who disapprove of her, and sad to say, they might wish to cause her harm. Better that she remain in the comfort of her own home than risk assassination, like her father. And perhaps a daily delivery of fresh fruit and flowers would further underscore the concern for her health? Oh, didn't everyone know she had been ailing? Wasn't this the very reason she was not roaming freely and creating her usual ruckus? Not that they minded if people made a little ruckus—children did it all the time—but it should not cause unrest. It should not lead to insurrection, violence, and widespread disrespect of leaders. After all, no government could tolerate that.

A good government had to guide its people, sometimes gently, sometimes strictly, just as parents did. It could allow certain freedoms, but in a *style* that suited the country. Only the leaders knew what that style should be. It was like fashion. In some countries, the women wore practically nothing, exposing their breasts, their bellies, the ugly creases of their buttocks. They were not critical of that style. But in their country, it was more beautiful to wear a longyi. It was a matter of cultural difference. For that reason, a country had to handle its own affairs. China handled its affairs. Why shouldn't Myanmar? China governed with its own style. Why should Myanmar be singled out for criticism for doing exactly the same?

This new campaign would work very well, the generals and the ministers agreed. Most important to its success was the demonstration that every effort was being made to find the missing people. The tourism office would be in touch with the military police to create a methodical plan. The world would be shown how hard the warmhearted people of Myanmar were seeking the group's whereabouts—searching high and low among the two thousand two hundred sacred temples and beautiful stupas of Bagan; in the intriguing monastery outside Mandalay, with its world-astounding collection of Buddhist statues; on a jetty taking in the most scenic part of the Ayeyarwaddy. When the cameras were turned on southern Shan State, where the tourists had last been seen, they would zoom in on photogenic "giraffe-necked" Padaung women in native costume, a dozen choker rings pushing down on their shoulders and giving them that elongated look—all tourists marveled at this. And the ladies, who would have been rehearsed in expressing concern for their foreign friends, would bob their heads gracefully above their ornamented throats as they waved, or rather, wept.

And if the tourists were found to be dead—not that this was

likely—it would be explained in an acceptable way, that it was mis-adventure, for example, that it was the tourists' own fault, but the good people of Myanmar did not blame them.

The officials with the Ministry of Hotels and Tourism decided to bring in an international public relations expert—not, however, the firm that helped them devise the failed "Visit Myanmar" campaign in 1996, or the one that helped give them their new, friendly name. The ministry found a consulting firm based in Washington with an impressive list of clients: Samuel Doe of Liberia, Saddam Hussein of Iraq, and Rwandan president Juvénal Habyarimana. The consultant would help create a multipoint plan to saturate the news with positive images.

The consultant arrived, and at first, the ministers were skeptical. He was a fairly young man, who smiled all the time, so who could take him seriously? He also made some insulting remarks about their standing in the world. And then he came up with an astonishing sug-gestion: Plant the words "the new Burma" and associate the phrase with "Myanmar."

"The situation, as we now know," the young man said, "that is, from discussions with high-level tour operators in other countries, is one of inadequate understanding of your country and its tourism potential." He cited research figures showing that upward of ninety-five percent of people polled outside Asia had no idea where Myan-mar was. They did not recognize the new name of the capital, Yangon, whereas they still recalled Rangoon.

He went on to point out that such people were, of course, un-informed and behind the times, and thus did not associate Myanmar with the famous glories and beauties of its past, all worthy of many visits and the spending of discretionary income. They did, however, remember the old name, Burma. To Western tourists, "Burma" sounded fun, friendly, and romantic.

One of the ministry staff added, "In that terrible way associated with British colonialism." They had already spent vast sums to promulgate the idea that "Myanma" had been the first name and a more egalitarian one, whereas "Burma" referred to the Bamar ruling class. Damn those people who said "Myanma" and "Bama" were merely variants of the same word! And it was a lie that most Burmese considered "Myanma" to be associated with the old ruling class. Where were those Burmese liars who said so?

"The research doesn't lie when it comes to public perception," the young man said. "That is why I suggest a bold strategy—and that is to *go backward* to keep step with the backward world perception, and in this way, you can then lead the world *forward* into the new Myanmar. Start with the tagline: 'The new Burma is Myanmar.'"

This proposal was met with silence. Everyone glanced about to see how to answer.

But then the senior man who oversaw propaganda nodded with a bland face and said, "It's unorthodox, yet well reasoned, forward-thinking even. The world is backward, and we must get them to follow us. The new Burma *is* Myanmar. That is the message. I like it." Loud bursts of acclaim sounded in the meeting hall. "The new Burma!"

The senior man fell into further contemplation and scratched his chin. "Or did you say, 'The old Burma is the new Myanmar'?"

Everyone grew silent as the boss thought about this. He nodded. "Yes, that was more the idea." And the room burst into fervent accord. "The old Burma is the new Myanmar! Excellent! A very wise refinement, sir."

And thus began a campaign by the military regime to recruit Harry as their spokesman for tourism. And of course, the visas for Mary Ellen and other members of the search party were granted forthright. But you already knew that.

HIGH IN THE RAINFOREST, Marlena, Vera, Heidi, and Moff tended to the sick. Marlena and Vera were in charge of Esmé, Bennie,

Wyatt, and Wendy. Heidi cared for Roxanne and Dwight, and Moff hovered over his son. The past few days had shaken them to the depths of their souls. For a while, it seemed impossible that they would be able to provide any relief beyond water, which they poured over their senseless charges to quell the brain-damaging fever. And when their patients' fever was exchanged for bone-shaking chills, they wrapped their arms around them, and rocked and cried. There was nothing more they could do.

While returning from the loo one day, Heidi caught two old grandmothers feeding Wyatt and Wendy a strong-smelling liquid. One of the women explained matter-of-factly what she was doing, but Heidi understood none of it. The woman drew out some leaves from a pouch, pointed, and smiled, as if to suggest, "See? I told you. It's only this."

Heidi inspected the leaves. They were green and feathery, looking very much like parsley or cilantro. She took a leaf to Black Spot and asked him what it was. "It is good," he said. "A plant, I am knowing the Burmese name, not the English name. But it is medicine for jungle fever." Heidi next sought Moff, who was sitting quietly next to his son. The boy was unconscious and moaning. She dropped the leaves in his lap. "What do you think this is?"

Moff picked them up, looked at them, with their slim bifurcating stems, then smelled them. "Ah yes, the telltale balsamic fragrance. In the States, you see this growing around garbage dumps and along the sides of roads. Also known as sweet wormwood, *Artemisia annua*. There are many species of *Artemisia*, and this one I've never seen before, but the leaf structure is characteristic. Grows fast and turns into a plant the shape of a soft-limbed Christmas tree. The fragrance is also typical." He put a leaf in his mouth and smacked his lips. "And the bitter taste. Where did you find it?"

"One of the old ladies made some kind of concoction and was giving it to Wyatt and Wendy to drink."

Moff's eyes lit up. "Brilliant! Dear God, she's absolutely right.

Artemisia annua does have an antibacterial property, maybe even antimalarial. Where is this woman?" He stood up. And then he and Heidi hurried off to find the lady with the herbs.

"TODAY, JANUARY FOURTH," the Myanmar official announced to TV cameras and the crowd at the airport in Mandalay, "the unified people of Myanmar proudly celebrate our Independence Day, our liberation in 1948 from British colonial rule. Today we will feast, hold festivals, pay respects, and give offerings, as well as play music and dance in our native dress. We will visit our holiest of pagodas and our greatest monuments in our beautiful golden land. And today we welcome at the new and modern Mandalay International Airport our honored guests from America, who join with us in looking for their compatriots and family members."

An interpreter translated the words into English for Mary Ellen Brookhyser Feingold Fong and Dot Fletcher. The two women were staggered by the size of the crowds. Were all these television cameras actually for them? They made Mary Ellen suspicious, but Dot was touched by the outpouring of concern from the Myanmar officials.

"Soon," the speaker continued, "we hope we will be celebrating the happy whereabouts of your family members, who can resume their visit of our beautiful country."

Dot Fletcher's boyfriend was openly impressed. "Can you beat that?" Gus Larsen said. And Saskia Hawley was happy to see that her two dogs had made it past customs without quarantine or even a glance at their health certificates. "They are search-and-rescue dogs," she explained to the interpreter, and the deputy minister of information exclaimed, "Search! Yes, we want you to search our lovely countryside. Search everywhere. We will help." And he pulled out brochures of some of Myanmar's most scenic spots, at each of which a camera crew was waiting.

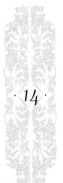

· 14 ·

THE INVENTION
OF NOODLES

By the end of the second week in No Name Place, my malaria-stricken friends were somewhat improved, enough to complain about the menu and the mosquitoes. They sat on two logs facing each other across a clearing that was grandly called "the dining room." Their faces, arms, and legs had been rubbed with termite powder, which Black Spot had given them to prevent mosquito bites. The powder came from a bark or mineral that was also effective against termites, hence the name, or so they thought. It was actually the ground-up bodies of termites. Had they known, they still would have continued to use it. They did not automatically question the advice that the tribe gave them anymore. Every day, at every meal, they drank the wormwood tea.

They also drank the soup that was made especially for their health. A bland rice broth had been suitable when they were finally able to keep down a bit of nourishment. But now their San Franciscan palates were being restored and they yearned for foods with more variety. They did not complain to their jungle hosts—that would have been ungracious—but among themselves they lamented the thrice-daily offerings of rice and the deplorable fermented sauces and dried creatures. They figured the tribe had an underground larder where food supplies rotted to the precise degree of slimy nastiness. They were grateful, however, that there was plenty of food. As they ate, birds cried to one another, shaking the leaves as they fluttered about to claim a branch above potential food droppings. The branch above Bennie made for the best territory, since he often spilled things.

Loot and Bootie were hunched at the edge of the camp smoking cheroots, and the old grandmothers who had given wormwood tea to the sick were happy to see their foreign friends heartily eating the meal they had prepared with American tastes in mind. They kept an eye on the Younger White Brother, who was seated in front of them.

"I wish we had something different to eat for a change," Bootie heard Rupert grumble.

"Like what?" Esmé said.

"Top Ramen," he said.

"We don't have noodles."

"Then I wish we had noodles."

A few minutes later, Bootie told Black Spot what the Younger White Brother had said. He nodded. He was on his way into town to get more supplies, the fermented fish and spices the grandmothers had asked for, betel-nut leaves, and cheroots. He would find noodles.

"THIS IS REALLY WEIRD," Rupert said that night at dinner. "I was just thinking about noodles, and here they are."

It was probably one of the tribe's staples, the others guessed, though it was curious that they hadn't brought them out earlier. The noodles were delicious. Tonight the vegetables were better, too, fresh bamboo shoots and forest mushrooms. The fermented stuff seemed less rancid, and blessedly, nothing looked black, crispy, or eight-legged.

"Who invented noodles, anyway?" Roxanne said.

Marlena answered brightly: "The Chinese did, of course."

Moff slapped his forehead. "Oh, of course. It's always the Chinese influence. For a moment there, I was going to blame the Italians."

"Marco Polo first ate noodles when he visited China," Marlena added.

"I saw a movie with Gary Cooper as Marco Polo," Wyatt said. "He's talking to this Chinese guy, who's played by Alan Hale senior and has this big ol' Fu Manchu moustache and slanted eye makeup. So Marco Polo is eating noodles and he says, 'Hey, Kemosabe, this stuff is pretty good, what is it?' And Alan Hale says, 'Spa-get.' Ha! Like 'spaghetti' is what the Chinese call it. It's hilarious. Spa-get, like the Chinese invented spa food as well."

Wendy laughed until Dwight broke in: "Well, there's another theory that the early ancestors of Italians invented noodles."

"That's not what the movie showed," Wyatt replied.

"I mean it," Dwight went on. "There are these Etruscan wall paintings that prove that noodles were around in eight hundred B.C., if not earlier. That means noodles are in the genetic heritage of many a modern-day Italian."

"Excuse me," Marlena said as evenly as she could. "The Chinese have been eating noodles for over *five* thousand years."

"Who says?" Dwight countered. "Did someone unearth a Chinese takeout menu from the Ping-Pong dynasty?" He laughed at his own little joke.

He kept his eyes fixed on Marlena. "We can debate the origins of anything," he said. "You make the case that all noodles originate from China. And to be fair, I say they likely evolved in different places around the same time, and that it may have been an accident the way they got invented. Doesn't take much culinary evolution for a cook to run out the door during battle, leave the dough behind, and find it dried hard as rock when he returns. Midafternoon there's a flash flood and—what do you know?—the dough is soft again. From there it was only a matter of time and refinement before someone discovered that cutting the dough into thin strips made it easier to boil up for a meal on the road. That's what you might call an evolutionary spandrel, spandrels being the supports when a dome was built that later were used as decorative elements, unrelated to their original use. You create something for one purpose and it gets used for another. So it is with spaghetti, an accident made purposeful. . . ."

Marlena sat in stony silence. Spandrels, schmandrels.

"That's what *we* need to find here," Dwight went on, "if we want to get out of this place. Spandrel ideas. Something that's here right now, which we can adapt to another purpose. Obvious and right under our nose. Look around at what we have here, think how we might use it. . . ."

Marlena knew she was right about the noodles. Noodles had likely been around since the start of Chinese civilization. She remembered that dumplings had been found in the tombs of emperors, so why not noodles? Both were made of dough. But then she did not know how old the tombs were in which the dumplings were found. What if the tombs were only two thousand years old? She thought about lying, telling Dwight that they were found as artifacts in Stone Age caves, maybe even in the excavation of Peking Man. That would make them six hundred thousand years old.

She wasn't one to lie; it's just that she became infuriated whenever someone tried to intimidate her. Inside she was a ball of static, snapping and crackling, but outwardly she presented the look of someone overly familiar with being dominated. This is not to say she acted cowed like the whipped and damned. Her posture remained erect, her neck long and regal. But she didn't defend herself. She sat like a cat with its ears back, ready to spring at the next provocation. That was what she had done all her life, turned quiet when her father belittled or bullied her, quashing any of her ideas or desires. Later in life, she was able to gain expertise in contemporary art and could exert her opinion among the elitest of the elite in the art world. In that regard, she and I had a lot in common. It was how we met. Like me, Marlena rarely backed down in her ideas about art. She learned that confidence and strong opinions are vital in presenting oneself as a curator of any collection. That manner was a cultivated skill and not part of her psyche, so outside her profession, she reverted to insecurity. I often wished I could give her the *umph* in triumph. God knows I had plenty left over from the battles I had fought.

I prodded Marlena to stand her ground now, to look Dwight in the eye with a determined scowl to match his and tell him his conjecture was so faulty it did not bear further discussion. "Speak up!" I shouted. "What do you have to lose?" But all I could muster from her was more internal sputtering-muttering.

The only person who had the confidence to argue with Dwight was his wife, and that was because Roxanne was smarter than he was and knew his specific deficits in logic, facts, and bluffing. Like the bit about spandrels: he was always inserting that term into conversations when he wanted to impress people into silence. They didn't know what the hell he was talking about, but it sounded conceptual and smart, so they couldn't counter him. Roxanne could have said in front of the others that the paradigm of spandrels, as the evolutionary biologist Stephen Jay Gould meant it, did not apply to dried-up dough turning into spaghetti. That was adaptation by accident, another form of evolutionary leap. Roxanne, however, never would have pointed this out to others. What—and show her intellectual superiority over Dwight once again? She had learned to not humiliate her husband in public. It was not an act of loyalty. He was insecure enough as it was, and she suffered the consequences. Once attacked, he fought with teeth bared, and if defeated, he would slink away and become remote and insular. She then had to bear the brunt of his wounded pride, his negativity toward everything, his anger beneath the surface. "Nothing's wrong," he would say, but the opposite was shown in even the littlest things. He would decline an invitation to go to the movies, telling her he was busy—couldn't she see that? He would play solitaire on his computer for hours. He rebuffed her, but in ways she could not challenge, leaving her feeling cut off and alone.

She had long known that their marriage was faltering. She guessed that he felt the same, but they could not openly admit it. That would have made the end inevitable. But the reality was clear: As a couple, they had evolved from well matched to mismatched. She wanted a baby so much it made her anxious, and at times depressed her with a vague sense of hopelessness. She was used to defining the parameters and controlling the outcomes, of creating academic success out of near disaster. Why wouldn't her body, of all things, cooperate? The baby was her priority in this marriage, and Dwight was her best chance at fulfilling that. Who knows, the baby might even give their marriage a purpose. She pictured a baby girl for some reason. Girls were about hope. If her marriage ended, the baby would still be hers, a gurgling bundle of burps. But what would happen if she did not get pregnant? How long before their marriage collapsed for good?

Like Marlena, Bennie viewed Dwight as an adversary. He found it maddening that Dwight made critical assessments of others in front of everybody. Dwight had insinuated that Bennie should be more assertive with the tribe and demand that they help the Americans get out. "I'm sorry," Bennie had said huffily, "but I just don't think that's appropriate. And I think we should wait until everyone is completely well."

Dwight also questioned Bennie's poor decision-making, his inability to set priorities. Bennie was sick of it. Who the hell was Dwight to say these things to him? These criticisms had been more frequent in recent days. If anyone objected to Dwight for his being either wrong or rude, he would say, "I'm just trying to point something out that might be helpful to you as a person. I'm a psychologist, so I have expertise on such matters. The fact that you interpret it as rude says something more about you than me." It drove Bennie crazy that Dwight could turn a situation around and make it seem that the other person was at fault. The night before, he had lain awake replaying Dwight's insults, then imagining verbiage he could fling at the brute the next time.

They were sitting around the fire one evening after dinner, when Dwight insulted him again. Yet another discussion had come up about how to be rescued without exposing the Lajamees to danger.

Dwight started by saying that the Lajamees might be suffering from paranoiac delusions. There were plenty of tribal people around Inle Lake who were not on the lam or in fear of their lives, he said. They'd seen the women in those turbans, wearing red-and-black clothes, Karen women. You couldn't miss them. And nobody was lining them up and shooting them, let alone doing what Black Spot said. Dwight knew of cults in America that were built around a shared culture of persecution when none really existed. The cults talked of mass suicide, just as the Lajamees did. Some actually carried through with it. The People's Temple, for instance—nine hundred people died, most of them forced to drink poison. What if that happened here? They didn't want to be caught in that insanity, did they? "We have to do whatever we can to get rescued," Dwight said. "We can keep fires going and draw attention with smoke. Or a couple of us who are strong enough can hack our way down and bring back help."

"But who knows for sure if the danger isn't real?" Heidi responded. "What if the soldiers kill the tribe? How can we face ourselves the rest of our lives?" She did not tell them that she had seen a man who had been murdered. "I'd be uncomfortable," she said, "putting them at risk."

"But we're already uncomfortable," Dwight retorted. "And *we* are at risk! Don't you realize where we are? We're in the fucking jungle. We already had malaria. What's next? Snakebite? Typhus? When do we factor *us* into the equation for what we do?"

He had brought up their unspoken worries and a series of morally ugly questions. Whom do you save? Can you save both? Or do you save only yourself? Do you do nothing and risk nothing, or die from whatever happens to come along as you sit on a log waiting for whatever comes?

They agitated over the questions in private thought, wishing to forget morals and just be out of this place. Who else had discarded morals and saved themselves? Could they live with themselves later? If they put away the concerns of the Lajamee, how soon would they push aside one another's welfare? At what point do people resort to "every man for himself"?

Dwight spoke again. "A few of us can try getting down." It was the idea they had discussed when they first learned they were stuck. They would follow the crevasse, the ancient dry stream. It was possible that the sinkhole closed farther down the mountain. They would have to go quite a ways, since Wyatt and Dwight had already done an initial exploration, and the split went on as far as the eye could see, before it disappeared around yet another bend.

Only a few people would go, Dwight said. They would borrow two machetes from the tribe, take food and gear, one of Heidi's headlamps, the extra batteries, some wormwood leaves. "Who's going to go with me?" Dwight asked.

Moff knew that he was logically the one who should go, but he couldn't leave Rupert. He had almost lost him. He had to watch over him from here on out.

"Anyone?" Dwight said.

Everyone remained silent, hoping he would take the clue that it wasn't a reasonable request. But Dwight had never registered silence as disapproval, just timidity and indecisiveness. He asked Bennie what he thought: "After all, you *are* our group leader. In fact, maybe *you* should go."

Bennie thought Dwight had said the words "group leader" with an excess of sarcasm. And to counter the slight, he wanted to say he was willing to go. But he had now been without his anti-seizure medication for more than two weeks. He had experienced some warnings: flashing lights, phantom smells, and more recently, that familiar sinking feeling of being pulled down into the earth, of his mind's dwindling as if he were becoming smaller yet heavier, shooting backward straight through the earth's core and out into hyperspace. He would get that warning sense of doom, and it took all his strength and concentration to resist panicking. In the past, some of these episodes had been auras that heralded the arrival of a more generalized pattern, the synchronous neuronal firings that spread throughout the whole brain and led to a grand mal. He felt he was building up to a big one, and that would make his going into the middle of nowhere a very bad idea. He could die out there, tumble off a cliff while unaware, or suffocate in all those sticky plants, while leeches and gigantic carnivorous ants crawled into his nostrils and eye sockets. And what if they ran into another tribe who still had a Stone Age mentality? They might think he was possessed by a bad spirit and beat him to set him free. He'd read stories of things like that; he remembered one in particular about an American diver in Indonesia who swam at night with a headlamp and was clubbed by fishermen who thought he was a magical manatee.

Before Bennie could respond to Dwight's suggestion that he go, Marlena interjected: "I don't think that's such a good idea, splitting up the group like that. What if you didn't come back when expected—

would we then send another bunch of people to look for you and risk those lives as well?"

Bennie nodded, relieved Marlena had provided such good logic for his excuse.

But then Dwight broke in: "I asked Bennie what he thought."

Bennie was caught off guard. "Well," he said, drawing out his thoughts, "I think Marlena has a point. But if everyone else thinks I should go, I will, of course." He smiled good-naturedly, feeling safe that no one shared Dwight's opinion.

"You know, Bennie," Dwight said with a tone of impatience, "I've been noticing this about you. You seem unable to make decisions or keep them. If you do, it's based more on what you think others want to hear. We don't need to be pleased and coddled. We need firm leadership, and well, to be frank, I don't think we've really gotten that from you since the beginning of this trip."

Bennie grew red-faced. All his practiced retorts flew from his mind. "I'm sorry you feel that way," was all he could manage to sputter.

The rest said nothing. They knew that this was Dwight's way of saying that Bennie was to blame for their current predicament, and privately, they thought the same. Bennie should have nixed the idea of going into the jungle for Christmas lunch with men they didn't even know. And now, by not defending Bennie, they were in some ways expressing their agreement with Dwight.

Bennie felt his head tingle. *Why are they looking at me that way? Why don't they say anything? My God! They blame me, too. They think I'm stupid. . . . I'm not! I'm overtrusting. I trusted that damn guide. Is it so wrong to trust people?*

Suddenly he gave out a deep cry and fell backward, hitting the ground hard. The others winced, thinking he had lost his balance. But then they saw his face was contorted and congested. Bennie's whole body was clenching, as if he were a large fish flopping out of water. A dark stain of urine formed at his crotch.

"Oh my God!" Roxanne shouted. "Do something!" She and Dwight tried to hold him still, and Moff kneeled to jam a stick in his mouth.

"No, no!" Heidi yelled. "That's not what you're supposed to do!" But they didn't hear her, so she pushed them off and grabbed the stick from Moff's hand and hurled it to the side. She, the consummate hypochondriac, had taken three first-aid courses and was the only one there who knew that what they were attempting to do was an outdated method, now considered dangerous. "Don't hold him down!" Her voice filled with an authority that surprised even her. "Just get him away from the fire. Make sure there's nothing sharp on the ground. And when he's done convulsing, try to roll him to his side, in case he vomits."

In a minute, it was over. Bennie lay still, breathing heavily. Heidi checked his pulse. He was groggy, and when he realized what had happened, he groaned and murmured, "Oh, shit. I'm sorry, I'm sorry." He felt he had let everyone down. Now they knew. Heidi brought over a mat for him to lie on, and though he was still upset, he had a terrific headache and felt an overwhelming pull toward sleep.

As for Dwight, he sensed that everyone blamed him for triggering Bennie's seizure. They avoided eye contact with him. There would be no more talk of bushwhacking that day.

OFF IN ANOTHER PART of the camp, Rupert and Esmé had given only a glance toward the ruckus. One person or another was always letting out a screech when a snake was spotted or a leech had attached itself to a leg. The leeches seemed to love Bennie especially, and would hurl themselves at the white meaty skin above his sockless ankle.

Rupert and Esmé, still weak from malaria, sat on a woven mat, their backs propped against a mossy, decaying log, termites teeming under its flaking bark. The youngsters were playing a pantomime game in which they took turns acting out a category of things they missed. Esmé made licking motions with a fisted hand.

"Dog licking your face!" Rupert yelled.

Esmé giggled and shook her head. "I have that," she said, and scratched Pup-pup's belly.

"Guy licking a girl!"

She shrieked and covered her face, then socked his arm.

He smiled. "I know. Ice cream in a cone."

She smiled. Next she weakly drew a circle in the air, then used her finger to dissect it into wobbly sections.

"Pizza!" Rupert guessed, and a second later: "Foods you miss eating!"

Esmé nodded and gleamed with happiness.

Marlena glanced up at the kids, dazed by what had just happened to Bennie. How innocent they were, enjoying each other's company, unworried about the future. Only two weeks before, they would have nothing to do with each other. But when Rupert had recovered somewhat, he saw that Esmé was lying nearby, delirious, and he found himself encouraging her to pull through, just as he had. "Hey there," he'd call to her. "Hey there." And now he showed a brotherly warmth toward the younger girl, feeling he was the main reason she had been saved, while Esmé, to judge by her giggles and watchful eyes, thought so, too.

A first crush, Marlena thought. She was both sad and glad that Esmé had a boy who filled her heart with hope, a boy who might keep her yearning for a future, a will to go on, when their lives were now so uncertain.

The malaria had frightened them badly. At least here in this camp they had shelter, clean water, and in a manner of speaking, food. Their hosts were kind and tried their best to make them comfortable, letting them have the most sheltered sleeping areas, giving them the larger portions of the daily fare. To supplement the rice and noodles, they foraged for fresh edibles, caught a variety of fine-boned rodents and birds, as well as the occasional monkey. No matter what it was, Marlena told Esmé the meat was chicken. And Esmé knew that it wasn't, but she took whatever there was so she could give it to Pup-pup.

Esmé doled out tasty treats for each play bow the little dog made. Before they had gotten lost, Harry Bailley had taught her how to train her puppy to do this. "There's no reason to delay training until a dog is doing behavior you don't like," he had said. "A puppy is quite happy to offer you what you want over and over again—but you have to reward her for what you want her to repeat. Is it a bark, a tail wag, a yawn? Or how about when she goes down on her front paws and leaves her backside in the air? That's when you give her the treat—as soon as you see that." Esmé had watched Harry dangle a treat above Pup-pup, and the dog immediately tipped her nose up to follow the scent. As Harry moved the tidbit up and down and side to side, Pup-pup's nose followed, as if tied to the treat with an invisible string. Up went her nose when the morsel was over her head, down it went when she did her play bow to the lowered treat. "Good girl!" Esmé cried, and doled out the treat. That was how she passed the long days in the jungle, and Pup-pup never failed to entertain her.

One day, Esmé said to Rupert, "Watch," and then she looked with serious intent at Pup-pup. "Bow to the king." Down Pup-pup went, her butt still in the air, tail wagging. And Rupert said, "Pretty cool," which sent paroxysms of shivery delight up Esmé's spine. He thought she was cool.

"Bow to the king!" Rupert commanded the dog, again and again.

Nearby, a group of children crouched and watched. Loot and Bootie were among them. When the dog-training session was finished, Bootie ran to Black Spot.

"The Younger White Brother has recognized who he is," she said. "All the creatures on earth know it. The dog bowed whenever the Lord of Nats cried out who he was. At last, the Lord is ready to make us strong."

BLACK SPOT SAT DOWN on the log bench next to Marlena. He sensed that this American was kind. With her Chinese face, she looked more like them and thus might be more sympathetic. "Miss," he began shyly. "I am asking you question?"

"Sure. Go ahead," Marlena said, giving her friendliest look.

"Miss, the boy Rupee, he can help us?"

Thinking that he meant that Rupert should help them with chores, she answered, "Yes, of course. I'm sure he would be glad to." And if he wasn't, Marlena said to herself, she would persuade his father to exert some pressure. "What would you like him to do?"

"Saving us," Black Spot said.

"I don't know what you mean," Marlena said, and thought, Why would they think Rupert could get them out of No Name Place any better than the rest of them?

"Saving us from SLORC soldiers," Black Spot said. "For many, many years, we are waiting for our Younger White Brother to come. Now he is here, he is bringing our book."

Marlena was baffled. It took ten minutes of intensive questioning before she understood the gist of what Black Spot was saying. This was their Christmas surprise! They had been kidnapped by a crazy tribe, who believed some mumbo jumbo about a savior who could make them invisible. Dwight had said they might have paranoiac delusions, and it was true.

But no, that couldn't be right, she told herself. After all, they weren't being held captive. They had not been tied up with ropes or blindfolds. No ransom demands had been made, as far as she knew.

The people here were gentle. They went without so that their guests could be more comfortable. And no one would have tried to stop them from leaving. It was just that the bridge was down, so they couldn't leave. No one could. She looked at Black Spot, at his haunted eyes. Maybe they had grown paranoid and delusional from seeing their families killed. Or perhaps he was delirious with the onset of malaria. He did look a bit feverish. Better get the old grandmothers to give him the sweet wormwood tea.

EACH MORNING, those who were strong enough paired up to do chores. They shook the bamboo blankets free of any insects that had collected on them overnight, sprinkled more of the termite powder on the mats. They had tried heating water on the stove, but now they bathed in the running-stream trough as the tribe people did. They took turns washing their clothing, whatever needed to be rotated among the clothes they had worn and what the tribe had given them, tunics and longyis that were often much nicer than what the tribe wore. Marlena and Vera were learning from the twins' grandmother how to make yarn out of pounded-thin strands of bamboo and weave it into a blouse. Bennie shaved with a razor that a one-eyed man kept sharp. The others let their stubble turn into beards.

One morning, Moff and Heidi borrowed two machetes from Black Spot, grabbed their hiking sticks, and plunged into the rainforest to forage for food. They were on the lookout for young bamboo shoots, which they found to be mild and tasty, not at all bitter like many of the other plants. The Karen people had showed them how to find the young sprouts. As they departed they could hear the happy shouts of children and adults watching Rupert doing a card trick.

To make sure they did not get lost, Moff and Heidi first positioned themselves with the small compass Heidi had sewn to the outside of her backpack. They walked straight into the jungle, and if they were forced to deviate because of obstacles, they slashed at vegetation to mark where they had been. They had wrapped the bottoms of their trousers with bands of cloth to keep out bugs, but they still had to use a bamboo comb to detach burrs and sticky leaf buds that clung to their clothing. The trees were tall and the connecting canopies served as sun umbrellas. This part of the jungle received scant light, and thus gave a feeling of perpetual dusk. But even in this dim world, they could not miss some peculiar-looking plants.

It was the color Heidi noticed first, a bright rubbery red. The plants resembled crimson bananas growing out of the spongy soil set deep in a pocket of the roots of a rotting tree. "Look. Such an intense red," she said, "almost fluorescent." Moff turned and saw what she had found. As they drew closer, Heidi gasped and was immediately embarrassed that she had. The projectiles were the perfect likeness of erect penises with bulbous hoods, and the red color made them appear turgid and full to bursting. She turned away as if scanning about for other edibles. But Moff was still inspecting the plant.

"Seven inches long," he reckoned. "What a coincidence." He winked at her and she laughed weakly. He thought about teasing her further, but stopped, realizing at that moment not only that he was attracted, but that he had grown fond of her, even her quirks, and especially her newfound daring in spite of her fears. He wondered whether she felt a similar attraction to him. And she did, yes indeed. She liked that quality in him that was both rough and gentle. He was overconfident at times, yet these days, after his son's illness, he seemed softer, protective, yet vulnerable. He could admit to his mistakes. All in all, she found him attractive. She liked the beard.

Moff bent down to inspect the plant more closely. "Might be a fungus," he guessed. "The question is, can we eat it? Some fungi are delicious, some will turn your liver into pâté." He noticed that a few of the plants sported small white waxy flowers. They looked like tiny chrysanthemums that had burst from wartlike bumps along the base of the hood.

"Hmmm, not a fungus," he said. "Fungi don't flower. The mystery deepens." He ran his finger delicately around the head of the plant, then pressed and probed to determine its structure and texture. "Ah, soft to the touch yet firm," he pronounced. He caught Heidi's eye, and for five seconds, which was approximately four point five seconds too long, they stared at each other with slight smiles. This was his usual tactic with women, the gaze that let the woman know he was about to draw her in. But this time it was not calculated, and Moff was unfamiliar with the awkwardness he felt when he finally looked away and turned back to the plant.

"Isn't it amazing how many things grow here?" Heidi said, trying to sound breezy. "There's hardly any sun."

"There are quite a few nonphotosynthetic plants," Moff replied. "Mushrooms for one. Truffles. A shady area is essential. That's why you find them in canopy environments. It's a pity that the rainforests are being razed worldwide by greedy assholes. They have no idea how many species of incredible things are being destroyed for good."

"They're destroying rainforests here in Burma as well?"

"As fast as they can clear them. Some for wood, some for heroin poppies, and a lot so they can run an oil pipeline to China, which, by the way, American companies are helping them build."

Heidi took a closer look at the plant. "Are these rare?"

"Could be. They're some kind of flowering parasite. See how they're latched on to the roots of this tree? They've been feeding off its root system."

"You know so much about plants," Heidi said. "I barely know the difference between a bush and a tree."

"It helps if you own a five-acre nursery," Moff said modestly. "I make my living growing the stuff that's found in rainforests. Bamboo, giant palms." He wiped at his damp brow with the back of his wrist. "Can't say I'm too fond of the abundance of bamboo out here. But if we ever get out, there's a hardy species I have my eye on that would be ideal for a zoo I'm working with." He carefully pulled out one of the strange red plants and held it up. It was attached to a twin, connected by a ball-like root. The thing looked even more obscene, Heidi thought, like the sexual organs of conjoined twin satyrs. She tried to act nonchalant.

"Aha!" Moff exclaimed. "I thought it might be. *Balanophora!* Yep, right ecosystem, grows in Asia—China and Thailand for sure. Quite a few species. Sixteen, as I recall. This may very well be the seventeenth. They're listed in the annals of *Weird Plant Morphology.* We're all familiar with the bizarre humor in plant life. See the shape of the head? Most have more of an acorn pattern, not quite this smooth." He extracted a few more plants. "I've never seen photos of anything like this," he said, growing more excited by the second. "If this is a new species, it's a beauty, longer and thicker than most, and completely red, instead of having a flesh-colored stem." He inspected it from all angles.

"What do you mean by new species?" Heidi said. "You mean it's a mutant?"

"Just that it's not identified, not in the taxonomy where people keep track of such things. Of course, the people here might have a name for it. Big Red, for all I know. Wow, this is incredible. . . ." He caught Heidi staring at him with a bemused expression.

He grinned. "Hey, if it's a new species, I could get it named after me." He drew his finger across as if reading a plaque: *"Balanophora moffetti."* He looked at Heidi again. "I'm kidding. Some scientist would first have to verify that it is indeed an undiscovered species, and it would probably be named after him. Though sometimes they name it after whoever found it."

"I saw it before you," Heidi teased.

"Right you did! So it would be *Balanophora moffetti-starki*."

"*Balanophora starki-moffetti*," she corrected.

"If I married you," he said, "it could be *Balanophora moffettorum* and cover us both."

Her mouth opened and she was about to speak, but she could not think fast enough for a witty rejoinder. *Married*. The word had surprised her. In the silence, they heard birds calling. He was about to tell her he was only joking, but that would make it seem as though he could not possibly see her in that light.

Finally she said, "I'd keep my name. But don't worry, I'm not keen on having a plant that looks like *that* named after me."

Now he felt reckless. He stood up. "We could still get married." The last two weeks had forced him to look at time and risk differently. His mind had once been focused on the future—future projects, future clients, future expansion. These days life existed in the context of before and now.

Heidi laughed. "You're ridiculous. Stop joking."

"I may not be," he said. She grew quiet and looked at him, full of wonder. He tipped her face toward him and gave her a light kiss. "Nice. Best kiss I've had in two weeks."

"Me, too," she said softly.

And with that permission, he slowly wrapped his arms around her, and she grabbed on with surprising fierceness. At this point, let me simply say that they let the wild side of the jungle overtake their senses. I shall leave it to your imagination as to what exactly transpired. After all, it would be inappropriate to reveal the details, which were, I might say, quite extensive.

AN HOUR LATER, Moff and Heidi gathered up their clothes and a few other plants that they knew for certain to be edible or useful:

plenty of ferns, young bamboo shoots, more of the medicinal sweet wormwood, and the lemon-scented leaves of a bush that, when ground into a powder, helped deter the creepy-crawlies from coming into their tree huts. They placed their haul in the woven rattan baskets they had brought along, and returned to camp with a sense of dual accomplishment. The children ran toward them, shouting welcome, tugging on their hands to lead them to a plank by the cook fire, where they set the morning's haul.

Black Spot's daughter picked up the red penile-looking plant. The women who did the cooking quickly took the plant from her. One of the old ladies called out to Black Spot, who in turn yelled for Grease and Salt.

"You've seen this before?" Moff asked Black Spot.

"Yes, yes," he said. "Many times. Very good plant."

Moff was disappointed. It seemed the plant was not undiscovered after all.

But in fact, the plant was not officially known to the rest of the world. The tribe had found it just a few years earlier, and in taste-testing it, they discovered that its shape was good advertising for its potency. It was an aphrodisiac, and quite an effective one. A sliver of the plant, chewed slowly, could endow a man with the prowess of a twenty-year-old. It also resolved any prostate plumbing problems. And it had a similar arousal effect on women, though this was not supposed to be discussed, for fear of an outbreak of lascivious ladies running amok.

Black Spot, Grease, and Salt would regularly make forays into the jungle. Whenever they found even one of these rare plants, they raised the bridge, scurried down the mountain with their treasure, and went into Nyaung Shwe, where they turned to a trusty network of sympathetic Karen and a man who was experienced in discretion and turning a huge profit.

Throughout Myanmar, the power of the plant had grown quickly into fabulist lore. One seller cautioned his customers to try only a small amount, for he knew of a formerly love-hungry wife and her once inattentive husband who were now both hospitalized for sexual exhaustion. There was also talk of an ancient man who fathered three sets of twins with three beautiful sisters. Then there was the middle-aged virgin lady who once was too rigid from disuse to bend into the shapes required for lovemaking and who now had the flexibility of an acrobat. The effects of the plant were reputed to last for at least a week. It was also a preventative against one of the most terrifying and deadly conditions a man could develop, *koro*, which caused the genitals to be sucked up into the body. Once they disappeared, the victim died. No wonder the red plants were revered as "Second Life."

With the money earned from selling the plant, Black Spot and his compatriots would buy supplies in discreet amounts from various shop owners, including dreamed-of foods, bolts of fabric, and of course, fermented delicacies. Then they would ascend the mountain and remain until they had more treasure to take down. It had been a long while, however, since they had found another plant.

Black Spot asked Heidi and Moff if they had seen more of the plants.

"A half-dozen," Moff answered.

Black Spot translated to his compatriots. "Where are you finding this?" he said. "You can show me?"

"Sure. Is it good to eat?"

"Very good, yes," Black Spot said. "But only for medicine. Not for everyday eating."

"For what sickness?" Moff asked.

"Oh, some very bad sicknesses. *Koro* is one. I am not knowing the English word. You having this, you are wanting to die." His compatriots nodded.

"I guess it's not what we thought it was," Moff told Heidi, and they laughed.

Black Spot motioned for Moff and Heidi to enter the thick rainforest and retrace their steps. With Heidi's compass, they pushed aside the cloak of green leaves, and forged their way back toward the jungle bed where they had so recently made love.

· 15 ·

A PROMISING LEAD

Tonight the ragtag citizens of the jungle were grouped in front of the television according to the hierarchy of the divine. The twin gods sat in front, their grandmother between them. Black Spot, his cousin, and other cohorts squatted in the second tier. The women and children stood behind, and those with missing limbs sat off to the side on mats. It was nearly time for the nightly rerun of *Darwin's Fittest*. My forlorn friends had not watched it over the past days; the demands of malaria had required their total attention.

Black Spot and the old grandmothers motioned that their honored guests should come join them. *Mes amis* declined. Instead, as had become their routine, they seated their morose and silent selves on logs and stumps by the campfire. Dwight sat next to Bennie. They had had a rapprochement: Dwight had apologized for taking his irritations out on Bennie, and Bennie had admitted that he was not adequately prepared for the trip. "You got thrown into this at the last minute," Dwight said. They recognized that they all needed one another. They did not know whom they might need in an emergency or for comfort if matters really became dire.

The ember-red logs threw a nervous dance of light on their faces. In the early days of their plight, they had spoken urgently of ways to get out of No Name Place. As their unscheduled stay lengthened, they anguished over the possible ways to be saved. During the malarial scare, they bargained with God and the tribal powers that be. And when all were on the potholed path to recovery, they learned that the boatman had lost his mind and now had delusions that Rupert was a god. Would they go insane as well?

They ruminated over what their families and friends back home might be doing to find them. Surely they must have contacted the U.S. Embassy in Myanmar. A search party of American planes was probably doing aerial scans right this minute. My friends did not know that the Myanmar military government limited where the Embassy staff could go searching. And thus, the search was going on only at tourist destinations that the junta wished to showcase, and where Harry Bailley, consummate television star with a mellifluous and persuasive voice, could give his poignant updates.

The mood that night was grimmer than usual. Earlier that evening, Esmé, in a burst of frustration, cried out: "Are we going to *die* out here?" Only a child could have voiced that taboo question. Marlena reassured her, but the question hung in the smoky air. They sat quietly, knowing that another exotic illness or a dwindling supply of food could place them on the brink of extinction. Would they indeed die? Each of them imagined the news of their demise.

Wyatt remembered that his mother, who had had breast cancer, pleaded that he stop going on his thrillingly dangerous adventures. "You risk not just yourself but my heart," she had said, "and if anything bad happens, it will be a hundred times worse than my cancer ever was." He had laughed off her fears. Now he saw in his mind's eye his mother staring at his photo: *How could you do this to me?*

Moff pictured his former wife raging for his having taken their son on a trip he knew was dangerous. She would try to believe with every inch of her soul that Rupert was still alive, while hoping that he, the husband she divorced for his insensitivity, had been snatched by the hands of fate and had his last breath choked out of him.

Vera remembered the stories of people who refused to believe that their loved one had perished in a plane crash, a sinking boat, or a collapsed mine. The words "no survivors" were only conjecture, and sure enough, days after the funerals had been held by other families more resigned to tragedy, the beliefs of those optimistic people were miraculously fulfilled when the presumed dead came home healthy and no worse for wear other than being famished for good ol' home cooking. Was it the strength of love that allowed the miracle? How much did her own children truly love her? If they were already mourning her, would that lessen her chances of ever being found?

Heidi was contemplating ways that would enable them to survive. Perhaps there were other medicines. The Karen grandmothers would know. And they'd better prepare now for rain. She made a list in her head of various situations they should be ready for, and the proper responses. Foremost, if the soldiers came and started firing indiscriminately, would be to run into the jungle and hide. And then she had another thought: Perhaps she and Moff might make another foray into the jungle to find a few secret places.

Bennie was the only one thinking of the future, of going home to a joyful celebration. Before leaving on the Burma Road trip, he and Timothy had agreed to open Christmas gifts after he returned. More than likely, Bennie thought, Timothy had rewrapped his gifts with yellow ribbons—so like him to do that—and perhaps he had added more lavish presents; cashmere would be nice. The store tags would already have been cut off, reflecting Timothy's certainty that his beloved would return. But then he pictured Timothy taking down the tree, paying the bills, and sifting clumps out of the cat-litter box, a chore that had been the source of their most frequent arguments. It was a mundane life they'd led, but even the mundane was precious and he wanted it back.

Out of the blue, Dwight laughed. "Tomorrow I have a teeth-cleaning appointment. I better call and reschedule."

Now others remembered unpleasant tasks waiting for them at home: A car that needed a dent taken out of the fender. Dry cleaning to pick up. Unwashed workout clothes left in a locker at the fitness center, probably mildewed by now. They focused on trivial matters they could most easily give up. All else was unbearable to consider.

Their voices dropped to silence again. The campfire flames illuminated their faces from below, giving their eyes dark hollows. I thought they resembled ghosts, which is ironic for me to say. Many imagine that the dead have the same spooky look, which is nonsense. In reality—and by the very fact that I have consciousness, I have a reality—I have no look other than what I picture myself to be. How strange that I still don't know the reason for my death, whereas I seem to know all else. But your thoughts and emotions after death are no different from what they were when you were alive, I suppose. You remember only what you want to remember. You know only what your heart allows you to know.

In the distance, by the jungle's entertainment center, the shrieks of children mixed with happy, animated chattering. "Numbah one! Numbah one!" they chanted, repeating the boast of the ratings for *Darwin's Fittest*. The show had begun, announced with its characteristic theme music and opening. Bass fiddles rubbed and vibrated in a borborygmus crescendo, lions roared, crocodile jaws snapped, and fragile-necked cranes honked warning.

Bennie stood up, his eyes stinging from the smoke. He secretly loved all the reality shows, the awfulness of them—the cruel elimination rounds, the role-switching with calamitous consequences, and the makeovers of people with missing teeth, bad hair, and recessive chins. He glanced toward the television. Oh, why not? Pabulum was better than the conscious pain of despair. He walked over to the happy side of the camp.

In the blackness of the jungle, the screen was bright as a beacon. He saw the female host of *Darwin's Fittest* in her same safari hat and dirt-stained khakis of two weeks or so ago. This time, she had artfully applied a swath of mud to her left cheekbone. The two teams of contestants were building canoes, carving them out of balsa wood. Their clothes were transparent with sweat, which left, as Bennie noted, no bulge or droop or crease unhidden. He could see that the fittest, whose bodies were fat-free specimens of healthy living, were detested by the others, as they should be.

"Are you ready?" the safari-hatted woman said. "Today's new challenge . . ." And she told them that holes would be punched into their canoes' hulls, to simulate an attack by a hippopotamus, and they would have to plug these leaks with any material they could find, hope it held fast, then paddle one hundred meters upstream, where they could obtain the fresh water and food necessary to sustain them for the next three days. "If you don't make it," she warned, "you're literally and figuratively sunk." She gave a rundown on the voracious creatures that lay in wait in the waters—rib-crunching crocodiles, flesh-nibbling fish, poisonous swimming snakes, and the most dangerous creature of them all, the people-hating hippos. The camera zoomed in on each contestant's face, and captured the fast-blinking eyes of the fearful, the pressed lips of the determined, the slack jaws of those who already knew they were doomed.

Bennie empathized with their fears and public humiliation. When they scratched at an itch, he did, too. When they swallowed in horror, he swallowed as well. They looked like prisoners on a chain gang, he thought. I should tell them we are in the same boat and should join forces. He walked closer and then caught himself. What was he doing? This is TV, you dope, it isn't real. His glazed eyes returned to the screen, and a minute later, his logic flipped once again, so that he was operating under the reasoning of dreams. It's a reality show, he told himself, and that means it *is* real. The people are real, the boats are real, the holes are real. The only thing that separates their reality from mine is a piece of glass. If I can just get them to see past the screen. . . . He threw his arms in the air, and this sudden action was enough to jolt him out of the delusion. Stop thinking crazy, he chastised himself. But like a person pulled irresistibly toward sleep, he gradually fell back into this semi-dream state. He sent a message with the power of his mind. *Look at me*, please. *God damn it, look at me! I'm stuck in the jungle, too. Look at me!*

I knew how he felt. Since my death, I have been overwhelmed with a frustration that alternates with despair. Imagine it: your consciousness separated from others by an invisible barrier that was erected in the blink of an eye. And now the eye no longer blinks. It never will again.

In Bennie's porous mind, he was now advising the teams: Tear up your clothes, mix them with mud to make a ball—no, no, not the coconut hair, forget that, and don't pick up the thatch, it's not going to bunch up tight enough. You idiots! I'm the leader! You're supposed to listen to me. . . . His disobedient team had just put their boat into the water, when a news crawl floated along the bottom of the screen: "Special report: More on the mystery of the eleven missing tourists in Myanmar."

Bennie was amazed that other tourists were in their same predicament. The only difference: eleven instead of twelve. Wait a second. *We* are only eleven. He blinked hard to push out the brain skitter. Was it merely wishful thinking? A hallucinatory manifestation? He ran closer to the TV, blocking everybody's view. But now the news crawl had disappeared.

"Did you see that?" he cried.

Loot ordered Bennie to get out of the way. No one in the tribe had read the words at the bottom, not even Black Spot, who could pick out one letter at a time with great effort. These English words had run across the bottom of the screen as fast as a beetle when you over-turned its home.

The crawl came back, slithering like a neon snake. "Special report: More on the mystery of the eleven missing tourists in Myanmar."

Bennie gasped. "Hey, guys!" he yelled. "Get over here, quick! We're going to be on TV!"

"What's he imagining now?" Dwight said softly. They had been taken in by other fantasies of Bennie's. Claims that the bridge was up (which it indeed had been when Black Spot went for more supplies). Shouts that he saw people on the other side of the rift (which he in-deed had, when Black Spot and Grease returned). And now he was saying they were on *Darwin's Fittest*? Poor Bennie, ever since his seizure, he had been coming apart, they concluded. They tried to humor him, and they also feared the possibility that others among them would go insane.

Bennie shouted to them again. "The news," he gasped. "We're on the news!"

"Your turn," Moff told Roxanne, and she sighed and went to Ben-nie to put to rest this latest false hope. If they didn't, he would not stop. But a few seconds later she yelled back, "Get over here! Quick!" They nearly fell over one another to reach the television.

"Look!" Bennie shouted, dancing up and down. "I told you so." An anchor for an Australian network was saying that new footage about the Missing Eleven had just been received. My friends stared hard at the screen. But what came on next was a letdown. A travel piece on Egypt or something. A figure was climbing to the top of a pyramid. He was scanning more of these pyramids, which stretched out toward the horizon. The camera zoomed in on a well-groomed man with dark hair and silver temples. He looked uncannily familiar.

"Harry!" Marlena shrieked.

"The aching splendor," Harry was now saying in a dreamy voice. He looked off into the distance toward a panorama of more than two thousand domes and spires. "To see such stoic magnificence"—and he turned to the camera—"reminds me of my brave friends. Once they are found, and I know that will be soon, I shall bring them here to glorious Bagan, where we can enjoy the sunrises and sunsets together."

Heidi laughed and then squealed. "He's talking about us! We're going back!" Moff gave her a happy squeeze.

"Omigod!" Wendy blubbered. "We're saved! We're going home!"

"Turn it up," Moff said calmly, belying his nervous anticipation. Dwight grabbed the remote control from Loot's hands. The people of No Name Place wondered what had made the Younger White Brother's friends so excited. Only Black Spot suspected, and the knot in his stomach tightened. Had they offended a Nat? Why did they need to endure so many trials?

"We have some very, very good news," the Missing Eleven heard Harry say in his best television voice of authority. A cheer went up among my friends. High fives were exchanged. Bennie was already thinking about hugging Timothy, taking a luxurious bath, then plopping into their plumped-up bed. The camera panned out to show Harry speaking to a Burmese reporter. "Our search team," Harry said, "has a new lead, a promising one, in Mandalay. It seems that a craftsman of papier-mâché marionettes saw something suspicious, as did two monks. They all reported seeing a tall gentleman with long hair tied back in a ponytail and wearing khaki short pants, and with him were a young Eurasian boy and girl. The marionette maker said he spotted them at the top of Mandalay Hill, and the monks glimpsed them later that same day at Mahamuni Pagoda."

The Burmese reporter cut in: "This man with a ponytail, this is a description of your friend, isn't it?"

"Correct," Harry was seen answering with authority. "That could very well be Mark Moffett and his son, Rupert, along with Esmé, the daughter of my fiancée, Marlena Chu, who is also missing." Four photos flashed up.

"That's me!" Esmé cried, and then instantly she pouted, saying, "I *hate* that picture."

Moff stamped his foot. "Shit! You blasted idiot, Harry! I'm here in bloody nowhere, not in Mandalay."

"Fiancée," Marlena whispered to herself.

"The worrisome part," Harry went on, "is that they were led around by two men—"

"But they were not Burmese," the reporter cut in, "as we confirmed earlier."

"Yes, that's right. The witnesses said they appeared to be Indian or Thai, maybe even Chinese, in any case, definitely not Burmese, because, as you so astutely pointed out, the Burmese witnesses said they couldn't understand a thing the thugs were saying. But what they did note, interestingly enough, is that they were speaking in gruff tones, and Moff—or rather, the man we think is Mark Moffett—plus the two youngsters, simply obeyed as if they were under the influence of something. The marionette maker and monks said it was a spell cast by Nats, which some Burmese believe are disturbed spirits who are very out of sorts because of a violent death centuries ago."

"Yes, they are very common here," the reporter said.

"Well, I believe they might have been drugged," Harry continued, "which is a more rational explanation. They were reported to have the glazed look of heroin users—"

The reporter broke in: "Heroin is strictly forbidden in Myanmar. The penalty for heroin using or selling is death."

"Yes, indeed. And none of my friends are of that ilk, absolutely not, I can guarantee that. But that is precisely why we are concerned about the people who were with them, who might have possibly drugged them. Regardless, this sighting represents a huge break for us, *huge*, and that's where we're going to focus our efforts over the next few days, in Mandalay, atop the hill, in the pagoda, anywhere our search team feels we should investigate based upon creditable sources of information. Creditable, that's the key. The government of Myanmar has been extremely helpful in that regard. As soon as I climb down this incredible specimen of Burmese history and architecture, we're off to Mandalay. In the meantime, if anyone sees anything else of importance, we ask them to call the special Bear Witness Hotline number on the screen."

Harry beckoned to a woman with two dogs. He vigorously scratched the neck of the black Labrador until the dog's back leg started thumping. "That's my little sausage," Harry said, and then bent down to the other member of the search team, a border collie. "Lushy-mush," he cooed with lips pursed for kissing. Before the dog could slurp him with her slick tongue, Harry deftly pulled back. "These beauties are better than the FBI," he gloated. "Search-and-rescue dogs, infallible noses, with a work ethic based on a simple reward of fetch. And this gorgeous lady here is their fearless trainer." The camera zoomed in on a woman in a perky shift of pink and yellow stretch cotton that clung to her thin, youthful body. "Saskia Hawley. She trained them herself," said Harry, "and did a top-notch job, if I say so myself."

"Using techniques you taught me and many thousands of others," she added generously, batting her eyelashes comically.

Harry gave his best bashful but charming little-boy smile and then turned to the camera: "That's all for now. We'll join you next from Mandalay. What do you say, Saskia? Lush and Topper, are you ready to work? Let's be going!" The dogs leapt up with tails twirling as fast as helicopter rotors. Saskia smiled at Harry, a little too adoringly, Marlena thought. With a soft command from Saskia, the dogs shot forward, sniffing the ground as they led the way.

My friends and the Lord's Army folk watched as Harry and Saskia strode side by side into a blindingly beautiful sunset. Their figures receded, and the camera panned out and did a slow fade to black, as if all hope had been extinguished.

The news anchor broke in: "For those of you tuning in late, that was a tape sent by TV Myanmar International, with Harry Bailley . . ."

For several seconds, my friends in No Name Place were too stunned to speak. "I can't believe it," Roxanne finally said in a low monotone.

Wendy started to cry, and leaned on Wyatt's shoulder.

Marlena wondered who that woman was, the one Harry had spoken to with such frank familiarity. Why had he called her "gorgeous"? Why the googly eyes? Was she a fiancée, too? She realized how little she knew about Harry.

Vera sat up straight. "Let's not be pessimistic. This is good news. They assume we are still alive, and they're looking for us. Let's talk about what this means and what we should do."

And so they struggled to do as Vera suggested. Late into the night, they discussed the best way to let their potential rescuers know their whereabouts. They also contemplated how to ensure the safety of the tribe. Perhaps the Lajamees could hide in the rainforest, and the eleven could tell their rescuers that they had found this abandoned camp. Or they could simply insist the Lajamees were heroes and should be protected from retribution.

Dwight sprang to his feet. "Well, now that we have a plan," he said, "I'm going to bushwhack my way out of here. Anyone else want to come along?"

"Don't be ridiculous," Roxanne said.

Dwight ignored her. "If I can get out of this rainforest to an open area where people can see us from above, that would be far better than waiting for God knows how long."

"Be serious," Roxanne said.

He did not look at her. The others shrugged, and Dwight strode away in disgust. Roxanne thought, Why did he have to be that way—and just when the two of them seemed to be getting along?

My friends now switched to a conversation that reflected their new optimism. First thing when she reached home, Marlena said, would be a long, hot bath. Roxanne said she would run the shower for a sinfully long hour to flush out all the grit that had adhered to her skin. Wendy wanted to get a massage, a haircut, a manicure-pedicure, and buy makeup, underwear, and socks. Bennie was going to buy all new suits because he had lost nearly twenty pounds. The malaria still came back in waves, making it impossible for him to eat much. But what a surprise Timothy would have when he saw Bennie's trim physique. Heidi wanted to lie in clean sheets. Moff wanted to lie in the clean sheets with her.

They were thinking of the future, the small things, the little luxuries. The big hope was already taken care of. Everybody was looking for them.

ELSEWHERE IN THE CAMP, the conversation was more solemn. Black Spot had recounted to his people what the tourists had seen on television. The man Harry Bailley had started his own television show. It was not in the jungles of *Darwin's Fittest*, but here in Burma. He was searching for the Younger White Brother and his followers and had elevated them to TV stars. Black Spot was sure the SLORC soldiers were helping the man to look for them. No one else would be allowed.

An old grandmother lamented, "We might as well jump into the cook pot right now and boil ourselves down to a soup of dead bones."

Salt agreed. "They are now bait for the tiger. And we're the ones who will be eaten."

"No more talk of soups and tigers," Black Spot said. "We need to make a plan to escape to another hiding place."

"The Younger White Brother will protect us when we go," Black Spot's wife said.

Some people nodded, but a man with a knee stump countered, "He's the one who got us into trouble. And what sign do we have that he is truly the Reincarnated One? The card and the book—perhaps he stole them."

Other doubters nodded. Soon they were arguing over whether the boy really was the Reincarnated One, the Younger White Brother. A true Younger Brother was supposed to make them stronger, not weaker. He was supposed to make them invisible. "But we are now more visible than ever," a man complained.

Black Spot shot to his feet. That was the answer! The Younger White Brother had come to make them not invisible but *visible*, seen by the whole world. He recalled for the tribe their wishful dream of having their own TV show. That's why the Younger White Brother had come with ten people and a moviemaking camera to record their story. They would show the world they were braver and had endured more hardships than those on *Darwin's Fittest*. Their perils were real. People would want them to survive. Their show would be number one, week after week, number one among wombats and kiwis, Americans and Burmese, too popular to cancel. The path had been placed right before their eyes: all they needed was to have Harry Bailley feature them on his show.

The little twin god Loot stood, removed his smoky cheroot, and extended both arms. His glazed eyes flew upward, and he cried out, "Let us pray."

My friends were still riveted to the TV, ready for it to illuminate their faces with further news of themselves and how they were doing. Those who were strong alternated in pedaling the bicycle to recharge whichever battery was not in use. Their faces were turned in one direction, and thus occupied, they did not notice Black Spot entering the strangler fig abode where Roxanne and Dwight kept their belongings. They did not see him remove the camcorder from the small backpack and take out the tape, nor did they notice him leave the camp with Grease, Salt, and Fishbones, and race down the path toward the chasm.

Fishbones stood watch for any of the foreigner guests who might be approaching. This was not likely, since it was dark and the friends of the Younger White Brother feared the split in the earth. Grease and Salt looped the rope around the tree-trunk winch and pulled until the bridge was raised high enough for them to grab the lines and fasten them to the tree stumps. Black Spot and Grease scurried across. Salt and Fishbones lowered the bridge. They would wait for their compatriots to return to bring it up again. By then it would be morning.

No Name Place was now a happy campground for its visitors. Hooting and laughter were heard at all hours of the day. The Americans danced around the TV set. The tribe sat more quietly on their mats, turning to look at whichever foreigner had his or her face shown on the screen.

My friends were relieved to find that Walter had not perished in the chasm after all. He was in a hospital with amnesia, caused by a bump on the head from a falling rock in the pagoda he was climbing while searching for Rupert. "See what can happen when others go looking for you?" Moff chastised his son. "Others are affected by what you do."

In the morning, GNN televised a parade that the city of Mayville, North Dakota, had put on to show support for Wyatt's safe return.

Children in yellow knitted caps and fat snowsuits rode in sleds pulled by their mothers, who also wore yellow. A trio of men, expelling clouds as they laughed and talked, held a large banner that said: "Mayville's 1,981 Folks Are Praying for Our Native Son." In the May-Port CG high school auditorium, yet another bake sale was going on, the fourth in the past week, with goods sold by the teachers. Hotcakes decorated with sugary yellow bows sold like hotcakes, and behind the tables a huge banner read: "American Crystal Sugar Company Wishes Our Best to the Fletcher Family."

"Brrrr! How cold is it in Mayville today?" the reporter asked one of the teachers.

"I heard it's six degrees," said the woman. "Balmy for us!"

In another part of the auditorium, the high school band was playing a passable rendition of "America the Beautiful." Several women sat behind tables laden with yellow scarves, a sign proclaiming: "Hand-knitted by the May-Port PTA."

The reporter was now leading the cameraman to a woman who claimed she was Wyatt's girlfriend.

"My what?" Wyatt said.

Wendy leaned forward, her heart racing. So Wyatt had a girlfriend all along. No wonder he seemed emotionally unavailable. "Tell our viewers," the reporter said, "what Wyatt is like," and he aimed the microphone at a short woman with frizzy bleached-blond hair. Her face sagged at the jowls, and she had drawn black liner around her eyes, Cleopatra style. "Who the hell is that?" Wyatt muttered. Moff and Dwight were hooting.

The reporter asked the woman to describe what Wyatt was like as a boyfriend. She hesitated, and then said in the deep, grating voice of a longtime smoker, "Hell, he'd do anything for you as a friend, and vice versa." She looked down and gave a coy smile. "He's a *real* nice man."

Jungle whoops went up among Moff, Dwight, and Roxanne. Moff socked Wyatt on the arm and said, "Way to go." Wyatt was shaking his head. "Who the hell is that? Why is she saying that she's my girlfriend?"

"Do you have a message for Wyatt right now?" the reporter asked the woman. He again pointed the microphone at her tiny mouth.

"Yeah, sure." She scrunched up her face and pondered the question. "I guess I'd say, 'Welcome home, Wyatt, whenever you come home.'" She blew a kiss and waved.

"That is *so* pathetic," Wendy said, now confident enough to be indignant for Wyatt. "What some people will do to get attention."

In the update that followed, Moff's ex-wife was shown sitting on a sofa in her living room, a place Moff had never been. He had always picked up and dropped off his son at the curb in front of Lana's house. His former wife still bore the appearance of someone in control of her looks, her life, her thoughts. But the interior of the house surprised him. The furnishings were cozy and casual, and not at all as neat and prissy as he had imagined they would be. In fact, the room looked messily lived in, a nice kind of messy, with newspapers strewn on the table, shoes lying about, a box of Kleenex and photo albums stacked haphazardly on the coffee table. It was surprising, considering how rigid she had been about keeping all surfaces absolutely pristine when they were married. She held a framed photo of Rupert and turned it toward the camera. She spoke in a calm and assured voice: "I know he's okay. His father is very protective. You see, Mark would never, *never* let anything bad happen to our son. He would do *everything* in his power to bring him back to me." Moff wondered dryly if that was a compliment or an order. But then Lana reached for a tissue, dabbed her eyes, and began to cry. "I'd give anything to have them both back," she added in a quavering whisper. *Both?* Moff was flummoxed. Was this an overture to be friends—or more? Heidi quietly watched him and prepared her heart for disaster.

At five o'clock, another special report with Harry Bailley aired, this time filmed on location in Mandalay. "We're at the top of gorgeous, *gorgeous* Mandalay Hill, where you can see for miles in all directions," he began, and my friends listened, hoping for clues as to where they might be found.

THE SPECIAL REPORT from Mandalay had been filmed only that morning. When the Burmese camera crew arrived at the base of the hill, Harry was disheartened to learn he would have to climb a staircase of one thousand seven hundred and twenty-nine stone steps. It looked like a fast ascent to heaven via a heart attack. But what he lacked in aerobic conditioning he made up for in hope that he would find clues to his friends' whereabouts. Thank God the staircase was covered with a canopy to keep the blazing sun off his back. As instructed, Harry removed his shoes, then held them up to the camera, saying: "No footwear allowed in holy places, which this is." He began the long march up.

The stone stairs were smooth and coolly sensual. He thought about the millions of bare soles that had climbed these same steps over the past centuries. What prayers did they come with, what fungus on their feet?

At first, he maintained a good pace, passing by tables of nibbana goods, Buddhas both crude and fine, replicas of pagodas, and lacquer bowls and boxes. But after a hundred steps, he found it difficult to breathe without making it sound like the death rattle. He gestured to the camera crew to stop filming, but they seemed to think he was asking for them to take a tighter shot. Never mind, then. He was experienced at this sort of thing, saving the shot, providing cutaways that would later make the editing easier. Ah, here was his opportunity for a transition: a small table full of cheap wooden Buddhas. Brilliant. He feigned having them catch his eye. With his back to the camera, he panted, out of breath. He held one of the wooden Buddhas up to the sun and examined it like a jeweler inspecting diamonds. He realized he was perspiring copiously, but unlike the set for his own show, this one lacked a hair and makeup artist with a powder puff at the ready to take off the shine of perspiration. The only puffs he saw were the smoky ones emitted by the nuns, monks, and kids sucking on their cheroots. He looked around for something that might do for a handkerchief and settled on his shirtsleeve. He faced the camera. Damn, they were still filming. What to do? He held the statue smack dab in front of the camera. "Cleverly carved, in a primitive sort of way so popular with art collectors now." He asked the woman to name her price and made no attempt to bargain, thinking it best to show American generosity. He peeled off the bills, the equivalent of three dollars in U.S. money. Now he'd have to resume the torture of the stairs.

God! It was bloody hot, and the air was thick, settling in his lungs like gravel. Well, if Moff, Rupert, and Esmé had climbed these bloody steps, he could, too. It was all part of his effort to do what he could. These on-location news spots were their best chance at keeping the attention focused on his friends. This way, if they had been abducted, the kidnappers would be afraid to kill them. If they were lost, a million people would be on the lookout for them. Filming the updates was as important as any *Fido Files* episode he had done— amend that to *more* important, even more than the ones he did during sweeps week. His friends depended on him. *Lives* depended on him. Love depended on it. Thus refreshed in spirit and body and heart, he looked right at the camera and said in a commanding voice: "All right, then, onward and upward."

This time, he paced himself, leisurely admiring the architecture, or the plains below and the increasingly expansive horizon. He took a lengthy rest at a temple located at the midway point. "They tell me this place contains three bones of the Buddha, first-class authenticated relics," he narrated. "It strikes me that this display is rather similar to what the Catholics do with saints. They enshrine a rib or a lock of hair, which can then be viewed centuries later by pilgrims seeking renewal." He was proud that he had thought to say that. It was important that people identify with the place and not think it was foreign and thus incomprehensible and bizarre.

A few flights more, and he saw another convenient excuse to stop: a statue of a woman kneeling before the Buddha, offering him some pies. He glanced down at his notes. Good Lord! Those weren't pies; they were breasts! What was this statue supposed to symbolize? And why was the Buddha smiling? What would the Buddha possibly do with the breasts? "And here we see a pious woman," he quickly thought to say, "offering a gift of . . . herself." He was about to make some cultural comparison to Christian martyrs, but decided against it. That would not benefit his friends in any way. With the image of severed breasts in his mind, he resumed climbing, now less buoyant, less certain.

Finally he reached the top, and a pagoda made of blue and silver glass. He was cheered to see the two search-and-rescue dogs. As he walked closer, he saw Saskia. She was sitting on one of a row of tall stools positioned for viewing the landscape from a bird's-eye advantage. She was not smiling, he noted, and fear ran down his scalp. Body parts, he guessed, the dogs had found body parts. The camera crew followed him as he walked toward Saskia.

"Any developments?" he asked as coolly as possible.

To his relief, she shook her head. "I gave them the scent samples. The dogs did a search. The entire terrace, the steps, and they came up with a big nothing."

Harry exhaled. "So we've eliminated this spot. False report. Well, we might as well enjoy the view before we head to the other side of town. And don't forget. If you see anything suspicious, any sign of the Americans, call the Bear Witness Hotline number on the screen."

Conscious of the camera still aimed in his direction, he walked to the edge of the terrace and looked out. The plain reached past pagodas, shrines, and turrets, edifices that contained things he could not understand: secrets, glory in death, tributes to Nats, ideas of worship and history foreign and bizarre. As his eyes scanned the panorama in a widening arc, he said quietly to Saskia, "Wasn't that a horrendous climb? I nearly passed out."

"Look behind you," she said. And he turned and saw on the other side of the terrace a Japanese tour group, all wearing identical hats and following like ducklings a women with a yellow flag held high. "I went up that side," Saskia said.

Harry looked again. He then saw the alternative route, a series of escalators that led to a parking lot just slightly below, where air-conditioned buses waited to whisk the tourists to their next destination.

An hour later, he stood with the camera crew before a massive gold statue of the Buddha in an elaborate alcove of the Mahamuni Pagoda. It was lit by fluorescent tubes and colored lights, giving it the look of the Coney Island arcade game Shoot the Freak. Good Lord, Harry thought, a twelve-foot-high monument of gold. Its eyes appeared to be staring down at its admirers. More than a hundred people sat cross-legged before it, their palms open. Dozens of men, the merit-seekers of the day, waited in line, holding tissue-thin square leaves of gold. The women, who were not allowed to touch the Buddha, gave their gold squares to a man in white. Harry watched as a merit-seeker reached the foot of the Buddha, climbed onto the Buddha's knee, and stood as high as he could to press his soft gold leaf onto the statue's arm and rub. With each rub, the gold melded into the Buddha's body. Others pressed their gold on the Buddha's hand, which over the years had swelled to enormous proportions from such daily devotion, the manicured fingernails so attentively gilded that they appeared to be piercing the platform.

The merit-seekers had bought their leaves from poor men who did nothing but pound gold for twelve hours a day with a hammer. They pounded the gold repeatedly, until it turned into a layer as fine as skin. Often the merit-seekers were also poor men, and to buy the gold, they and their families had to sacrifice a few necessities of life. But they did this gladly. For how else would they advance themselves in the next life, if not by doing this? Merit was better than food. Merit was hope.

Saskia waved from the other side of the vestibule, and Harry waved back. She threaded her way through the crowd, the two dogs following. When they were reunited, Harry bent down and gave the dogs hearty slaps on their rumps and scratches behind their ears. The cameras started to record, and Harry was aware of this. "Hello, love," he cooed to Lush. "Tell old Harry where you've been and what you've seen." The dog thumped her tail in response. "Hey, mate," Harry called to Topper. He pointed to his watch and the Lab directed his nose that way. "What say you give me another ten minutes, and then we'll go for a game of seek. How's that?" The dog emitted a throaty gurgle in response. Harry looked up at the face of the Buddha, so the camera crew could get a shot before he explained where he was.

A soused old man with a bent back watched all this. He had once pounded the gold all day until it shook loose his bones and caused them to crumble. He went up to the movie star and looked him right in the face, trying to get his attention, but to no avail. Harry was busy expressing wonderment as he stared up at the Buddha's downcast eyes. Ah, the gold-pounder said to himself, the foreign man is so mesmerized by the manifestation of Buddha that he is unable to see another person. He had seen many do that when he was standing next to the Buddha. The tourists never saw him. He turned toward the statue and stood side by side with Harry.

"I see you are a rich and famous man," he mumbled in Burmese. "And you can see I am a poor man. I have no shoes to take off before entering this pagoda. But I washed my feet today, so the Buddha knows my respect is great. Though I have no gold leaves to bring, for many years I made them for others. So with my labor I, too, have given the Buddha many leaves. In my mind, I take each leaf I have ever made and I put them all on the Buddha's legs, his hands, his arms, his chest. I have fattened his body. I have given up many material things in life to bring him this gold. In my mind, the Buddha knows this, and I am receiving merit. And so, as you can see, although I am poor, my respect is great, and I am as welcome to come here as anyone else." He gestured to the people around them. "You can be poor. You can be rich. You can talk to dogs. I talk and no one hears me. But in the next life, we may change places. You might be the dog I will talk to. . . ." The man laughed and wheezed.

While waiting for the crazy man to leave, Harry concentrated on what to say. Finally one of the camera crew shooed away the lunatic, and Harry turned to the camera. "We are in this gorgeous pagoda with a fantastic gold Buddha. Take a look. People are actually putting pure gold on the Buddha as we speak. It's a constant renovation of sorts. This place is also where monks saw my friend Mark Moffett being led by two suspicious-looking men—"

The Burmese reporter accompanying Harry reminded him to say that the men spotted with his friend looked Thai or Indian but were definitely not Burmese. Harry nodded, although he was starting to get annoyed at being told once again what to say. The man had also told him to say "Myanmar" and not "Burma," "Bagan" not "Pagan," "Yangon" not "Rangoon." "Would you like to call *me* something else?" Harry teased the reporter, who simply answered no. He now directed Harry to return to the entry of the hall and then walk toward the statue as if coming upon it for the first time. Over the next half-hour, Harry walked up to the Buddha repeatedly and from different angles, forever evincing newfound awe.

It was finally time to show the dogs in action. Harry called for Saskia and the "poochies" to step in front of the camera. "We've been given special dispensation," Harry said, "to have the dogs roam this holy pagoda, go where their noses lead them—and rest assured, these highly trained dogs will not do anything to desecrate the place, not a drop." He reached into a daypack and pulled out three pieces of footwear, a desert boot, a Nike sneaker, and a pink sandal with a daisy at the V of the toe.

"These belong to my missing friends," Harry explained. "I have taken the liberty of borrowing them from possessions they left behind at the resort. They will prove highly useful. You see, we figure that like everyone here, my friends had to take off their shoes before they entered this pagoda. And as they walked barefoot—in a trance, we are told—they would have left invisible but telltale scentprints on this polished stone floor. What I have in my hand contains their same individual scents. You see where I am going, of course. We'll have the dogs take a whiff from one of the shoes, that will be the scent sample, and they will use their highly developed noses to match this scent to a scent on the floor. That's how they will pick up the trail. From there it is a piece of cake, as straightforward as following Hansel and Gretel's trail of bread crumbs." Saskia interrupted to remind Harry that in that particular tale, birds ate up the crumbs, which was why the two children became lost.

"We should edit out the bit about Hansel and Gretel," Harry told the reporter. He faced the camera again and walked slowly, gesturing to the stone floor. "Even in a heavily trafficked area like this, where thousands have roamed over the last few days, it is quite easy for trained dogs to pick up a scent. Once they've found it, we'll reward the dogs with a game of fetch." He held up a tennis ball. He called the dogs, and they bounded over with sprightly wagging tails. "All right, then, my little sausages. Let's have a deep sniff." Saskia offered the desert boot to Lush and then to Topper. The dogs sniffed with interest, pawed the air in excitement, then sat, their signal that this was the scent they knew they should find. With a barely audible cue from

Saskia, they stood and began their work, moving forward in a widening arc, their noses twitching like bumblebees in flight.

"We'll soon have our answer," Harry said with confidence and swelling hope.

An hour and a half later, a grim-faced Harry called off the search. There would be no fetch today.

HOW THEY MADE
THE NEWS

Harry's disappointment did not last long. The next morning, soon after he ordered a large American breakfast from his suite at the Golden Pagoda Hotel, he heard two quick raps. Room service? That was certainly fast. He threw on a bathrobe. But when he opened the door, he saw a man in an unstylish longyi, wearing the white cap of the bellhops but not the crisp white jacket and gloves. The man presented him with a small package wrapped in plain white cloth. Unbeknownst to Harry, this package had come via the same network of people who had helped Black Spot pass along the "Second Life" potency plants. Harry tipped the out-of-uniform bellhop with the first bill he grabbed from his wallet—he never could calculate the equivalent dollar amount, but whatever it was, the recipient seemed highly pleased.

Attached to the package was a small note, folded in half. The outside of the note was addressed, in crudely printed letters, to "Mr. Hary BAily." Inside, the note said: "Special for you. Please see quick." The wrapped object was light and as small as a matchbox, and in fact when Harry laid open the cloth, he saw that it *was* a matchbox, decorated with a picture of two natives leading an elephant. On the sides were elegant squiggles of Burmese writing. Who would give him matches? He didn't smoke. He shook it. Ah, something was inside—a camcorder tape. Its label said in neat script: "Trip to China/Myanmar." On the other side was written: "Tape #1: 12/16/00."

Harry saw no interesting significance in these words. He guessed that the tape contained material that the reporter wanted him to review before the next day's shoot. In the late afternoon they would leave Mandalay for Rangoon, where, according to three other eyewitness reports, Moff and the children had been seen wandering in a daze in the jade market. Terribly thoughtful that the Burmese TV station provided him with background material, but why the devil didn't they include something with which to watch the bloody thing? He was accustomed to having the production of *his* TV shows run in an efficient manner, with the underlings thinking ahead for what his needs and preferences might be. Best go find a camcorder, so he could study the contents while having his breakfast. He put on a freshly pressed white shirt and tan shorts fastened with a crocodile belt that matched his loafers, which he wore sockless. When you're a TV personality, you have to look the part twenty-four hours a day. He slipped the tape into his shirt pocket and headed down to the lobby to search for a suitably equipped tourist. They certainly worked him hard, and without paying him a cent. But it was worth it, anything to keep his friends in the public eye.

Surprisingly enough, there were a fair number of guests, whereas only the previous week all the hotels had been nearly empty in the wake of panic over the missing tourists. Harry reasoned that his reports might have encouraged people to return—astonishing, really, how one person can make a difference in the world. All the tourists had rushed out of the country when the news of the disappearance was known, couldn't pack their bags fast enough. Now, after his first report, from Bagan, and the Mandalay episode just yesterday, the hotel lobby was packed with tourists. What would the place be like after his third episode? Not that he wanted to help bring in the tourists, but the numbers meant something—it was the power he had to change people's perception. This was visible proof. He breezed through the lobby and saw that none of these travelers had any decent video equipment, only those outmoded models that took the larger cassettes. And those horrible clothes they had on—the tour operators must have slashed the price for coming here, to have attracted such an obviously lower class of tourist. He continued past the double glass doors that led to the pool.

The air temperature was pleasantly warm. He gazed upon the Olympic-sized pool, its waters unmolested by any of the slicked-up sunbathers lying on deck chairs draped with monogrammed hotel towels. On the far side was a tent-shaped cabana with mahogany flourishes that gave it the romantic aura of an old colonial backwater. Ah, there, on the table by that woman with a hat, a silvery object standing upright, that *had* to be a camcorder. He sped toward it, and then saw its young bikinied owner turn and look at his approach. Even with the oversized hat and dark glasses obscuring her peepers, she was fetching. As he drew closer, she tilted back her sunglasses, and he reassessed the bronzed princess with long chocolatey hair to have a shaggability rating of eight plus—not that he was in the game, but there was nothing wrong with keeping his analytical skills sharp.

Across from her was a boyish-looking woman consulting a guidebook. He reckoned she was in her late thirties, what he once considered close to the end of shelf life, but that was before he met Marlena. To his tastes, this woman had never made the shelf. She had a spiky hairdo and a no-nonsense face. She was toned, on the extreme side, an anatomical model of pectorals, deltoids, and biceps hardened through much disciplined exercise. Harry had found that women who loved to exercise usually suffered from frigidity. For this reason, athletic women were not his type. Besides, this one had a certain Sapphic quality, that hirsute area above the lip a deliberate Frida Kahlo statement.

It was not by coincidence that Harry had run into these two women. They were both reporters for Global News Network. Since the story of the missing tourists broke, a dozen news bureaus had sent teams disguised as tourists to flesh it out. The networks could do only so many interviews with the missing travelers' families, friends, neighbors, co-workers, former teachers, former colleagues, former spouses, ex-girlfriends, stepchildren, and ex-stepchildren. One reporter had gone so far as to interview Marlena's housekeeper.

The TV networks had not had a human interest story this riveting since that baby girl fell into a well in Texas more than a dozen years before. As in the baby's case, the hour-by-hour updates on the missing tourists trumped news on wars and bombings, AIDS and unrest in Angola. New advertisers came on board—dog food companies, manufacturers of anti-anxiety medications—and bought thirty-second spots. But now, if they were going to take advantage of the public's hunger for more, the networks needed more leads, more angles, and, if possible, a juicy scoop to distinguish themselves from other networks in close competition.

Late-night meetings were called among the news producers. Proposals flew, and this one emerged: How about sending a team of reporters disguised as ordinary, bumbling tourists to get the real story? We'll equip them with what appear to be outdated and cheap video recorders, and they'll wear Hawaiian shirts, and socks with their sandals. They'll fumble with maps and guidebooks. Well, hop to it!

So that was what Harry saw when he strolled through the lobby of

the Golden Pagoda: a dozen or so journalists, all secretly congratu-
lating themselves for blending in with the real tourists. They were
wearing loud Hawaiian shirts and toting repulsively outdated video
equipment that no bona fide journalist would ever be caught with,
unless as camouflage. Of course, the inner workings had been retro-
fitted to record film-quality images.

As you might guess, the mandate of every network was an exclusive interview with Harry Bailley. GNN told its journalists to tape
Harry secretly. The man was just too savvy about saying the right
thing, which was far less interesting than the off-camera truth. Wasn't
it illegal to record someone without permission? Not to worry, in
Myanmar, the question wasn't "Is it legal?" but "Is it lethal?" Everybody, watch your step.

To help coax Harry into baring his soul, GNN sent Belinda
Merkin, its most strategically equipped reporter, a green-eyed, big-
haired brunette and former figure skater, who also had been a Ful-
bright scholar in China and was a graduate of Columbia's School of
Journalism. Accompanying her was Zilpha Wexlar, a sound engineer who had a superb digital recording device, and the critical ears
to match it. The device was attached to the inside of her well-worn
backpack, its microphone peering out of a frayed, bullet-sized hole.
This duo had been lurking for nearly two days, searching the bars
that Harry might frequent. Their original plan was to appear befuddled and ask him for recommendations on places to visit and things
to do. And where are you going next, they'd inquire, with Belinda
sprinkling enough flirtatious hints to get him to suggest that they tag
along. As their researchers had told them, given Harry's reputation
and his eye for attractive young women, they'd probably have no
trouble getting the invitation.

"Pardon me, miss," Harry now said to the long-haired reporter.
"You probably have no idea who I am. . . ." He paused, waiting for
her to recognize him.

"Of course I do," Belinda said brightly. "Doesn't everybody? You're Harry Bailley. I'm so honored to meet you." She extended her hand. What irony, she chortled to herself. *He* was pursuing her. When the researchers said he'd be easy, they underestimated how much so.

"You've seen me?" Harry appeared to be both astonished and flattered. "On the telly here or in the States?"

"Both," she said. "Back home, everyone is watching you. I've always been a fan of *The Fido Files*—I have a naughty papillon. And this 'Mystery in Myanmar' series is the best reality show around. Everybody says so."

"Actually," Harry said, with a twitch of his head, "the program that I do here isn't a reality show, it's more of an investigative documentary."

"That's what I meant," she graciously amended.

Harry returned an amiable grin. "And who are you who means so much?"

"Belinda Merkin."

"Merkin. Interesting name. May I call you Ms. Merkin . . . Mrs. Merkin . . . ?"

"Just Belinda is fine."

"Lovely. Well, Just Belinda, I wonder if I might bother you to let me use your camcorder for a short while? Of course, if you're in a hurry to go off and do some sightseeing . . ."

"No hurry. My sister and I haven't even figured out where we want to go."

"Forgive me," Harry said to the bogus, more boyish sister, "we haven't formally met."

"Zilpha." She gave Harry a slight smile and a firm, businesslike handshake.

"Please to meet you, Sylvia," Harry said.

Belinda picked up the camcorder. "Do you need me to show you how to use it?"

Although Harry knew perfectly well how the camcorder operated, he said, already full of gratitude, "Oh, would you?"

As Belinda took out her tape and loaded the camcorder with his, he said nonchalantly, "It's just some material I have to review before my next segment. You're welcome to watch, if you like." He knew it was a tantalizing offer.

And just as expected, she replied: "Really? That would be so exciting." She scooted over, and Harry slid in and mumbled apologies about needing to be as much out of the sun as possible to better view the tape. His scratchy bare thigh rested against her recently waxed one. Belinda resisted laughing aloud at this obvious and adolescent ploy. She held the camcorder between them, and Harry squinted, choosing not to put on the reading glasses tucked in his shirt pocket.

An image appeared on the tiny screen, and they were jarred by the sudden blare of shouts and hoots, road noise, and engine drone as the camera's eye took in the scenery from a speeding vehicle. "Hey, everybody," a female voice yelled above the racket, "look this way." Belinda set the camcorder on its side to adjust the volume until it was barely audible. "Much better," Harry said. By the time they resumed watching, they had passed the section showing the smiling faces of the tourists on the bus.

Even without his reading glasses, Harry could tell this was not a professionally shot backgrounder. It was hardly better than what a tourist might video-record of a temple-a-day package tour. Why did TV Myanmar International think this would be informative? Look at this crap: An airport terminal. A cluster of tiny figures bunched up for the requisite group shot. Distant buildings in some typically rustic village. The footage was pathetic. It displayed all the faults of home movies: camera shakes, two feet of empty space above each person's head, and too many panoramas that were probably breath-taking when viewed in real life but dully one-dimensional on video. The better shots, which were few, captured the universal subjects of coffee-table books: local people in colorful costumes, snaky canals, smoky alleys. And those ethnic women with crisscross halters and heavy bundles of pine needles, those women he and Marlena had seen outside Lijiang. What were they called? The tribe name was like "Nazi" or "taxi." Naxi!—that was it. Evidently that same tribe was also in Myanmar. Ha, maybe they were the same ladies, professional photographic natives who circulated everywhere, like those Peruvian flute players who popped up no matter where you were in the world.

The images came in unconnected bursts, reflecting the mind of a person with attention deficit disorder. Harry watched in snatches, while taking ample opportunities to admire Belinda's luscious thighs, the plush delta separated from his naked eye by a flimsy bit of Lycra. Back to the camcorder screen: A fleeting field, a swoosh of sky, primitive pagodas and bewildered grandmothers, then buffalo cows, more buffalo cows, a child riding a buffalo cow, now signs and more signs, signs with innovative applications of the English language. Belinda read aloud: "Lodging and Fooding," "Restaurant and Bare." And then she came to a group of people, barely more distinguishable than ants on the screen. They stood behind a sign: "Sincerely Welcoming You to Farmous Grottoe of Female Genitalia."

At the same instant that she saw the Westerners were Harry and the missing tourists, Harry's heart flip-flopped. *Grotto of Female Genitalia?* All the scenes just viewed now took on the eerie quality of déjà vu. Zilpha saw that Belinda had a look of intense focus.

"May I?" Harry said, and before Belinda could answer, he seized the camcorder from her hands and deftly pushed the rewind button, then whipped out his reading glasses. *Play.* There it was, the familiar sign, and there they were: Dwight, Heidi, Moff . . . and sweet, darling

Marlena! Curious, she looked older than he remembered her. But there she was, next to him in China, his arm around her waist, and around them were the others. Alive, so alive, so happy then. And *now*? He realized that in his hands, in that tiny rectangle of circular reels, was a parallel world, the past seen as present, reexperienced as here, as now, unchanged, able to repeat itself over and over. "It's us," he said.

"Can I see?" Belinda asked.

Sorry." He punched up the sound and let her see. "It's us," he announced. "It's a tape of us, my friends, before they disappeared."

Belinda feigned surprise. "Oh my God, really?"

More snippets of the past rolled by, and not a glimmer of disaster in any of them. As he watched these ten-to-twenty-second spurts, his mind was a tangle of worry. Where did this tape come from? Did TV Myanmar really mean to give it to him? Couldn't be. They would have called to tell him what they were sending. So who sent it? His heart raced, not knowing which way to go, up or down? Was it a sign they were alive, or was it—

Belinda broke into his thoughts. "Where did the tape come from?"

"It was handed to me by a bellhop this morning," Harry said. "At least, I assume it was a bellhop. Roxanne made the video. She's with our group."

Belinda nodded. Of course, she knew the name. She knew all of them, as well as their ages, occupations, physical attributes, and names of family members. How could she have been so stupid not to recognize earlier what they had been viewing? She didn't even have the excuse of not wearing reading glasses like Harry. No matter, because here it was, in her hands. The scoop. She felt killer instincts surge in her brain, and saw all the signs leading to "top of the news hour," an in-depth special, a fast-track promotion to anchor the evening news or produce her own weekly show, numerous Emmys, and her ultimate dream, a Peabody.

As they watched with absolute attention, Belinda tried to remain concerned but not delighted. My God, what a scoop this would be, and it had literally fallen into her lap, along with Harry, the number-one interviewee! Surely this was fate sent down by the ratings god. Only one question remained: How would she get that tape out of Harry's hands and into those of her producer at GNN? She wrinkled her nose at Zilpha to indicate she had sniffed out a fish that needed to be hooked and landed, and her colleague acknowledged her with a sudden yawn to let her know she could "rest assured."

Belinda tried to be optimistic. "This must mean they're alive. It was slipped to you to let you know that."

Harry nodded and sighed. He still pictured Rupert shivering on the tape.

Zilpha leaned forward. "You know, I have a computer in my room. We can see this more clearly if we plug the camcorder into it. That way the video will be the size of the computer screen and you'll be able to make out the details."

Belinda looked questioningly at Harry, and he responded, "Yes, yes, by all means, yes." They hurried to the room. With a deft movement, Zilpha connected the camcorder to the jack in her computer, and surreptitiously inserted a recording disc in the DVD drive. They started the video again, and the images jumped onto the screen. When she saw that Harry was fully absorbed, Zilpha reached into her backpack and turned on the recording device, then aimed the microphone toward Harry.

Harry now saw that the frames were date-and-time-stamped. December 18th, 10:55 P.M., December 19th, 3:16 A.M. . . . He frowned. "I don't remember this happening then."

"It didn't," Belinda said. "The date never got changed from Pacific Standard Time."

Harry's brows flew up. "Amazing that you thought of that."

"Not really," she said. "I forget to reset my watch all the time when

I'm on—" She coughed, having almost said "assignment." "On vacation," she quickly recovered, while mentally kicking herself. No more slips.

"Even so," Harry said admiringly. He pressed the fast-forward button and the lives of his friends zipped by, complete with squiggly voices, until he saw their arrival at Floating Island Resort. There's Heinrich, he noted, old slobberchops and greasy palms, meeting them at the dock. Harry turned up the volume and heard Roxanne narrating as she recorded: "The Intha fishermen here stand on one leg to fish. . . ." The next image was Harry's cottage with its partially burned roof. *Criminy, she filmed that?* Roxanne was giving a wry description: ". . . He set his bungalow on fire last night." She giggled, then snorted out the rest: "And he tried to stomp out the flames, wearing only his birthday suit!"

Harry reddened, but when he glanced at Belinda, he saw she was straight-faced, watching the video with serious intent. And then, like evidence of ghosts, eleven shadows climbed into longboats. The date and time stamp indicated December 24th, 3:47 P.M., which was stupid o'clock on Christmas morning in Myanmar, so damn early it had still been dark. His heart was drumming in his ears.

He is with them now, in that lost time now found.

He hears Marlena call out to Esmé, "Honey, did you bring your coat?" The throaty sounds of the outboard engine drown out the answer. Cut.

Moff is looking toward the mountains, the only sounds the soft plash of water on the boat's sides. As sabers of light slice at the mountains' purple silhouette and open the sky, everyone murmurs in unison. Cut.

They're amid the rhythmic clacking in a weaving mill. Cut.

Noisy banter and bargaining in a cheroot factory. Moff and Dwight waggle cigars out of one side of their mouths and utter Groucho Marx witticisms. Cut.

His friends are watching a man pour a gooey mixture onto an artisan's screened frame. Harry realizes this must have been the papermaker's place. All the things that these witnesses had reported were true! So what happened after? Harry can barely breathe. Cut.

And here it is: A flash of green, a patch of sky, and bodies jostling about with shouts and groans. An engine grinds into gear, and someone—it sounds like Moff—yells: "Hang on!" The world is heaving from side to side, and Dwight lurches into view and then out. Roxanne shouts in a sarcastic voice: "As you can see, we're on this *ultra-deluxe* bus, making our way to a Christmas surprise in the rainforest. . . ." "This better be good!" Wendy's voice is heard to yell back. Cut.

All is quiet, save for a bird calling and the creaking bend and snap of young ferns being stepped upon. The camera eye looks ahead and sees the travelers' backs trudging upward in single file. A man is complaining: Bennie. A woman is, too: Vera. Cut.

Some are sitting on a log, others leaning against it. The camera eye closes in on an oil-coated paper umbrella, and when Roxanne calls, "Hey, you," it tips back, and underneath is Esmé, snuggling the white puppy. She wrinkles her nose at the camera. Cut.

What's this? A river? A gully? Definitely some sort of deep chasm, but even though the eye drops down and down and down, the bottom can't be seen. It looks sickeningly deep. Cut.

Long ropes run over the perilous rift—oh, it's a suspended bridge. "Hell, no," Bennie says off camera. A hiss of words follow: "Safe?" "Scared." "Shit!" Are his friends actually going to cross it? Good God, there goes Moff! Now Rupert! Heidi! And Marlena—she makes it, too—good girl! There goes Esmé, Dwight, Vera, Wyatt, Wendy, Bennie . . . Roxanne calls for Dwight to take the camcorder from Black Spot, and the camera blurs and then is on fixed on her, and she, too, crosses with a wobble and a shout. Cheers and laughter. Cut.

Dark faces, Burmese, perhaps tribal. Two old women in turbans are behind Dwight's partially viewed head. They look up and wave to the camera. "These are the Karen tribe," Roxanne says. "As you can see, it's really primitive here, untouched by the twentieth century." Cut.

Dwight is inspecting a small hut made of tree roots. The camera's eye looks up, then down. "This is the finest hotel in the region," Roxanne says. The camera surveys a set of trees. Cut.

A feast and smiling faces. His friends are eating. They wave: "Hi, Mom!" "Hi, Mom." "Hi, Mom." "Our new home . . ." "We're going to learn how to make food just like this . . ." "Hi, Daddy, this tribe is the coolest. . . ." "Man, this is so great we never want to leave. . . ." *They never want to leave?* Harry is aghast. Did they actually stay on purpose? Are they sympathizers? Cut.

Rupert is showing card tricks to two small cheroot-smoking children with reddish hair. "In magical lands, magic can happen, but only if we believe. Do you believe?" The little girl answers, "We belief in God." Cut.

The eye of the camera glides across in a blur and stops on an unknown object, a fallen tree branch . . . wait, what is that? Good Lord, it's not a tree but the stump of a leg! The eye moves upward. And its owner also has a sewn-shut eye. And look at this poor girl, horrible, horrible, she's missing her arm. This one, part of a leg. This one, a foot. The camera sweeps to the face of a somber-looking young man. He has smooth cheek planes, large, almost black eyes. He looks like an Asian god. And he can speak English, but his accent and soft voice make what he is saying hard to understand: "When the mine is exploding, the mine is no more danger, and the soldiers are very happy, because now path is safe for walking."

The eye of the camera sweeps to the mutilated body parts and comes in close so that fused vermilion flesh fills the screen. Roxanne speaks in a shaky voice. "It's heartbreaking. . . . They forced them!

The fucking military took away their land, burned their villages, en-slaved them. God, this is so sickening. . . . It really makes you appreciate . . ." Her voice drops to a fierce whisper, and it is obvious she is crying. "Oh God, it makes you appreciate not ever knowing such things. . . . We have to help them. . . . We can't just give them sympathy or a token bit of help. We want to help in a bigger way, a substantial way that can make a difference." Cut.

The chasm again. Voices are grumbling, arguing, nay-saying, insisting. "This is the shits," Roxanne says. The eye of the camera veers toward a ladder of ropes running straight down the other side of the crevasse. The bridge has collapsed! They're looking down? Has someone fallen in? *Who?* How many? Marlena? Esmé, Moff? No? No! Thank God. They're fine. There they are. All there? Yes, they must be, since no one is acting crazed with grief, just pissed. So that's it. They can't get out. The bridge is down. They meant to come back all along. And they're alive. They're simply stuck. They must be okay. They had food. Thank God! Cut.

It's night. Why has so much time gone by without any video? The date stamp says December 30th, so it is the 31st, New Year's Eve. Rupert is lying on the ground, his eyes looking upward, perhaps at stars. Whoever is holding the camera is shaking it. It makes Rupert look jittery. Rupert is mumbling, but it's impossible to hear what he is saying. Every now and then, he lets out a shout. A night moth flutters by, dancing with the light of the smoke.

Vera is speaking. "You shouldn't do that." She isn't scolding. She sounds very gentle. She must be telling Rupert to not be so noisy, because others are sleeping.

Rupert doesn't answer. The camera continues shaking. No, wait, it's Rupert who's shaking. He's shivering, shivering violently. He must be sick, terribly sick. It is now Moff who is speaking, although he is not seen. "His mother," he says in uneven breaths, and the camera heaves with him. "She'll want to feel she was next to him . . .

taking care of him, too. . . ." Oh God, he's crying. Moff is crying! Harry has never known his friend to do that. What does this mean? Rupert lets out a shout again.

"Honey, please," Vera is saying, so tenderly. "His mother is going to hug him in person. Nothing bad is going to happen. We won't let it. Come on, turn off the camera. Sit down, get some rest. We still need you to help with the others. . . ." *Others?* What's happened to them? Are they sick, too? Is it too late? Does she mean graves must be dug to bury them? Was it poison, malaria, no food? Or did someone hurt them? Did they try to run away and someone stopped them? What happened? What could cause this kind of sadness? Would knowing be even worse than wondering?

Vera comes into the eye of the camera, her hand is reaching, and then the eye of the camera is a blur, and Moff is weeping like a baby, and when the eye can see clearly again, the world is askew, full of smoke and ashes rising. She must have put the camcorder on top of something, so that now it is looking up. Red words are flashing: "Battery low," pulsating like a heart. Its eye does not flinch, never looks farther ahead into the dark or to the sides. It stares straight up, observing flecks of ash rising in golden smoke and the red flashing words. Its ear listens without favoring any particular sound, it is simply acting as witness to the babble and shouts, the shuffles and sobs, the occasional crackle of wood as it is consumed. It is calmly tucking these final moments into itself for safekeeping, into memory that winds back in time and will one day move forward.

That is what Harry is watching. He has entered that world and has become the eye blurred by smoke, brushed by the haphazard flight of moths, stuck in a mise en scène, the entire world, his only existence. He cannot blink and lose even a millisecond. He is memorizing all there is, this moment to the next, to another and another . . . until all at once the screen goes back, and there is nothing more to memorize.

He was so dazed he did not hear Belinda. "Are you okay?"

Zilpha leaned toward him. "Do you want to watch it again?"

Harry shook his head. He was emotionally exhausted. He took the tape from the camcorder and gently wrapped it in the white cloth, then slipped it into his shirt pocket. Walter and Heinrich never mentioned a Christmas surprise in the jungle. But what did Walter remember? He was probably brain-damaged from that brick that hit his head. And Heinrich was perpetually soused, that Teutonic drunkard.

"Are you still going to Rangoon?"

"Yes, of course . . . No . . . I don't know."

"You think they're still in the jungle?"

Harry's mind was racing. The witnesses had said they were in Rangoon. But on the tape, they were stuck because the bridge had collapsed. The tribe wasn't able to lead them around Bagan, Mandalay, Rangoon. . . . The next minute the truth sprang forward. The lousy bastards had set him up! All those tour sites and witnesses, rubbish. What a bloody blinkered fool he had been. And then he remembered that his reports had kept the focus on his friends. Belinda said that the story was splashed all over the news in the United States. That had been part of his plan—in fact, he rationalized, that was the main one. So now what? Was Marlena still in the jungle? Anything could have happened in the days since the tape ended.

Belinda and Zilpha remained silent, waiting patiently for Harry to announce his decision. Even before meeting him, the two had discussed the possibility that the TV Myanmar search was a sham, and that Harry had been their sucker. He was like many people who were desperate, needing to hang on to any kind of hope. Several networks besides GNN suspected a public relations ruse, but they had decided not to raise doubt yet about the possibility of concocted eyewitnesses, since there was nothing solid to counter either Harry's belief or popular opinion.

He turned to the women. "I have to get back to the lake, to that damn resort. They're somewhere near there, that's clear."

Belinda and Zilpha looked at him quizzically. It was a reporter technique to elicit more information.

"Look," he said, now fully under control again, "the group was never in any of those cities where the witnesses reported them to be. I had a feeling that was the case, but I went along with it so we'd continue to get coverage. I didn't want my friends to be forgotten. The media can make things happen, you see. I know, because I work in television."

Belinda and Zilpha nodded. "Listen, this might be a stupid question," Belinda said, "but how are you going to search for them? Who's going to take you? If it's true what they said on camera about the minesweeping and all, the military isn't going to rescue them. They might do something that isn't what you have in mind, especially if your friends are linked up with Karen rebels."

"Wait a minute," Harry yelped. "Who said they were rebels?"

"The military thinks all Karen tribes hiding in the jungle are rebels."

Harry frowned. "How do you know that?"

Belinda kept a straight face. "They've been doing special reports on the military regime on Global News Network."

Harry thought fast. "I'll get the American Embassy to intervene."

"They can't do anything at the lake," Zilpha said. "They aren't allowed to leave Rangoon without permission."

Harry recalled someone else's saying that—the expatriate at that other resort on the lake. Damn. "I still have to speak to someone at the Embassy. They can put the pressure on and make sure we find my friends without anyone being harmed."

"Maybe you should go to Rangoon as planned," Belinda said. "That way you can meet with the Embassy people personally."

Brilliant, Harry said to himself. Why hadn't he thought of that? "Yes," he said, "I had been considering that. And I'll give them the tape. They'll see that it gets aired, and that way, the whole world will be watching."

Belinda looked at Zilpha out of the corner of her eye. They'd have to work fast to return to the bureau in Bangkok. The disc they'd recorded had to reach Global News Network before Harry gave his tape to the Embassy; otherwise, bye-bye, exclusive.

Belinda asked if Harry was still going to do the update in Rangoon with TV Myanmar. He snapped a brisk no. He'd play along with them and let them fly him to Rangoon and pay for his hotel, and then he'd feign food poisoning before the shoot. Let them get a dose of their own medicine, he said to himself.

Before leaving Zilpha's room, Harry said, "I can't thank you enough for letting me use your camcorder and computer. You're a godsend. Say, what is it you two do?"

"We're teachers," Belinda said immediately. "Zilpha teaches kindergarten, and I've got first grade."

Harry broke into a smile. "I thought it might have been something like that."

THE NEXT MORNING, in Rangoon, Harry arose at five and went over his plan. He would wait for the reporter to call him at seven. He'd make his voice hoarse to sound deathly ill and to ensure that it was impossible for him to speak on camera. A couple of retches might be good, too. He'd play the part thoroughly. No shaving today, and no shower. He mussed his hair, put on rumpled clothes. At eighty forty-five, he would take a taxi to the American Embassy. If anyone from TV Myanmar saw him leave the hotel, he would say he was trying to find a Western doctor. Had he covered all the bases? Brilliant. He was about to order breakfast, but thought better of it. So he took out his notes and the rough draft of *Come. Sit. Stay.*

At seven, the reporter called, but before Harry could launch into his excuse, the man said tersely, "Today we are not filming. Everything has been canceled."

"Oh," Harry said, forgetting to sound sick. "Why is that?" The reporter was elliptical in his answers. The more Harry asked, the more opaque his comments became. The reporter would say no more.

Harry was baffled. Had there been a national crisis? He turned on the television. Nothing. Whatever the reason, at least it had nothing to do with him.

THE APPEARANCE
OF MIRACLES

For the past few days, my friends in the jungle had taken turns pedaling the bicycle to keep the car batteries charged. Night and day, they watched the news on the various satellite channels: the BBC, CNN, Star out of Hong Kong, TV Myanmar International, and what they believed to be the most informative, Global News Network.

For some reason, tonight TV Myanmar was no longer showing Harry's reports from Bagan and Mandalay, which used to repeat every other hour. My friends had enjoyed tuning in to those segments when there was nothing new on the other international channels, and having watched them so many times, they could recite the words before they came out of Harry's mouth: "The aching splendor . . ." When Harry turned to the camera and said those words, my friends always burst into laughter. Their antics had annoyed Marlena. Why were they making fun of him? It was his show that had gotten them on the international news. Tonight she was worried to find no reruns. According to Harry's report, he was supposed to be in Rangoon today. He was moving farther away, and yet watching him every other hour had made her feel that they were emotionally close.

My other friends had turned their attention to a Global News Network special. They were watching interviews about themselves, padded with comments from family and friends. For the next hour, they learned there were heroes and heroines among them. Who knew that Heidi had discovered the body of her murdered boyfriend? No wonder she was so cautious yet, they now understood with appreciation, skillfully prepared. He was a housemate not a boyfriend, she tried to explain, and they praised her even more for downplaying her trauma.

They also had not known—not even Roxanne—that Dwight had served for three years as a Big Brother to a kid who had been bullied in grade school and had become a truant to escape the torment. The former kid was now a young man on a track scholarship at Stanford and, inspired by Dwight's example, also a volunteer at an after-school program for troubled teens. (The kid had not seen Dwight for ten years or so. He had told Dwight he was the biggest bully of them all, which had left Dwight embittered about the whole experience.)

Vera, they discovered, had two grown children, who recalled the time she gave money to the disadvantaged in lieu of buying Christmas presents. (Vera had actually bought them bicycles but not the boom boxes they wanted.) They'd been angry at the time, they admitted, but later they realized, as one of them said, that "she was as much a saint then as she is today."

Whatever portion of truth those televised comments held, hearing them moved my friends to tears and increased their affection for one another. They hugged the recipient of each tribute. From now on, they promised, they would celebrate every Thanksgiving together, no matter where they might be. Within that vow, they voiced their belief they would get out of the jungle alive and well.

THE PEOPLE of the Lord's Army were also listening to tributes, not on television but told to one another as they crouched in a circle. Their mood was somber, and they had reason to believe that their days were numbered.

Black Spot had taken the tape down to Nyaung Shwe Town days earlier. He had given it to their trusted source, the same man who took the "Second Life" plants they found. But the tape had not appeared on either of the Harry Bailley shows. And today, TV Myanmar had removed the program, and all the reruns as well. The tribe knew the reason. The generals in charge were angry. They now knew the faces of the Lord's Army. They would hunt them down and kill them as rebels. They would go to Nyaung Shwe Town and post photographs of tribe members, and the longboat pilots whom they once beat out of fares would say, "Hey, that's Black Spot! He took those people to Floating Island." Arms would be twisted, twisted off, if necessary, until someone blurted out where the Lord's Army was hiding. And at least one person had a fairly good idea where that was. The tape had not helped them after all. They would not be TV stars on Harry's show. The show had been canceled, and that meant they would soon be canceled, too.

All day they had been telling stories, the familiar ones, and also the ones that had never been said aloud. Loot and Bootie crouched in the middle, near the campfire, rocking rhythmically while they sucked cheroots.

A bowl of water was passed around the circle, and whoever took a sip told a story of a brave soldier in the Lord's Army: A brother who refused to carry the food that would nourish the SLORC army. A mother, whose children had already been shot, who never looked away as the mouth of the gun rose to her mouth. A young man who could have jumped on a truck taking the others to safety, but instead went back in the direction where his sweetheart had been captured by the army. A grandfather who refused to leave his burning home. A sister, only twelve years old, dragged by six soldiers into the hidden parts of the forest, where she screamed, then stopped, screamed then stopped, until the rifle shot came and she made no sounds forever-more. She was brave. They all were brave. Those now listening would try to be brave.

When it was close to dusk, the old grandmothers brought out the red singing shawls they had repaired that morning. They had threaded the iridescent mantles of one hundred emerald beetles onto the long rope fringes, twenty carapaces on each string, knotted off with a small brass bell at the end. Their granddaughters carried out fifty-three blankets and placed them on the mats to air. The married women brought forth the best of their now tattered clothes, so that they might show their sisters the secret weave and knot they had carefully guarded as their own. No need for secrets now. The grand-mothers hung the singing shawls on the arms of trees, since the un-married girls would not be there to wear them and mourn. Soon they would put on these best clothes, and fifty-three people, young and old, would each lie on top of a blanket and roll into a cocoon. They would have already eaten the poison mushrooms the twins had found. They would wriggle and writhe like moths bursting against their sacks. The fringe of the blankets would brush their unfeeling faces, a sign that sleep this time had no end. And when their breath was the departing breeze, the emerald wings would flap and fly, sounding the bells and singing to the dead, "Go home, go home."

Loot stood and picked up a bowl of food made with the last of the hoarded spices. The food was passed around the circle, with all tak-ing a pinch, so they could give offerings. Loot cried out: To the Nats, who kindly did not give us too much mischief. The refrain chant came back in English. *God is great!* To the Lord of Land and Water, who owns all of nature and let us dwell in it. *God is great!* To the Crop Grandmother, who had no crops to watch, but that was not her fault. *God is great!* And to the Great God in the sky and His son, Lord Jesus, who will welcome us into the Kingdom of Everlasting Rice Fields and bottomless bottles of sweet toddy, which we will drink while watching the greatest dances, puppet dramas, and number-one TV shows. *God is great! God is great!* We will grow strong and then stronger still, so that when our enemies die and try to sneak into our kingdom, we will knock them down and beat their heads, until they are as soft as egg yolks. *God is great! God is great!* We will smash their bones and grind their hearts, until the pieces are like moldy manure. *God is great! God is great!* We will toss this stink into a burning river. *God is great! God is great!* Away they will be swept, boiling and bubbling, screaming and crying, over a cliff and down a firefall into the fang-toothed jaws of Hell, just as the Lord of Nats has foretold. *God is great!*

Now our people will be ready to be resurrected as soldiers for the Lord's Army—*God is great!*—and at last they will return to earth and take back our stolen lands. *God is great!* But before we plant and harvest the fields, we will find the scattered bones of our dear families, mother, father, sister, brother, child, child, baby, baby. We will wrap them tenderly in blankets woven with the secret knots, and as we talk to them, soothe them, we will lay them in the earth—not in a secret place with no name—but on the top of a mountain, with a clear view of the sky. *Amen.*

DURING A BREAK in the news, my friends came over to watch the ceremony that the Lajamees were holding. They sat on logs and low stools. Today must be some sort of a holiday, hence the celebration with the passing of the bowl, the loud oration and ritual chanting. Wendy went over to Black Spot. "What's the occasion?" she asked.

He looked somber. "Day of our death, miss."

Like the Day of the Dead in Mexico, Wendy thought. "Does everyone in Myanmar celebrate this holiday?"

"No, miss. This is not holiday-making. This is ready-making for death. Tomorrow, maybe next day, we are dying. We think it is soon."

Wendy ran back to the group and related what Black Spot had said. A mass suicide? The eleven Americans had talked about this before, but during the past week the tribe had seemed so cheerful. What had changed their minds? And here was a scary thought: Did the tribe expect that their guests would join them in the exodus? They'd have to put a halt to that notion right now.

Bennie went to Black Spot and asked him what he meant by "ready-making for death."

"SLORC soldiers are coming," Black Spot said. "We are already telling you before. When they are finding you, they are finding us. They are saving you, they are killing us."

"Oh, come on," Bennie said, trying to calm his own rattled nerves. "That won't happen."

"Why not?" Black Spot said, and walked away. He went into the woods, where those who had died after coming to No Name Place were now buried. He was feeling very bad for his people. He was ashamed to realize that the boy was not the Reincarnated One. The boy was not the Younger White Brother or the Lord of Nats. And the ten other people were not his disciples or his retinue of soldiers. They were tourists who had attracted nothing but bad luck. What a disaster Black Spot had brought upon his people.

Over the next hour, there was much talk among my friends. What should they do? These poor folks had been kind to them, had shared their food, their blankets, their clothes. It wasn't their fault the bridge fell down. One thing was certain: The eleven of them would help the tribe. They would tell whoever saved them that tribe people here were not guerrilla rebels. They had no weapons. They were regular folks—all except the twins and their grandmother, poor thing, brain-damaged from all that past violence, thinking she could talk to God. And if the military still caused trouble for their jungle friends, they would use influential contacts in the States. A senator, the mayor, they would figure that out later—the point was, they would help.

Yet what if the SLORC soldiers rushed in and started shooting before asking? What if they shot *them* before they could yell that they were Americans? Would being Americans help them? What if it had the opposite effect?

Two hours after the sun went down, Loot and Bootie stepped onto the tree stump where the spirit of the Crop Grandmother once stood watch over nothing. Loot raised his arms high and shouted in Karen dialect, "Let us pray." He rocked on his heels, his eyes rolled back, and my friends heard again the mumble of gibberish. Above that came Bootie's higher-pitched voice leading the people into a chanting refrain: *God is great, God is great.*

Loot shouted that the Younger White Brother was not among them. The boy was merely a mortal, but they did not blame him. They did not blame the Nats, who made them think that, for they were merely being playful. But now it was time to go find the real Younger Brother in the Kingdom of Everlasting Rice Fields. And before they ate the last supper of life-ending mushrooms, they would pound the drums and sound the horns. They would ready the souls of their bodies, the soul of the eyes, the soul of the mouth, all of them one by one. They would know to be ready, to not dillydally and get left behind. Soon the soldiers would arrive. They would stab them with their bayonets, shoot them with their rifles, but they would already be gone, their bodies empty like the hollow husks of the emerald beetles.

Souls, be ready!

The men on the inner edge of the circle readied their drums, the bronze one and those made of hide stretched over a wood frame. The women on the other side picked up their instruments: the bamboo flutes and hollowed tree knots carved like spiny frogs. When they trilled the flutes and ran a stick over the frog bumps, the sound was of water trickling over rock, much loved by the Lord of Land and Water, a pleasing song to any god who was listening.

Black Spot brought forth chicken bones, feathers, and a small bag of rice. He placed them next to Bootie, who tossed them bit by bit into the fire. These had been the twins' divining tools. Best to burn these shaman tools now, lest their enemies use them to trick their souls and send them to the wrong realm or into a weak person's body.

My friends watched as the tribe's personal goods were thrown into the fire: worn mats and carved sticks, the woven rattan that covered their meager verandahs when it rained. Bennie regretted seeing a wooden bowl with etchings also sacrificed in this way. The fire burned higher and higher.

"Lord God," Bootie cried in English above the inferno, "we coming soon. Bo-Cheesus, we coming soon. Heavy Fazzer, we coming soon. In life, we serf You, in dess we serf You. We Your servants, we Your children, we Your sheep. And we Your soldiers, onward marching, we the Lord's Army. . . ."

Roxanne nudged Dwight. "Did she say 'Lord's Army'?" He nodded. "We the Lord's Army," she repeated, then rolled the words around on her tongue. *We the Lajamee.* How wrong they had been about so many things. What else had they misunderstood?

The chanting grew louder, and the drums, horns, gourds, and flutes fell into the rhythm of an excited heart: *Boom-tock, boom-tock.* Faster and faster, louder and louder. The repetitious din made it hard to think or move. Bennie was afraid his brain would lock on to the repetitive beat and he would have a seizure. The pounding and chanting had become a communal heartbeat.

With a single last bang of the bronze drum, all the souls in No Name Place were jolted out of their bodies, my friends' souls, too. Were they dead? Had they been shot? They did not feel wounded. They felt bigger and lighter. They seemed to see themselves, not their physical bodies, but their own thoughts and truths, as if there were a mind mirror that could reflect such things. They all had those mirrors. Now that they were outside their bodies, they could hear without the distortions of ears, speak without the tangle of tongues, see without the blinders of experience. They were open portals to many minds, and the minds flew into the soul, and the soul was contained in the minds of everyone. They knew this was not normal, and yet it was natural. They struggled for words to describe what they felt, that they were every thought they had ever had and those of others, an open repository containing bright particles and endless strands, microscopic stars and infinite trajectories, endless constellations that were holograms within holograms within themselves, the invisible as visible, the impossible as obvious, the greatest knowledge now effortlessly known, and the greatest knowledge was love. Just love. And I knew this, too.

"Amen," Loot said.

With another jolt, my friends instantly returned to their separate bodies, separate minds, separate hearts, leaving them one among many and no longer many in one. They looked around, at one another, at Loot and Bootie, waiting to see if the sensation would burst through again. But the experience began to fade as dreams do, despite their trying to resurrect it or grasp at it as if at motes of dust. They had their senses back, yet never had they felt less sensible.

The light from the television flickered. They walked over and sat on the rattan and bamboo stools, waiting for the morning news from New York. Among themselves they slowly began to talk. Had they just experienced a religious ecstasy? Had they glimpsed the edge before death? Maybe you got the same effect when you'd gone without eating or sleeping for days. . . . They guessed at it until they lost it. And yet, without their knowing, some change had already taken fragile root. Some part of their souls had broken free.

THAT NIGHT, the first of four miracles occurred. Or five, depending on how you look at it.

The first revealed itself when my friends were standing in front of the television. "Our top story this morning," said the anchor on Global News Network, "a videotape has been found, belonging to one of the eleven tourists missing in Myanmar, showing us exactly what happened after they were last seen. Belinda Merkin is with us, live in Bangkok. Belinda, can you tell us how this tape came into your possession?"

Belinda was standing at the night market in Bangkok. "Ed, as you know, we've been working underground in Burma, finding credible leads and following them into the secret recesses of a country that exists behind a veil of secrecy. And because Burma is ruled by a repressive regime, we have to protect the identity of our sources. Let's just say a birdie dropped it from the sky and into our hands." She held up a bogus camcorder tape, the real contents having been copied onto the disc and sent to GNN headquarters from Bangkok via a high-speed digital link.

"Your life must have been in danger, too, wasn't it, Belinda?"

"Well, Ed, let me just say, I'm glad to be in Bangkok, with Burma behind me. But what's more important now are the missing Americans. And within this tape are important clues. It is a home video shot by one of the missing, Roxanne Scarangello. . . ."

"What!" Roxanne yelped. "That can't be."

"And now," said the anchor, "we're going to show you at home exactly what the tape captured. Viewer discretion is advised. Some of the scenes are disturbing and not suitable for children. . . ."

Once the tape had been shown, Roxanne ran to retrieve her backpack. "It's gone! It's gone!" she shouted, loud enough to catch Black Spot's attention. She stood there with her camcorder, its cartridge holder open and empty. Black Spot walked over to hear what was being discussed.

The visitors were chattering wildly. With the bridge down, there was no way the reporter could have sneaked in and stolen the tape. And no one in this camp could have taken it to the local post office to mail to GNN. "Maybe a bird really did find the tape," Bennie said. "Crows are known to take all kinds of things to line their nests. How else would you explain it?"

Black Spot held his arms outstretched. "It is miracle," he said.

My friends considered the possibility. The release of their souls only moments earlier had opened them to the mysterious and inexplicable.

"However it got to them," Roxanne said, "I'm worried about where the tape leaves off. Rupert was delirious, Moff was out of his mind—"

"I don't think it shows that at all," Moff said, careful not to look at his son. "You can tell in the tape that I was exhausted."

The group analyzed whether it might look to outside viewers elsewhere that everyone had died. Would the search still go on in Rangoon? They hoped not. Would searchers come to the jungle, to the mountains around the lake?

"There's a lot of jungle," Heidi said, and then added: "But maybe another miracle will happen."

ALTHOUGH BLACK SPOT knew how the tape had made its way to Mandalay, he still believed it was a miracle. How else would Harry have known to give it to the lady reporter? The story on the tape was even better than he had remembered. Sister Roxanne had spoken with great heart about their suffering and used just the right words about the cruelty of the SLORC soldiers. She showed the tribe's wounds, the maimed, the faces of good people. She spoke of their kindness. Their story was not on TV Myanmar but on Global News Network. His heart pounded. The whole world knew their story. Their story of survival was greater than any of those on *Darwin's Fittest*. A leaky boat was a small problem. The hippopotamus did not really exist, nor did the crocodiles. For those TV people, it was all pretend. But his people had a true story, and so it was better. The world now knew who they were, and their hearts would find them in No Name Place. Their show would be number one, week after week, too popular to cancel. They would be TV stars, and never again would they have to worry that they would be hunted and killed.

He already knew what to call the show: *The Lord's Fittest*. He went to spread the good news.

MY FRIENDS' ELATION dissipated in the next hour.

This began when their backs were turned to the TV, when they felt they no longer needed to watch out or worry. They did not realize that in the jungle a TV is a not just a TV. It is a Nat. You must watch it continually, or it will get angry and change the story.

The TV Nat had been talking and talking, and no one had been listening. His attendants were jabbering among themselves and changing the past. That troublesome tape of Roxanne's? Now it was funny! Remember when we were in the back of the truck, they said, going to the Christmas surprise, and Roxanne was telling us to wave? And Wendy was saying, This better be good! Ha. Ha, ha. Who could have known?

Black Spot went to my friends and apologized for all the trouble caused by his bringing them to No Name Place: "When Walter is not coming and no one is knowing why, we are saying to ourselves, No Name Place is also a very good Christmas surprise. And yes, of course, we are also hoping already you are bringing the Younger White Brother so he can meeting his tribe. The Great God is helping us, miss. I am thinking he is helping you, too."

The TV Nat was irritated. No one was thanking him. So for a moment he left No Name Place and flew to New York.

At GNN headquarters there, the anchor walked from his desk to an area off camera designed to look like a cozy library filled with books. When my friends turned their attention back to the news on TV, an interview that had obviously started several minutes earlier was on.

The anchor was sitting in a boxy armchair. "They've been known to imprison even those foreign journalists who report unfavorably about them."

A young man sitting on a sofa said in a British accent: "Right, and spies are treated even more harshly. You'd be rather lucky to be imprisoned for twenty years—and that, my friend, would be after the torture."

"Like Belinda, you took a substantial risk getting this footage, didn't you?"

He nodded modestly. "But not nearly as big of a risk as those eleven Americans may be facing. Wouldn't want to be in their running shoes."

Chills ran down the spines of my friends.

The anchor leaned forward. "Do you believe those Americans have joined the Karen tribe as underground rebels?"

"No," Heidi whispered. "We haven't."

The man pressed his lips together, as if reluctant to answer. "To be honest, what I really think? Well, I really, really, *really* hope not."

My friends felt a vise pressing on their throats.

The man continued, "The Karen tribe are known for having insurgents among them. It's not the whole tribe, mind you, but they are a fairly large ethnic group. Many have passively resisted the junta, while others have engaged in guerrilla warfare. The junta doesn't seem to see much difference between the two. A number of Karen are hiding up in the jungle, including, apparently, where the Missing Eleven were last heard from."

The anchor shook his head sadly and said: "And now we've just heard on the home video, which was made by the American woman Roxanne Scarangello, that they wanted to help the Karen tribe, not in a token way but, and I quote, in 'a substantial way that can make a difference.'"

Roxanne whispered, "A hundred dollars."

The anchor looked concerned. "That's not going to sit well with the regime, is it?"

The British man sighed heavily. "It was a brave thing to do, but also very foolish. Forgive me for saying this, but Americans tend to operate under their own rules in other people's backyards. The truth is, in Burma, foreigners are treated under the same laws as the natives. The penalty for drugs is death. The penalty for insurrection is death. The penalty for engaging in warfare with insurrectionists is death."

The anchor sat up, clearly unhappy to end on that note. "Yes, well, we certainly hope it won't lead to that. But now let's switch gears. You're a documentary filmmaker. You've done quite a bit of investigating on the regime's treatment of dissidents, those who have spoken out against them in even the mildest of ways. And now you've put together a documentary on this very subject. . . ."

"It's a work in progress—"

The anchor faced the camera: "Our viewers should know that this entire documentary will be aired on GNN later this week. But right now, we're going to have a look at a portion of it, a GNN exclusive. It may be a bit rough in spots, but we know our viewers will overlook that so as to be informed on what is the very latest in our series *Democracy Goes to the Jungle.*

The anchor turned back to the filmmaker. "So Garrett, tell us what we're going to see."

"It's called *Oppressed and Suppressed. . . .*"

An hour later, my friends sat on two logs facing each other. Roxanne felt especially bad. The documentary had shown gruesome details of what had happened to members of ethnic tribes, as well as Burmese journalists and students who had criticized the regime and were now wasting away in jail. Appearing at the bottom of the screen throughout the documentary were photos of missing Burmese. My friends felt sorry for their Karen friends here in the jungle, but they felt sorrier for themselves.

"The soldiers *can't* kill us. We don't deserve this," Bennie cried.

"The Karens don't deserve it, either," Heidi said.

"I know that," Bennie replied fiercely, "but we aren't here because we wanted to be rebels. We got stuck and we gave a hundred dollars each. We shouldn't have to be tortured to death because a bridge fell down and we wanted to be generous."

Esmé said nothing. She was stroking Pup-pup. Marlena assumed she was too frightened to speak. But Esmé was blessed with a child's point of view—that adults overreacted to everything, and while things were indeed scary, her main concern was making sure no one hurt her dog.

My friends had exhausted themselves from a long day of bicycle riding, the trance ceremony, the elation of near salvation, and now a plunge into an abyss as deep as the one that prevented them from leaving No Name Place. Without anything more to say, they drifted off to their own bed mats to weep or pray or curse until oblivion mercifully could take over.

The people of the Lord's Army crouched in another area of the camp, smoking cheroots and drinking hot water. The latest TV program had shown their bravery in the face of death. This would only help to increase the popularity of their show. They were giving thanks now to Loot and Bootie, to the Nats, to the Lord of Land and Water, to the Great God, and yes, to the Younger White Brother, even if he did not recognize who he was. They had had doubts, but now those were banished. Whether he knew it, he was manifesting the miracles. He had made them visible around the world.

The TV Nat was abandoned. The twins forgot to turn him off so he could sleep and be less mischievous. And thus he continued to cast light and shadows on the world before him. He was at his luminous best, calling out prophecies, changing fate, creating catastrophes, then retracting them in the next update.

My friends awoke at dawn to a profusion of birdcalls. They had never heard the birds sing so insistently, so ominously. The Karen people had never listened to such beautiful morning songs. In spite of this avian chorus, the camp seemed unusually quiet. Moff walked over to the television set. It was stone-cold dead. Right away, Grease jumped on the bicycle generator and began to pedal. The other members of the tribe gathered fuel for the campfire and foraged for food. They were happy to carry out their routines, the daily habits of living.

At noon, one of the batteries was considered sufficiently charged to turn the television on. Global News Network came back on the air. My friends were afraid to move closer to an object that had delivered such a painful shock the night before. They sat quietly on their two facing logs, listening to the birds, wondering what their shrill cries meant.

HARRY HAD GONE through a similar roller coaster of emotion. He was sitting in an office in Rangoon, being interviewed by five men. Saskia and the dogs were also there, as were Wyatt's mother, Dot Fletcher; her boyfriend, Gus Larsen; and Wendy's mother, Mary

Ellen Brookhyser Feingold Fong. Harry was sipping a cup of English Breakfast tea.

Thank God, the consular officers had come that morning to take him and the others to the U.S. Embassy. It could have been the Myanmar military. And in fact, the SLORC soldiers had appeared at his hotel a half-hour after Harry had been whisked away.

"Why didn't you people show up ages ago, when my friends were first reported missing?" Harry griped.

A consular officer named Ralph Anzenberger answered in a droll voice. "Well, you see, Mr. Bailley, we were sitting on our duffs, waiting for the Burmese government to give us permission to leave Rangoon and do a search. We were still waiting, actually, when you finally materialized in Rangoon to do another public relations show for the military regime."

Harry squawked. He was not doing any such thing! He had taken the only route he knew to keep attention focused on his friends.

"It did that," Anzenberger agreed, "but the junta has also benefited by turning your reality show into propaganda to boost tourism. And by the way, there were no witnesses who saw your friends in Pagan, Mandalay, and Rangoon. You knew that, didn't you?"

Harry's face flushed at the obvious truth that had only recently dawned on him. "Of course," he maintained. "What kind of fool do you take me for? I was playing along." Saskia cocked an eye and gave him the same doubting look she used years before, when he denied flirting with others.

Anzenberger looked at a file. "How did you know to give the tape to the GNN reporter, Belinda Merkin?"

"Her? Ha. She's not really a reporter." Harry was glad he knew something Anzenberger didn't. "She's a kindergarten teacher I ran into at the hotel pool in Mandalay. I borrowed her camcorder, and we watched the tape together, that's all. But I didn't give it to her. It's right here. See?" And he pulled the tape out of his pocket.

Anzenberger bunched his eyebrows and glanced at his colleagues. "Mr. Bailley," he said. "Belinda Merkin is a reporter with Global News Network. She's been there for a number of years. And she did give some interesting footage to her employer. It aired last night on the international broadcasts and caused quite a stir. Shall we watch?"

Twenty minutes later, Harry sat in a stupor. Was he dreaming? Did he have malaria? None of this made sense. It was the same tape, all right. Had Roxanne given out several of them? And that vixen Belinda. Kindergarten teacher! Bet they had a laugh over that one! Anzenberger was speaking to him. He said they would now show him some other footage, the aftermath.

"AND NOW from GNN headquarters in New York, the latest on the Missing Eleven and their new role as freedom fighters for democracy. . . ." What followed were quick scenes from cities all across America, holding what looked to Harry to be parades. There were rallies and demonstrations, with marchers carrying placards and banners: "Free the American Eleven," "Hurrah, Freedom Fighters," "Go, Karens, Go," and one that said "Nuke SLORC." There were shots of vigils and fasts in Tokyo, Oslo, Madrid, and Rome, and in Germany, a silent march where candles illuminated poster-sized photos of the missing carried by demonstrators—and pictures not just of the American Eleven but of Burmese students, journalists, and supporters of the National League for Democracy as well. A thousand photos of the missing. A thousand of the dead. A sea of people.

"As support for the American Eleven grows," the anchor said, "so do denouncements of the Burmese military regime around the globe. People in many nations are calling upon their governments to do something. We'll be talking soon to foreign policy experts on what this might mean in regard to U.S. relations with Burma—and yes, that is what people are going back to calling the country that was renamed Myanmar by the junta. Coming up next." A logo sprang up on the screen: "Democracy Goes to the Jungle." It was superimposed on an image of bare-chested natives leading an elephant, the same image that had appeared on the box of matches delivered to Harry's hotel room and countless tour brochures.

When the segment was over, Harry gave silent thanks. "They've always been good-hearted people," he remarked to the Embassy staff, "quick to empathize with the disadvantaged. That's why we came to Burma, you know, to see for ourselves what the conditions really are, and to determine if we might help in any small way—not through violence, of course, but in ways that rely on gentle persuasiveness, a kind presence. Actually, it is not unlike the techniques we use in shaping dog behavior. . . ."

Harry remained in the room with the Embassy staff and watched GNN unfold the next batch of scoops. The updates continued hour after hour throughout the day. Policymakers in those countries that had not announced boycotts in previous years were now meeting in special sessions to discuss doing so. ASEAN was calling an emergency meeting to determine how to handle this situation that was so damaging to their joint reputation. This was a very delicate matter, for according to their rotation plan of shared leadership, Myanmar would take over as the chair of ASEAN in the not too distant future. Perhaps it was time to apply more forceful guidance on the country. Trade restraint, a delay in that pipeline construction, no more sales of arms, the withholding of development aid, even a suspension of membership in ASEAN. Yes, the other member countries would look into all these measures as friendly encouragement.

THE DRUMS AND GOURDS were sounding in No Name Place. The flutes played like morning birds. The Karen people were performing a dance, enacting the arrival of the Younger White Brother and the overthrow of their enemies. Meanwhile, Heidi and Moff were improvising a jig, Wyatt and Wendy were doing a do-si-do, linking arms and skipping one way and then the other. They had all watched TV coverage of the international rallies supporting them and honoring the Burmese dead. Black Spot said to Marlena, "Miss, I am sure telling you, everything now is good. It is a miracle."

On January 15th, after days of international rallies and denunciations of the military regime, plus some confidential arm-twisting from ASEAN members, the government of Myanmar issued a statement composed by its newly hired image-consulting agency based in Washington, D.C. It was broadcast on television around the world. "The State Peace and Development Council of Myanmar is concerned that other nations have been given incorrect information. We do not persecute any ethnic minorities. We welcome and treasure diversity of all people, including tourists. Even with tribes that have created unrest and unstable conditions, we have offered truces and signed peace agreements. We have several tribal leaders who can testify to this. . . ." TV screens showed a lineup of smiling ethnic-costumed actors behind the spokesman.

"Lies! Lies!" Bootie shouted. "Bo-Cheesus will punish you and you and you."

"Unfortunately, some tribes in the hills have not heard of these truces. They live far away and have not come down in many years. Some of these people did step on land mines, it is true, not as part of any jobs forced on them, but because they trespassed into restricted areas with mines planted by other ethnic hill tribes years ago, maybe even their own. In the interests of safety to our people, we closed off those areas and marked them with big danger signs. Perhaps they could not read. Illiteracy is high among those who live in remote places, and we are working on educational development as well. So we give our heartfelt sympathy that they were wounded. And if these Karen people come to our new modern hospitals, they will receive free care, even though it was their fault for trespassing and injuring themselves."

"Lies! Lies!" Bootie shouted.

"But most important of all, today, we are showing the Karen tribe in the jungle our true sincerity. Today, on this television broadcast throughout the world, we are signing an important agreement. It guarantees the safety and freedom of the Karen tribe and the Americans who are with them.

"Of course, the Americans should not have gone into the jungle when there are so many other beautiful places to see that are safe and comfortable. In these places, bridges do not fall down. So when the Americans return safely, we sincerely offer them a special getaway package to Bagan to visit its two thousand two hundred monuments and experience the aching splendor Dr. Harry Bailley has made so famous. We think our American tourists will be pleased with the excellent roads, the world-class restaurants, the eight-star hotels with private bath. They can even take advantage of bonus bungee-jumping activities, provided by our friendly military air force.

"For our Karen friends, we have agreed to give them their own land, the place where they are now, wherever they are, and the outlying areas of that, up to ten thousand acres. They can decide what they wish to do with it—they can clear the rainforest and plant crops, sell the teak wood, whatever they wish.

"These are the things we promise—deluxe vacation getaways for our American friends, ten thousand acres for our Karen family of Myanmar. And now, *with the entire world watching*, we will sign this document, and to show our sincerity and honesty, we have a special person to bear witness, our good friend and TV star, Dr. Harry Bailley."

So that was the third miracle. The fourth happened only hours after that. After the dance and the pounding of drums, a similar spirit of ecstasy overcame my friends and the Karen people. They were feeling quite fond toward one another, when suddenly Salt ran through the camp, yelling, "Miracle! Miracle!" Black Spot translated what Salt said. "The bridge is resurrect, risen from dead!"

Sixty-four people ran to the ravine and saw that it was true. Grease ran across the bridge and jumped on it to show that it was sturdy. My friends screamed in joy, and many cried. The Karen people shouted: "*God is great!* Praise be the Younger White Brother!" When they returned to camp, the Karen came up to Rupert, who had gone over to the TV with my other friends. They bowed deeply, telling him in the Karen language, "We thank you for coming. We thank you for bringing us the miracles, for bringing peace to our people, the end of our suffering."

"Why do they keep doing that?" Rupert complained.

"What! You still not knowing who you are?" Black Spot said. And he bowed and said, "Our Younger White Brother, Lord of Nats."

Once again, Black Spot told Rupert about the man who had come more than a hundred years before. He told them about the Holy Signs. Loot held up Rupert's playing cards. Bootie held up the black book of Important Writings. Truly, the Younger White Brother had made them strong. Surely, he now knew who he was.

When Black Spot was finished, my friends looked at one another and spoke silently with their eyes. Should we tell them? What difference will it make if we do?

But it was Rupert who decided. "I'm not anybody's white brother. I'm an only child." He turned over the pack of cards. "See this? Cathay Pacific. That's how I got here. Not through reincarnation, through customs, like everybody else. And this book is a paperback I borrowed from a guy in my class. It's called *Misery*, and it's not a history of your tribe. It's a made-up story by a guy named Stephen King. See? Here, take it, read it yourself."

Black Spot took the book. "We are treasuring it forever," he said. "Thank you." He had understood almost none of Rupert's jabber of words except for "King." But it was evident that the Younger White Brother was still confused. One day he would know who he was. He would remember that before he came, no one knew of the Lord's Army and their suffering. No one cared. They used to hide, now everyone knew them. They had been given land. They had a TV show with number-one ratings. What other proof did they need to know the Younger White Brother was among them?

My friends were at last able to leave No Name Place. But how would they walk down the mountain to the truck? "Not far," Black Spot said. "Walking, it is taking only one hour most."

"I can try," Bennie said. He was still quite weak from the malaria, as was Esmé. Obviously, neither of them would be able to walk even a hundred yards. Perhaps a few could go down and bring help? But the idea of being left behind frightened Esmé, who cried: "What if you can't find your way back? What if the bridge falls down again?"

"Maybe we can telephoning now and asking people for help?" Black Spot suggested.

Telephone? Was he daft? "I forgot telling you," he said. "There is so many miracle." Black Spot went off to the edge of the camp and into the bamboo stands, and when he stepped out, he pulled from a satchel an oblong of blue plastic: Heinrich Glick's satellite phone.

In their elation, in their desire to leave in whatever way possible, the Americans did not question how this phone was manifested. "Who should we call?" Marlena asked.

"Bear Witness Hotline," Black Spot said. "We are telling them we see ourselves." He put the phone in the satchel, stepped into the loop at the base of a teak tree, and like a frog, leapt to the top, above the canopy, where there was a clear view of the sky.

· *18* ·

THE NATURE
OF HAPPY ENDINGS

On January 16th, Global News Network broadcast the dramatic rescue of my friends and the Lord's Army by a brand-new Mi-8MPS helicopter generously supplied by the Indian government. Most of the tribe could have walked down, but after the twins said they wanted to be airlifted by the giant sling, everyone else did, too. Why not? It made for great TV visuals, all day long.

And so fate—if you can call it that—changed course over the rainforest canopy, and kindnesses and miracles poured like quenching rain after a drought. Such is the nature of happy endings.

Before going their separate ways, my friends, a few of whose personalities had clashed, decided they were as close as kin and promised to meet for a "Celebration of Life" once a month, in addition to the annual Thanksgiving reunion. They would share potluck dinners of rainforest recipes, spiritually deepening discoveries, survival health tips, and support during personal turmoil. But they enthusi-astically agreed that they should buy native drums and gourds to re-create the communal heartbeat and elation they had shared on that incredible night. That experience had opened them to possibilities beyond their Western-acculturated senses. Immersion, however, into their American lives soon restored them to a more rational view. The more they looked into it, the more they saw that simple causal forces had led from one thing to another. It was this and this and this—a cascade of events combined with a good wallop of sidespin. None-theless, the drumming was amazing, wasn't it? They agreed they should still do the drumming at their gatherings.

Speaking of drumming, Dwight had actually purchased a drum and had to smuggle it past both Burmese and U.S. customs. He found it in a shop in Mandalay that promised "genuine antiquities and rar-ities." The yellowed tag described it as: "Circa 1890, from the bank-rupt estate of Lord Phineas Andrews, human skull drum, produces a sound like no other." The shop owner believed it was a holy instru-ment brought to Burma by a visiting Tibetan priest. Although one tribe in Burma was famous for having been headhunters, they were not very musical. The shop offered other odd items: fans made from the feathers of now extinct birds, a tiger-skin carpet, elephant-leg stools, and the like. But Dwight passed on those.

The tide also turned for the tribe. Just as was hoped, a film studio demonstrated interest in their starring in "the greatest reality show of all time." Fortunately, the studio owned a subsidiary in Burma, a clothes-manufacturing company that had been doing business before the sanctions. And through various loopholes and exemptions, plus a dose of lobbying, the green light was granted. As Harry would say, On with the show!

One minor change: The show would not be called *The Lord's Fittest*, as Black Spot had hoped. The studio "execs," as Black Spot and his friends learned to call them, had conducted a focus group in

Fallbrook, California, and concluded that this title would not play well with Muslim audiences, which could be plentiful in some countries, or with Christian conservatives, who might object to putting their Lord in the same company as the Lord of Nats and the Younger White Brother. Most disappointing of all, the name received loud boos from the studio's target audience, boys between the ages of twelve and nineteen. For a better title, the studio execs went to shopping malls across America, and soon they had their name: *Junglemaniacs!*—the peppy exclamation point capturing the excitement of watching the real perils of real contestants in a real jungle, where elimination by real and excruciating death was always a possibility and might even occur live during broadcast.

Thanks to friendly negotiations lasting several hours, instead of the months of squabbling that stalled most deals, the tribe members were told they would receive a generous share of the profits on the "back end," with "points over net," which would be subjected to strict accounting by expensive lawyers, and not to worry there, those fees would be paid entirely by the film studio, for which the tribe was grateful. The profits were certain to be huge, given how popular the tribe had become, and because they would likely get millions of kyats, no money would be paid up front. This was a tradition, in fact, known as "standard for the industry." Was this satisfactory with the tribe? "God is great," chanted the twins. "It's a miracle," cried their grandmother.

When the series got under way, predictions were fulfilled. The TV ratings went sky-high in just the first two weeks—number one among reality shows airing in the United States on Thursday during prime time. The ratings dipped a bit the third week, but were revived when two guests on the show, Mark Moffett and Heidi Stark, revealed they had discovered a new species of plant.

During that episode, Moff recounted the thrilling moment that he, or rather, Heidi and he, discovered and prepared the specimen in its habitat and documented its secret location. The rare plant had a bulbous shape on top, like "W. C. Fields's proboscis," as he circumspectly described it for general audiences, right before the shocking image was flashed on screen. A botanist at the California Academy of Sciences had already confirmed that the plant was not in the taxonomy, and he coauthored a paper with Moff, which was sent to a respected journal for peer review. After the paper was published, Moff said, the plant would officially be known as *Balanophora moffettorum*, named after both Heidi and him, who were soon going to marry. Moff proudly published a scientific article in *Weird Plant Morphology*, and *Weekly World News* did a huge spread on the discovery, complete with testimony from happy middle-aged women.

The episode of *Junglemaniacs!* on which Moff and Heidi appeared was widely watched; the night before it aired, they had been on *Late Show with David Letterman*. Letterman had started the interview by remarking that Moff and Heidi looked positively "radiant." He leaned in close, as a confidant might. "Could it be the aphrodisiac plant you've just discovered?" Moff laughed and said there was no scientific evidence that the plant had any effects on libido, performance, or stamina. But a bit of probing from Letterman led him to divulge that some people, in service to science, had bravely subjected themselves to experiments over a period of two months. The "empirical findings" were merely anecdotal, hardly scientific; however, they suggested—did not *prove*, mind you—that consumers could enhance and maintain "reproductive-oriented activity" for days, and most interesting of all, the plant was equally effective for women, if not more so. Headlines in the media ran the gamut from "Women Say: It's About Time" to "Church Leaders Fear Rise in Infidelity." To assess potential medical benefits, a start-up was formed with venture capitalists, and some of the profits were promised to the tribe. "God is great," chanted the twins. "It's a miracle," cried their grandmother.

Ratings for *Junglemaniacs!* rose again, although not quite so spectacularly, when botanists who went to study *Balanophora* in its native habitat stumbled across a new species of sweet wormwood that contained the compound artemisinin in highly concentrated amounts. They had chanced upon two old tribal ladies giving the medicine to the show's Burmese boom operator, who had contracted malaria and lay in a sweaty, senseless heap. Days later, the boom operator was practically swinging on vines through the jungle. This newfound wormwood, the initial findings showed, was a highly effective antimalarial, possibly up to a hundred times more potent than the plants that were being cultivated in other parts of Asia to provide antimalarial compounds. Amazing to tell, this species was also effective against drug-resistant cases. What's more, it grew faster, maturing in nine months instead of eighteen. And in contrast to related and less effective species, it did not require much sun, filtered or low light being sufficient, or perhaps even necessary, and a good soak from a monsoon every now and then was beneficial. Damp rainforests, instead of sunny fields, were the best environment for this particular species, ideal for rampant growth in the millions of acres of uncultivated jungle.

A ready cure! Naturally, people in tropical countries were overjoyed to have a cheap and ready remedy. In Africa alone, three thousand children were dying each day, a million a year. The pharmaceutical companies were the only ones not pleased. No research or complicated extraction process, no clinical trials, no FDA approval required for use in other countries. Just an old Karen grandmother was needed, to show people how to distill the plant into a tea. The Lord's Army would reap millions, even billions, by selling their supplies to the World Health Organization. "God is great," chanted the twins. "It's a miracle," cried their grandmother.

The newly renamed State Peace and Innovation Network— SPIN—took a benevolent interest in the plant. A new law would be ruthlessly applied. No more deforestation of teak forests! No more clearance of rainforests for pipelines! No more cutting of trees for heroin cultivation! Those who harmed the environment would be tortured and then executed. Moff commented with a sardonic laugh: "Where ecological conservation has failed, commerce prevails."

Happy days and high ratings reigned a bit longer. But if miracles are like rain after a drought, then greed is the flash flood that follows. Heroin growers and fortune hunters, who had bribed SPIN members, came with AK-47s and shovels. They raped the hills until there was hardly a tendril of *Balanophora* remaining. The military's consumption of the plant led to a resumption of rape of ethnic tribal women, which some military leaders justified as a natural way to assimilate tribes, for who could wage civil war with a new generation of mixed-blood babies? The junta, declaring the destruction of the plant's habitat a "mismanagement situation requiring intervention," took control of the land, so that damage would not extend to the valuable wormwood. No one was allowed to pick so much as a leaf of the plant, not even the tribe. A small outcry rose from human rights groups around the world. But by then, *Junglemaniacs!* was no longer prime-time but relegated to the less popular seven a.m. Sunday-morning slot. The SPIN council explained that the Karen tribe had never really *owned* the land. The regime had granted them "responsible use" of the land, and the tribe surely understood that, since, as all Burmese knew, there was no private land ownership in the country. The land belonged to the people, the junta said, and thus in the interests of all Burmese, the members of the junta had to step in and protect their assets. They felt that the Lord's Army, being patriotic people, should understand this completely. Some of the military brass met with them to confirm that this was true.

Another month passed, by which time the ratings for *Junglemaniacs!* had plummeted to the depths of a sinkhole. Not even the tragic deaths of a few members of the tribe from untreated malaria could resuscitate it. The show was canceled, having never earned a single red cent or Burmese kyat and having spent huge sums on publicity and miscellaneous.

Soon after, the stars of *Junglemaniacs!* disappeared as suddenly as their American guests had on that Christmas morning. Meanwhile, the names of my friends appeared in a few magazine articles— "What's In and What's Out," "Where Are They Now?" and "Fifteen Seconds."

A few months after the Lord's Army dropped from sight, they resurfaced in a refugee camp on the Thai border. In preparation for death, they had begun their trek to the border in their best clothes, items given to them earlier for use as product placement on the TV show: T-shirts from Bugger-Off bug spray, jeans from Ripped & Ready, and baseball caps from Global News Network. The grandmothers carried the singing shawls. In doing health checks, doctors in the camp ascertained that the twins Loot and Bootie were not seven- or eight-year-olds, as my friends had thought, but twelve-year-olds stunted by incessant cheroot-smoking. An American psychiatrist visiting the camp diagnosed the twins' grandmother with posttraumatic stress disorder. Ten to twenty-five percent of the refugees suffered from the disorder, he claimed. In the old woman's case, it stemmed from having seen one hundred and five members of her village being killed. This, he said, had led to her "magical thinking" that the twins were deities. The twins admitted they had gone along with their grandmother's "make-believe" stories to keep her happy, and also because they were given as many cheroots to smoke as they wanted.

A few NGOs worked briefly with the tribe to counsel them on ways they could become self-sufficient. Among the suggestions: creating a business doing satellite-dish installations in remote areas, running a bicycle-generator franchise, or opening an eBay store selling the interesting emerald beetle singing shawls with the "secret knots." Black Spot explained that the tribe's desire was simply to find a scrap of land where they could plant their crops, preserve their stories, live in harmony, and wait for the Younger White Brother to find them once again.

At the end of the summer, the Thai government decided that not all the Karen people in the many refugee camps were refugees. Those who had not fled from persecution faced no danger and had to go back to Burma. As far as authorities could tell, fifteen hundred fell into this category, including the Lord's Army, who not only had not been persecuted but had been given star treatment. They were taken to the other side of the border, where a military welcome party was waiting for them. Some feared the regime would retaliate against these runaways, but they need not have worried. Thus far, none of the people deported has been heard to complain, not a single one. In fact, they have not been heard from at all.

While being transported, a terse military report later stated, the hill-tribe insurgents, once known as the Lord's Army, escaped and then drowned when they foolishly jumped into a swollen river.

My American friends were devastated when the news reached them, months after the incident. They had not seen one another since their return home, and they called for a reunion. There were hugs and tears all around. What had happened to Black Spot, Grease, Salt, and Fishbones? Where were the cheroot-smoking twins Loot and Bootie and their loony old grandmother? Did they really drown, or had they been shot in the water? Were they alive but now porters, pipeline workers, or land-mine sweepers? Were they in the jungle right this minute, hiding quietly as soldiers walked by, hunting for goats?

With the Mind of Others, I could see where they were. There is a place in the jungle called Somewhere Else, a split that divides Life from Death, and it is darker and deeper than the other ravine. They lie on their mats, all in a row, and they stare at the tree canopy that hides the sky.

When the sun is gone and there are no stars above, they turn to their memory. They hear a hundred bronze drums, a hundred cow horns, a hundred wood gourds in the shape of frogs. They hear flutes chirp and bells echo. They hear the gurgling brook music any god would love. Together, they sing in perfect harmony: We are together and that is what matters.

LET ME first confess that I was wrong about Heinrich. I had never been able to discern his true feelings. He was a master at subterfuge, and I had made up my mind that there was nothing more I wanted to know about him.

But gossip had it right: He was indeed a former CIA agent. In 1970, he disagreed with U.S. policy on Vietnam, and if you must know, it was the Phoenix Program, when National Liberation Front members were classified as Vietcong and then killed. He left the service a disillusioned idealist, and since his cover had been as hospitality consultant, he saw no reason why he should not continue in that capacity in Bangkok. Oh, and the accent was fake, at least it started off so. He was born in Los Angeles, the land of movie stars, to a Swiss German father and an Austrian mother, and by familial ear he was able to affect the accent, using it so constantly that it was second nature to him, even when he was drunk. The alcoholic stupor, however, was not a cover. Heinrich was a sad and angry man who was happiest when absent from his senses.

What surprised me was his connection to the hill tribe, specifically, the Lord's Army. He had met Black Spot during the boatman's many forays bringing in resort guests. In Heinrich, Black Spot found a friend in spirit. He had heard the German utter hateful words about the regime. Eventually, he and Heinrich made a pact, one that Heinrich kept from his own staff. Heinrich would buy supplies for the resort and then—cursed bad luck!—they would be "stolen." In recent times, it was a bicycle and a television set, a satellite dish, a bicycle generator, and car batteries. Food often went missing, especially spices and fermented fish. But Heinrich *never* said that Black Spot could "steal" his satellite phone. And he most certainly never said that Black Spot and his friends should steal his *guests.*

Well, looking back, he saw that perhaps he had *inadvertently* said this. He recalled the day Black Spot told him with great excitement that they had found the Younger White Brother. They spoke in Burmese in front of the guests. See him there? The tall young man kicking the caneball? Soon, Black Spot predicted, they would reunite him with his followers up in No Name Place. Heinrich sought to discourage the delusion. The boy was merely an American tourist, he counseled, not a deity. But he did magic with the cards, Black Spot said. Back and forth they tussled over Rupert's qualifications as god versus tourist. To underscore the futility of getting Rupert to go to No Name Place, Heinrich remarked: "The only chance of that happening is if the whole lot of them agrees to come along for the fun of it."

And now he recalled Black Spot saying, "Thank you for your wisdom."

When the tourists didn't return on Christmas Day, Heinrich tried not to show that he was concerned. He had to steer the military away from the truth, as well as he could. If the authorities learned they were all in cahoots, that would be a death sentence for the tribe and possibly him. And he had to get that bastard Bailley to stop stirring up the waters. When Black Spot next came to the resort for supplies, Heinrich collared him. The white brothers and sisters are fine, Black Spot assured him. They *love* their Karen people. They said so on their movie camera. And they are very, very comfortable, so this is not a problem at all. They think it is a great adventure to sleep in trees. At each meal, they praise the unusual food, saying they have never eaten so many unknown delicacies and tasty insects. Heinrich was astounded that the tourists believed that cockamamie story about the bridge being down. But he was relieved to have more time to extricate them from calamity. He would wait a few more days, hoping that the tourists would tire of their adventure and that the tribe would realize the boy wasn't their savior. In the meantime, he made sure that Black Spot brought them plenty of provisions lest they starve, tasty insects notwithstanding. He also berated Black Spot for stealing his satellite phone. He told him it was senseless for the tribe to have a phone in the jungle; you couldn't get reception below those trees. Black Spot replied that his people seemed helpless without a phone, and they could order many things to happen when they had one. He assured Heinrich he would pay for it soon.

Black Spot came three more times. Once it was to pick up food supplies, including noodles, which the Younger White Brother said he craved. On the second visit, he delivered the curious red plants, which would indeed raise money for a new satellite phone. On the third, he handed over the camcorder tape that would make the Lord's Army TV stars. He asked Heinrich to give this to Harry, who already had a popular show that appeared all over the world. Heinrich had watched the tape twice, trying to decide whether it would hurt or help. Who knew for certain? He went into his office, closed the door, and poured two jiggers of a very old port, one for himself and one for the Nat who lived in his liquor cabinet. Several days and many jiggers later, the Nat finally agreed not to make mischief.

WALTER RECOVERED his memory two days after he was found in the pagoda, knocked unconscious by the corner of a loose brick. He recalled exactly what had happened:

They had been on the dock, waiting for Rupert. The guests and longboats were waiting to take them to their Christmas surprise, the school on the other side of the lake, where a classroom of children would sing carols. To find the troublesome boy, one of the boatmen went in one direction, and he in the other. Minutes later, the boatman ran to him saying he thought he had seen the boy, but he might be hurt. He had glimpsed a boy climbing a sacred pagoda that was under repair, he said, and then the boy slipped and fell out of sight. The boatman cried out to the boy many times but received no answer. He suggested that Walter climb up to find the boy, and he would seek help to carry the boy back.

The pagoda was in very bad shape. Bricks and stones had fallen out in several places and the Buddhas inside the recessed walls had no faces left. Against the interior back wall, Walter found a wooden ladder. He climbed up and searched carefully, but there was no sign of Rupert. Was he even in the right pagoda? He went to climb down, but found the ladder had toppled (thanks to the boatman, who had set it down to waylay him while he and the other boatmen spirited the tourists away). Twenty feet lay between Walter and the ground. What to do? He shouted. Surely someone would come looking for him. But after a quarter-hour went by, he worried that the tourists would be impatient and angry, and he decided he should descend without the ladder. He dug his fingers into the cracks between the stones and placed his feet onto tiny perches, while apologizing to the Nat of the pagoda for stepping on the fragile wall. But he must have displeased the Nat anyway. When he was only two feet from the ground, the stone slab he was hanging on to with his left hand slid out like a rotted tooth yanked from moldering gums. In a flash of pain, he fell into a bottomless place, and there he saw his father for the first time in more than ten years.

That day and into the next, he stayed in the bottomless place, where he and his father had long conversations. What a good talk it was, both joyful and sad. His father said he should not think of his family's inheritance as a curse. English could save him. He should go away and study, let his mind wander freely. Until then, he should not be obeisant in spirit to those who trampled it. His father then gave him a photograph of himself with his own father. On the back he had written: "With hope, a mind is always free. Honor your family and not those who destroyed us." Walter nodded and put the photograph under the stone that had hit his head and loosened his thoughts.

When Walter woke in the green room, his head was a pounding drum. There were three military policemen nearby. He learned that the American tourists had disappeared. He was about to tell the police what he knew, but then he clearly remembered his father's words. He remembered the sound of his voice. He remembered the pain of losing him. "I remember nothing," he told the military police.

Walter remained as dependable and as efficient as I had always known him to be. As soon as he heard that his charges would be airlifted, he arranged to have their luggage retrieved from Floating Island Resort and sent to the American Embassy in Rangoon. He secured airline tickets for their flight to the capital, where they met with Embassy officials for a debriefing. When my friends insisted he have dinner with them the night before most of them departed, he was able to speak to them openly, knowing they would safeguard what he said. He told them of his father, the journalist and professor, of his steadfastness to the truth, and later the cost of it. "I wanted to be a journalist at one time," Walter said, "but I became afraid, more concerned with my own life than that of my country."

"Come to the United States. You can study journalism there," Wendy said. "Your English is perfect, so you'd have no problems keeping up."

Many of the tourists he had met had said he should go to the States. It was a nice gesture, and only that, since it was nearly impossible for anyone to secure a visa. First you had to speak English fluently, which he did. Second, you had to have an unblemished academic record, which he had, in English literature. And last, you had to have sufficient funds to get there, and then to buy your food and books and pay your tuition and rent. He was short by about twenty-five thousand dollars.

"Come," Wendy repeated. "We'll take care of you."

Walter's heart quickened. It was terrible to have such a great hope casually dangled before him.

"You are too kind," he said with a smile.

"I'm not just being kind," Wendy told him. "I'm offering to put money in the bank so you can come study journalism. We need people like you to do that."

Walter took the TOEFL exam and received a perfect score. He was accepted into the UC Berkeley School of Journalism with a fellowship that would cover his tuition. And true to her word, Wendy opened an account in his name and deposited twenty-five thousand dollars. The consular officers at the American Embassy in Rangoon knew him well by then, and all the paperwork was approved with deliberate good speed. But before he could leave, the United States was attacked. The tallest buildings in New York fell, and so did Walter's dreams of going to America. He had not learned of the attacks in the newspapers or on TV Myanmar. The government had banned all mention of them. An American consular officer told him when he explained to Walter why his application had been put on hold indefinitely. Like so many with similar hopes, he was on a waiting list, at the mercy of many unknown factors.

The day he was told this, he returned to Inle Lake, to the pagoda with his life-changing stone under it, he removed his father's photograph, turned it over, and read the words that would keep him free.

A YEAR AFTER THE RESCUE, Moff and Heidi had not yet married. Heidi was the one who was hesitant. She knew that both love and fear were reduced states of consciousness, not good for making important decisions. For now, living together was risky enough.

On weekends, Moff took her to the Laguna Seca Raceway, near the bamboo farm. The cars shrieked and her heart boomed, nearly shooting out of her chest. She loved the sensation, the release of terror. She would close her eyes and listen to the cycle of the deafening and diminishing whine. Approach and retreat, dread and thrill, a rhythm that repeated, that didn't stop. The racers were hurtling at the speed of love, on the verge of leaving the track and colliding into her. But they always held to the course, and she did, too, safe from disaster, lap after lap. Whenever the old dread rose and threatened to consume her, she recalled that she had already been through what she had prepared for. She had survived the jungle. She had also enrolled in a paramedics training course, the first of many she would need to take, because one day, she would jump into a van and zoom toward disaster, and that would be her choice.

Moff, on the other hand, was becoming more cautious. He had never been the worrying kind of dad. But he had agonized over Rupert's near death. The camera had not lied. When his son was shaking hard enough to break Moff's teeth and crack his skull, he knew that the terrors of remorse would deepen and widen, encompassing the rest of him, consuming his heart with baby teeth. In dreams, he saw it happening, like the camcorder tape he had watched, rewinding, replaying, trying again and again to save his son, then failing, each time failing. When he told Heidi about this recurring nightmare, she said, "I know." That was exactly what he needed to hear. She knew that his fear almost wasn't enough. He would worry. He would always be watching for ways in which he needed to be more careful.

ALTHOUGH RUPERT had acted annoyed to be treated like a god, he now fantasized about the Younger White Brother and the Lord of Nats. He played an anime version of himself in these two roles. Sometimes he became a tree, or a bird or a rock. Other times he wore the mask of a martyr with a grimace of agony. He pictured himself scaling temples and throwing bricks on advancing soldiers of the regime. One day he would return to Burma and save his people. He would make them invisible.

In the meantime, he practiced new card tricks and surfed the Internet. Out of curiosity, he searched for references to "Younger White Brother." He was surprised to find mention of it in several websites as a myth among the Karen hill tribes. He thought that what those people believed was weird, but this was weirder than that. It said the Younger White Brother would bring back the Lost Important Writings and end their suffering. He did more searches and found an article that was part of an unpublished memoir by the wife of a captain with the Raj. In lively prose, she recounted meeting an Englishman in "the wild part of the jungle inhabited by the Karen hill-tribe." He called himself a lord. But she could see he had "the mistaken arrogance of one raised to peerage, not through merit, but with filthy lucre." The hill-tribe people, she said, being isolated from the modern world, believed this Englishman was the "fabled Younger White Brother." He went by the odd Christian name of Seraphineas, and he fathered many children with his two dozen "perpetual virgins."

Rupert spent most of the night searching like a dog on a scent trail until he found a clue that made him shiver. His favorite book, *The Expert at the Card Table,* was at one time called *Artifice, Ruse, and Subterfuge at the Card Table,* and the author was S. W. Erdnase, which was "E. S. Andrews" in reverse. I am not suggesting that Rupert is indeed the Reincarnated One, as the Karen hill tribe called him. I will simply remind you of Rupert's own words: *In magical lands, magic can happen. But only if we believe.* Rupert believed.

WENDY AND WYATT were no longer a couple. But you guessed that already. Wyatt left her for a hero's welcome in Mayville and never returned. He wrote only to thank her for the "unforgettable trip to Burma," and said he hoped to be back soon, so he could attend some of those reunions they talked about. Wendy cried for a solid day and then off and on for several weeks.

Eventually she threw herself into her work. She was a full-time activist with Free to Speak now, who denounced the regime and spoke of the Burmese people's plight. Phil Gutman coached her. "You can't soft-pedal this," he said. "You have to denounce the fucking regime. People who believe this constructive-engagement shit usually turn out to be public relations consultants and lobbyists hired by companies doing business there. And the lobbyists get people all hopeful by saying the military is going to start talks with Aung San Suu Kyi. Get real. It's all a sham to make people think they're going to reform."

"How do you know that this time it's not for real?" Wendy said.

"They've done it before," Phil told her. "They let her out, arrest her again, let her out, arrest her again. It's the old cat-and-mouse tease. You can't reform psychopathic killers, serial rapists, and torturers. Would anyone in their right mind let people like that out of jail? Why would they let them run a country?"

Thus prepared with purpose, Wendy took up investigative journalism, writing about human rights causes, not that she could write, but it is heartening nonetheless that she found a passion and was acting on it. Yes, she was immature, quite silly, and no doubt she would make embarrassing mistakes, yet none of them too serious, one could hope. But Wendy had the desire to make a difference. One day she would mature enough to do that in small or even large ways. She had already persuaded her mother to become the biggest contributor to Free to Speak's meager coffers. Wendy was glad she had made her mother more politically aware. She even asked her to fund another trip to Burma, so that she and Phil could go as human rights observers, incognito, of course. Her mother nodded and said, "That is so brave of you," but I knew that would never happen. The last rescue aged Mary Ellen twenty years, so that now she looked her age. I also felt Wendy shouldn't go. The junta had put her name on a special list of visitors. If she ever stepped foot in Burma, they'd lop it off.

Wendy admired Phil as her mentor so much she slept with him, in fact, enough times for them to qualify as lovers. Hard bodies, she decided, were not that important anymore. He was smart and articulate, and that was a form of seduction. She liked it that Phil worried she didn't care enough for him—which was the opposite of how things were with Wyatt. Actually, she noticed that Phil could even be somewhat clingy. He asked little test questions, like, "I was thinking about your tush today. Were you thinking about mine?" Sometimes he came across as desperate. She wished he were as confident in bed as he was with the press.

Every now and then, when she did think of Wyatt, which was "hardly ever," she told herself she was "so totally over him." He was a brief infatuation, and she convinced herself it was a hypomanic side effect induced by a change in her medication. Wyatt was a loser, and not very smart. Plus he had no idea what responsibility to others was. He didn't ever think about having a real job or having a goal in life beyond mooching off people so he could take off on his next adventure. He would never do anything to distinguish himself, just as he hadn't when they were stuck in No Name Place. There was nothing much to him, she concluded several times a day when he sprang to mind, besides his cute butt and a certain jackhammer talent of the pelvis.

WYATT DID indeed return to Mayville, which held another parade and a grand banquet in his honor. For weeks, he was invited to one luncheon after another. His high school held a victory dance in the auditorium, and there he ran into a woman who laughingly said, "Don'cha know it's me?" It was the ditzy woman with heavy black eyeliner who had been interviewed on Global News Network, the one who called herself his girlfriend.

He said, "Ma'am, I have *no* idea who you are."

She shrugged and said with a friendly smile, "That's how time is, isn't it, it just goes away before you know it, and in between, people grow older and some get old. I guess I look like nobody you ever woulda knowed." She gave a rueful laugh. "Don't matter. Like everybody, I just wanted to say, Glad you're back."

He knew that laugh. Sherleen, the woman who introduced him to sex. At the time, he was sixteen, half the age he was now, and she was thirty-one, younger than he was now. She had worked at the ranch where his mother boarded his horse, the gift he received from his father shortly before he died of emphysema. He was the rich kid, and she was the gal who described herself as "rich in heart and heartaches." She had been his secret haven, somewhere between comfort and escape. When he was twenty, he left to take a car trip to the Southwest. He sent her postcards, but she had no way to write back, and when he returned, he heard she had moved.

He was embarrassed to remember this. "What you been up to, Sherleen?"

"Kind of the usual," she said, "which is not a whole lot." And he knew it was hard times by the number of times she said "Oh, well" as she talked about all the "usual" things. He could see it in his mind, her getting bucked and kicked while breaking in horses, her hooking up with the seasonal ranch hands, this "bad-ass" and that "mean sucker," who kicked the shit out of her after they rode her like a bucking horse in bed. That was back when she could still work. Not anymore. She had a scrunched-up back, miserable pain eased by bottles of whatever was cheap. She had come to town when she heard that he was missing in Burma. For old times' sake, she had worried a lot.

Sherleen was also the mother of his eleven-year-old son. He immediately recognized that fact when he saw the boy come up to them holding a plate piled high with turkey and mashed potatoes. It was like seeing himself at that age, down to his facial expressions and loping walk. So those get inherited, too, he thought. And just as he expected, the boy said, "Wyatt," when asked his name.

After that day, he knew he had to do what was necessary to make amends and be a dad. How he dealt with Sherleen was another matter. He talked to his mom and her new husband, Gus Larsen. A family's got to take care of its own, Dot said, and the Fletchers knew how to do right by other people. She told him they would send Sherleen to a county rehab program—they'd pay, of course—and while she was drying out, they'd go to court and file papers saying she was an unfit mother, so they could get custody of the boy. That was best for the boy's sake, the mother's, too.

But Wyatt was reluctant to do anything backhanded. The woman was a mess, that's for sure, but she still laughed an honest laugh, and at one time in his life he had thought she was beautiful, the sweetest angel on earth. So many afternoons, he had told her, "I love you. I promise, Sherleen, I'll always love you." That counted for something, didn't it?

He could offer to set her up in an apartment near his mom's house. That way he could drop by and take his son fishing, to a ball game, or even on one of his expeditions when the boy was older. To Sherleen, Wyatt would say he'd like to be her friend. He knew she would understand it would be only that. He knew her well. She would say what she had always said, "Anything you want."

Roxanne and Dwight were still together, but not in the way you might think. Even before she reached home, she started to justify why she should end the marriage. All those weeks in No Name Place should have strengthened them as a couple, but instead they magnified her loneliness at being with him. His insecurity kept him apart from her. His abrasiveness drove others away. She could not share her successes with him, because he reacted only with terse comments— "Another one for the trophy case"—and that angered her and made her think that all they shared were different disappointments.

Dwight sensed what Roxanne was thinking. The thought of his marriage's ending both scared and saddened him, but he could not tell her that. Early in their relationship, he had wanted to protect her—emotionally—and he knew she needed that, even though she appeared strong to others. But she had rebuffed his efforts, maybe unknowingly, and he felt useless, then a stranger, alone. She wanted so little of him. He wasn't as smart as she was, not as strong, not even as athletic. Her disdain had been evident on this trip. She never wanted his help or suggestions. If she didn't reject his ideas outright, she was quietly unsupportive. He could see it in her eyes. She was tender only when he was weak, when he was sick.

After their rescue, neither of them spoke about the inevitable, yet they felt it sharply, the lack of jubilation in at last being alone together. They made separate arrangements: she caught a plane back to San Francisco, and he went to Mandalay to explore the areas around the Irrawaddy. That was what he had come to see. Along those shores his great-great-grandfather had been killed.

He pictured his ancestor looking much like himself, around his age, his same coloring, having a similar feeling of being displaced, alienated from his disappointed wife, squeezed by the tyranny of a society that would give him nothing by which he could distinguish himself. He was just another cog. He had come to Burma to work with a timber company, to see what his chances were, if his soul was still alive. He looked at the river and its broad expanse. And then came shouts, and he was surprised that death was happening so fast. Crossbow arrows rained down and sharp knives went through him with surprising ease, as if he had no muscle or bone. And then he was lying in his mess, his face close to the water, not feeling his body, but his thoughts still rushing out. He was going to die a stranger on these shores. And as the fiery sparks filled his vision, he had a startling thought—that long after he was dead, this river would still flow and so would he. He pictured a young man, who looked very much like him, about his age, his same coloring. He marveled that his blood would run through this young man, that perhaps it would draw the young man to this wild and beautiful place. And later the young man would have these same thoughts, that one day there would be another and another, with their same coloring and thoughts, who understood them both. And when that happened, neither of them would feel he was alone. They would live on together in the flow of this endless river. He died in peace believing it. And this peace would have been Dwight's, but for the fact that he had no children.

When he returned to San Francisco, he and Roxanne agreed to a divorce. There was no fight leading up to it. They agreed without tears or argument that the marriage was over. Two weeks after he moved out and a week after they filed the papers, he learned that Roxanne was three months pregnant. He knew she had wanted a girl. But the sonogram revealed it was a boy. She hadn't said anything before, she explained, because she felt it shouldn't enter into their decision whether to divorce. He wanted to cry over this sad irony. But he nodded.

Fate kept changing course. Roxanne nearly lost the baby and had to take drastic measures. Her doctor sewed up her cervix, ordered complete bed rest, and advised she avoid stress. Without being asked, Dwight returned home. He cooked and brought her meals, cleaned up after she finished, and washed the dishes. He collected the mail, sorted out the junk, paid the bills, answered the phone and took messages when she was sleeping. He helped her bathe and pushed her in a wheelchair the short distance to the bathroom. These were the menial things they had never done for each other.

Surprisingly, they got along well. Without expectations, they no longer had to face disappointment. Without disappointment, they were often surprised at finding what they had failed to find in the past. But it was too late, and they knew it. Dwight didn't hope for reconciliation, and neither did Roxanne. They continued to meet with lawyers to divide up the community property and had determined that they would share equal custody of the boy.

Roxanne was grateful to Dwight for the help, and that was enough for him, just thank you, I needed your help. And she knew that was enough, and also that he wasn't doing this for her. It was for the baby. He was protecting the baby. The baby was a kind of hope for him— she could see that in the expression on his face, not of love for her, but of a sense of peace, of ease. He had abandoned the fight against himself. She didn't know what the fight was; it had always been part of their problem together. If she had asked why he felt so serene, he wouldn't have been able to tell her. It was a vague yet satisfying feeling, a strong memory that would last to the end of his life.

In that future memory that he is yet to have, his child is a man who is very much like himself. He has come to a point in life where he feels lost and rudderless. He has been pulled to a place where he is the stranger. He stands on the shore of the Irrawaddy and thinks about who went before him and who will come after and how together but in separate times they will watch the same flow and feel it in their blood. They were never strangers.

WHEN LUCAS WAS BORN, Roxanne had sudden attacks of fear several times a day. She was afraid that she would forget to do something critical, like feed the baby, change his diapers, or recognize that he had a fever or was not breathing. She worried she would absent-mindedly walk into a room and leave the baby there, forgetting where she had last put him, as she did often with keys. The baby was so demanding, and it was draining to keep track of all his needs—so many of them in such a tiny person.

Roxanne's research project demanded her attention as well, but she was too tired to keep herself and her graduate students organized and focused. She had an ocean of data from various expeditions that needed to be documented and analyzed, research from her students that she had to review, grant proposals to write, an article for a journal she had promised her coauthor she would finish and submit promptly. On top of all this, her office had to be boxed up for a move to another building. She vacillated between tending to her baby and her work. She refused to give up working, yet she did nothing with her work except fret over it. She had never felt so ambivalent about her priorities, and when she could no longer decide, she became depressed. Whenever Dwight picked up the baby to take him to his place or to the doctor's for a checkup, she felt relief. Freed of responsibility, she went to bed, but she could not sleep.

"What's wrong with me?" she wondered to herself. "I wanted this baby so much. A billion women have babies. It can't be that difficult to raise one." She attributed her problem to hormonal changes, and blamed her trepidations on her confinement in the jungle. Why else would she feel so helpless now?

Yet she could not accept help when offered. That was proof she was failing her son and always would. Accepting help was like taking drugs. It would be addictive and in the end leave her worse off than before, she believed. Yet everyone could see that she would soon collapse.

Dwight moved back in. He had to insist and ignore her protests, her fury that he was implying she could not handle things. Although it had cost him a new romantic relationship with a woman, how could he not help when his son was at stake? Later, when Roxanne apologized and thanked him, he said, "Don't worry about it," and she cried. Dwight set up the routines and the schedule. She watched how relaxed he was while feeding and changing Lucas. Dwight had no worries. He sang made-up songs to him about his nose and toes. Roxanne saw how easily Dwight organized the baby supplies. He did not coddle his son, or her. He let her feed and change the baby, and when it was his turn, Roxanne saw his look of wonder and adoration. He had shown her the same expression when she first met him as her graduate student. He had worshipped her. She had unconsciously expected that he always would.

It gradually occurred to her that she had never known how to put herself second and defer to anyone else. All her life, from toddlerhood on, everyone had catered to her, had lavished praise and encouragement. To her parents and teachers, she was a genius, who required special attention to ensure that her full potential bloomed. Everybody looked upon her as extraordinary, powerful, and infallible, but all along, their solicitous attitude had made her weak, for she did not know what to do with her life now that this bundle in her arms cried and shrieked that he, not Roxanne, must be the only consideration in the entire world. Roxanne still tried to be extraordinary and infallible as a mother. But she failed time and again, or so she thought. She felt that her baby's cries of distress and anger were accusing her of that.

With Dwight's calm and confident presence, her anxiety ebbed. She had not become stronger but more aware of how little she had given him. He was not as selfish as she had accused him of being. She had never allowed him to take care of her, beyond her demands that he acquiesce to her preferences. Now she had come to know him better in a few months than she had in ten years. And she admired him. She still had an affection for him. It was not love, but there was trust in the mix, comfort too, in knowing he did not think less of her for being needy. So what was her feeling for him called? Was it enough for them to be a couple again? Would he ever want that? Did he need her in any way?

. . .

My dear friend Vera wrote the book on self-reliance that she had been hashing out in her mind during her time in the jungle. Thinking about it had kept her going, had given her a focus. Putting her thoughts to paper freed her of some burden she never knew she carried. She wondered whether she had captured what her great-grandmother had written in her book, the one she never found.

Vera wrote about the funny techniques she came up with to survive mentally. When she felt she could not bear to walk another step, she conjugated verbs in French. She had always wanted to go to France and spend a whole month there. Years earlier, she had signed up for French classes, but she was always too busy to go. She could study in the jungle, where it served no use except to practice it. As she conjugated, she had no room in her brain to think about fear or discomfort or the futility of asking, Why me? *"Je tombe de la montagne,"* she had recited. *"Je tombais de la montagne. Je tomberai de la montagne."*

And then she came to the uncomfortable questions. She had once been so sure of what she meant by helping others. Wendy had wanted to give Tibet back to the Tibetans. And Vera argued in turn that you had to give up idealism and make the Tibetans self-reliant. You had to find them jobs. Her intention was to make them strong. Her organization tackled social problems in exactly that way.

But how did you know whether your intention would help, or whether it would only lead to worse problems? Sanctions or engagement? How could anyone know which approach would work? Who could guarantee it? And if it failed, who suffered the consequences? Who took responsibility? Who would undo the mess? Would anyone be around to care?

No one had any answers. And it made Vera want to shout and cry.

She did not write that in her book. Instead she recalled the night when she was overcome by the pounding drums. She and the others believed for a moment that they inhabited one another's minds, and that was because they became the same mind. She wrote that it was a delusion, of course. Yet it was a delusion worth having from time to time. Sympathy wasn't enough. You had to be that person and know that person's life and hopes as your own. You had to feel the desperation of wanting to stay alive.

The book had been more difficult to write than she expected. The swirl of important ideas and powerful epiphanies seemed diminished on the page. They became fixed words and were no longer fresh internal debate. Still, she finished, and was excited and nervous to see what people would think, how her work might change their lives. It could have a ripple effect. She did not want to get her expectations up too high, yet writing about personal discovery could prove to be her calling.

And then she could not find a publisher. She kept sending out the manuscript and received only rejections or never heard back. It had been a waste of time to write the damn thing. She was going to throw it in the trash—it pained her to see it, this big lump of wasted time. But then she reconsidered. She was stronger than that. It wasn't a failure. She simply had not come out of the jungle yet. She needed perspective. She needed to revise her life before she could revise her book.

No more excuses about obligations. No more thinking she was indispensable. She bought a ticket for Paris. On the plane, she conjugated verbs that would soon have real meaning: *Je crie au monde. J'ai crié au monde. Je crierai pour que le monde m'entende.* I will shout to the world to hear me.

BENNIE REUNITED with Timothy and their children, the three cats. He discovered that Timothy had indeed read his mind. It was amazing, they said over and over: Christmas had waited for them. It was all there: The decorations and the gingerbread house with gumdrops. The twinkling lights around the window frames and the electric candles on the sills. The embroidered runner from the 1950s was on the mantel, the stockings were hanging with their embroidered names. The Franklin Mint plates illustrating the twelve days of Christmas still graced the dining room table, and in the center were pomegranates and tangerines in a bowl; fresh supplies had been required when mold set in.

"Good thing I came back," Bennie said. "This place would have wound up looking like Miss Havisham's wedding boudoir." He then burst into tears, hugged Timothy, and whispered, "We never let go."

Because the fir tree had to be removed for reasons of fire safety, the presents lay under a silk palm tree, which had been sprayed with balsam scent. Their presents waited, unopened and rewrapped with yellow ribbon. There was an extra gift, purchased after Timothy had learned that Bennie was missing. It was a cashmere sweater—and way too big, Bennie said proudly. The sentiment fit just right, he added, and he would keep the sweater, which I thought was wise. The daily celebrations of cake and champagne, plus bacon and eggs every morning, then baby back ribs at night, were bound to restore to him the twenty pounds he had lost, and fairly soon.

But most everything else fit the same. Nothing had changed, except his sense of gratitude, his appreciation of everything he had. It was just as you expect you should feel and what seldom actually happens without ugly little twists. What Bennie was grateful for most was love. He felt it so deeply that several times a day he cried, just at realizing how lucky he was. He had the kind of satisfaction I never felt when I was alive.

MARLENA AND HARRY finally had their long-awaited night of passion. When they came out of the jungle, Esmé's father was waiting to take her home. Harry and Marlena flew to Bangkok and checked into a luxury hotel. The lovemaking was again delayed, because Harry had to do dozens of exclusive interviews. When they were finally alone, they took inventory. No mosquito nets over the bed, no citronella candles, no chance of ritual burning of designer sheaths. She was shy and he was bold, but there was no hesitation or awkwardness. With the secret aid of a sliver of *Balanophora* that Moff had given him as a send-off gift, their night of passion was a great and prolonged success.

When they had exhausted themselves, she cried, and he was concerned, until she told him it was for joy that she felt free enough to lose her senses. What an endearing girl! Only a few other women had confessed that at the end of lovemaking. He never tired of hearing it. Of course, he was done with other women, he reminded himself, especially the younger girls. It was a strain to keep up with them, especially when he could not always be Johnny-on-the-spot, so to speak. Marlena would understand—not that it had happened with her, but in case it did. She would accept this with love and never pity or laughter. Of course, they could always get more of the *Balanophora*. Lord, that was a bit of all right.

Over the months, their love affair continued to be wonderful, a brilliant match. Harry called her his fiancée, as he had declared on the news. He still needed to choose a wedding ring. He told Marlena he was thinking of having one custom-made, but he had not found the perfect designer. The perfect designer would come after they had signed the prenuptial agreement. That shouldn't be a problem, he reasoned, since Marlena made almost as much money as he did—even more when you considered she didn't pay anyone alimony or child support, as he did. She probably had the same practical attitude about these sorts of things. Then again, women often took legal matters in entirely the wrong way.

Somehow things would work out, he was confident of that. Their love was based on understanding, on overlooking their small defects and seeing what was most important. Love with companionship. He wanted to slap himself for having been so blind to it. He had sought women in the past as a way to reflect himself. The women's eyes, their pulsating irises, had been a mirror of what he wanted them to adore. His strength. His knowledge. His social ease. His confidence. His well-timed words. All the qualities of a man above men. He had presented a parody of the male god, rather like his televised self. Well, banish that, at least after hours. And at home with Marlena he would simply be himself. He might have to learn what that was, which was frightening, but he was ready.

His show was doing superbly. Ratings were higher than ever. He won another Emmy. All that criticism he received for being a stooge to the Burmese military regime dissipated once he had a chance to explain how he used the limelight to make people aware of the plight of his friends and of all those who lived in Burma under fear. After all, hadn't things turned out well for everyone?

Harry continued working on his book, *Come. Sit. Stay.* His chapter on adaptability included real-life examples from his friends' stint in the jungle. It was the perfect opportunity to look at attributes of human behavior in groups under stress and pack behavior among dogs. He had interviewed his friends about the alliances they forged for the good of the group. Who became the leader? How were decisions made? Were there any problems in making decisions? My friends, however, were circumspect, which is a trait that dogs do not possess. They lied for the sake of the group. They said Bennie was the leader from start to finish. He received input from the group, conferred with Black Spot, the leader of the other group, and together they reached consensus. So what if these reports were not reliable? In some instances, lying is admirable.

Marlena wished Harry would change his mind and stay at her place every now and then. She had a lovely home in Parnassus

Heights, but she moved into Harry's apartment on Russian Hill when he declared it their love nest. It was smaller than her place, and made even smaller by serving as a kennel to several dogs, including an Italian spinone and a briard, which were the size of ponies. Because Harry was an expert on dog training, she had expected his dogs would know all kinds of useful tricks, like fetching the newspaper. She didn't expect their wagging tails would knock over valuable pieces of art on the coffee table. She found them sprawled on the floor in the most inconvenient places. And lounging on the best spots were two little furry foot slippers, Pup-pup and my sweet Poochini, who, I was glad to see, had settled in comfortably. He no longer sat by the door waiting for me to come and take him home.

After a month of living together, Marlena worked up the reasons that she and Harry should alternate homes. She had a big fenced-in yard for the dogs, she pointed out, and a view of the city almost as nice as his overlooking the Bay. Plus it was roomier, with extra space for an office for each of them, as well as a future media room. He said it sounded heavenly. If only his damn schedule were not so demanding and unpredictable—the early-morning calls, last-minute glitches, and unforeseen disasters. That very morning at the studio, a chow dog had eaten a whole box of chocolates that his cretin-brained owner left on the table as a gift to the crew. They had to call Doggie 911 and then work late to make up for that fiasco. Marlena right away agreed that her place was too far from the studio, another fifteen minutes, twenty if traffic was bad. She understood completely. She and Esmé would continue to stay at her home every now and then, especially when he was immersed in the writing of his book and needed solitude. Dear Harry responded, "Darling, if you really want me to stay at your house from time to time..." No! She wouldn't hear of it. But it was sweet of him to offer. Later, she wondered whether he really had offered.

While the sex continued to be fantastic, sometimes Harry was too plastered to make love. Marlena had been having twinges of worry. The plain truth was, Harry drank too much. It took a while to let this enter her consciousness. But there was no denying it. He lived from cocktail to cocktail, with meetings, lunches, dinners, and parties accompanied by social lubricants. She enjoyed, at most, the occasional half-glass of a bold and expensive French burgundy. He enjoyed bold and expensive as well, a couple of bottles' worth. She once tried to hint that "they" should drink less—and he joked that her *less* would take her down to dribbles. But he was responsive. He heard the hint, and that night he had only one martini before dinner, but after dinner his math and memory were not working properly, and he increased the postprandial refreshments by several additional nightcaps.

Perhaps she was fretting for nothing. Harry wasn't exactly in the gutter. He never drove when he was tipsy, or rather, he didn't seem tipsy when he was driving. Furthermore, he was a successful and respected man, and she was lucky that he loved her. He was a playful and resourceful lover, always trying new adventures, open to every intimacy. He loved every freckle and mole, not that she had many of those. But he named the ones he found. And he spoke of love in all the ways she had dreamed of—of knowing each other's foibles and laughing about them, of growing old and holding hands, of giving each other secret looks that were part of their language. And he promised they would still do this when they were senile and too aged to lock loins without throwing out their backs or artificial hips. He vowed they would remember it all, and they would be more in love than ever as the years rolled by. He said all those remarkable things to her. If only he remembered the next morning that he had.

Would it last until they were senile? Hard to say. They had been through trial by fire, and it would either forge them like iron or break them apart like untempered glass. But there was this: They both desired the same thing. They wanted to be loved for who they were.

They just had to discover who they were beneath the habits of foray and retreat.

There was also Esmé to consider. If anything, she might become the force that kept them together.

ESMÉ ADORED the little bedroom Harry gave her in his apartment. It was on its own level and was very private. She was now thirteen. A girl needed her privacy. The room had a bed built into an alcove with round windows on three sides, and when she looked at the Bay waters, she imagined she was on a flying boat. There was also a low doorway that led to a glassed-in balcony with a view of Alcatraz Island. At night she could hear the sea lions at Pier 31 barking their heads off. Pup-pup liked to bark back, but stopped as soon as Esmé told her to shush.

Sometimes Rupert came over with his father. He and Esmé no longer played those baby games about naming foods they missed most. That was so long ago. She was also not her mother's "wawa," thanks to a growth spurt, and was a few inches taller. She now had breasts and wore a bra and tight low-slung jeans. Her breasts were noticeable, she knew, because she caught Rupert glancing down at them many times. One day he touched them. He asked, sort of. He stared at them a long time, then looked up at her and said, "Hey." Right away, she gave a little cock of her head, then shrugged and smiled at the same time. He touched them, the tips. He didn't kiss her, like she wanted. He squeezed her breasts through her clothes. His hand was crawling under her jeans, and she would have let him go farther if only her mother hadn't yelled, "Esmé! Rupert! Dinner!" They heard her clanking halfway down the metal spiral staircase to call out again. Rupert jumped up like a person who had burned his hand, then lost his balance, hit the wall, and slid down. (Of course, this moment of embarrassment reminded me of the night Harry and

Marlena's passion got a good dousing.) Esmé knew right away she shouldn't have laughed so hard. She should have pretended she didn't even see it. But once the giggles came, she couldn't stop them. She was still giggling as he made his way up the stairs.

When he next came over, they were too embarrassed to say anything about the breasts, or the hand in her pants, or her laughing at him. They sat on her bed together, and hardly said anything. They watched anime movies on her computer. Her mother found reasons to call down, it seemed, every fifteen minutes. Esmé thought about "it." If he wanted to do it again, she would let him. Not that she would take off her clothes and do the other "it." That would be too weird. She was curious, though, what she would feel when a boy touched her. Would she go insane with something she never felt before? Would she become a different person?

The other thing Esmé liked about her room was the carpeted staircase to her bed that Harry made so that Pup-pup could go up and down as she pleased. Esmé appreciated that Harry thought of these things. He knew all about dogs. She often went to the TV studio when they filmed on weekends. She would be "on set"—she knew not to call it a stage anymore. And she sometimes went "on location," whenever Harry did the show at people's homes. She noticed that he called out a lot, "People! Shush!" And everyone immediately shut up. He was very important on the show, the most respected person there, and everyone tried to get his attention and please him. But all she had to say was "I'm hungry" or "I'm cold," and he bossed people around and told them to get her a sandwich or a blanket. She thought her mom should come to the set more often and see how people treated Harry there. If she did, she wouldn't argue with him so much. Her mother was never satisfied with anything he did.

The best thing Harry did, Esmé thought, was to feature her and Pup-pup to show that kids can be excellent dog trainers. "Esmé here," he said on that segment, "has patience, an observant eye, and perfect timing." Pup-pup was almost a year old, and Esmé had demonstrated that her dog could follow her cues to sit, lie down, come, speak, shake hands, dance, retrieve a toy, and stay in one place even when Esmé left the room. She watched this *Fido Files* episode at least fifty times. She decided she would become an animal behaviorist like Harry. Only she didn't want to be on a TV show. She wanted to go back to Burma and rescue dogs. If they treated people that bad over there, imagine what they did to dogs.

IT IS MY TURN. I now know how I died.

Yesterday, the police detective called Vera. She was trustee of my estate and, by the way, the one negotiating the addition of my name to a second new building of the Asian Art Museum—and no, not just a wing—the seed money for which would come from my twenty-million-dollar bequest.

The detective said he had a few items that belonged to me. They included the carpet I fell on, the Miao textile that covered me, and the things I broke when I fell: a wooden lattice screen, a Ming bowl, two Tang dynasty figurines of dancing maidens, which were replicas but very nicely done. And there were the two gruesome objects: the murderous metal comb and the tasseled tie-back that had gone around my throat. Did she want them?

No, Vera said, thank you.

He remembered one more thing: There was a personal letter.

Vera wanted to see the letter. She thought I might have written it, and would keep and treasure it if I had. She made an appointment to see the detective.

They sat at the detective's desk. "Can you tell me anything else about the accident?" Vera said. "Why was that little rake thing in her throat? And what about the bloody shoe prints? I still can't understand how you can call Bibi's death an accident." I was glad she asked these questions, for they were the same ones I had.

"We have a hypothesis," the detective said, "but it's only that. See, there was a small stool, close to the window. We believe Miss Chen mounted the stool, and was facing the window, about to put up some Christmas lights. Why she was doing this after midnight is anybody's guess."

"It was the first weekend in December," Vera said, "and all the stores had their lights and decorations up. Bibi told me she'd have to stay up all night to get hers done."

"The lights and decorations," the detective continued, "were on a long wooden table—"

"An altar table," Vera said. "She always put small items there for display."

"I'm not a decorator," the detective said. "Anyway, she must have reached back, lost her balance, and fallen. A haircomb was on the table and she fell straight on it. The comb is curved metal—silver, I think—and the top part broke off. I included it in the list of items. Maybe you'll want to see it, since it may be valuable. Some of the decorations on it look like diamonds." He slid over a box of things, most of them broken.

"Looks like costume jewelry to me," Vera said. "You could never be sure what Bibi would come up with fashion-wise. She favored fun over jaw-dropping. This must have been one of her fun pieces."

"I'm not a decorator," the detective repeated. He looked at his file. "As to the bloody footprints, they were trickier to figure out, but we're fairly confident we know what happened there. A man walking by probably saw Miss Chen bleeding in the display window. He broke open the door and jumped onto the platform. He knelt beside her—that accounts for the blood on the knees of the pants that were found elsewhere. In all likelihood, she was unconscious. In her fall to the floor, she hit the back of her head on a bronze Buddha statue. The autopsy showed trauma there. The man pulled out the comb from her throat, and in all likelihood, he was shocked by the amount of blood spurting out. So he grabbed a red tasseled cord from a curtain in the display window and wrapped that around her neck to stanch the flow. Despite these heroics, she died, drowned in her own blood."

The detective let Vera absorb this news. She was crying a little, imagining the horror and the futility of the stranger's actions.

"We think the man was terrified he'd be caught there," the detective went on. "His hands were covered with blood. We found fingerprints on the metal comb. He must have run out pretty fast. I'm guessing he ditched his pants and shoes close to where his car was parked. Now you know as much as we do."

Vera dabbed her eyes and said she could see how this made sense. I could, too. Nonetheless, it was so *unsatisfying*. Clumsiness? That was the reason for so much drama and blood? And what about the stranger? I wished I could thank him for trying. And as I thought this, I saw in an instant who he was, a man I had known for twenty-seven years. I saw him nearly every few days, yet I hardly knew him. He was Najib, the Lebanese grocer around the corner from my apartment building. He had been on his way home from a late-night supper with friends. He, who never gave me any special discounts at his store, had tried to save my life.

"We don't know who the man was," the detective told Vera. "But if I did, I wouldn't press charges."

Vera stood up, and the detective reached into his file and gave her the letter. It was written in Chinese. He said that he'd found it near my body and had given it to a Chinese guy in the department, who looked at it quickly and determined it was a chatty letter from a female relative in China.

"Someone might want to send back a note to this person," the detective said, "in case she doesn't know. Here's the address." He handed Vera his colleague's translation of the address.

If a soul can tremble, that was what I was doing. I remembered that letter. I had read it.

It was from my cousin Yuhang. She was my confidante in childhood, the one who told me the family gossip when she and her family came to visit us once a year. When the Communists were on the verge of taking over Shanghai, and our family left, hers stayed. This was one of her occasional letters, which arrived in a package of gifts the morning before I died. I was in the display window area, rearranging items, when the postman handed it to me. I put it on the altar table, and time flew by before I remembered it. As the detective guessed, I was indeed standing on a stool, hanging Christmas lights. I spotted my cousin's package, reached down, and slipped out the letter. It began with the usual chitchat about weather and health. And then my cousin got to what she called "the interesting news."

"The other day," she wrote, "I was at the dirt market to find some things for my eBay business. You know how the foreigners like to buy all the old stuff still in worn condition. Sometimes I take the old junk, roll it in dirt to give it an antique look. Don't tell anyone!

"You should go to the early-morning market with me the next time you come to Shanghai. They always have good bargains, many imperialist things that families hid during the Cultural Revolution. I saw some mah jong sets with original boxes. Those are especially popular with foreigners. I also saw a woman who was selling a few pieces of jewelry. The gems were real, not what you'd expect to find with a woman that coarse, a downriver person—you know what I'm saying.

"I asked her, just to be friendly, 'How is it that you came to have such fancy things?' And she boasted back, 'These belonged to my family. My father was a really rich man before the change. We had tons of servants, and lived in a great house with four floors and five Western toilets on Rue Massenet.'

"*What?* Massenet? You know what I was thinking! So next I asked her, 'What did your father do?' And she said with a proud smile: 'He owned a big department store called Honesty, a very famous one. It doesn't exist anymore, but in the old heydays it made money faster than you could stuff it in your pants.'

"I looked hard in her lying eyes, and I said, 'What's your father's name?' I knew that a person of her type wouldn't lie about that for fear her ancestors would strike her dead. Sure enough, she said, 'Luo.' And I said, 'So you're the daughter of Gatekeeper Luo, the infected leech who stole our family's gold and jewels!' You should have seen how round her eyes and mouth grew. She began to wail and said her father had been killed because a few of those jewels were found in the lining of his jacket. (I wrote to you about this, do you remember?) She went on to say that the Red Army took him and the gold, and she next saw him in a cart being brought to the stadium field, with words of condemnation written on a board tied to his back, and a blindfold that had slipped down so that you could see his frightened eyes. After he was shot, the family buried the other valuables. But when the great famine came, they took their chances. One by one, they sold the pieces. One by one, a family member died for having the valuables. 'No one cares what imperialist things we have now,' the crying woman said, and she was selling the last few pieces, because she didn't want the curse to get her son.

"I said it was ghosts who demanded she give the valuables back to the family they were stolen from. That was the only way to get rid of the curse. So that was how I retrieved these trinkets for you. Clever, no? They're just a few souvenirs from your family's past. Nothing that valuable, but perhaps they will give you pleasure as you think about those days again. . . .'"

I put down my cousin's letter and unwrapped those souvenirs. And right away I saw it. It was a haircomb with a hundred tiny jade leaves, and peony blossoms in the form of diamonds. Sweet Ma had stolen this from me. I had stolen it from her, and Gatekeeper Luo had stolen it as well.

Here it was in my hands again, my true mother's haircomb—yes, a *haircomb* and not a hairpin, as I had mistakenly remembered it. The haircomb and I were the two things remaining that had belonged to my mother.

I rubbed my mother's haircomb against my cheek and pressed it near my heart. I rocked it as one might a baby. For the first time, I felt the emptiness of her loss replaced with the fullness of her love. I was about to burst with joy. And then my knees grew weak. They wobbled and grew rubbery. I felt a softening wave and I tried to push it away. But then I recognized what this was, me holding back my feelings so I wouldn't fall. Why should I not feel it? Why have I denied myself the beauty of love? And so I did not stop myself. I let joy and love and sorrow wash over me. And with that haircomb close to my heart, I plummeted off the stool.

When I died, I thought that was the end. But it was not. When my friends were found, I thought that would be the end. But it was not. And when forty-nine days had passed, I thought I would instantly be gone, as some Buddhists think a person will. But here I am. That is the nature of endings, it seems. They never end. When all the missing pieces of your life are found, put together with the glue of memory and reason, there are more pieces to be found.

But I won't stay much longer. I now know what's beyond here. My friends once had a glimpse of it. It was in the breath that lifted a hundred emerald beetles. It was in the echoes that followed each beat of the drum. It was in the absolute stillness when all minds were one. I can't say more than that, for it should remain a mystery, one that never ends.

· *genuine gratitude* ·

MY THANKS to many who may not even be aware of their contributions. Like a "dragonfly who skims the waters," I picked up all sorts of tidbits from Rabih Alameddine, Dave Barry, David Blaine, Lou DeMattei, Sandra Dijkstra, Ian Dunbar, Matthea Falco, Molly Giles, Stephen Jay Gould, Vicky Gray, Mike Hawley, Mike Hearn, Barry Humphries, Lucinda Jacobs, Anna Jardine, Ken Kamler, Stephen King, Karen Lundegaard, Terry McMillan, Mark Moffett, Ellen Moore, Pamela Nelson, Deborah Newell, Aldis Porietis, Emily Scott Pottruck, Faith Sale, Roxanne Scarangello, Orville Schell, Rhonda Shearer, Lizzie Spender, Frank Sulloway, Bubba Tan, Daisy Tan, John Tan, Lilli Tan, Oscar Tang, Sarina Tang, Aimee Taub, Christian Tice, Robert Tornello, Ken Zaloom, Vivian Zaloom, the members of the Alta 16, the Burma Road Gang, the Friends of Sarina, the Philosophical Club, and The Rock Bottom Remainders. I have been forever changed by the necessarily anonymous: the water buffalo outside Stone Bell Mountain, the pig near Ruili, the fish in Muse, the tour guides in Yunnan Province and Burma, and those who disappeared.

I owe Bill Wu many Chinese dinners for opening my senses and my mind to nature and nuance, to art and the art of the bargain.

For

LOU DEMATTEI,

SANDRA DIJKSTRA,

and

MOLLY GILES

for saving me countless times